Intercepted!

"Free freighter eff-cee-five-five-niner, match velocities for boarding. Transmit your zone passage license immediately."

If ever I get home, Ming vowed, *I'll never set foot on a spacecraft again!* Taking a swipe at her wet forehead, she leaned away from Jiadra's board to check Shan's screen. Still the Renasco ship maintained position. The wormhole discontinuity loomed just ahead.

Abruptly, Ming plunged into an infinite abyss, her body destroyed. She fell, reduced to atoms. Fell, screaming, knowing no one could hear. Fell . . .

And reformed safely at the other end of the wormhole . . .

Where a second Renasco ship filled Shan's screen.

Lur braced both arms against the command chair. "Hot sweat," he growled. "They've got us in range."

CRYSTAL WITNESS

Kathy Tyers

BANTAM BOOKS
TORONTO • NEW YORK • LONDON • SYDNEY • AUCKLAND

CRYSTAL WITNESS
A Bantam Spectra Book/June 1989

ISBN 0-553-27984-X

Published simultaneously in the United States and Canada

Bantam Books are published by Bantam Books, a division of
Bantam Doubleday Dell Publishing Group, Inc. Its trademark,
consisting of the words "Bantam Books" and the portrayal of
a rooster, is Registered in U.S. Patent and Trademark Office
and in other countries. Marca Registrada. Bantam Books,
666 Fifth Avenue, New York, New York 10103.

Printed in the United States of America

OPM 0 9 8 7 6 5 4 3 2 1

I'm grateful to my Thursday night confederates—Janine, Paula, Diane, Laulette, Ben, Judy, Gwen, Bob, Chris, both Barbaras, Marjorie, and Marnia—for encouragement, ideas, and unflagging pickiness.

Special thanks to Amy Stout, Janna Silverstein, and Patrick Delahunt; to Jerry Oltion; to Anne Conklin, calligrapher; and to Marnia and Gayla, who know art.

To Mark, who believes.

PART ONE

A

For the first time since leaving Cabra Minor, Ming Dalamani felt like a smuggler.

The rest of *Opa*'s crew waited without speaking as Ming adjusted her radio transceiver. Her overwebbed acceleration chair felt hard, and the other crew members stared, making her wonder if she was somehow responsible for the silence answering her first transmission. Ming was new to this. Had she done something wrong? She raised the trans-C communications frequency five cycles, then spoke again toward the tiny, omnidirectional mike on her console. "Grant One, this is your contact. Do you read?"

Who might hear, besides the ship *Opa* hoped to hail? That coded radio-frequency burst should read as static to anyone but their contact, unless Renasco had intercepted and broken *Opa*'s codes. In that case, it would reveal them as smugglers to any enforcement vessel in the area.

A trickle of perspiration started down her chest, following deceleration's pseudogravity. No Cabran had crossed the void between Cabra and the Nexos system since the gamma-ray storm began a hundred years ago, and excitement gripped her throat. She pressed the key several times, swept plus and minus ten cycles around her assigned frequency, then cleared her throat and spoke. "Grant One, this is *Opa*. Do you copy?"

No answer. Touching one earring in the automatic gesture of apology, she glanced up over her left shoulder at her uncle, Lur Dalamani, for orders. Senior officer and cofinancier of this smuggling run, and her favorite of many clan uncles, he had left his command chair to help her if necessary.

He scratched the side of his thick, muscular neck with

one hand, grasping a metal brace that arched over Shan's
station. "They're only being cautious." He rapped the
brace with his knuckles. "Give them a few minutes to be
certain they aren't being monitored."

Ming reclined her chair to better see crew engineer
Shan Dalamani's supersized visual monitor, a meter to her
left. Nexos's gas-giant companion planet loomed so close,
the monochrome screen's entire background glowed a
pale sickly green. In her headphone and on the cabin
speakers, near space sounded empty. She couldn't criticize
the Nexan contact for caution, though. *Opa* carried two
thousand Cabran sunstones, enough exotic jewels to give
any pickup man the cold sweats, even on a legal run. The
Dalamani-Grazi clan's Caucus of Elders insisted every trip
bring a rich return, to counter the risk of interception by
the Renasco monopoly. The financially troubled clan
needed this mission to succeed. Yet once *Opa* left the
Cabra system, it trespassed. Renasco controlled intersystem space, creating a law of armed scoutships, ruling no
worlds except its colonies, allowing other worlds commerce only on its carriers.

If *Opa* were caught . . .

Ming had heard rumors. In light of her own small en-
counters with Renasco personnel, she tended to believe.
Summary execution was one of the milder alleged punish-
ments for trying to circumvent the monopoly.

Ming's monitor hissed softly, steadily. On Ming's right,
Jiadra Grazi scowled, shifted her own chair, and rested a
hand against the vertical weapons console, where Ming
could see the sleek white curve of her duty-suit sleeve,
tapering from shoulder to wrist. Her black-brown eyes
narrowed. "That's long enough. Try again."

Ming flinched at Jiadra's perpetual bossing. She shook
her narrow shoulders, settling the long, loose black clan-
tails of her hair behind them, then reached back to finger
the closely trimmed stubble between tails. Jiadra would
not hurry her into a mistake. According to Uncle Lur,
they'd chosen Ming instead of a more experienced appli-
cant because of her careful nature and her deep desire to
excel.

Before she could touch the transmission key, a voice
boomed in her left ear and through the overhead cabin

speaker. *"Opa,* this is Grant One. We have you on screen. Maintain your present vector. Transmit beacon in ten seconds."

Ming exchanged relieved smiles with her cousin Shan. A ticking pulse followed the transmission. Again she glanced over her shoulder for orders. Uncle Lur—*Captain* Lur—nodded, and she poised her finger over the beacon key, counting with the pulse.

On cue, she touched it again and announced *Opa's* presence to everyone within transmitter range.

Four seconds later, Shan pointed to the visual screen. "There."

Two steps took Lur from Ming's shoulder to Shan's. "It's either our contact or Renasco," he said, pressing together the heels of his hands. "Arm up, Jiadra. Ming, transmit the recognition code."

As Jiadra Grazi flipped a row of levers on her weaponry board, Ming set two dials and pressed the appropriate tabs, then glanced at Shan's screen, its image processor set for maximum resolution. She tracked a tiny mote as it slipped out of its hiding place in a thickening of the gas giant's outermost ring. It did not return code: The dark square near Ming's coding dials high on her board remained dark.

Within ten minutes, the mote resolved into the distinctive oblong shape of an approaching ship. It should be a tramp freighter, but at this range it also looked disconcertingly like a Renasco scout.

"They're being careful." Shan rested a muscular arm on her chair's edge. "Engines down, but hot. They're coasting. Backward."

"Could fry us with their blast," Jiadra muttered. "Ming, be ready to assist."

Sitting this close, Ming imagined she could feel Jiadra's stone-stubborn temper as her elder cousin tilted her chin toward the half-sphere ceiling.

Ming swiveled her stool toward Lur. "Why aren't they returning code?"

Lur stepped back to the helm, awkward in low pseudogravity. "For all they know, we could be Renasco ourselves." He seemed so calm, never fidgeting, never raising his voice.

Opa's main engine idled, humming low. The cabin

smelled stuffy. Jiadra drummed shapely fingers on her board. Her lips moved; once, Ming thought she heard her curse.

"Relax, Jiadra," said Shan. "It's them."

Immediately, Ming's headset rang with a burst of rapid tones. The code I.D. panel glowed absinthe green. *Three parts clear green, one maurin yellow*, Ming thought irrelevantly, one part of her mind fleeing to the serene milieu of her artwork. "Code confirmation," Ming called. As she spoke, Shan's husky voice rang out, "Confirm freighter, Captain." At last the other ship fired braking rockets.

Ming bent sideways to eye Shan's screen. This tramp was no Company scoutship. It looked every meter a local carrier, too big to have been freighted in from outsystem, too small to carry the radiation shielding necessary for cross-space travel, and obviously—from the scratches and pits along its sides—built decades before Nexos requested Renasco service six years ago.

The carrier slowed relative to *Opa*'s direction of travel, drifted alongside, then fired a series of directional bursts to match deceleration ratios. At last *Opa* lurched, and docking latches closed together with a clang. Jiadra unclasped the webbing that cocooned her curve-heavy torso into her chair. "Take my station, Ming."

Now Ming relaxed. The older woman never surrendered her post when she anticipated trouble. For a few seconds, Ming sat still, breathing tension out of her body.

"Ming Dalamani." Jiadra wheeled. "You have an order. Move."

Controlling her urge to answer back sharply, Ming shifted. She must obey without argument and follow shipboard discipline, even if Jiadra grew pushier under tension. Ming glanced aside to where Jiadra now leaned on a bulkhead. *If some day I had my own command, would I be different?*

It took Lur only a few minutes to finish the docking sequence. Then he pushed up from the helm. Sweat darkened his duty suit. *So he's worried after all*, she thought. *I'd never have believed it.* "Shan." He beckoned.

Her shriveled legs spread, arching in exaggerated, reversed bows over twisted feet, Shan shuffled to the middeck helm. Although Shan's upper body was hard with muscles built to compensate, those congenitally shrunken legs were of little use in an operation that might require walking speed. Her clan-tails, each trimmed at the bottom to a V, dangled halfway down her back.

From the ordnance post, Ming watched Lur ease open the boarding hatch, two meters to her right around the bulkhead's curve. A couple of tall men stepped through, too strong-chinned to be Cabran, with odd yellowish curling hair like she'd seen in ancient outsystem vids. Now Ming knew she was really in another star system. The second Nexan carried a small cubical vault. From the bent stance of his well-muscled body, Ming saw that even in the low decel "gravity" his burden weighed him down. "I'm Barrick Tunny," said the first. Intriguing, how little accent he seemed to have. The muscular man presented the vault to Lur and touched a catch. Its lid sprang open.

"Lur Dalamani. Welcome aboard." Her uncle braced one foot on a bulkhead projection and balanced the metal cube on his thigh, then drew out a gleaming yellow bar and touched a bulkhead tab. A wide slot opened. He set the bar inside, twisted a dial, then touched a second tab. Ming could not see the display over the window, but Lur stood fully alert, even with all that weight balanced on one thigh. Gold, the Nexan contact had promised. Sitting straight on Jiadra's acceleration chair, Ming held her breath.

Lur's shoulders relaxed, and he tucked the metal bar back into the security box, smiling. "This way, sirs."

Gold. Found almost everywhere man explored, but always rare—and in the molecularly pure state, untraceable.

Not so the sunstones. To Ming's knowledge, sunstones were mined only on Cabra Minor. Perhaps with her earnings from this trip, Ming would buy one of the rosy hearted yellow crystals for herself; and perhaps Lur and the Caucus would allow her a bit of the gleaming Nexan gold in addition to her pay, to plate a miniature honoring her father's cosponsorship of the *Opa* run.

Lur led the strange men along the far edge of deck one to the ladderway. Beside them he looked like a wrestler; Jiadra, following, a veil dancer. What a caricature that would make! Lur and Jiadra descended the spiral second and third to give the Nexans right-of-watch, common cour-

tesy to uneasy strangers. Wishing she'd been granted
drawing paper in her weight allowance, Ming watched as
they vanished downship. Soon thumps and clanging echoed below.

Webbed in for comfort more than safety, Shan grasped
opposite ends of the helm chair and pulled her arms taut in
an isometric—not posturing, but taking advantage of a
break, exercising and stretching the upper body that was
all her strength. Glumly Ming glanced down at her own
thin, bony arms. Not long before her mother died, she'd
used a term in conversation that now titled Ming's self-
concept: "fragile."

What did it matter? She was a smallform sculptor . . .
and now, an apprentice communication tech.

"Fifty thousand gildens," Shan said in her low, husky
voice—as rough as concrete blocks, and as familiar to Ming
as her own lean face in the mirror. One corner of Shan's
mouth crinkled upward. "You're going to be cozy."

"You, too. But you should have more." Ming twisted
her body left on Jiadra's chair to face her cousin sitting at
the helm. "You got us the shielding."

Shan shrugged, then stretched again. "If Caucus gives
me more, I'll take it." Subdued laughter filtered up the
ladderway. "But there's no rush. If we make it this time,
we'll have plenty of chances to turn a profit. Buy our own
ship someday, you and me."

"And maybe enough space back home for a studio."
Ming understood wealth as time to spend drawing, and
twist-welding miniature sculptures from wire and thin
rods, though if pressed she would confess she was already
fulfilling one lifelong fantasy, escaping the Cabran system
to deep space.

The clan's fathers had colonized Cabra two centuries
before the gamma-ray storm separated it from other in-
habited worlds. Renasco, with its own secret electrostatic
radiation shielding, now held a monopoly on intersystem
travel, as the storm's trailing edge passed. Though Nexos
entered Renasco's camp six years back, Cabra signed for
Renasco service just this year. Before Renasco could adjust
its security systems against Cabra's local codes and inquisi-
tive genius, Shan Dalamani had broken the data bank. As
nervous as Ming felt about illegal shipping, she took pride

in her clansmen. The Dalamani-Grazis meant to reopen commerce for independents. (They also meant to pay their debts.)

If *Opa* proved non-Company groups could learn to shield themselves, then Cabra Major, Secundis, and Ming's scorching homeworld, Cabra Minor—forced to develop marginal self-sufficiency on three planets never intended for independence—might forge links of their own with other worlds.

The room speakers began to boom again. "Unidentified ship docked to freighter en-kay-six, retransmit I.D. beacon. Unidentified ship docked to—" The baritone voice spoke mechanically, but a menacing note droned beneath its sharp diction. Running footsteps clanged in the ladderway. Ming gripped Jiadra's console, certain she'd better not retransmit that beacon.

Lur emerged headfirst. Shan dropped from the helm chair and hurried back to her post. Jiadra hustled hard on Lur's heels and evicted Ming from ordnance.

"Trans-C silence," grunted Lur. He swept past the helm, pausing only to reach down to his command chair's sideboard controls. "Where is he, Shan?"

The two strangers rushed from the ladderway. One carried a small locker of Cabran manufacture, the sunstone crystals, as they plunged through *Opa*'s hatch. A second hatch swung shut behind them.

"I can't read him, sir." Shan shook her head. One clantail half slid over her shoulder.

Lur sealed *Opa* and strode back to his cushioned black seat.

"They caught the beacon." Jiadra flicked yellow-barred safety panels off her row of armament switches. "The clanless, motherless—"

"Secure stations," ordered Lur. "Prepare for reorient." Ming reached down her chair and locked it into automatic mode. A clanging on her left and a lurch to the right told her the freighter had disengaged its electromagnets.

Her stomach took a turn. *Opa* slid through zero-g and began to accelerate.

For a sickening instant "down" had no meaning, then Lur fired attitude jets and established course.

Where was the Company? She stared hard into Shan's

huge screen on her left. A Renasco patrol might be hiding nearby in the huge outer planet's ring system, or at the far edge of radio range, reading *Opa*'s presence by satellite relay.

Only one way to find out: run.

"Ming." Jiadra beckoned fiercely.

Ming unlocked her chair. Across an intensifying press of acceleration, she slid it along the metal track that connected their stations, then secured it again. As she watched Jiadra's tracking screen for blips, she prayed it would not prove necessary to fire. If they shot at a Company ship and did not escape . . .

Acceleration mounted. Ming steadied her wrists against Jiadra's board. A minute passed, and she craned her neck around. Lur watched Shan's screen. From the sudden unknotting of neck muscles below his shorter arrow-tails, she saw he too felt the crisis nearly, slowly passing.

"Radiation shielding," he ordered. Ming understood his unspoken implication: *We're going to make it.*

"Sir," answered Shan, bending forward.

Silently Ming chanted, *Go. Hurry. Go.*

Shan twisted a dial to activate the shielding, a system stuck together with spare parts and hope. Thus far it had performed well . . . enough.

Bulkheads began to hum. Acceleration eased as the electrostatic shielding drained off engine power. Ming remained at Jiadra's screen, on watch.

Within minutes, *Opa* began to moan. The sound came shuddering from bulkheads where the shielding generators lay.

No, Ming groaned silently.

"Sir." Shan's gravel voice rang in the cabin. Twisting aside to face her secondary computer board, she asked, "Permission to run checks?"

"Go," Lur exclaimed. Ming's stomach protested as engine power dropped. "Ming. To Shielding."

Ming slid her chair left and reached for Shan's mainstation controls. The moan around her continued, low and steady.

"Keep the shielding on, unless I tell you." Shan bent to her small computer screen.

"Right," said Ming. In just over an hour they would approach the first "wormhole" discontinuity in the series between Nexos and Cabra, where thrust along a carefully plotted vector would instantaneously drive them through the "hole" in space to a location light-years distant. Thank the All no Company ships challenged, not yet. But Ming knew how raw her nerves had become when Lur's chair squeaked, a silent half hour later, and she jumped. She pivoted to see. Lur leaned toward his helm. Acceleration pressed her hipbones again.

"No clue, Shan?" asked Lur.

"Nothing."

"All right." Lur moved a hand across his controls. "We're going for vector speed."

Ming remained at Shan's station, one hand on the board, drawing comfort from her cousin's proximity. As acceleration shoved her harder and harder against her seat, the moan rose to a howl. She glanced to all sides. Either the shielding was about to fail or the bulkheads were stressing.

Ming stared at Shan's screen and counted off the minutes. Twenty till approach. Nineteen . . . twelve . . .

A blip appeared. "Sir!" Ming craned her neck toward the helm. "Ship ahead—I think."

"Track it." Lur never turned from his navigational screen. "Is it moving?"

Ming stared at the blip until her eyes hurt. "No, sir," she said at last.

"Then maybe it's not a ship."

"And maybe it is." Ming wheeled at the sound of Jiadra's voice. On the far side of Ming's own station, Jiadra sat erect, barely smiling.

She wants a fight, Ming thought.

Beneath Ming's feet, the main engines hummed a deep background to the bulkheads' howl. Ming still stared at the bright high-contrast blip.

Shan glanced away from her terminal just long enough to eye the screen, then hastened back to work. "It's a ship, all right," she announced.

How can she tell?

"Renasco," mumbled Jiadra.

Lur's chair creaked again. "Who else?"

But if this distant ship had challenged them back at the rings, it made no attempt at contact now. Ming glanced repeatedly at the trans-C board over at her own station. It remained dark.

"All right," Lur said, three anxious minutes later. "We're going for passage. We can get around them as we accelerate."

Ming looked back over her shoulder. On the control panel of the command chair, Lur keyed in the long sequence of vector coordinates for the first wormhole jump.

Shan punched another series of commands into her terminal. "Hot sweat," she muttered. "That doesn't fix it, either."

"Double magnification," Lur snapped.

Ming stabbed a key to make the correction on Shan's screen. The tiny green pip resolved into a shape every one of them knew and dreaded. Distinctly a Renasco scoutship.

Inertial pressure shifted in Ming's hips and against her shoulders—shifted, and decreased. On the right side of Ming's own station, a light pulsed erratically. She slid over, thumbing the search panel while recording. "Permission to amplify transmission, sir."

Every muscle on Lur's heavy frame looked tense now, and his white duty suit clung in dark wet patches. "Amplify."

Ming hit another panel. Two seconds later, *Opa*'s comm search mode found the appropriate frequency, and the transmission Ming's board had prerecorded came through in its entirety: "Silent ship. What is your operating number? You are in restricted space."

Lur gave no order. Ming stilled her hands against the edge of her console and waited. Another burst of acceleration thrust her chair against seat and shoulders.

"Silent ship." The voice in the speaker changed. It sounded tired, condescending, as if Renasco crews played disinformation games with one another. "Give your operating number, please."

"Ming." Jiadra, stiff in her chair, commanded her over with one imperious headshake.

Weapons. And this time, with a real threat in view.

Ming's stomach twisted. She glanced aside. Shan's focus

remained riveted to her terminal. Lur watched the screens.

Jiadra gestured again, this time with obvious anger. Ming reached for the pullbar and unlocked her seat, then slid it along the track until she sat beside Jiadra at the weapons board. She was expected to fill in wherever needed, and she would do so.

But . . . weapons.

"You'll do fine, Ming," Shan said quietly aside.

Ming swallowed on a dry throat and kept half an eye on the captain. Lur reached for a sideboard. "We are a free freighter." He laid just the right amount of casual slur over his voice to mimic a Nexan. "Eff-cee-five-five-niner, outbound slowcourse."

Ming bit her lip, aching with the hope it would work. Renasco did allow minimal, heavily taxed, free-freight traffic within its client systems. She rested an elbow on the console. It felt hard against her bones. Particle gun, laser, missiles. She was not sculpted to sit at this board.

"Free freighter eff-cee-five-five-niner, match velocities for boarding. Transmit your zone passage license immediately." The voice sounded crisper now, less bored.

"Lur Dalamani." Jiadra took a scornful tone, and Ming hated the implied disrespect toward her uncle. "Fire now. We have them at a disadvantage."

"Negative." Lur touched another panel. *Opa* lurched, still accelerating for the wormhole, but if caught in the Renasco ship's tractor, they would go no farther.

Unless they destroyed the Renasco ship.

"Free freighter eff-cee-five-five-niner, please confirm. You are to match velocities for boarding. Transmit zone passage license. Confirm, please." The voice was all business now.

Jiadra dropped one hand from the board and balled it into a fist on her hip. "Captain, *sir*. I suggest we fire while we have them at the disadvantage of surprise."

"Prepare for full acceleration," Lur said tightly. Inside the bowl overhead, howling shield units lifted their voices to a scream.

If ever I get home, Ming vowed, *I'll never set foot on a spacecraft again!* Taking a swipe at her wet forehead, she leaned away from Jiadra's board to check Shan's screen.

Still the Renasco ship maintained position. The wormhole discontinuity, invisible but plotted on-screen, loomed just ahead.

Abruptly, Ming plunged into an infinite abyss, her body destroyed. She fell, reduced to atoms. Fell, screaming, knowing no one could hear. Fell . . .

And reformed safely at the other end of the wormhole . . .

Where a second Renasco ship filled Shan's screen.

Lur braced both arms against the command chair. "Hot sweat," he growled. "They've got us in range."

B

Sunstone.

Abriel Innig twisted the ring on her finger and shivered for joy. She had wanted one of the jewels for years, since her school days. With her birthday approaching, perhaps she could justify it to Keath as a gift—from him—since he surely hadn't bought her anything yet.

She glanced around the sunny afterdeck of the cross-county shuttle, making sure no other passengers looked her way. Satisfied, Abriel twisted the gem back around to the outside of her hand and extended her fingers in a graceful pose. Set in six plain gold prongs, the crystal pulsed with red and golden light, giving back all the radiance of the late afternoon Nexan sun that poured through the shuttle's windows, and adding the faint glow of its thermoluminescent heart.

Leaning against a cushioned headrest, Abriel raised her hand into a beam from Nexos's sun. The crystal appeared to catch fire, incandescence flickering a barely discernible, erratic rhythm. Smiling, she hid the ring in her lap again, bowed her head, and twisted the band so only plain gold showed.

Bless Gib. Bless him!

Her line foreman, Gib Tunny, had come unannounced to her office that morning. Sitting in her position of authority, behind her desk and in front of the third-floor window of Associated Propellants, she'd looked him over. Small and proud as a cock, Gib carried his gray shift cap in one hand and approached with a sheepish manner that suggested a confession forthcoming.

Abriel struck the pose, both shoulders turned toward him, that she felt gave her the most supervisory air. New to this level of management, she knew she must carry off every encounter. Gib had never been one for transgressing, so she decided before he spoke that she would be lenient.

"What is it, Gib?" she asked. She added a slight, weary fall of voice that implied she already knew what he meant to say, and all could be confessed with impunity.

"Well, I . . ." The grizzled little man hrrm'd and thrust both hands into gray coverall pockets. "Mem Innig, last month I bought something I couldn't really afford. I mean, Mem, it was cheap, it was too cheap to resist, and I jumped. Wanted it for my wife. But grateful as she was, she reminded me how badly we need a new digester for the recycle unit. I guess I thought first of you, Mem, because you're the kind of woman for this kind of things, and you don't wear enough of them, if you'll forgive boldness. It'd look nice on you. I'm hoping you could buy it and maybe forget who sold it to you?"

He pulled his right hand free of the pocket and drew off the ring to hold out between his rough thumb and forefinger. Even under cold office light, the rosy hearted crystal glistened like a tiny living sun.

Abriel spread her elbows on the desk, trying to maintain her self-control. "How much?"

"Well, I only paid six hundred creds for it." He laid it in her open palm as she blinked at the bargain price. "I'd give it to you for five-fifty, though."

*   *   *

Abriel stared out the shuttle window, smiling and re-membering a time much further in the past. She had stud-ied management at an excellent school, but she'd been hard put to live peaceably with those who attended it for prestige, whose parents could afford baubles such as sun-stones. And when she fell in love—and signed marriage papers—with a musician, those classmates had scowled down long noses. She'd become pregnant right away, had wasted her maternity leave before seeking employment.

Sunstone.

The shuttle backbraked preparatory to its first landing on her side of Nexos's largest city, Vinnsing. "Block eighty-seven," said the mechanical voice from a speaker beside her left elbow. Clutching her briefcase, Abriel waited. The shuttle landed with a jarring double-thud. She kept her seat while several other passengers moved forward.

This gem hadn't been freighted by Renasco. Not at half the going market value.

Abriel fingered threadbare fabric at the edge of her shuttle seat. It had seemed such a good idea, back when Nexos contracted for Renasco service. A single group would provide intrasystem and cross-space commerce, to reforge Nexos's link with the Jarnik Belt and the homeworld. As time wore on, though, as import prices rose and Nexan salaries fell, Abriel's sentiments reflected those of Nexos at large. Renasco demanded compliance and tried to force respect, but Renasco could make no one like it. "Unity of mankind," the Company preached. Yes, Nexos agreed, the Company offered unity, but only under its control.

Apparently, others disdained that control too. There were smugglers out there, risking their lives in the radia-tion. *Nexans or Cabrans?* wondered Abriel.

The shuttle took off again, and she stared out at Vinnsing's streets. So many trees bloomed now that she felt almost guilty for adoring a cold gem.

The shuttle began to brake again. "Blocks eighty-five and -six," droned the speaker.

Wedging her briefcase under one arm and holding a safety cord that stretched from seat to seat, Abriel stepped up the main aisle to the shuttle's rear door. Closed inside her palm, the sunstone seemed to quiver—which was ridiculous. She was only feeling her own pulse run fast.

Spring blossoms burst their buds all around her, like blue- and yellow-hatted line gangs working the flowerbeds along each housing row. Her coat, closed for the air-conditioned shuttle, began to feel hot. She opened it absent-mindedly, walking a little slower, wondering how best to explain the ring to Keath.

Keath had a right to professional pride, but he often found it difficult to find steady work to supplement music income, and impossible, thus far, to find a permanent patron. Yet he had more about him than either pride or skill. She'd been drawn by his easy good looks and talent. She remained because of his kindness and devotion.

Abriel stepped down a curb and crossed a quiet residential avenue. To her right, a single car pulled away and began to accelerate. She stepped a little quicker and flicked a strand of blond hair off her face. Would Keath be willing to "give" her the ring? *He'll be glad to escape having to find something on his own. He needs time for work.* For her gift of time—he had to impress this client, or quickly find a seasonal job to pay for their gifted son's next year of school—surely he would be grateful.

She let herself into a tidy home near one end of a housing row. As she laid her keys on her kitchen work counter just inside the front door, an electronic choir rose in rapturous song. She paused, standing motionless beside the three-stool dining counter, gauging the melody's effect on her own emotions. As she did, she curled open her fingers again. Summer was coming, and she owned a sunstone.

"Mom. What've you got?"

A small, skinny boy, eight years old and crowned with his father's dark blond curls, sprang up from under the dining counter.

Abriel backed away. "Tieg!" Panting in exaggerated shock, she balled her hands into fists. "Don't do that to me."

"What is it, Mom?" He reached up for her wrist. For an instant she resisted, then she had to share her treasure. Tieg's feelings always mirrored her own. "Ooh," he said. "That's outsystem, isn't it?"

"Tieg!" Quick pride warmed her. Tieg was always surprising her. Evidently he remembered each irrelevant detail he read, or heard, or studied at that expensive school. "Yes, love." She rubbed his sharp chin with its mounting. "It's a Cabran sunstone."

He seized her wrist and held the stone to his eye, so close that it almost nestled into the socket beneath eyebrows that grew thickly for his age. His fingers squeezed. Then, taking her hand by the thumb and last finger, he pushed it away. "It's even brighter up close. Is it yours? Who gave it to you?"

"Yes, Tieg," she said, settling onto one of the high dining stools. "It's mine. I bought it."

"Bought it." Her son wormed between her knees. "How'd you do that?"

"What's this?" Keath Innig appeared in the doorway. Solid with muscle from manual labor, he retained a gentle manner that even after nine years seemed incongruous to Abriel. "Tieg," he said, the light of teasing reprimand in his eye, "are you playing Invaders with your poor mother again?"

"Look, Dad. She's got a sunstone." Tieg put just enough awe in his voice to mimic a character on one of his favorite vids. "A real one. Look at it glow."

Keath paused, then ambled over to the counter.

Since obviously she couldn't conceal the bauble until a better time, Abriel twisted the ring around to display the gem on the outside of her hand, where it belonged. She held it up to her husband.

"What . . . how much . . . why?" Keath stepped back. He too seemed struck by the spell of the exotic crystal and unable to easily look away. Again Abriel felt a swirl of awe, of how-in-the-world-can-it-do-this, just as when she first saw one. The pale luminescence drew energy from her hand's warmth, she knew, its fluorite-related heart sheathed in a hard, amberlike matrix. But she'd have to take off the ring to watch it fade, and she didn't want to. Glints from its fiery center played in Keath's blue eyes.

"I didn't pay much for it, actually. Nowhere near the going rate."

"How much?" he asked again.

"Five hundred."

She watched him consider. It constituted less than a month's wages at her new supervisory salary, not so much to spend on such a treasure. It cost far too little, and she knew it. Eventually, he would draw the obvious conclusion.

To her surprise, Tieg voiced it first. "Eee, Mom," he said with open admiration. "It must be smuggled."

Keath Innig reached down and gave their bony-shouldered son a smack, then took the stool beside Abriel's. "What do you know about smugglers, you little skink?"

Abriel's cheeks tugged with a controlled smile. Smuggling would seem a romantic notion to a bright eight-year-old. Between them, Tieg spread his legs and planted both hands on the hips of his pale green uniform jumpsuit. "Pell was talking about them just yesterday, after school. Said Renasco couldn't hold the monopoly on deep space forever. He's right."

A pang of jealousy twisted Abriel's insides. Tieg still understood Right, his mind not yet a filter of adult ideas like Practical and Appropriate. She felt surprised—delighted, really—that he clung to the childish notions.

Keath stared at her above Tieg's head. "I did hear a rumor that the Company caught a smuggling ship last week. Cabran, if they had it right."

Little Tieg affected a somber expression. "Do you know what Renasco does with smugglers, Mom?"

Abriel folded her hands in her lap. "I think they memory-wipe them," she said, with a cautionary glance at Keath. "And . . . often take them aboard Renasco ships, as manual labor."

"*I* heard they execute them." Again Tieg's voice took on the note of drama. "By—"

"That amounts to about the same thing, Tieg." Keath reached across the counter for a tickle-me from the bowl, then sat, elbows on the slick white counter, carefully peeling the chartreuse fruit. "Losing all your memories. Wouldn't that be the end of your life as you knew it? But I heard that the memory wiping is often done selectively. Saves Renasco retraining time, if they don't have to begin with baby talk."

"Locational electroconvulsion." Abriel glanced down

at the ring, wondering. Would she have risked memory wiping for a crystal such as this?

"Loca-tional electro-convulsion," Tieg mumbled, practicing. "Locational . . ."

Keath laid thin, hairy peeling back into the fruit basket. "Do you think it's illegal, then?"

Tieg examined the crystal again. Abriel let her hand go limp in his grasp. "Gib Tunny, one of my linemen at work, brought it in," she said. "He's had it a couple of months. So he told me."

"Oh," said Keath. "Then we're probably safe from the tracer team on this particular smuggler. Let's thank the All for that."

I can keep it! Abriel crowed silently. Then, as an afterthought, she asked, "Should I ask Gib where he got it, though?"

"No, Mom!" Tieg gripped her hand. "The less you know, the better. You can't tell the Company what you don't know. If there are other smugglers—independents—" he spoke the word firmly, "working the Cabra run, give them a chance."

Independents. His vocabulary! Abriel smiled down at Tieg and resisted the urge to muss his hair. "Tieg, you're going to be a politician."

He stepped away from the counter and smirked. "Nope. Pell and I talked about it already. We're going to Renasco school. We're going to get inside the Company and make trouble. I'm going to be a drive man."

Abriel fought off a qualm of uneasy maternal fear. She'd heard stories about that Renasco academy. She hated to think what their kind of schooling might do to the honest idealism of her young son.

Oh, he'll change his mind long before he's old enough for academy, she assured herself.

A second, uneasy voice inside her head quickly answered, *And when have you ever known Tieg Innig to change his mind?*

PART TWO

C

"Passenger Dalamani, proceed to level two briefing, room three-fourteen. Immediately."

As the deep voice faded from a speaker over her head, Ming groaned and pushed up to a sitting position. Her head ached. Her eyes throbbed. Her muscles sagged like overstretched rubber belts. She would feel less nausea soon, the medic assured her. The malady was an ordinary one requiring little treatment, the natural result of twenty years' suspended animation. Ming dangled her legs over the side, waiting. Would she black out? The previous morning she knocked herself silly trying this.

And what about the holes in her memory? Waking had been misery, these five days since she'd been brought up out of suspension.

No, her vision remained steady. She really felt better. Vitamin cocktails, motion therapy, low-wavelength irradiation of her muscles—they helped.

But she hurt all over, and the gaps in her recollections remained. Briefly, she struggled for a grip on the times the Company let her remember: four months in training, twenty years in cold sleep, and then—then, while still sleep-sick and weak, two days of agonizing "mnemonic therapy."

Shuffling forward, she caught the glance of an attendant standing at one end of a long row of beds, near the sickbay's door. "Sir," she said. "Excuse me." Her own voice like gravel sparked a sudden fleeting echo of Shan's voice. Ming grasped at the shred of memory but it vanished, leaving only grief. Shan was someone she had loved. Decades, light-years, and now memory blocks, too, separated

her from any life she had known before they . . . before.
"Where's level two?" she asked the attendant.

With slow disdain, he gave directions. On his white
tunic rode Renasco copper-on-blue collar points.

"Thangyou," she mumbled and headed down the
gleaming corridor, its brilliance terrible and wonderful
after so long a sleep. *The more I move, the quicker this will
wear off,* she reminded herself. Small comfort when every
motion hurt, when every nerve must relearn to fire after
twenty years' quiescence.

The level two corridor hummed with foot traffic and
too-loud voices. All the strangers wore gleaming copper-
on-blue, and none looked at her. She glanced down at her
clothing.

A slick-fitting jumpsuit of electric blue, belted in cop-
per-edged white: She looked like one of Them.

She was one of Them.

Ming leaned against the wall, dizzy again. *"Company
property,"* the medic had greeted her, upon waking her
from the twenty-year sleep that followed her training.

Conditioning, she corrected herself. Dimly she recalled
a lifelong desire to be a part of something bigger.

Shan was twenty years dead—executed, Renasco
hinted—and best forgotten. Renasco said the others'
crimes had been worse than her own. How many others?
What had the passage of years meant to her homeworld, to
her . . . her widowed father, now childless too?

Not now, she warned herself. *Don't add time-disorien-
tation to everything else. Get your bearings "here." Later,
get them in the "now."* Although she could remember
months of "readjustment" and her training in three-dimensional calligraphy, no crime, no glimmer of plans, no
shred of actuality remained.

What had she done?

Traffic thinned. She pushed away from the wall and
headed blindly to her right. By now, whoever wanted to
see her would be waiting with the famous Company patience: none.

Luck must have guided her. The first door she found
was numbered three-fourteen. It opened, and she stepped
inside.

Three men—no, the red-haired one was a woman—sat

waiting at one end of a long, high-gloss table meant for twenty. They wore the same copper-on-blue as everyone else she'd seen shipboard, but on these it was a sharp dress uniform, black with blue-trimmed copper collar bands. A folder lay closed on the table in front of one man.

Something looked wrong about his eyes. Ming peered closer, then recoiled. They opened side-to-side, the slits oriented in the vertical. He looked half human, half . . . reptile. Had mankind contacted almost-human aliens during her twenty-year sleep, or was this some new kind of cosmetic surgery?

Several places down from his end of the table, Ming laid her hands on the back of a chair.

"Over here." The normal-eyed Company man gestured her toward a seat cornerside of his cohort. She hurried toward it, stumbling along the way. If only her muscles would respond like a normal person's! Everything was too loud and too bright, the floor too rough.

"You need only be told a few things." The woman spoke, her posture aggressively erect, her voice an imperious whine. "Your employer is our current Company rep on Mannheim, the world we are presently orbiting. Personal slab-calligraphers have become unexpectedly difficult to place, which is the reason you have been in storage for so long. Your term of servitude shall be forty years Standard, unless by meritorious service to the Company you are able to distinguish yourself beyond expectation. We encourage you to work diligently toward that remission."

Ming stared ahead, seething at the woman's condescension.

"At such time as your debt to humankind, as represented by the Renascence Shielding Corporation, is fulfilled, we shall provide you additional training and relocate you on a world of your choice within our region of operation, with modest but adequate resources. A small percentage will be withheld from each unit of your pay, until your sentence is served. New colonies as well as our established client worlds will be open to you." She paused as if waiting for an answer.

Ming rubbed the slick table. Her instructors hadn't spoken in terms of years when training her, only that she must repay her "debt to humankind." Only now, nearing the world on which she would serve it, did they deliver her sentence.

Forty years would take her past youth. Past childbearing, even if they let her take rejuv treatments. Severed forever from the clan, condemned to an empty future. Any family she would ever have . . .

Would be the children of a sentenced worker. Company property, like herself. She lived now by the company's mercy, and no planetary government could gainsay the owners of the High Ground.

It wasn't right. This couldn't be real. Her eyelids began to flutter from the sleep sickness. Ashamed of her weakness, she let her head droop onto folded hands.

"She'll be all right," a male voice said dispassionately. "Cold hangover. Shipper, check her collar."

The way he said "collar" brought her back upright. Had they made her forget that, too, until now?

The lizard-eyed man walked around behind her. "Put your head back down."

Ming leaned forward and squeezed her eyes closed. Cold fingers pressed the base of her neck. "Established and operational," the man said, ignoring her shiver.

Wired into her fourth vertebra and through her spinal column, the Renasco collar utilized the electrical impulses of her nervous system as its power source, and its halves could be radio signaled to paralyze her. If no one chose to help her, she might die of simple thirst. Nausea thickened the back of her tongue.

The man's footsteps retreated, and his chair scraped again. She pressed up with her elbows and sat erect, shuddering with anger at this Company that could submit a human to such a device.

The woman ran a hand over her close-shorn red hair, then lifted something hand-sized and pale green off the top of her folder and held it up. "Your I.D. disc," she said. "You will carry it at all times. On Mannheim, citizens use them as access to finances, proof of employment, and evidence of security clearance." She smiled. "Yours, at present, is zero."

"Yes, madam."

"Oh, you can talk." Lizard-eyes blinked slowly at her, his leering expression proof he well knew his eyes' effect on others. "Excellent. Here, take it." He took the plastic disc from the woman and slid it over. Ming picked it up. One ring of tiny grooves ran around its rim; at its center, in another ring, "Ming Dalamani" was printed in black letters: block typeface. Her training gave her a new appreciation of print styles.

The woman reclined her chair and shook her shoulders languorously before speaking again. "As your debt is paid, we will perhaps upgrade that. A low-security check will reveal you as a law-abiding citizen—you see, you will be allowed to end your life with a modicum of dignity. Assuming we have no . . . mishaps along the way."

"I see." Ming flipped the disc and found its other side blank.

The Renasco woman pulled herself upright. "It may interest you to know that the Mannheim system is a corporate colony. We settled it, we own it. The local economy is open but controlled, based on agriculture and organic chemical processing. There are occasional transgressions of Company policy. Any you can find and report will doubtless shorten your time of service and lessen your debt to humankind, as represented by Renasco."

"I see." Following the announcement of her sentence as it did, she understood the half-promise of parole was meant as powerful motivation. "You want me to spy, Madam?"

"No, simply to report when you find . . . troublemakers." The leering man blinked again, his eyes closing slowly like slashes. "The Company can afford more subtle, better trained operatives, naturally. You are offered that opportunity as a way to prove your commitment."

Opportunity—the lizard! Ming no longer cared if the man carried alien blood. Whether alien or surgically altered human, he disgusted her.

From his left, the other man pulled up a long blue satchel by white straps, then dropped it onto the table with a soft *plump*. "Your tools," he said. "All you'll need to begin work, supplied by the school. Your clothing, housing, and additional materials will be provided by your employer."

"Sir," said Ming. "What will his name be?"

Both men turned toward the red-haired woman.

"Our current Company rep on Mannheim," she an-

swered, folding her hands and glaring narrow-eyed at
Ming, "is a woman. Her Grace the Podacan ambassador,
Holdj-peep Lang-lick," she said distinctly, then handed
Ming a small card lettered in castil font, HOLJPIP LANGEL-
LEIK, RENASCENCE SHIELDING CORPORATION, ONE
PRIME ROW. ANSLANDING, MANNHEIM. "She has a reputation for callous use of her employees. You are to use your
position as calligrapher to get as close to her as possible and
await further orders. That, calligrapher, is the capacity in
which you stand to serve the company best. Do you understand?"

Frowning, Ming returned the woman's stare. "I . . .
believe so, Madam. I am to await further orders."

"If you prove able to fulfill them on Mannheim, they
will be given. If not, your time there will be short."

Ming nodded, understanding the veiled threat and not
anxious for details of possible removal.

Lizard-eyes leaned on the table and blinked again.
"Your shuttle leaves in fifteen minutes. The waiting area is
on level thirty. You'll need to hurry."

The woman waved her away. Ming seized her satchel
and sidled along the table to the door.

For a moment, standing outside, she wondered why no
guards shadowed her. Then, as she boarded an elevator,
she guessed. Naturally, they would let her roam the ship.
She wore the collar. Skin pulled tight at the back of her
neck. Further orders: What would they be?

She found her destination with no more effort than
before and boarded the shuttle with five minutes to spare.
Directed toward its rear compartment, she sank on a soft
acceleration chair. Three passengers already sat in this
economy section with neither windows nor a viewscreen.
Disappointed to be denied one glimpse of her new
homeworld from space, and ignored by the other passengers—one pulled a periodical from his satchel—she sat and
fumed for what seemed hours.

They wanted her to spy? On whom? *For* whom? Was
she to insinuate herself into one regime's favor, then to
help bring it down and fall with it?

Not fair. She wasn't trained for spy work! Gulping hangover nausea, she swung her feet hard to work away at the
sickness and peered around the cabin for loose periodicals.

She'd give a lot to know what was happening in this decade.

Rancor spent, she pulled down her satchel to examine her tools.

Her own tools. It felt odd to possess things again. No one had owned anything in training.

Digging through the satchel, she found she had a goodly supply of the powders necessary to mix (and later set) the injectable three-dimensional calligraphy slab medium. Ten injection pens, eight with nibs varying from needle fineness to the width of her little fingernail, and two of variable width for tapering effects, nestled in cases tucked into compartments along one side of the satchel. Three ruled working trays, inks, Standard cards for six alphabet "hands," and three thick pads of white paper lay below . . . and one small completed slab.

She drew it out, squinting to admire the delicate work of the unknown calligrapher whose original was duplicated for reference. Threaded through this centimeter-thick piece of clear hard medium that nestled comfortably in her palm, four alphabets glistened, eight marching lines of micro hand. The thin black ribbons of ink twisted with beautiful and perfect accuracy, circular and triangular counters, ascenders and descenders, entrances and exits.

Someday she would do as well, if Renasco gave her enough time to learn. She must establish a rigid practice schedule the day she arrived. Today.

Clutching two pens, Ming rested her head against the chair's high back and shut her eyes, remembering *home.* Renasco had sparked out sections of her memory, not the whole.

Her Renasco testing, gruelingly thorough, found her unfit for physical labor. Ruefully, she glanced down again at her thin, bony arms. Perhaps fragility had saved her from a life of miserable drudge work. And now that they'd placed an unspecified number of memory overrides on the left side of her brain, causing recollections that snapped into blackness, art remained as her only trained talent. By the time recall returned in full (five to ten years hence, the tech had forecast), she'd have made a new place for herself, a place she wouldn't want to give up for antiquated hopes. She would feel only shame regarding that dim past life.

But someday she would remember. She had a vague guess already, for if she had transgressed against a space-travel and colonization monopoly, only a few acts would offend it.

A tear puddled at the corner of one eye. Fiercely she wiped it away. She would remember it all, one day. Her standards and morals remained intact, centered in her nonverbal right hemisphere, which Renasco's "therapy" ignored. She couldn't have committed anything shameful or violent. Still Ming Dalamani, she would be true to herself. Every mental block she discovered offered a clue to her past—such as mathematics, now a jumble ridiculous for one of her age. She would have to relearn multiplication. And the Cabran economy . . .

She shook herself. She'd answer to an ambassador, now. Ming pulled out the card and eyed the queer name. HOLJPIP LANGELLEIK. "HOLDJ-peep," she whispered, trying out the Renasco woman's inflection. "HOLDJ-peep LANG-lick." Why did Podaca, a Belt world, place an ambassador on a Renasco-owned colony? And what was her relationship with the Company? If Ming read the whining woman correctly, Holjpip Langelleik was either in some kind of trouble or under consideration for promotion.

Ming felt her body ease forward in the padded seat and wished for a window. Her compartment-mate turned another page.

At last the shuttle landed. She could not mistake the sensation of backthrust while engines roared close to her compartment. An attendant sidestepped into the cabin and called, "Mannheim. Anslanding, capitol city," then eased out again.

Anslanding, the city named on the card. They'd made her do everything else for herself, they would expect her to disembark unassisted. Renasco asked her to be oddly independent, for a prisoner.

They wanted to present her as an ordinary employee. Ming unbuckled, secured her satchel over one shoulder, and slid up the long corridor into a cabin that did have windows, one side darkened against glare. Several passengers sat waiting for the shuttle to take off again. First class unloaded first, she observed. Renasco efficiency.

Left turn into brilliant light, and she stepped out. A breeze flowed through her hair and thin blue jumpsuit. From atop a long, curved ramp cast of white concrete, the light seemed fierce, but cool air suggested early morning. And the fragrance . . . Ming inhaled an incredible sweetness.

Something jostled her hard from behind. *"Go,"* said an irritated male voice at her back.

She marched on down the ramp, savoring every breath. Flowers, but where? And was their scent truly this intense, or heightened by her body's long sleep? And there were—she gulped—puddles on the ground. Puddles of *water*.

At the foot of the ramp, several people clustered together and one man stood alone—at least, she assumed this one was a man. The sleeves of a long robe flowed off his shoulders to join its sides, and a cascade of V's chevroned in brilliant shades of blue and green down from his collar, widening to fill all the fabric. When he shifted it shimmered, hurting her eyes.

At the bottom of the ramp, she realized he was returning her appraising stare. His short, curling blond hair sparked a self-aborting memory. (Where had she seen that kind of hair before?) Above the center of his forehead, however, lay one lock so white, so symmetrical, it had to be false. Tall but not towering, the man tilted his strong chin and looked down with blue-gray eyes under his curling brows. "Would you be the calligrapher?"

His slight, casually slurred accent also stirred recollection. "Yes, sir."

"Your name?"

She took herself in hand. "Ming." Suddenly she realized her physical wooziness had passed. Perhaps the sweet, cool, free-flowing air roused her. "Ming Dalamani." Hitching satchel straps higher on her shoulder, she took a tentative step left and away from the ramp.

"This way." The shimmering figure moved off toward a line of four-wheeled cars parked along a straight avenue, beneath a double row of rhythmically swaying trees. Dark clouds scudded away overhead. When she caught up, he said, "I'm Tieg Innig, Her Grace's tone poet. Today neither she nor her staff require my services, so I came for you." He gave her a sidelong glance. "You're not what I expected."

Ming opened her mouth to ask what he did expect, when engines rose behind her. She pivoted in time to see the shuttle point its nose toward the runway and move out.

She fought the temptation to cover her ears and cower at the roar. "You're a . . . singer, then?"

"That's close. This way." He led her toward a silver car. Above it drooped an incredible tree; long branches covered with long, tender-looking leaves dangled within a meter of the ground. "Instrumentalist," he said as she marveled at the leaves' pendant delicacy and the slender stems on which they fluttered. What a damp world this must be. "All sorts of instruments, ancient and modern," the man in robes went on. "Her Grace enjoys a pleasant synthesizer as background, like anyone else, but she has also preserved a taste for the instruments a synthesizer mocks."

Ming gazed up into the tree's crown. A spectacular series of whistled notes trilled down out of its branches.

Enchanted, she stared at the musician. "What was that?"

"Daylark." Puckering his lips, he whistled back the song. The breeze caught one sleeve of his robe and blew it aside far enough for her to catch a glimpse of muscular forearm.

Oh. Not so effeminate. Professional musicians she remembered from Cabra Minor tended to unhealthy stringiness. This man in woman's dress was a contradiction.

Tieg Innig slid open a panel in the back of the car. She handed him the satchel. He packed it away, then came around to the front, and she followed him step for step.

He blinked up from under bushy eyebrows, then jerked his head. "Other side."

Rounding the car's tapered prow, she reached another door that stood open a crack. It felt odd to sit down into a car. Like a dream fragment, she glimpsed another world from the high seat of a three-wheeler. As she tucked her feet in, the door closed by itself.

"All set?"

Ming exhaled. "Yes. Right."

He pressed a tab; the car rose several centimeters on its wheels, and he steered out into the traffic lane, then a wider highway. Few cars traveled the main road, and none passed them. She stared as lines of trees whipped by.

"This is Newport. Twenty minutes to Anslanding."

"Oh." In little more than a minute, the car sped out into a treeless area without buildings. Wide fields lay on either side of the road, carpeted in intense yellow. "Oh," she said again, blinking. "Beautiful."

Tieg pulled one hand off the half-wheel and rubbed the back of his head. "Cryllia. You probably smelled it when you got off the shuttle. Its perfume is one of Mannheim's exports. They'll be harvested in about a week, and after that the johnnistars will come into bloom. Pegsbreath is next. You've just missed the foggy season. It will be spring to the point of insanity now, for several months. Nice time to arrive." He turned to study her, and again she thought how ludicrously false that white shock of hair looked. "Enjoy your trip?"

Ming frowned and stared down the long highway, across fields of yellow glory. "I slept all the way."

"I'd had the impression Company employees traveled first class."

He thought of her as an employee, not a sentenced laborer? Good. "Tell me about Madam . . . uh . . ." She made the plunge and tried to pronounce it. "Madam Langlick?"

"Her Grace isn't just the Company rep here." He laid both hands in his lap, the folds of his caftan shimmering around them. Ming glanced ahead. The black road ran on without any hint of a turn, and the car appeared to track perfectly; but still, this no-hands driving did little for her nerves.

"The Renasco position is top grade but only half-time. She's also the ambassador from Podaca, her home system, and major stockholder of a third of the industry on the continent. She doesn't seem to mind the low population here; it's landed her a pair of choice positions. This is her fourth professional station, and she's dug in well. She's lived here six years. What else do you want to know?"

"Ambassador? From one Renasco world to another?"

He exhaled, sounding self-important. "Renasco owns Mannheim, but not Podaca. Podaca contracted for service and has its own trade board, so it maintains an office here for its interests."

"No conflict of priorities on Her Grace's part?"

"Evidently not. Podacan visitors and Renasco inspection teams come and go, and we remain a colonial entity."

Silently Ming repeated all this, then asked, "How long have you been here?"

"Almost as long as Her Grace. Four years, going on five."

Tieg Innig, tone poet to a woman with that kind of power, would be a good one not to cross, no matter what kind of hair and dress he affected, and he might be able to help her "get close."

"Have you any idea what my position will involve?"

"That's for Her Grace to say. Frankly, I have no idea. I've never heard of a professional calligrapher before. Sounds exquisitely boring, if you'll forgive my saying so."

Ming set her chin forward. "I find it satisfying."

"How did you come to be in Company employ?"

Alarm bells clanged in Ming's mind. Whatever she told him, it must be close enough to have the ring of truth, simple enough to remember, and able to stand up under investigation. "I . . . come from a very minor world, and I was born into a minor clan there. My people have always run counter to everyone else, and I—I have always wished to be a part of something bigger. To serve humankind." So far as it went, it was truth. She must make the best of this sentence, and never give away her hatred and resentment.

To her surprise, Tieg snorted softly and took hold of the half-wheel again. "How do you come to equate humankind with Renasco?"

"I—" Automatically she reached up to touch an earring in apology, but her fingers grasped only soft earlobe. Earrings. She'd worn earrings, and they'd been taken away. "I don't. But humankind is scattered and broken, and for all its faults, the Company is trying to piece it back together."

After a minute, he said in a smoother voice, "Yes, that's policy."

Ming fumed. He wore no collar. He could say what he

liked. She stared out the window at yellow-green hills beyond level cryllia fields under cultivation. "You're not a Renasco employee, then?"

"I work for Her Grace under contract."

The car topped a rise. In the western distance, a river valley winding down its long plain ended in a glimmering city. One white sweep of stone caught the sunlight and gleamed atop a dark forested ridge.

"There," said Tieg Innig. "Our home, Ming. The ambassador's official residence, Holjpip's villa."

D

The road dropped between fields of pale shrubbery, affording Ming time to scan the villa. From this distance, it looked long enough to land a shuttle on, and she could only guess at its width.

"Is that a penthouse there on the right?"

"No, a hangar. Landings take place over the staff wing; Holjpip has North Upper—the left side, from here—for herself, guests, top staff, and dining. I'd guess they'll house you below ground."

"They need another floor under that?"

"Yes, three dormitory halls and the garage. You'll see."

The road passed under an arch and into Anslanding. Ming marveled at the stretch of land they'd crossed, free for cultivation, under no dome. (And why was that so important in her anchorless memory?) But Anslanding seemed familiar enough, with heavy vehicular and foot traffic. Tall, ordinary-looking, black-haired men and women jostled along the sidewalks with brunets and blonds of all shades. Four pale young women sat nearly

naked under the high sun in one grassy yard, and Ming
gaped as Tieg drove past. On Cabra Minor, people *blistered* themselves at midday.

The spotty pattern of things she did remember baffled
her, evidence of the convolutions her mind used to store
data. One long leap of a concrete bridge took them over a
roaring torrent thick with logs and other debris. "Riddle
River," Tieg said absently. "It's flood season."

Ming set her thoughts forward. She would have time to
see Anslanding. For now, she'd better prepare to meet this
mysterious employer who was headed either up or out.
She reached toward the floor.

In half a second she caught herself. She owned tools and
a single set of clothes, but nothing with which to wipe
perspiration from her forehead or comb her hair. *Maybe
she won't want to see me right away. Maybe she'll be busy.*

Ming's stomach lurched. The road began to rise again,
walled on the left by a hillside covered with deep green
vines. They passed a black-suited guard at a gate; Tieg
Innig drove through without pause. *Well. Whatever Tieg
is, he's known here.*

On Ming's right, the hill dropped away. She watched
town, river, and—heavens! That long, flat, glimmering
stretch of slate blue beyond the city—could it be an ocean?

She stared spellbound. It was, it was; covered with
shadowed rippling waves. After several seconds, she
wrenched her gaze left. Behind a grove of trees, a single
broken row of dark, reflective windows strung the high
white facade like a line of code. Tieg drove slowly now. On
his left, a blacktop ramp lined with parked cars curved off
this access road. At last, he steered into a cutting that
became a tunnel, then a huge chamber lit in pure artificial
white. Lines and rows of silver cars like the one she rode in
. . . longer models that made her gape . . . a blockhouse
ahead, and Tieg headed for it. Beside the curb, he stopped
and shut down the car. She felt it sink.

He leaned toward her. "This is it, Ming Dalamani.
Good luck here. I hope you can be happy, just to spite
them." He gave her a knowing look and pressed another
button. Her door clacked open.

Ming struggled out and up to her feet. When she

reached the back of the car, sniffing at unfamiliar exhaust fumes, Tieg handed up her satchel.

Silently, resenting his ease, she followed him into the blockhouse. Inside, at its far end, gleamed a glass-walled elevator. Another guard stood just indoors, and a young man in eye-searing purple sat behind a computer terminal.

"This is the calligrapher," Tieg said without elaborating, then strode to the elevator. In his brilliant chevrons Tieg Innig rose, clearly visible through glass, to pass out of sight above the ceiling.

Ming took a step closer to the man at the work station. His purple jumpsuit fairly glowed, recalling a flux she had used when welding sculpture. *(Another inexplicable, irrelevant memory. Why?)* As she approached him, she felt a qualm of uncertainty *(suppose there's been a delay in transmissions, and they don't know I'm coming),* and then a too-brief surge of elation *(I'd be free!—for a little while).*

But he said in a bored tone, "Mere Dalamani. I.D. disc, please."

She fumbled it free of the breast pocket of her blue issue tunic. The man dropped it onto a square panel dished out precisely to hold that circle, eyed the pattern of white lights that sprang on beside it, then handed it back. "Take this." He handed her a slippery, rectangular chip of brilliant pink plastic just large enough to fit in her palm. "Groundside, right above this room, you'll find Staff Central. Show Mere Bertelsen the pink chip and she'll see you set up."

"Thank you, sir." Ming clutched chip and disc as she walked to the glass tube, uneasy under the man's stare. Seeing no call tab, she waited on a hunch.

Sure enough, a half-moon of floor descended, a door slid aside, and she stepped on. *There's room for only one passenger,* she observed as the quarter-round door panel slid back into place, *and they can watch you coming up.* Grudgingly she forgave Tieg Innig for abandoning her to ride alone. She guessed she would find other security systems, here in this headquarters for Renasco operations, which doubled as an ambassador's residence and the All knew what else.

The ceiling sank past her feet through smoky glass.

Another black-suited guard on the next floor watched as she rose. A thin cord of bright violet trimmed his shoulders and collar.

Cool uplevel air raised bumps on her arms. Ming stepped off and across into a windowless chamber, where a heavy, black-haired young woman occupied the computer chair. Ming walked forward, extending her chip and disc like shields. "I'm Ming Dalamani," she said. "Are you Mere Bertelsen? I hope—"

With a cool, officious glance, the girl snatched the disc and chip and swiveled the chair so Ming saw only her back.

"—you're expecting me," Ming finished. *She's young. Has she got the money for rejuv?* she wondered fleetingly. Then she wondered why she had not had the same eerie suspicion about Tieg Innig.

Mere Bertelsen turned again. "I'm drawing you a map." She gestured toward the printer beside her keyboard. It whined and vibrated as it rolled out a swath of paper. Bertelsen, whose pale violet-colored jumpsuit bunched at her waist, neatly tore it free and spread it over a second keyboard, this one on her left, protruding into the room. Ming leaned forward. On two long rectangles drawn side by side, Ming saw black lines that must be walls, dotted lines she could not interpret, and a slurry of other inexplicable symbols.

"Don't lose this," Bertelsen said in a slightly lisping voice. She glanced upward, and at last Ming saw a hint of a smile at the edges of her eyes. "You can always get someone to bring you back to Staff Central, but getting lost is a colossal waste of time. Yours, and others'."

Ming listened intently to directions to room twenty-one sixteen, downlevel. "Load the pink chip in the palm-lock slot," Mere Bertelsen went on. "Then press the black panel firmly with your dominant hand. Got it so far?"

"I . . . think so," Ming said slowly. The morning bout of sleep sickness had long passed, but her back was beginning to ache again.

"Everything inside is issued to you. For now. You'll find a display screen over your desk. Switch it on and leave it on. It'll alert you audibly if you have instructions. Till then—" She looked up. "It looks like sleep and a bath will be your first orders."

The upper corridors, busy but not crowded, again gave Ming a sense of lost home, but in women's quarters downlevel, her footsteps fell into silence. She found her room with only one wrong turn and one backtrack. Below its number, drawn in darker brown on spruce–brown paneling, a black rectangle gleamed at shoulder height with no obvious place to insert the chip. Careful not to touch the reading surface, she fingered all around it, then examined the door frame.

It would make sense to look for help, but in this silent hall she feared she'd wander off and get lost. One minute away from deciding to drop and nap right there on the carpet, she saw a large woman swing into view at the far end of her corridor. "Say!" Ming waved. "Can you help me?"

The woman strolled up the carpeted hall. Comfortably shaped and dressed in white coveralls that showed a single broad, yellowed stain on the fronts, she walked nevertheless with a spring in her step.

"I'm new," Ming said. "And I'm locked out. Where do I put this?" She held up the bright pink rectangle.

"Oh. Um." An incongruously refined nose wrinkled on the woman's round face. "It's been a long time. Oh." She pressed her palm to the panel, and it hummed as it extended outward several centimeters from the wall. "There. *Now* drop the chip in. At the top."

Standing tiptoe, Ming spotted a slot behind the slab. She slid in the chip, wiped her right hand on her tunic, then pressed hard against the black panel. It gave way until once again it lay nearly flush against the wall.

"Thank you." Ming pressed the black rectangle again, and the door slid open. "I'm Ming Dalamani," she said, extending a hand to touch fingertips.

The woman clasped her whole hand in a soft, smooth palm. "Lyra Dusenfeld. I live in twenty-twelve, and I serve in Staff Dining. You?"

Ming tucked her satchel under her arm. "Calligraphy. And who knows what else." She glanced through the door. The room looked huge, almost as spacious as her father's living room. Hers, without having to share. This was no crowded dome-world.

"You're probably right about the what else. We get the

oddest jobs occasionally. Here, why don't I show you how everything works?"

Following Lyra Dusenfeld into the carpeted room, Ming found a narrow, bare-mattressed cot, a full room for wet needs, an efficient desk with silvery shelves overhead, and two—*two*—hard orange desk chairs. Along one wall, at a long wooden table, she could work comfortably. From the ventilator screen over the table drifted a faint scent of flowers.

Lyra vanished into a walk-in closet and emerged with a pile of folded linens. "Help you with the bed?"

Ming copied the other woman's movements, tucking down the single blanket with a final tug that pulled it tight. "Soft," she said, fingering its hem. To her supersensitive skin, it felt like the woven essence of sleep. "But is this really warm enough for here?" She straightened. Again, the inexplicable sense of memory.

"I suppose that depends on how hot you're used to sleeping." Lyra shrugged. "You have to excuse me. I keep forgetting that new people are likely to come from anywhere."

Ming leaned against the wall, groping . . . groping . . . she had it! "Where I lived last, only the poles are livable," she said, keeping her voice steady. "With full-time, full-dome refrigeration."

"I see." Lyra stepped across to the closet. "In that case," came her muffled voice from inside, and she reemerged carrying two more soft gray covers, "spring on Mannheim might be a little chilly for you."

Together they wrapped the second blanket. "The old lady's all right," Lyra said unexpectedly. "Treats us well. Pays well, too." She smiled. "But I guess you know that. We like to say Holjpip is headed for the top—probably the head of Renasco, someday. Her mutant, though—watch out for him."

Ming scratched one elbow. "Who?"

"Hookey, or something like that. I've seen him, and I've heard nasty things—oh, here I am, worrying you. You'll probably never meet the man. Not if you're art staff."

"Do you know others on the art staff?"

"Not to speak with them. The tone poet I've met, but

he's a little scary. Someone told me once they'd heard he'd killed someone. Accident . . . maybe."

The hint made her uneasy. *Yes, but I'm a criminal too. Maybe Tieg Innig just hasn't been caught yet.*

When the third blanket lay wrapped neatly around the mattress, Ming sat on it. "Mh," she grunted. "My feet."

"There's some great powder in the wet room." Lyra made a shaking motion with one hand. "Half-close the shower drain and dissolve it in the water that collects when you bathe."

Glancing around the room—huge, and all hers—Ming caught sight of the data screen. "Oh, no. I forgot." She walked back toward the desk and reached for a switch.

From behind, Lyra caught her hand. "Wait."

Ming hesitated.

"It's not official wisdom." Lyra shook pale reddish-brown curls. "And it may only be rumor. But supposedly security can watch *you* through that screen, if they want. That's one reason we're not allowed to turn it off, once it's activated. Just thought you'd like to know. *I* dress in the wet room."

"Oh," Ming said blankly. "Thank you." Then she flicked on the screen. No instruction appeared, so she walked across and sank back down onto the bed, reaching for one shoe. Her foot throbbed as she freed it. "Thank you for everything, Lyra. Will I see you again soon?"

"Uh, sure, Ming." Lyra still stood by the door, absently circling her palms against her coverall fronts. "You, um, have to let me out."

"Oh. Sorry." Ming padded back to the door and palmed the inner locking panel. Smiling, Lyra eased back through.

E

Ming sighed. She was standing again. She pulled open the walk-in closet to explore, wondering if Lyra Dusenfeld would be as friendly if she knew what kind of collar Ming Dalamani wore beneath her clothes.

Under a broad shelf that still held two pillows, a number of jumpsuits hung alongside a loose-fitting tunic for bed, and one long white wraparound nightrobe. Ming took the robe, tunic, and a pair of room slippers into the wet room and shut the door before undressing.

The private shower swept her sticky flesh clean, then she slipped into the velvety tunic. Relaxed at last, she laid the robe across the foot of her bed and fell in. It was smooth, and warm. Beautiful . . .

An irritating, repetitive buzz woke her. With no idea how long she had dozed, she felt sleep-sick all over again, her head pulsing. Throwing off the covers, she began to shiver. She yanked the robe on over her tunic before staggering to the screen, her bare feet scuffing on short, nubbly carpet.

+REPORT SUITE 1011+, it read. Hurriedly she searched the keyboard for an "acknowledge" tab. There, at bottom right: ACK. The noise stopped, but her screen did not entirely clear. On its lower margin blinked a cluster of numbers: 0812. As she watched, it changed to 0813.

Unfortunately, she hadn't noticed the time when she lay down.

She pulled out Staff Central's map and squinted at it, wondering when the day would come that she'd wake feeling rested instead of sick. Along the map's corridors marched hundreds of tiny numbers. The thousands lay

42

right above her—the ambassador's wing, according to Tieg Innig.

The ambassador. This is it.

She changed into the darkest blue jumpsuit. In the wet room she splashed her face, found a brush, and made her short black hair lie down. As an afterthought, she seized her satchel and the map. Refreshed but still unsteady, and wishing for time to enjoy that delectable shower again, she headed in search of an elevator. One of the glass bulges blistered a wall around the first bend. She stepped in and immediately began to rise. *There must only be the two floors*, she observed, *if no passenger control is necessary*. Then she remembered the hangars and garages. Four floors. The others must be accessed by special elevator or . . . something.

Ming expected opulence at the top of the ride, but her notion of opulence rested on what standards of Cabra Minor she could recall. From a high, wide ceiling that was a single frosted skylight, light gleamed on deep gold carpet, moldings, and door frames carved of blond wood with a whitish grain. Cream-colored rough fabric lined the walls nearly to ceiling height, where just below the skylight they gave way to blond wood once again. Soft music sounded from somewhere, a soothing melody played by something that sounded like, yet unlike, a Cabran string-synthesizer. She recognized the scent of the flowers blooming out in the fields. What had Tieg Innig called them? Daystars?

A woman in violet-on-black watched her from three doors away, and in a few moments walked over. "Do you have business here?"

"I'm to report to ten-eleven. Can you direct me?"

"Operations. That way." Towering over Ming, she pointed left, southward. "You new?"

"Yes." Ming adjusted her satchel over one shoulder.

"Then for your own sake, you should learn a house rule right now. Except Security, mere-class staff doesn't stand around in North Upper."

What other rules will I learn only when I break them? And at what point do they start punishing infractions? Ming walked off in the direction the guard pointed. The carpet cradled her feet with each step, and her soft shoes sank in—yet when she glanced back, she saw no footprints.

Room numbers. She remembered to check a door frame. Sure enough, in the proper spot to the right of the blond wood, a number gleamed in pale light, cut through the fabric.

It's beautiful, she breathed to herself. *Oh, Shan. I wish you could see this.* She paused between steps. Her cousin had been congenitally crippled. Wincing at the flash of memory, she walked on. The music grew louder, then began to fade as she passed a door. Farther on, the phenomenon repeated itself: same music, different rooms.

She could see the end of the passage now. The wall looked green and moving, as if indoor trees lined the corridor's end. But before she reached it, along the left wall she found the room numbered 1011. A pair of guards waited outside at attention, holding some kind of rifles at rest, butt to the floor.

"Ming Dalamani," she said to the one nearest her. "I'm to report."

He neither answered nor challenged her. She brushed past him and inside. That same music played softly in here.

The room's back wall was a single long window. Ming controlled a gasp when she saw the ocean again, but she didn't get time to gaze, for against that window stood two more motionless guards and two women. One, tall and quite young, wore the most incredible version of a Renasco uniform Ming had ever seen: belted in copper, not blue but a pale amethyst, with flared shoulders, gathered full sleeves, and a heavy bracelet cuff on each wrist. A high collar graced her long, stately throat, matching elbow-length hair in a rich shade of copper.

Smaller than her long-haired companion, the older woman wore violet too, the same intense shade Ming recalled seeing on the staffer in the garage blockhouse, and she carried a holster on her belt.

Ming inclined her head, not quite sure how to behave toward Holjpip Langelleik, Company representative, Podacan ambassador, manufacturing magnate, and patron of the arts. Nor was Ming sure which one of these two she was, though she guessed at the younger. At least she remembered the title Tieg Innig used. "Your Grace." She bowed toward a space between the women. "How may I serve you?"

The young one tipped back her head so copper-colored hair cascaded behind her shoulders. "Come here, calligrapher."

Ming took several steps closer, threading a way between elegant gilded chairs. The near wall sparkled with electronic gear, including several silent screens that displayed scenes in other rooms. A man and a woman sat on stools before the wall, wearing headphones, watching.

So Lyra had been right about the computer monitors. But Lyra had also never seen this room, or she would know the "rumor" for a fact—and how few rooms Renasco watched at any moment. Ming's position, then, entailed a good deal of contact with individuals other staffers served from afar.

"You have your tools?" asked the slender girl in a strident, brassy voice.

The worst of it was that she looked familiar. "Yes, Madam." Ming displayed the satchel, groping into the dim past for recollection. How did she know Holjpip Langelleik?

"Stand at attention," the girl snapped.

Ming obeyed, silently fuming. Did they expect her to know their local customs without a protocol briefing? Or were these women other than whom she expected? Yet, the guards at the door—and two more outside the long window, beside its corners—suggested Someone inside who wanted guarding.

Standing stiff-legged, she studied the girl's face and saw a network of tiny lines framing deep, hard eyes. This woman had gone on rejuv very young.

This was Her Grace, Holjpip Langelleik.

"In the future," Holjpip said, "we shall likely have our staff deal directly with you." Then she spoke to her companion. "Did you ever see such a human antenna?"

"Not an overeater." Holjpip's associate made a wry face. "Mere Dalamani, have you brought samples of your work?"

"No, Madam. It was explained that I would not be allowed the extra mass of set gels shipboard."

The smaller, older looking woman raised a hand. "I am *Missara* Claude Yerren, adjutant to Her Grace. We shall ask for several sample alphabets, as quickly as you can produce them."

Missara? She'd never heard that title before. Her stomach rumbled, and her cheeks warmed at the rudeness. She glanced left. The glare from outdoors made Holjpip's hair a gleaming nimbus. "Excuse me, Your Grace."

Holjpip laughed unpleasantly. "Haven't found Staff Dining yet, I hear."

"No, Your Grace. May I ask—"

"Questions are to be directed to Staff Central." Holjpip stepped toward her desk. The curly haired woman held Holjpip's chair. Adjutant? That could mean almost anything. Claude Yerren didn't carry herself like a menial, and the amethyst ring she wore, deep-shaded and cut in myriad facets, circled a long, aristocratic finger.

Behind the desk, Holjpip Langelleik sat rigidly, arching her long neck. Now Ming saw from direct gestures and attentive eye movements that she had worn authority for a long time. Ming waited, having no words except rebuffed requests for help.

"Have you any experience with facial art?" Holjpip asked abruptly.

"What is that?"

The breadth of Holjpip's mouth remained flat and narrow-lipped; only its corners lifted. It chilled Ming. She existed only to please this enormously wealthy woman, and Holjpip was making sure she knew it. "You were an artist, I read in your file."

"Yes, Your Grace." Her employer would know much from that record.

She would also have a frequency-coded transmitter that could cripple Ming from who-knew-what-distance.

"Then we shall have you trained in makeup, so that you may attend us on occasions. You are all bones, girl, but your hands and face show the artistic temperament. I shall give you a try." She flattened her mouth into that odd, hollow smile again. "You may practice on Missara Yerren, perhaps."

The smaller woman raised a heavy, dark eyebrow.

"Dismissed." Holjpip's strident voice rose, and the audience ended.

Ming bowed again. Clutching her satchel, she hurried

out, totally disoriented. Was it evening? Morning? How long had she slept? She was ordered to produce samples. But where would she eat?

Questions are to be directed to Staff Central, Adjutant-Missara Claude Yerren said. Uncommunicative Mere Bertelsen might have gone off-duty. *Or,* Ming reflected as she hurried forward, *I might not have asked the right questions.*

Staff Central. South. Ming pivoted toward the wall that had looked green and moving from down the hall. From this closer vantage, she saw through glass a line of fountains along the center of a huge room, their showery rank crossed by a long, marble-floored reflecting pool; and raised beds of multicolored blossoms lay between curtains of drooping trees. A guard blocked the glass wall's only opening. "Sir?" she asked. "I need to get to Staff Central."

"Then you'll take an elevator and go around." Apparently seeing her confusion, he softened. "Are you new? The centrum is off-limits to staff except by express order."

"Oh. All right."

Turning back, she caught a glitter of gold and red behind the guard and paused, hugging her satchel for warmth.

Tieg Innig sat on a bench beneath one of those drooping pale trees, wearing a loose, red tunic trimmed in gold and a gold-toned kilt, three women at his feet. Some kind of wooden instrument lay on his lap; his hands moved, but she could hear only the wired-in music of the hallways.

Remembering his casually friendly conversation of— the day before? earlier today?—and Lyra's warning, she watched a little longer, half eyeing the guard. The burly man in purple-bordered black wouldn't let her pass but didn't seem to mind if she stared.

Tieg's fingers moved deftly, each banded to a short wooden rod, to pluck strings on the wooden lap-frame. One strand of white hair fell loose, toward his face.

She leaned closer. Despite what he'd said about Holjpip's tastes, she had thought a manufacturing world would prefer synthetic music over old, elegant, one-person-one-melody instruments. Perhaps Holjpip encouraged others to develop an appreciation of the arts, making the staff calligrapher position possible.

Ming headed back down the corridor. If she hoped to "get close" to the haughty, young-looking woman back in that Operations room and win freedom early, her first job was to impress Holjpip Langelleik—if she could.

Later that morning, in a North Upper conference room, six of the youngest and brightest rising Renasco officials on Mannheim sat, in varying degrees of comfort, in front of Holjpip. All lived here in her villa but worked in Anslanding, and she had seen few in six calendar months. From her chair at center table she accepted their reports, the fingers of one hand curled beneath her chin.

"Our stimulation program has the nilly pines' time to maturity down to six years, estimated from vegetative growth, but that still leaves nearly three years until the first artificially developed crop comes in." The speaker, an agriculture man in his twenties, tapped a pen against the tabletop, his slender build typical of the Little Yorkers who colonized southern Mannheim. "Your Grace, I'm sorry, but we still can work no faster."

Holjpip inhaled, smelling perfume at her wrist. "And synthesis of the active chemical—" She barely shrugged, making the motion an exercise in dignity, "isn't working. Missars, Missaras, HolLanCorp therefore has a bind." She let her employees sit in silence long enough to grow uneasy. At the first restless movement, she spoke again. "This does, on the other hand, provide allowance for the time necessary to train production and packaging personnel. Goodsprings School will graduate its first class next year?"

The woman on her right adjusted thick glasses on the bridge of her nose. Though she looked forty, Holjpip knew her for sixty-plus. "Yes, one year more, Madam. Some graduates may go over to General and ALPEX, but HolLanCorp's incentive system will logically keep the best graduates for our work."

Beyond the spectacled educator, another woman spoke up. "So long as Renasco wants our products for its own use rather than distribution, we have a waiting market."

"In other words," said the thin Little York transplant, "the market is steady; the price remains high until we bring in the cultivated crop. But dealing with an arboreal product—"

Holjpip cut him off. "We know. We are settled, then, on maintenance of current programs for another calendar year."

"If we do stimulate cone production sooner, Madam, we will inform you immediately."

"If you stimulate cone production sooner, Missar," she answered, stretching her fingers, "your division of Hol-LanCorp will receive an additional half percent of net profit, for distribution as you see fit."

She smiled to herself at the slight widening of his eyes, but in forty years of Renasco employment Holjpip had learned control of even those tiny muscles that might give away her own emotion.

Renasco wanted increased production of nilly beans, seeds of "pines" native to Mannheim, which stimulated the metabolism to the point that the user felt time speeding up. Renasco would have production in quantity soon enough.

Until now, Holjpip had followed Renasco's orders where it sent her. Renasco could be worked to suit her, despite the hostage they held against her good conduct, and south of Anslanding, in the groves of wild native "pines," seed cones and parasitic pods grew steadily. Holjpip intended to stay, this time.

How to get talent and industry to Mannheim, quickly, efficiently?

Inwardly she shrugged. All success was hollow, bitter, short-lived without joy. So she would build herself as a memory. An entity without pain, without vulnerability.

Silently, without displaying her expression to her employees, she laughed. *Easy* . . .

North, down, and south again. After her long detour below the centrum, Ming found the same girl on duty at Staff Central, but Mere Bertelsen proved willing to answer direct questions. Ming had slept away afternoon, evening, and the long night of a twenty-five-and-a-half-hour planetary day, and she would find breakfast at Staff Dining in North Upper, back the way she had come.

Half an hour after leaving the Ops room, warm and full now, Ming spread her tools on her work table, mixed a quarter liter of gel, and spread it in her working tray.

Fifteen centimeters by twenty, crisscrossed by the reference grid, the tray was as fundamental to technique as the injection pens. Thirty minutes to preset. She marked the time and turned to her faintly glowing screen.

Here, perhaps, she could learn a little more about her world and employer without embarrassing herself. She pressed the USER tab, and a blinking prompter appeared. *Data base,* she typed. The prompter vanished. Sure enough, it took Renasco commands.

Though unsettled, knowing the screen might be watching her, too (this villa had rooms numbered in the thousands; how could they watch all employees at once?), she explored subheadings for three-fourths of an hour. Under +CLIMATE+ she found Anslanding's average temperature for this time of year, almost frigid by Cabran standards—it sounded lovely—and that the foggy season was ending. +HISTORY+: First planetfall had been here at the delta of the Riddle River, a crew of twelve under Captain Ann Draper of Renasco's headquarters world, Little York. Hence the name of the fifty-year-old town, Anslanding.

Under the +HUMANITIES+ BIO section, she perused a long file on Holjpip Langelleik. The woman was sixty-seven, Standard, and—if all this was true—brilliant, capable, and shrewd. Born on the Belt world of Podaca, she climbed the Podacan Foreign Service ladder while performing a similar ascent within Renasco's Trade Board branch. Now, as a full ambassador stationed on Mannheim to facilitate trade via Renasco, she served Renasco as a planetary rep, supplying the Company with refined agricultural products. Value of her investments in one biochemical export company, HolLanCorp, had risen tenfold in two years, and HolLanCorp recently passed Allegiance Pharmochemical Export (ALPEX) as leading exporter. To Ming's surprise, Holjpip also claimed twenty-five percent ownership in the Newport Space Travel Authority.

No hint of trouble with Renasco here. She shifted her weight on the desk chair and tried a search for Tieg Innig.

The entry she found was oddly, laughably short.

Perhaps elsewhere. She glanced at the time panel flashing at the bottom right corner of the screen. Time to get to work—past time. The gel would not harden until she sprayed it to set, but she had a long job ahead, her first real task for a new employer.

Her sentence, her instructors had said, was formulated to use her most valuable skills in the way she'd find the most tedious and unpleasant. Besides testing all motor and intellectual abilities, they'd given her a full psych battery, so they guaranteed she would hate whatever work they trained her for—but that she'd excel at it.

Where in the Belt would a professional calligrapher find an employer? she'd wondered.

Now she knew. Someone wealthy, fond of entertaining, desiring a talented designer of invitations or gifts, someone the Company wanted watched.

She filled one pen with black ink, checked it for free flow over a cellose blotter-block, then eased it into one edge of the gel. Castil hand was her favorite; she'd start with that one. Deep breath.

Capital *A*. With painstaking control she swept a triangular counter: straight stroke, change pen angle sixty degrees, second side, change angle again, third side. Quickly she shut down ink flow, retraced half the final side, then added a straight-down exit stroke.

She exhaled the held breath. Those hand and forearm muscles, twenty years out of tone, were unsteady. In three-dimensional work, few strokes allowed the hand to rest on the working surface's frame or a handbridge. All her other art training helped not one whit with this, for this work rested solely on drilled technique, without creativity.

"Art will come later," the instructor had sneered, a tall, full-hipped woman who reminded her vaguely of a second cousin, "when you custom-illuminate to your employer's specifications. Personal calligraphy is still an art, and original slabs cannot be created by artificial means. But for now, you must master counters and strokes." She glanced down. "And yours, Mere Dalamani, are irregular."

Strokes and counters, counters and strokes. Entries and exits, rate of flow, the pen nib traveling precisely one centimeter per second through gel. Too fast, and swirl currents ruined unset letters, or the ink ribbon broke; too slow, and pigment pooled and blobbed. Recurring dreams shrank her to nib width, swimming in gel under the baleful eye of that implacable instructor, at the precise rate of one centimeter per second.

Slowly she pulled the pen to the right, trailing a thin black thread behind it. Now, lowercase *a*. At the proper spacing, she gave her hand a slight twist and began to pull. The thin thread became a ribbon again, the width of her nib. This letter had to twist precisely ninety degrees per ninety degrees of arc. When her pen hand came down almost to touch the gel, she shut down the ink, waited an instant, and pulled it free in preparation to join the second stroke.

"Sweat," she muttered. A trail of ink marked the nib's exit from the gel, not a mistake but a malfunction. Growling to herself, she opened her solvent and cleaned the nib. She nearly poured out the gel plate, too, then thought better of it. She'd do well to readjust all her new pens before one malfunctioned on the Zed of a virtually finished alphabet slab. Carefully she ran the thick-barreled instrument at hand through each of its control cycles, chaining circles until they satisfied her. Her hand relaxed as the chains grew.

She was beginning to take pride in her new skill. They could not rob her of all pleasure while she served out her sentence. If she learned to enjoy the work Renasco meant for her punishment, she could not be defeated, not in forty years.

Ming glanced across at the time blinking at the bottom of her screen. She couldn't finish today. The six alphabet gels she'd hoped to submit would take her till midnight at least, barring mistakes. She took up the second pen and meticulously repeated the tests.

That afternoon, while punching up files and waiting for a fourth tray to preset, she happened upon her link to Staff Central on the screen. *Is there anything like a rule book here?* she typed with hands growing tired and shaky, cramped like her shoulders and neck. Her back ached, too, and both eyes stung. She would be lucky to finish the third alphabet; she'd already discarded two faulted trays.

+STAND BY+ Paper began to flow from a slot she hadn't noticed below the screen. Ming grabbed it between black-spotted fingers just before its leading edge dropped into her gel tray. Now she'd have an idea of what was expected of her. *Thanks,* she typed in, but SC did not respond.

When the screen buzzed some time later, Ming—fortunately caught with her pen free of the medium—dropped the pen on the desk. She snatched it back up, seized her cellose blotter, and with it sucked the drip from her nib while shutting down ink flow with her other hand.

+PLEASE ACK+

She complied one-handed while scrubbing ink off her desk with the blotter.

+HOW MANY ALPHABETS ARE FINISHED?+

("Be brief and make no excuses," she'd read between pen tests.) *Two finished and set, one nearly limned.*

There was a pause. Then: +REPORT 1011 WITH FINISHED SAMPLES+

Ming glanced over at the clear, thin, jelled slabs she'd sprayed to set, and then stepped to one side of her working area. How to transport them without mounts? It never occurred to her that her supervisor would not examine them here, in place.

+PLEASE ACK+

Sighing, she complied. Her working trays would do in a pinch to support the set gels, but the display effect would be poor, and she would have to pour the gel she'd begun down the sink.

Nothing else to do.

F

Ten minutes later, Ming tipped the set gels out of her working trays in the beautiful uplevel suite.

"Two." Holjpip pushed them back to Ming across the blond wood desk. "Why aren't any others finished?" She gestured for Ming to sit down.

Ming obeyed, bemused to find herself dealing with Holjpip, not the adjutant, after all. The chair felt as comfortable as it looked, though she didn't dare lean back. She clenched the empty ruled trays on her lap. "It took me some time to prepare my tools, Your Grace. Tomorrow I should be able to work more quickly, though my hands are . . . stiff."

"Yes." Her keen brown eyes narrowed. "They would be. Do you need more materials?" That voice cracked like a lash.

"I could use more—"

"Staff Central will see you are supplied." Holjpip tapped an elegant, purple-tipped nail on the desk. "How long did these take?"

Ming stared at them critically. "Two hours each, more or less, Madam."

One thin brow arched. "That's too long."

"I am still learning speed, Your Grace." Ming felt herself examined, weighed. Perhaps the ambassador found her too slow, too expensive to keep, for the output she could produce. Or perhaps Holjpip would ask how she'd wasted so much time.

"You work in other media?"

"Yes, Madam—"

"I want . . ." Holjpip gestured to someone behind Ming. Claude Yerren appeared again, her deep blue eyes stern. She pulled back the ambassador's chair, and Holjpip wandered toward the window. Outside, dusk darkened the eastern sea. Holjpip struck an elegant pose. ("Remain at attention when speaking with Senior Officials.") Ming waited motionless, straight-backed in her chair.

"Tomorrow—" Holjpip said as she turned, "draw my likeness, a preliminary study for a portrait. Central will give you paper. Come up at nine hundred hours." Ming must have flinched, for the woman arched a single thin eyebrow. "You are reluctant."

"Madam," Ming stammered. "I have never done portraits." It was true enough. The sort she did remember doing—caricatures of various "Renasco monkeys" sketched for her friends—Her Grace, the ambassador and Company rep, would find distasteful. "And it . . . would be difficult to capture your features perfectly as a first exercise. Would you permit me to draw someone else first, as practice, so that I might not disappoint you when I feel ready to fulfill your request?"

Holjpip barked out a laugh. "Another politician. Very well. Draw for me . . ." She pressed one palm against the window. "Draw for me Tieg Innig, whom you met yesterday. Begin a folio: pencil portraits, line drawings, impressions. Central will arrange times, if you require assistance with a schedule. Meanwhile, continue with your alphabets. When they are complete, I need to see what sort of illumination you may be capable of. An *H* will do, capital, as large as one of these slabs. . . ." She turned half a pirouette on one foot. "Fill it in with vine work. You will collect appropriate botanical specimens locally to copy.

"I shall ask for all these in a week. That should give your hands time to recover from sleep stiffness, but it will be your final chance. Do not come to me until you can show your best work."

It was not a protocol dismissal, but Ming recognized "Good-bye and go away." Not wishing to show the potentate her back, she bumped backward out of the room, gripping her trays. Three steps up the hall, she realized she'd left the gels behind.

A black-skinned woman in trim yellow suiting hurried up the hall while Ming hesitated below the long, dimming skylight. When she drew abreast, Ming smelled smoked meat and a warm, sweet something.

She stopped, thunderstruck. She'd missed lunch. No wonder she was cold. Her body was trying to tell her something.

Abandoning her day's workmanship to Holjpip, Ming set her face toward the bright, cavernous staff dining room.

Half an hour later, stuffed to bursting by Lyra (who dished her double helpings of everything to make up for the skipped meal), she took one ruled tray toward Staff Central.

"Ming," said a voice behind her in the long hallway.

She stopped. Someone knew her name?

Tieg Innig strode alongside, dressed in a tight jumpsuit with broad white stripes spiraling in ungainly oddity along his limbs. After seeing so much sameness in training school and so many uniforms here, Ming discovered she liked the unique outfit. "Come in here for a minute," he said. "I'd like to talk with you." He opened a side door into a narrow stairwell.

She followed him through. "Yes?"

He stared down at her. "I've been thinking about something you said yesterday in the car. You have a pretty way about you, Ming Dalamani, but there's a haunted look in your eye. I think I know what you are."

She took a step backward, wondering how he'd found out; then, frightened enough to be angry, she stood her ground. "I don't know what you mean."

"I have a guess," said Tieg Innig, "that you are one of the select and lucky few to cross the Company and survive, because they felt they could use you. I guess—" He glanced left, away from her. "No, I don't guess. They've put one of their abominable collars on you, haven't they? You're not one of Them. You're one of Theirs."

Lyra was right about him—scary. "Your manners," she managed to sputter, "are atrocious, sir."

"Got it in one, then. I won't tell, Mere Ming. You can have your second chance with a clean reputation. That is, if you'll consider assisting me while you serve our mistress."

Ming glared. *And I hoped this man might prove a friend.*

He stood straight-backed and fidgeted two fingers together. "They're not watching you all the time. The staff's too large. And this is not a major matter, nothing that threatens Renasco. I could use a pair of eyes and ears privy to the female hallways. I am rather conspicuous, don't you think?"

"Um." Ming glanced up and down the stairwell, its walls enameled off-white in the direction of pale blue. "Yes, I think so."

"It's my job to be conspicuous."

"I see that."

"Listen, then. I've been curious for some time about the way Holjpip is staffing the villa. In the last two years, she has hired a number of odd talents—such as staff calligraphers."

"Why are you worried about that?"

He shifted one foot. "You don't want rumors started about Renasco collars, do you?"

He was actually threatening her. But she was Company property, protected by Company law. It was an interplanetary crime to harm her.

Harm her, yes. Humiliate her, no.

Asked shipboard by the Company to watch for transgressors of policy, she thought she could guess one here and now. Forty years of servitude—and the chance to shorten it.

But why trust them to make good that promise?

With a wrench, she admitted that if she couldn't believe in Renasco's promise, only despair remained.

Her stomach twisted around the huge meal she had just eaten. She hated to betray anyone to the memory blockers, after what they had done to her. Cast friendless into the future, she walked alone.

"I need an answer, Ming," Tieg Innig said softly, glancing over the railing.

He acted confident she would not mention him to her superiors. Either he thought his position invulnerable, or he was a real Renasco spy, sent to test her loyalty.

Why would Holjpip choose him for a portrait model before any other employee? It looked like coincidence, but that had to be answered, too, before she did anything about reporting him.

"Yes," she said with an effort. "I'll watch people for you. But it will take me a while to get to know this place."

"That's why you could be so valuable to me. You're still in the noticing stage. Thank you, Ming Dalamani."

"Is that all, Tieg Innig?"

He opened the door back into the hallway.

At last she reached Staff Central with her request. "Do you have anything like this?" She laid the ruled rectangular tray in front of the man who now occupied the seat of organizational authority.

He lifted one lip of the gel tray between his brown thumb and middle finger. "Probably." Rotating his stool, he set the tray onto a broad shelf protruding from a black wall behind him. The shelf slid inward, taking the tray with it, and Ming wondered if it would emerge doubled.

It did not. But as the man in purple handed it back, he asked, "How many do you need?"

"I could use ten. And four about . . ." She spread her hands to shoulder-width apart, "half a meter on each side. For transport."

As he made marks on a piece of paper, Ming admired the rich shade of his skin, lighter than sienna, yet not at all ruddy. Then she thought of Tieg Innig, curly eyebrows throwing shadows over his hard gray eyes. Why choose her to threaten, why ask her to watch people for him, the dome-rat? "And a carrying case," she hurried on. "Paper, drawing pens—"

"Slow *down.*"

Ming glanced at a pair of screens over his work table. On each, some villa room showed in an overhead view. "I'm sorry." She wondered whose rooms those might be, and why and how they were being watched. "First, I need a carrying case. Cloth would be fine. About a meter long, and . . ."

Weary now, feeling every day of her twenty-year cold sleep, Ming stumbled through the doorway into her room. She sighed in anticipation; the incomprehensible expanse of space, all hers. . . .

A shape on the bed's edge moved. Ming jumped backward, ready to apologize for trespassing. It was a man, sitting. She must have the wrong room.

But the door had opened to the touch of her hand. Her pens lay ordered on the long bureau, and this was women's quarters.

In that half second, the man rose. Barely shoulder height to her when standing, his body proportions looked all wrong, his chest too deep and round, his arms too short, his chin impossibly pointed opposite a large dome of short-furred skull.

"Welcome to Anslanding," he said, surprising her again. By its pitch it was a child's voice, yet its bored inflection had seen servants come, toil, and vanish. He raised a child-length arm and touched his huge chest with one finger. "I am Zardir Huekk, Mere Dalamani. Missar Huekk, you shall call me. Her Grace's lieutenant, giver of gifts. Watcher of the waters." He smiled, a twist of the lower half of his face that looked as if it pained him.

A mutant: genetic victim of the radiation storm, isolation, and inbreeding. Many such congenital cripples lived on Cabra Minor. "Show me the collar, Mere Dalamani."

Ming's first impulse was to refuse, but Missar Zardir Huekk had entered her locked room. That suggested authority. How did he know? From the lizard-eyed supervisor, or had Tieg told him, or Holjpip?

She dipped her head and held the pose. At the edge of vision she watched him bend forward, examining the back of her neck.

He wouldn't see much. Two small metal stubs showed if one knew where to look, but that was all. She'd searched with a mirror.

He snorted. "Now, sit. I want to talk to you."

Ming sank onto the orange chair beside her work table in a state of shivery awareness.

Huekk stood over her. He smiled more naturally now, as if he felt most comfortable looking downward. "Sedition and piracy. Tried at Vinnsing, Nexos system, forty-five twelve New Age. Ming Dalamani." Scratching one cheek, he paused. "Also Lur Dalamani, Ashan Dalamani, and Jiadra Grazi." He pronounced it "gray-zee." "Did my stylish colleagues shipboard tell you what happened to them?"

Ming seized the information, tried to hold it, couldn't.
Blocks slammed down to disrupt her conscious reflection
on the memory. What had he just said? This was how the
blocks worked, disrupting the mind's filing system. What
was he doing, tormenting her?

"The . . . others." His question, at least, stuck in her
mind. "Tell me."

"The mandatory sentence for sedition is death."

"I . . ." She clenched the chair's edge, down by her
thighs. "Then why am I alive?"

"Mitigating conditions," he intoned. "Young, dominated by the crimes of others."

Which crimes? she wanted to shout. *What did we do?*
He was toying with her, to control her, but she would
control herself. Maybe she could prompt him to give away
secrets. "They are dead," she said cautiously.

Huekk's face twisted again in his disagreeable grin. He
pulled the other chair away from her terminal, spun it to
face a quarter away, and sat down across it, leaning one
arm against its back. "And what hope have you of getting
your term mitigated, Sentenced Laborer?"

He wasn't telling. Crestfallen, she sat silent for a moment, then quoted, "Meritorious service to humankind, as
represented by Renasco."

"You have, I assume, been asked to watch for habitual
transgressors?"

"Yes," she murmured, glancing up at an empty, silver-
toned shelf above his head.

"Well." He touched his chest. "You report to me."

This would be her official channel. One of his eyes half
closed, and with his body draped sideways over the back of
her desk chair, he looked less like a figure of authority than
a misshapen balloon. Strange that Ambassador Holjpip
Langelleik, patron of the arts, employed a mutant this ugly
in both appearance and manner. Would her "further orders" from Renasco come through him, as well?

Huekk pushed off the chair back to sit almost upright.
"You will have to show yourself above the average woman.
Have you keen—*keen*—powers of observation?"

"I am a visual artist." She mustn't sound as if she were
trying to justify herself to this . . . creature, yet possibly
he held the access codes for her future freedom.

And, she realized bleakly, she still wanted to do what was legal and right. Huekk couldn't help his deformities.

He rose. "Then, Mere Visual Artist, there is reason to believe—for Renasco to believe—that there is among us at least one spy, someone with cause and means to watch inner Renasco operations here on Mannheim for the unknown purposes of some seditious network." He paced to the end of the table, then back toward the wet room's door. "We have hired your eyes. Your visual artistry, as it were. We want that spy. We will repay you well, even if all you can do is point your long, lovely finger in the proper direction." Ming glanced down at her bony hands. "Fail us, and you've a long road ahead of you. Remember what you are, and what you have been promised."

This made twice, now—in one hour!—she had been asked to spy for someone. What kind of secrets could any Mannheim concern hold from the Renasco monopoly?

Fields of blossoms spread before her mind's eye. Pharmaceuticals? It had to be. HolLanCorp had two rival companies mentioned in that database program. Perhaps one had found some new kind of naturally occurring chemical, some catalyst, or stimulant, or hallucinogen, and the HolLanCorp division of Renasco wanted that secret, and Holjpip wasn't moving quickly enough toward ferreting out the criminals. The apparent wealth of this system had to be due to something marginally legal, and before Ming worked here much longer, she meant to know more.

Huekk kept speaking. "No one is to be considered above suspicion, except—" he gave her another twisted smile; this one made her shiver, as if he wished to hurt someone, "myself, of course, and Madam. Find us the eyes and ears of the outsider, Mere Dalamani, and we will give you freedom. A new name, a new world." He sniffed. "A chance for a family of your own that is not the Company's property."

And Madam. Then she did not report to him on Holjpip. Circles within circles! Whatever he was, he knew her world's priorities and was wedging her into a position for which he knew she had no qualifications. Again, to torment her?

Maybe she would surprise him. Innig, she thought without doubt, Tieg Innig, making independent queries.

Why did Innig need to know about women with odd talents? Here was a chance to free herself—immediately!—of Tieg's threat of exposure, if his activities didn't bear scrutiny.

Yet she hesitated. Implicating a favorite of Holjpip's might cause her own dismissal, prevent her from "getting close," make her start this whole wretched process over again. Another cold sleep, while Renasco made her another assignment.

She could wait to speak until she knew more.

Ming pressed her arms hard against the arms of the chair, straightening her spine. "I am . . . my powers of observation are at your service."

He laughed and paced over to stand staring down at her from too close: She smelled musty heat. "They are, Mere Visual, pretty virgin. You are." When he touched her face, it was as if insects crept up her cheek. "Anyone you wish to discuss as yet? While your initial impressions of Anslanding, of this household, are yet fresh?"

"Ah," she said, as if thinking over every soul at Holjpip's villa. "I can think of no one as yet who seemed suspicious to me. But perhaps it is my system of perception at fault. I was raised far from Mannheim. What appears normal to me might be entirely irregular by your standards."

Huekk shifted his weight from one foot to another. He wore heavy thonged sandals, the first she remembered ever seeing.

"But I shall do my best for you, sir."

"Missar." He pronounced the word with an upward tilt of his chin. "Tonight, access the protocol program and straighten your terms of address, as well as the prescribed manner of dress for your class—*Mere* Dalamani." He started for the door.

"I—"

As he paused, Ming felt a sudden overwhelming urge to see his misshapen form vanish through the doorway, to have these spacious rooms to herself. She swallowed the compulsion to explain.

"I thank you for your time and your advice, *Missar* Huekk." She stood up and dipped the top half of her body toward him. It probably wasn't a proper bow, not in this system (or any other), but it seemed to please him.

"I shall call on you again, Mere Visual." He touched her interior lock panel with the tip of his thumb. The door slid open for him.

Expelling a long breath, she fell backward onto the bed. She would escape this place someday, call a new world home and walk free, where no one could stand with his finger on a collar transmitter and watch her. All the aches in her body returned at once, as if she'd been painted in hot oranges and reds. She was so tired. She ought to get up and soak her feet, as Lyra . . .

Ming wasn't sure what woke her, but when she rolled over, groaning, the blinking time on her computer read 0444. While she stood getting her balance, she realized for the first time since her long sleep she had wakened without nausea.

She felt fully human again, with strength for a day's work. Barefoot, she padded to her printout "rule book" to see how she was expected to dress. Under several status headings in that protocol program, she found that a member of the arts corps was to dress "tastefully," with a touch of the amethyst-purple of Holjpip Langelleik's service. Terms of address she found under another subheading. At her level, the lowest, "Mere" served for both men and women. Workers under independent contract, seven percent of villa staff, were "Missar," or "Missara."

Ah, she thought, flipping a page. *Missara Claude Yerren —and, then, Missar Tieg Innig.*

"Madam" was reserved on Mannheim for Holjpip Langelleik.

She needed an emblem, then, of the proper color, to wear with her "tasteful" assigned wardrobe. She rifled her cabinets. A glimmer against the wall, on the silver shelf over the console screen, snagged her attention. There: a small, hexagonal cloisonné pin.

Now I have time for a shower.

The luxurious excess of pressurized water raised her spirits yet further. After pinning the emblem to the shoulder of a clean cream-colored jumpsuit, she rummaged in her kit for pencils and a sketch pad, then settled in to warm up her hands for a day's work. Leaning back, she crossed her ankles on the desktop to try a contour drawing. Her first attempt looked like her big toe had been squashed, but she enjoyed straightening a crooked crease in the skin of one little toe. She blended shadows to make the drawing look more finished.

A little wooden, but accurate. Better than accurate, in one way. Ming laid her pad on the table and ambled into the wet room for a drink of water.

Eyeing her image in the mirror, Ming had a thought so simple she blushed not to have thought of it sooner. She returned for the chair, hauled it across the carpet and onto the smooth flooring of the wet room, and perched on the chair's high back, between the large mirror and a small one she mounted in a wall bracket.

A long, round oval. It was so tempting to caricature a skinny skull and shadowy eyes! For another hour she struggled, sketching and erasing, but when she finished the face, she was almost pleased with the result, and it was after ten, late enough for the villa to be waking.

So, now do Tieg, she told herself, discarding the sketch. 1014, answered her clock.

Tucking her pad under her arm, she went in search of him.

He was playing in the centrum again, and wearing the caftan, surrounded by a bright bouquet of gowned women, all of whom looked young and extremely lovely, and one of whom was Holjpip. A security guard, muscles round and hard under his black suit, watched the glass wall's opening. Ming rallied herself. She had been assigned to draw Tieg Innig. If she did not disturb him or his audience, this would be an excellent time to catch him sitting still.

As she stepped closer to the guard, he glared in her direction. "Mere," she began boldly, "Madam has asked that I sketch Missar Innig. Might I sit back a distance and draw quietly?"

The muscleman looked down at her, then turned aside, as if wondering whether this merited interrupting his mistress for permission while the ladies paid her court over morning c'fee.

"Quietly," he said, "and be sure you are unobtrusive." He stepped aside, and Ming crossed the threshold.

G

Ming eased through a large doorway, careful not to make noise. In this warm, humid expanse, Tieg's music rang sweetly, filtered through countless drooping trees, many of which supported vines covered with bright pink flowers. The air was alive, smelling of blossoms and soil. Tiny bright birds of all colors flitted from branch to branch, and beneath her feet, stepping stones lay flush in mossy turf that appeared from a distance to be carpet. She heard trickling water clearly enough to feel suddenly thirsty, but couldn't see it.

Tieg Innig sat on the edge of a massive planter made of red stone, with his left foot pulled up beside him and a new instrument resting on his right thigh. Similar to the tarra of Cabra Minor, this body looked leaner in proportion than the tarra's, its neck longer. Below him, the ambassador and her ladies lounged in white webbed chairs, facing away from Ming, some sipping at small cups. She could only see a few of their faces.

But she saw Tieg's, even from this distance, under brilliant skylights. Taking her cue from his choice of seat, she hopped up onto a nearby planter and rested her sketch pad against her knee.

Forced to evaluate his features and not caricature him in her mind, Ming stared, studying with an artist's detachment. Jawline, square across the chin; good cheekbones— by Cabran standards, at least—noticeable but not protruding; a straight, cleanly chiseled nose; thick eyebrows, and blue-gray eyes. She hadn't requisitioned colored pencils yet, but she would remember the hue, and that of his skin, too: tanned, barely ruddy. Most of his hair was dark blond, curly but short.

Still staring, she let her pencil begin to slip over the paper. The contour drawing would look like nothing, but it helped . . . free . . .

Thoughts blank, she shifted into the half-aware state of serious drawing.

After a few minutes, she allowed herself a break.

This person could hold powerful women rapt. Frowning, Ming set down her pencil and flexed her fingers, clinging to an edge of the harmonic whirlpool that held Holjpip motionless.

What relationship does she have with him? The ambassador's hair flowed like beaten copper over her shoulders, her profile sharp-chinned and sharp-nosed; yet here, a hint of softness played in her expression.

Seven-tenths of the way to the top of Renasco, Holjpip sat surrounded by intrigue. The Renasco woman with her lizard-eyed friends watching. Tieg Innig, evaluating the staff for . . . for whom? ALPEX, or General Co-Op, or some other company? And Zardir Huekk, looking for Innig. For the present, Ming could wait—to tell Zardir Huekk that Tieg was the man he wanted—to warn Tieg Innig that Huekk guessed his presence, depending on which side looked more right, when she knew this place better. Ming smiled to herself. "Hired" by both men with a threat and a pittance, she had orders neither guessed, and if she was careful, she would find a way to play the situation to her advantage. Meanwhile, she must bring her skills to bear on paper.

She set to work again. Two women left when one suite ended, but the rest of Tieg's audience remained, and after an hour Ming laid her pencil down again. Her glance flicking from paper to model and back again, she evaluated the sketch, liked the face well enough, and turned the page. Penciling suggestions of collar and caftan, she made a fast drawing on the next sheet.

She stared down at the paper one more time, then up at Tieg. Another long, ancient-sounding suite over, he rested his instrument on one knee to receive his audience's admiration, his expression grateful with a touch of pride. He'd done a job well. She knew the feeling. What were his secrets? And where was his "tasteful" touch of amethyst purple?

He glanced her direction.

She hopped down, clutching her pad. Passing through the door, she checked the time high on the blond wood of the hallway. A little past noon, the dark clock-face told her. Ming strode off. Today she was not going to miss lunch, and once she ate, she meant to try a new branch of the data base. Someone here must know something about Tieg Innig.

Tieg Innig received his meal in his studio an hour later. Barely noticing the white-aproned domestic who brought it, he touched a cleared spot on his U-shaped desk. "There," he said. The woman set down his tray, backed out of the darkened room, and left through a white-carpeted living area.

Only partly distracted by the interruption, Tieg touched a playback button for memory unit number four and listened hard. He preferred to compose after performing, when the rush of his audience's approval freed his creative energies. A synthesized eight-bar theme played through. One hand went to his tray and brought up something to eat, and he chewed without tasting.

He didn't like what he heard. Touching the keyboard again, he stared at a brown curtain while a second melody ran. Holjpip's next major occasion, a retirement reception for some employee of her Goodsprings processing plant, required a variety of moods he had attempted recently, and he'd used that theme today. She would notice. For a woman with primary interests in processing and politics, Holjpip Langelleik had a remarkable ear.

The second theme suited him better. Like Holjpip, it hid steel beneath beauty. She had ordered attention to focus on herself midway through the upcoming reception, but in a subliminal way. Then she would present a retirement gift.

Tieg picked up his fork and ate rapidly. He had arrived on Mannheim a year before meeting Holjpip, living the lonely, half-employed life of his father's profession, familiarizing himself with this world's ways and gradually establishing a clientele. Then she'd advertised the tone poet position, as he'd been told to expect, and he came for an audition.

She heard him in the centrum, third out of a group of seven men who waited together with thinly concealed competitive hostility. Four came in by Renasco passenger liner from Belt worlds, for this was billed as steady, high-paying work, rare in the music field. Tieg watched Holjpip as she heard the first two performers, his amusement touched with awe, that this woman was already building a sphere of influence so broad the Old School wanted it infiltrated.

The Old School, a loosely organized band of reactionary spirits from all the Renasco worlds, existed to end Renasco's hold over transportation, however it must be done. To search out knowledge of the shielding that allowed space travel, and someday seed mankind with that knowledge. Because Renasco practiced violence, Old School trained its agents in violence. Tieg knew to exercise caution until necessity demanded, then move without self-doubt. But when the time came, could he?

His aborted Renasco training in drive technology made him Old School's logical choice to play for Holjpip's favor, to try to discover why she was hiring so much talent—talent of all sorts, arts and engineering, production and processing. Holjpip appeared to have goals Old School could turn to its ends, Renasco puppet though she was. This might prove to be a world where the shielding secrets could be cracked, by careful proselytizing of the right caliber of Renasco employees.

Evidently the seeds planted far back in his childhood, during music lessons taken at his father's side, had rooted in good soil. Holjpip Langelleik, Podacan ambassador, Renasco Company rep, and patron of the arts, had hired him without calling the remaining four applicants.

Over the next year, he formed an admiration for the woman he'd been set to watch. Then came the nilly beans and mellow pods. Holjpip began to collect staff like tickle-me blossoms collected bees, and Tieg could no longer watch the whole villa for Old School. Mannheim developed at an unprecedented rate, but its character remained refined, unlike other Renasco boomworlds. Surely she was building Mannheim for a new Company center. If he maintained his position as court favorite, he would be here, watching it. In Mannheim's flowering might grow the seeds of Renasco's defeat.

He ran the theme once more, emptying himself of native emotion and letting the music rouse him as it would. How would it affect someone unaccustomed to his personal style?

The oval, ivory-skinned face of Ming Dalamani, framed in short black hair, appeared in his memory. He let his hands fall from the keyboard and stared at the curtain. Soft-chinned in an odd racial type, eyes narrow and bright black, Ming's supple way of moving suggested she would come alive one day, like a dancer, for the right man. Frowning, he added a bass drone to his sequence. What had lithe, slender Ming done to earn a crippling Renasco collar? How was she reacting to Holjpip Langelleik?

Tieg splayed his fingers into the hair above his forehead and pulled back hard. He didn't mind Holjpip hiring quality. He believed in quality. It had galled him to maintain low scores on evaluations during Renasco training to keep them from watching him too closely.

The soft whine of his entry's motion sensor and a rapping sound in the outer room startled him. He laid his fork on the empty tray and walked toward the hall door, past the Renasco console he knew could watch him—had watched him, in the past, for Claude Yerren had questioned him about an Anslander woman he invited up for drinks. Holjpip allowed him his studio unmonitored, and part of the living room, but his bed was watched by the Madam, though she demonstrated no wish to lie there. Even the court favorite had to endure Renasco's eye. He touched the lock.

Lounging, one shoulder against Tieg's doorjamb, stood a man Tieg hadn't seen in years: Joash McMikall, his head freshly shaved, just as Tieg remembered him, wearing Renasco copper-on-blue and a wry, mocking smile. "Innig, you old son-of-a-breeder. It is you."

"Well, for . . . Mc—Mikall. McMikall, come in." Mentally cursing, Tieg stepped in front of the console while his guest passed by. This marginally competent snitch from Renasco school knew his past, far too much of it. Tieg had taken less care of his tongue in those days, even mentioning Old School to classmates he did not implicitly trust.

Joash McMikall made for the dining table, in full view of the screen. "No," Tieg said, gesturing aside, "over there. Much more comfortable."

"How nice," drawled his guest, and he sank onto the pure white brocade love seat. The copper-on-blue of Joash McMikall's tunic made a brazen statement on the pristine background.

"Have you been on Mannheim long?" Tieg asked.

"No, just transferred. I came into a nice little fortune, and I'm laying in a supply of your lady's mellow pods, though if they do extend your lifespan, I may need a double batch." He rubbed his shaven head. "How have you been keeping? I'm enjoying the villa this morning, as part of my tour of town. Found your name on—I don't remember where, but I said to myself, 'There couldn't be two men of that name in all the Belt,' and left the tour group. Music's your game, now? That's a long way from drive tech."

Another dupe for the fountain of youth. Tieg never liked Joash McMikall, although no hostility had ever broken out between them. He moved his lightweight wicker occasional chair out into the room, to mark the precise edge of the console's viewing radius. Already he disliked the situation. If Renasco had come to suspect him of Old School involvement, his cover was blown, his watching post vacant, and he was effectively dead. Mind-wiped at the least, like his—

No. He wouldn't think of her.

"Yes," he answered, surprised even a trained voice could sound so smooth, "but my father was a musician. I don't know if I ever mentioned that."

"I'm in planetside traffic, now. Good post, no family to support. Money for myself, and spaceport women." He winked one brown eye at Tieg and rubbed his shining head. "The best. No inhibitions. But now that I think of it . . ." He glanced around, a gesture taking in all Tieg's outer room. "Nothing like what I'll bet you've got. Her Grace keeps you well, I hear. How is she under the sheets?" He sniffled and swallowed.

Tieg had heard those rumors, though never spoken boldly to his face before. "Holjpip takes her pleasure in ruling people, McMikall, not dalliance. It's an excellent job. May I get you something to drink?"

"Of course. Something expensive."

Tieg knew petty jealousy when he heard it. McMikall would enjoy casting suspicion on him, if he had not done so already. While Tieg strolled across the room, McMikall went on talking. "Things are a little odd, here. Don't you think?"

Careful! "What do you mean?"

"Oh, rumors. The Company's asking everyone to watch. I don't know what you've heard. . . ."

He rattled on, repeating a number of stories, some reasonable, some ludicrous, that circulated in Anslanding over the past year. Tieg had heard them all, at one point or another, and others.

The man was sniffing for someone, yet Renasco could afford better spies. Without turning his back on his visitor, Tieg opened his liquor cabinet and drew out a corked carafe of Podacan whiskey, a gift from Holjpip. It seemed wrong to waste it like this. He poured two tiny crystal glasses.

"Nice place, Innig," he heard. "Amazing, isn't it, I should find you here? After all these years—and you didn't exactly make yourself easy to follow, when you left school. You didn't come here directly, did you?"

Follow. Be careful, Innig.

Beside the carafe, behind the support for the shelf above it, lay a tiny dart pistol, built without metal or composites and therefore easier to carry past Holjpip's inspection points at villa entrances. With a smooth motion, Tieg tucked it into the voluminous caftan's left sleeve band.

"Not directly," he said, balancing the glasses on his left palm—an awkward trick for a right-hander. "Had some odd jobs. The usual. Settled for Mannheim because I like the climate. It's a garden world, and still not too crowded."

"Right." McMikall nodded as Tieg recrossed the room. McMikall put down half his drink in a gulp. "My sentiments, exactly. We both like it uncrowded. What would it be worth to keep a few certain parties from knowing you're here?"

So. McMikall did remember. He wasn't a spy but an opportunistic blackmailer, and stupid enough to come

alone. Tieg was probably still unsuspected at official levels.
But Joash McMikall, left to himself, would carry Tieg's trail
back to Renasco. Tieg gripped his glass, still left-handed.
"It would be worth something, McMikall. What are you
after?" Lowering himself into the wicker chair, Tieg took a
tiny sip of whiskey. Even if he paid blackmail, he doubted
McMikall would keep quiet.

Midway through that five-year training stint, misplaced
trust had gotten him betrayed and expelled. He had
learned hard lessons from that incident.

"Well." McMikall sniffed the whiskey and then finished
it. "I'm glad you're reasonable. I think I'd take three hundred creds a month." He snuffled again. "To start."

"I don't make that much."

Joash McMikall opened the hand that held his glass. As
the tiny tumbler fell and shattered, Tieg saw black plastic
gleam. "You do have a choice," said McMikall.

A dart pistol of his own. Tieg folded his hands toward
each other as if making a pleading gesture and slid his
fingers into the sleeve band.

McMikall raised his pistol and leveled it at Tieg. "Well,
Innig?"

"All right."

McMikall smiled and glanced away. Tieg whipped his
hands apart and placed a single dart below the man's ear.
McMikall's blank face whipped toward him. One hand
groped for the dart and dropped, limp, on the couch.

Tieg inhaled and watched McMikall die. It took only
seconds. His own heart pounded. A fraction of a second
slower, and that would be him slumping dead. Ancient
Gods, he had done it.

Still keeping out of the console's line of sight, Tieg
examined the papers in McMikall's breast pocket. He un-
folded a hand-scribbled column of names. His own headed
the list.

Where did he get those? Tieg straightened. If that list
came from official sources, his cover wasn't worth hydro-
gen. It could be names from school. . . .

He refolded the paper and tucked it into his own
pocket, then heaved the limp body up, over the couch's
back, and dropped it behind. After dark he could pass the
console and get down to the beach unnoticed, and strong

offshore currents washing the villa's bay would take Joash McMikall and his weapon far out to sea.

Tieg's pulse throbbed. He wasn't in the clear yet. If Holjpip's Company colleagues had sent McMikall to check on him, they would notice McMikall gone.

Someone would notice him gone eventually.

Rising, Tieg went to wash his hands and the remaining whiskey glass. For the second time, he had watched a man die. This one was not a friend, but he was going to be sick anyway.

In still night air, Able Tatarka scratched at his uncomfortable uniform collar and withdrew deeper into leafy bushes. Weary of guard duty, he'd come out for a breath and heard footsteps. A stem poked at his ear, but he held still in covering shadows.

A dark form strode up the beach path. As the man approached the villa entrance, Able recognized him. *The tone poet, at this time of night?*

Several breaths after Innig passed inside, Able strolled toward the path. *Wet footprints.* Curiosity piqued, Able followed the path down to the beach and examined the ground. After a year's work on Her Grace's security force, he ought to be considered for promotion soon, and then he could afford to marry and start a family. What could be found here?

He reached the sand, drew out his pocket light, and knelt beside a long furrow. Something had been dragged from the lower-level beach elevator down to the water. He tried the door and found it locked to the outside, as it should be at this hour.

A call to Her Grace's security chief seemed in order.

Ming groaned, straightened to stretch her aching back, and pulled a breath of outdoor air. She had spent the days since sketching Tieg largely locked into her basement room, practicing and experimenting, drilling herself in alphabet details all day and then trying foliage patterns all evening. In less than two days more, now, she must prove her worth to Holjpip. Renasco had trained her in technique, not creativity; yet Ming had discovered that even ribbon lines' width and points of branching could become creative endeavors. Shaping new letters of similar style became a favorite pastime, conditioning her hand musculature without tedious drill.

She *was* learning to enjoy the work they had assigned for her punishment. Some day, free again, she could forget all this. From the data base she had nothing on Tieg yet, but her familiarity with base systems, wiped clean, was only now beginning to reestablish.

Her spine gave a satisfying *pop*. She bent again to probe the villa's shadow for samples of native vines, clutching a small, sharp knife procured at Staff Central. Six varieties of ground cover lay underfoot. It was difficult to concentrate, though, even on greenery, when at her back rolled the sea.

The sea . . . she gave in, straightened once more, and gazed into the onshore wind. Water rippled a thousand shades of blue, gray, and purple beneath darkening sky. Clutching tough stems in her left hand and the knife in her right, she followed one wave far below as it formed, swept into magnificent curls, and plunged suicidally toward the strand, dying in foam, buried in foam, dissolved whispering back to sea. In midair she traced its motion with her fingers.

She had enough botanical samples to copy for one evening's practice. Surely one from this batch would suit Her Grace's large-sized initial. She turned her face toward the villa's seaward door, hoping she could return to her room without having to speak to anyone and break the intensity of her kinship with Mannheim's vast ocean.

Passing into the villa, she sensed a new ambience in the hallways. The music had changed. The soft undertone generally pervading the upper level now carried something heady. It coiled around her emotions and intensified them. As rapt as she had already been, this made her almost giddy. Hardly thinking what she did, she hurried toward the centrum.

Gaily robed men and women gathered in groups inside the green-grown area. Most looked young, some with faces painted to resemble exotic animals, some wearing jewels and little else. The skylights darkened, but high above the highest trees, banks of lamps caught the hue of true daylight and directed it downward.

Beside the wall nearest her, half hidden behind several planters, curved an array of electronic machinery. Intent between two black-dialed consoles, Tieg Innig hunched over.

She hadn't seen him in four days, since the morning of her first preliminary sketch. Still clutching her vine samples, Ming moved a step closer to the glass wall. Head bowed, hair falling over his forehead, he reached down with both hands. One settled on a panel, the other twisted, and the music changed. Two bass notes she had barely heard before began to swell, at odds with the harmonies above them; then the harmonies resolved, dominated by the deeper mastery, while above this struggle two high melodies interwove, each painted in a different timbre. Incredible, that one performer could create such complex music.

A vision sprang into Ming's memory: She sat in an acceleration chair, the ceiling arched overhead—then came the tearing, falling sensation of wormhole passage. It went on, and on—they broke through, with their cargo. . . .

Ming startled loose from the vision. Cargo? What had they been doing? Panting, she reached for the glassy wall to steady herself.

Tieg's right hand touched a higher panel, and the intoxicating melody repeated—but slightly altered. Ming's wakened memory faded. She clutched at it.

It wouldn't come back.

Oh! It had been so vivid! She closed her eyes and tried to reweave the shreds into a whole. From the door into the centrum, a black-suited guard started toward her.

Touching her ear in apology, Ming backed away and hurried down the cream-carpeted hall. The music followed until the glass elevator closed around her, yet in her mind it played on, echoing like that glimpse of the past she had lost, its details irrecoverable, its essence unforgettable.

She had to hear more.

In her room, she ran a basin of cool water and laid the vines in it. She needed more than a single preliminary sketch of Tieg Innig, anyway. She could finish the illuminated initial tomorrow. How better to capture the natural postures of Tieg, the musician, than at his job?

Hurriedly she showered, dressed in the only suit in her

closet that included a long skirt, then pinned the amethyst
cloisonné emblem at her neckline.

"Calm down," she muttered as she dug in a drawer for
her sketch pad. "It's early and the party's only beginning.
He'll be at work for hours."

Nevertheless, she breathed hard by the time she
reached the centrum. Holding four pencils low at her side
and brandishing her pad, she approached the door guard.
"Her Grace has asked that I draw her tone poet's likeness,
Mere." Already the music took its hypnotic hold, and Ming
knew she would draw something better than she'd ever
stretched her skills. "I wish," she went on, "to sit quietly,
along the wall."

He wrinkled his nose. "No food. That's for guests, not
staff."

"I'm not hungry." She laughed a little crazily as she slid
through the doorway.

It was louder in here. Wide-footed, Ming braced herself
against the music's effect. Why did it hold her so?

Emotional manipulation. It had to be part of the job.

Ah, she thought. *I think I understand you now, Tieg
Innig. I want my freedom, but you're chasing power.*

Ming edged around an earthy-smelling planter toward
the wall near Tieg. His deep-set eyes evidently saw nothing but his bank of instruments, if those black boards and
silver consoles could be called musical instruments. Tonight he wore black pants and a shimmering orange, black,
and white striped shirt, with long furred fringes along each
arm that drifted like feathers in the wind when he moved.

A hand grasped the back of her neck. Wriggling, she
tried to turn around, and the hand dropped.

"We are partygoing tonight, Mere Dalamani?" Zardir
Huekk's tiny child's voice thrust through the enchantment
of music and scene. Ming completed her turn. Huekk,
dressed in formal black, stood in a deep shadow, likely
invisible to everyone but her.

"The best of evenings to you, Missar Huekk," she said
with a small bow. In the days since he appeared unannounced in her room, she had accumulated new confidence. "I am attempting to fulfill our mistress' orders. She
asked for a portrait of Missar Innig."

The twisted smile appeared. "Her Grace's tone poet. He does his work well, does he not?"

She glanced over her shoulder.

"It's all in his *memory.*" Huekk stressed the word by primly drawing out the second *m*.

Ming sniffed at the deliberate reminder of her mind wipe. She'd used the word herself, for letter practice.

"I shall not detain you from your duty, little Mere Visual. However—" he paused and twisted his misshapen head first one way and then the other, "I will ask for whatever news you gather tonight. This is a group of spaceport employees, invited here for a minor celebration Her Grace really doesn't have time for. Do keep your eyes moving. You belong to the Company. Never forget that."

H

Backing away, Huekk vanished behind a group of white-clad women at a nearby fountain. Ming shut her eyes. *"Do keep your eyes moving"*—as though drawing took no concentration! Perhaps Huekk inherited bitterness with his deformities. She drew a deep breath and glanced toward Tieg Innig.

Though the music went on, he was staring at her. Their eyes met, then he looked aside again.

Slowly, watching all around her (Huekk meant every word. She must find some tidbit to throw at him tomorrow!), Ming made her way to the planter nearest Tieg's station. Laying her sketch pad on the high red stone wall, she scrambled up, mindful of her loose black skirt, then surveyed the centrum from that vantage.

The entire middle area of the high room centered on

the long rectangular pool and six fountains. Greenery draped the fountains' sides and trailed from their bowls into the pool, cascading in shimmering textures like Tieg Innig's music. A small yellow-orange bird splashed in one end of the long pool. Delighted, Ming watched until it shook dry like a small explosion. Under the feet of the ambassador's guests, tiles laid in concentric hexagons faded from deep green, through pale shades of spring, then mixed out to almost white, so that the nearer one approached the fountains, the less the contrast between mossy ground and the floor tiles.

Ming shifted her weight on the stone seat. The centrum had been designed by an artistic master. Holjpip could afford the best, including Tieg Innig.

She set to work.

Tieg remained between two black-surfaced banks of electronics. All she wanted tonight was contour drawing, a series of natural poses, but he didn't hold any position long. Ming felt like an imager with very slow graphics.

A knot of women passed in front of her. They carried full, clear glasses and they spoke louder than perhaps they realized.

". . . if HolLanCorp is going to make a move, anyway." The tallest of the group, willowy and dressed in a floor-length gown on which tiny red and silver jewels spiraled from shoulder to floor, tossed off her drink and smiled knowingly at her two companions.

Another, silver-haired, whose face was painted catlike in black and white, shook her head so hard her hair flopped against pigmented cheeks. "The woman knows her risk tables better than Renasco knows Holjpip. A year at most."

Glancing in Ming's direction, the third, whose jeweled, dangling belt and breastband made her transparent blue leotard barely suitable for public wear, reached for the willowy one's elbow. "Look. He's bringing out a tray of mellow pods." They passed out of earshot.

Ming hadn't understood a word of that, but Huekk might. She flipped a page, and with a few sure strokes she drew memory caricatures of the three. This might have to do with the marginally legal activity she suspected, some competitive firm hiding new products from HolLanCorp and Renasco. At least, His Exalted Missar Lieutenantship would appreciate having someone to suspect.

Finished, she returned her attention to Tieg. These fast impressions had begun to gel in her mind. She might try a preliminary portrait sketch soon, if he consented to sit. With flat strokes of a pencil's edge, she shaded irregular stripes on the pad, dark on his chest, and then faintly, like hints of camouflage, around his head to frame it. She found herself wondering whether she'd find this drawing accurate tomorrow, when the music no longer made her certain she could accomplish anything. No one could complain of lassitude in this atmosphere.

Twenty minutes of calm passed. Then Tieg glanced toward Holjpip and brought his theme to a close. Ming couldn't believe how suddenly the music changed, nor its effect on her. One moment she was leafing back through the pad, half clinging to a shred of memory Tieg's playing suggested. The next moment the star-filled void fled from her mind, and the charisma of the man who made this exotic music drew her like iron to magnetic north.

Tieg touched several additional tabs and stepped from his station. The music went on, quickening her blood. He seemed to see her again, sitting high on her planter. His eyes narrowed, he hesitated, then he strode her way, the fringes on his sleeves rippling behind him. He planted his feet on the tiles and looked up. "Working?"

She turned the pad to show him, feeling shy and hypnotized. Her drawings did not do him justice.

"Come down."

She could do nothing else. The vortex sucked her in, heated her. Beneath shimmering, striped fabric, his muscular chest rose and fell.

He pulled her from the centrum by one hand. She came willingly, her heart dancing to the music's pulse. At the first bend in the hallway he drew her through a door, and they emerged under bright lights onto a lawn-covered bluff on the ocean side of the villa. There he let go.

Ming shivered in brisk evening air, her skirt fluttering at her ankles. *What am I doing here?* she wailed to herself. *This isn't right!*

Tieg took two steps away and gathered a handful of fringe in his fingers. With his eyes half closed, he looked like he might be laughing. "Feel better now, out of that heat room?" he asked.

"Better?" Oh, dear clancestors, how could she get back indoors? This man was Holjpip's, and probably in more ways than one.

Tieg spread his hands. "You were glassy-eyed, Ming, but it's not your fault. Holjpip just signaled for seduction music. If you'd stayed in there, you'd be rolling in the moss by now. With anyone. Music often requested by the Loyal Brothers of Shipping. You chose a particularly rank party to intrude on."

He'd brought her out of it, to safety. She must thank him. But first, she needed to know: "Does Her Grace . . ."

"Holjpip," he said quietly, "keeps her men in glass cages and her women in the workplace. She's married to Mannheim." Tieg turned to the sea, and Ming stared at his profile. *His best angle*, she realized. The hypnotic music might lie silenced behind heavy doors, but it had awakened an attraction she could not so easily mute. That profile belonged on a sculpture, a proud one, facing the sea. "There's something more than human about Ambassador Langelleik," he added.

Hearing him lead the conversation away from the jeweled spaceport crowd, Ming walked forward on dark, microcrystalline stepping stones set into the lawn grass. "She hasn't put you in any cage, has she?"

His posture went formal and stiff. "Why do you ask that?"

"What—"

"What does it matter, what I think of Her Grace's ways?" he asked, staring out to sea. "Ming, do you want your true status broadcast?"

"Tieg, I—"

"I don't care to answer questions about my personal affairs."

In the low voice of this new, frightening Tieg Innig, Ming caught the undercurrent of violence Lyra had warned about. "Good night, Missar Innig." She fled indoors.

Tieg watched her go, his emotions less steady than he'd have liked. He shouldn't have admitted anything about

Holjpip to Ming. Why did he want to tell her secrets? After watching her stand alone with Zardir Huekk, he feared more than ever that he might have to silence Ming Dalamani, too.

No, he groaned to himself. Four nights ago, after giving McMikall to the sea, he had barely made it back to his room before being sick again, then spent two tormented nights before sleep came easily. Ming Dalamani, warm, alive, and one step away from his arms, made the notion of killing even more repulsive.

What do you believe in? insisted his inner voice. *You need time to finish your work here. You made a mistake, asking for her help, and both of you may have to pay.*

Yes. Later. Maybe. Shut up, he told the grim voice.

He strolled to the cliff's edge, uncertain where he meant to go. Between two shrubs lay the head of the downhill trail. He wasn't dressed for walking; this shirt would need dust washed out of its fringe again.

Ming. Poor, lost Ming, her tapering, graceful hands a testament to artistic beauty. He strode down the path.

There she had stood, cheek to jowl with Holjpip's mutant, the most obnoxious Renasco man on Mannheim, the one Tieg wished he dared silence. And then she started asking questions. Why had Ming sat sketching him twice already? He couldn't afford to rouse suspicion now, with Old School's deepspace probe drifting back across the system from a mysterious lump of rock.

Circling this sun one-eighty degrees from Mannheim and sharing its orbit, the captured asteroid—mined for palladium in Mannheim's early days—had emitted odd energies in recent months. Tieg needed at least another month unsuspected, to get offplanet, intercept the probe, and finish his investigation. Thank the Ancient Ones no one had come looking for McMikall yet, or asked about him at tonight's party.

The girl was Renasco trained, memory-blocked. Forget her night-black eyes *(if you can, Tieg Innig).* Forget the collar in her spine, always ready to paralyze her.

His loyalty to Old School was worth the price of his own life, he had decided years before, worth months and years of secreting himself on Mannheim and working his way to the ambassador's inner circle. Therefore, it was worth the life of young Ming Dalamani, the moment she began to ask the wrong kind of questions.

Inhaling salty air, he stepped off the path onto the beach, and his dress boots dug into fine sand. Surveillance down here was sporadic, more trouble and money than Holjpip wanted to spend when funds could flow into parties and production. He glanced from side to side. Strong cross-shore currents had obliterated the furrow McMikall's body had gouged.

How do you trust a woman Renasco has collared—and then undoubtedly promised an early release, if she serves them well? Trust no one. It's safer.

He cast his stare out to sea, and it returned slowly: the moonless sky, intense with stars, silver-gray wave crests forming, beginning to gleam with a pale phosphorescence near the shore, then crashing, dissolving to lap at his feet.

And at his back, the villa. He stared up the cliff at long gleaming walls.

He had done little to win her trust tonight, though he brought her out of the centrum with honorable intentions. In that little way, at least, he'd been able to protect her.

Protect her, so she can give you away to Renasco.

The shell of a dead crustacean lay on the shore. Channeling his frustration into one foot, he kicked it out to sea, where it landed inside a wave and vanished. His head still ached with warring compulsions, and he still could give Ming Dalamani nothing.

The next morning Ming's week of grace ended, but she was ready. On her work table lay six sample alphabets, executed twice in two nib widths; an original alphabet hand created after innumerable experiments; and most delicate of all, Holjpip's capital *H*, presented as twin columns covered with the pale arrow-leafed vines that spiraled the villa's entrance pillars. Newly sprayed, it lay setting now.

And a series of studies, sketches, and contour drawings of Tieg Innig. Nothing in any of them hinted at the sinister side he'd shown on the bluff, but examining them gave Ming confused feelings of fear and admiration.

You're lonely, she told herself. *Get to know Lyra better. Meet some other art staff.* For a minute she stood looking at her work, proud of the hours this spread represented—hours of practice time spent on discarded sketches and gels, more hours preparing the works themselves. Then she began to interleaf set gels and cellose tissue, layer on layer, in the carrying case she had obtained from Staff Central. She checked the blinking timer on her screen. Eleven-twelve, it read. Plenty of time to relax, shower, catch a good lunch, and mentally prepare for her afternoon appointment with the ambassador.

Some slight noise and movement to her right caught her peripheral vision. Zardir Huekk hesitated, framed in the doorway, then paced into her room. "Mere Dalamani, little artist," he said, taking her desk chair without waiting for a greeting. "What did you see at the party last night?"

Even for him, she was ready. From a second sketch pad, lying closed on one end of the work table, she pulled the three caricatures from the spaceport gathering. "These women." She presented the sheet to Huekk but remained a respectful two paces away. "Last night, they were talking about Her Grace—scornfully. They sounded as if their loyalty lay elsewhere, Missar Huekk. Very much elsewhere." She tried to repeat their conversation.

"Ah." The little man eyed the paper. When he sat on her orange chair, his body looked less grotesque, though the unnatural point of his chin and the bulging, domed back of his head made her feel she faced an outsized insect. "Yes," he said when he looked up. "This is a useful ability you have, a vital skill for a noticing person."

"My—?"

"Your ability to draw caricature, Mere Ming. You see, I know these women. Anyone who knows them would recognize them from this paper. Anyone who needs to communicate her visual impressions would do well to learn the art of caricature."

For once, someone appreciated it. That ability had caused hours of trouble, in school and at home. Ming managed to look him in the eye and smile.

"Unfortunately for you," he added, "I also know they have been watched and cleared. This is nothing new, for Renasco. We need more, Ming Dalamani. More, or we will find it necessary to have you transferred."

"Missar," she dared. "I am the employee of Madam Langelleik—"

"And not Zardir Huekk," he finished for her. "Oh, yes, little Mere, that's true. But Madam Langelleik is the representative of the Renascence Shielding Corporation, and Mannheim itself is Renasco's property." He slid forward off the chair, gliding down to land on tiny legs. "Keep trying."

Once he left, Ming sat for a while, staring at her work, half of it still lying on the table and half neatly laid in the carrying case. For one instant she wanted to destroy it all and deny Renasco her service.

That flare of temper cooled quickly. It was her own work, good work. Holjpip set these tasks, and she had made a beginning; but there was more to be done. Huekk ordered her to sniff out counter-Renasco spies, too, and Tieg Innig demanded her help—which she hadn't yet been able to give. She stood in a precarious three-way balance.

Yes, she reminded herself, *and there are the others. And if I watch, watch and wait, Ming Dalamani will give the right information to the right person and walk free. Free, with a clear conscience.*

Conscience. She scratched around the irritating metal stubs at her spine. A convicted criminal, and she worried about conscience.

It did worry her. What had she done?

She reached Staff Dining late enough that Lyra Dusenfeld sat at a table, waving a bare, fleshy arm in the air for Ming to join her. Lyra had come back to her room three days ago and answered questions while Ming practiced raza hand: Ming cajoled her into helping her practice multiplication tables, too, offering overdependence on a calculator as her excuse and a desire to better herself as motivation. Today Lyra looked so round and animated that Ming laughed quietly. For all Zardir Huekk's threats, Renasco could not rob her of lighthearted moments.

"I'm glad to see you eating." Lyra spread jelly on a slice of yellow bread as Ming sat down on a low stool.

"Yes," Ming said, "being cold improves my appetite. How are things on the casserole line?"

"Not bad. I have a vacation in two days. My sister lives

about eight hundred klicks south of here, and I'm going to see her."

"Oh. A vacation. How lovely." Ming swallowed a mouthful of some insipid, spiceless, but steaming mixture of ground meat and grain. "There are more settlements on Mannheim than Anslanding and Newport, then?"

"Oh, Ming." Lyra laughed, took a long drink of c'fee, and wiped her mouth. "The Pomona Valley is where things are *really* happening this year." She paused as if expecting a reaction.

Ming heard an odd word. "Pomona?"

"Minor goddess of springtime and fruits," said Lyra. "Way, way, *way* back. I don't suppose you've heard of nilly beans, either?"

"Where would I have?"

"Hots, some people call them?"

Ming shook her head.

"Well." Lyra tossed dramatic glances to left and right, then leaned forward on her elbows and cocked her head at Ming. "About two years back, settlers down in the Pomona Valley—they grow fruit, mostly, it's a pretty place—began to wonder why the nutchuckers—little lizards that live there—could move so fast. You can't shoot one without a laser from two meters away. Turns out they live on the seeds of a local tree. And those seeds are loaded with something about a hundred times more powerful than this." She touched her half-finished c'fee.

"New industry, then?" Ming sopped a roll in broth and tucked the soggy morsel into her mouth.

"That's only half of it. There's a parasite that lives on the nilly pines. Mellow pod, they've taken to calling it. *It* has a fruit with just the opposite effect. Slows you down. So well, in fact, some settlers' kids have quit growing." She pressed her palms together, still leaning forward. "It stops aging."

"It does what?"

"Better than rejuv treatments, in some ways. You probably haven't heard about it yet, because of two things. One, Her Grace doesn't allow free use of either at the villa. And two, she's sitting on a platinum mine. Renasco is buying nillies for its pilots, execs, and anyone else who has to think fast in a crisis. Holjpip is supplying them and *also* doing the only research-in-progress on the stuff. So for the last two years, she's been able to spend money like never before. ALPEX and General are beating themselves silly at the gates, but the forest is walled for HolLanCorp."

Ming laid her fork on her plate and took a sip of cold water. Money like never before, and so catching others' attention.

And hiring odd talents. This fit.

Lyra picked up her cup and swirled it, then drained the last swallow. "You should see the nilly pines. Weirdest things that ever grew."

"Weird?"

"Unique. I . . . can't describe them. You probably could."

Lifting another forkful of hot mash, Ming had a second notion. If this new pair of pharmaceuticals constituted Holjpip's hope for the future, a metal miniature in the shape of one of those "weird" nilly pines might work as a gift. She was ordered to try to win the ambassador's favor.

But should she know about these products? Ming caught a whiff of something spicy as a small man hurried past her table with his tray. If she read Holjpip right, taking risks to win her favor might win Ming sanction and approval. "Huh," she said aloud. "If I could get the time off, might I come along? I wouldn't be a bother."

Lyra swatted Ming's arm. "Staff Central's in charge of vac time. And it's my experience *art staff*—" she folded thick fingers daintily on the table, "are always vanishing for research vacations. You've got pay coming, too, you know."

"Where do I get that?"

"Central will clear your account. It's on your credit disc. Ask."

Ming asked. Sure enough, art staff could take two-day vacations from the first week on duty. Having worked nine days, Ming was entitled to four for herself, "for purposes of research."

She left Lyra a message on the intervilla comm net by typing a message on her console, then touching up Lyra's room number: *When did you say we were leaving?*

Then, cautiously balancing her loaded satchel on both forearms, she went to meet with Madam Langelleik.

Holjpip remained at her work as evening darkened the drawn, decorative fiber curtains of her Operations room, half conscious of the guardians with whom she surrounded herself, thinking of Ming Dalamani.

The meeting had gone well, the week's reprieve worth the wait. Resting her arms on her desk, Holjpip stared between seaside curtains and the wall of observation screens. Ming Dalamani's first set of samples had shown muscular shakiness. The later set, presented this afternoon, demonstrated a steady hand, and Ming herself showed respect, pride, and satisfaction.

She touched a red glass vase of fragrant cryllia. One day the pleasant, unspoiled temperate world of Mannheim would be a haven for the proud, the talented, the able. They would look to her as their guardian and bless her name, and cherish her memory, one day when neither rejuv treatments nor pharmaceutical research could prolong her life. Holjpip's life would have counted for something, and for that cause, it was worth prolonging.

Idly she reached for the touchboard recessed into the left side of her desk. From this room, she could access Renasco files at many levels—and, if she managed to break through Renasco's file-security codes without tripping alarms, the Company would never know. Now that Ming Dalamani had proven herself worthy of retention, what was her past? Why did Renasco own her? What potentials did she hide that Holjpip might tap for her own uses, with or without the approval of her superiors in the Renascence Shielding Corporation?

Once only in her career, Holjpip had ordered "mnemonic therapy." The man she paid for Renasco codebreaking sequences did not recall, now, how he gained his sudden wealth, and lived contentedly on Little York. Few people, on Mannheim or any other world, could breach certain levels of Renasco security. Holjpip's choice had been simple: She must have those keystroke sequences without Renasco's notice. She had to force him to forget his brief transgression or else silence him permanently.

With twenty carefully chosen taps, she brought the

Renasco file on Ming Dalamani onto her small screen. She blinked, stared, then blinked again.

Piracy?

That was what it read. Sedition and piracy.

Cabra Minor, declaimed the background abstract, had delayed contracting Renasco service for almost a decade after first recontact, much longer than its neighbor system Nexos. *Hoping to duplicate our shielding,* she observed. *Evidently, someone succeeded.* Holjpip tapped a fingernail on her desktop. The shielding was installed only on Little York. Even Mannheim's Company rep had never breached that secret.

Holjpip pressed her body back onto her chair, one hand steady on the edge of her desk. *Right in my hand. Renasco, you may regret collaring this girl.*

She considered the entry again. Ming didn't look it, but what would a pirate look like?

Mere Dalamani had no recall, of course, of what she had done, nor of how she and her coworkers—surely this byte of a girl had not worked alone—accomplished the shielding miracle.

But was memory blockage infallible?

The electrode work was performed on the left, verbal hemisphere; she had watched it, that once. Holjpip allowed herself to straighten in the chair as an old notion resurfaced. Men or women trained in the arts allegedly possessed excellent cross-hemispheric connections.

Holjpip cradled a pen inside one palm. Was it worth pursuing? She lifted one line drawing of Tieg Innig, done with a lute in his hand.

As the Company rep, she would be the last person to whom Ming admitted any return of memory.

Still, Tieg Innig could evoke the mood of space travel. She had uncovered her handsome, opinionated tone poet's "old scholastic" affiliation years ago, through sources Renasco knew nothing about. Another piece dropped into place on the huge mental gameboard Holjpip maintained.

She gave a little relaxing sigh. She would slide her pair of pirates closer together and order several more studies, as preparation for the formal portrait. What moods would she ask her tone poet to evoke while Ming worked, then, to spark the kind of memories Holjpip hoped to unearth in

Ming's electrically untouched right brain? It would be good to know what kind of pirate she was dealing with, as well.

Holjpip had contacts on Nexos, where Ming's conviction was registered. It would take time to reach them, but that was all part of the game.

/

Caught packing three changes of tough-fabric outdoor clothes into her Renasco-blue duffel the following night, Ming heard her door slide open. Zardir Huekk stepped through. She wheeled to face him, grim thoughts chasing each other through her mind: *I should have reported to him that I was leaving!* Then: *He's going to make me stay.*

He's going to do worse than that, to make sure I don't forget to check in again.

What's the range on that collar transmitter?

Standing just inside the doorway, his feet apart, he stared up as if he read each of those thoughts and approved them all. "Mere Dalamani, I require you to take a trip for me. Tomorrow morning, no later."

Oh, she groaned, again meeting his half-drooped gaze and trying to show neither fear nor revulsion. "Yes, Missar Huekk?" she asked, wistfully touching her vacation clothing.

"I need a parcel taken to a man whose name I shall give you. He works at one of Her Grace's processing plants, this one in Goodsprings."

He paused as if waiting for her reaction, but the name meant nothing to her. "Yes?"

"In the Pomona Valley." His crooked smile appeared again, tearing the lower half of his face.

Pomona Valley. Sweat. He already knows I was going. How did he find out? Would he take me to task if he didn't need a parcel run up?

"I shall . . . be pleased to oblige you, Missar Huekk." She waited for him to reprimand, or threaten, or explain how he knew she intended to leave.

Huekk did none of these. "I shall send it down by messenger in about an hour. Do not leave without it."

"Missar."

"You will not tell your heavy friend from Staff Dining you are delivering it."

"Missar."

Huekk remained where he stood for another minute, not speaking, irking her by his very presence. Ming stared at his cleated sandals, trying for patience.

He left without another word.

She pulled another khaki-brown jumpsuit from its Staff Central cello packet. Discarding the cello, she laid the jumpsuit on top of another, beside a pair of new, leather-fragrant walking boots.

Forty minutes later, a thin man Ming did not remember seeing delivered the parcel. Cube-shaped, it fit into her two hands and felt heavy for its size, possibly metallic. Tucked into a stiff clear band tying it was a note lettered in the small, blocky typeface of a portable printer:

The parcel is to be delivered to Rayman Dourthe, at Goodsprings One. Your collar can be closed at any distance on this continent, Mere Visual. Have a care.

With damp palms, she slipped the parcel into a pocket at one end of her duffel. Where was Goodsprings One, and how could she escape Lyra long enough to make a delivery? Lyra loved company, and probably had every intention of staying at Ming's side.

With a brisk motion, Ming snapped the duffel's pocket closed. She would manage. She was beginning to trust her luck.

She did not escape the villa, however, without one more encounter. Her buzzing screen awakened her, a message glowing at its center:

+CAN YOU COME TO THE CENTRUM FOR A MINUTE?
T.+

T for Tieg, she thought through a fog. *What time is it?*
2317. She'd slept only an hour. After hitting the ACK
tab, she stood staring at the darkened screen. *He must be
getting off work.*

She ran a comb through her hair. He wanted to know
what she'd found, who down here in the women's wing
had extraordinary talent. As she laid down the comb, a
thought struck her with all the vehemence of just-awaken-
ing jealousy. What if Tieg Innig were simply looking for a
talented woman for himself?

*Stop it. That music wasn't written for you alone. You're
acting like a spacebreather in heat.*

Ming stared into her mirror at a long face, all eyes and
bone. In that case, Tieg might not be the conspirator
Zardir Huekk sought. Easing out into the hallway, she
worked on repressing that thought, but it would not leave.

She found him wearing the blue-and-green caftan
again, sitting beside the long pool. Even at this late hour,
the fountains still played beneath a bank of overhead
lights. When he rose to greet her, air currents off the fountain caught the long, set-in sleeves of the garment, making
it ripple around his body. "Ming. Thank you for coming."

She took a seat on the pool's brim, just far enough from
him that their knees did not touch. "You're wanting to
know who I've found, I take it."

"Yes?" He dipped a hand into the water.

Seeing it was allowed, Ming did the same and found
cool, liquid pleasure between her fingers. A fountain like
this, back at home, would be beyond price. "Calla Whitney, I met one day at lunch. She's a specialist in
hypermagnetic fields. And," Ming added, conscience forc-
ing her to speak on, "she's lovely. Silver hair to her waist,
and—"

"Calla. Yes, I think I know who you mean." Tieg nodded. "Go on."

"I . . . also thought of Tieralyn. I don't know her last
name. Very young, top honors in her class on Jarnik, back
in the Belt, in city planning. Not," she added, "as pretty as
Calla."

She watched Tieg for a reaction, but his face did not change. He only said, "Go on."

Pursing her lips, she reached for her earlobe. "That's . . . all, Tieg. I'm not the eyes for you. I stay mostly in my rooms."

He stared, his expression dark and serious. *Holjpip's favorite,* she reminded herself, *in his glass cage. About as far above the likes of you as a man could rise. Be polite, and warm—and remember, your freedom does not lie with him.*

"I enjoyed your music very much, Tieg, when I was working on those sketches for Madam Langelleik."

"Including . . . ?" His eyes sparkled deep in their hollows.

A nervous laugh escaped before she could squelch it. "Yes. That was . . . particularly beautiful. Very, um, effective. Your own? I mean, original, I assume?"

"The melody is folk, from one of the Belt worlds. I added harmonies, though, and reworked the orchestration." His expression darkened. "Ming, do you have anything else for me? I didn't come for compliments. I'd like information."

The cocoon of sleepiness vanished from around her. This man could change in an instant, and she must never let her guard rest. "I wish I could tell you more, Tieg."

He leaned aside to flick water across the pool. "Thank you, then. Sleep well."

Some threat underlay those calm words. Perhaps she should mention him to Huekk. She glanced once over her shoulder as she strolled through a glass door, past the middle-sized, black-haired guard who had admitted her when told she was asked to speak with Tieg Innig. Tieg still sat inside, reaching into the water, showing the profile that made her want to stare.

It was a good thing she would leave on vacation tomorrow. She needed distance from this man.

Lyra Dusenfeld drove confidently, but as Ming expected, she talked every klick of the way from Anslanding up the Riddle River Valley.

At first Ming listened attentively while Lyra explained how she came to Holjpip. Settled in the right-hand seat of a low, silver two-passenger car, Ming fingered soft sky-blue upholstery while Lyra talked them past the outskirts of Newport. "I was born up there." Lyra lifted one finger off the half-wheel to point ahead and left, southwest toward their destination. "My family has worked the Pomona Valley since it was first planted. It's really pretty, you'll like it if all you grew up with was desert. But my mother was the kind who simply couldn't let go. Had to know where I was every minute of the day and night. She's got three of us, and I don't know how she spares the energy. Anyway, when my sister, Rimi, married a worker there at the old processing plant, I panicked and left for the big city."

Ming gazed out the window, tracing patterns on her lap with one hand. Fragrant white johnnistars drooped in clusters from thin-stemmed bushes with tiny leaves, in fields on fields. "Was that hard to do?" she asked.

"Yes. And no." Lyra shifted on her own seat. "I wanted good pay, a future, and a husband who wasn't a plant worker. I've found the first, and probably the second, and serving in Holjpip's dining area seems like a good way to meet the other."

"How long have you worked at the villa, then?"

"About a year. After I finished school in Newport, I lived there another five years. Mother's gone north to see my brother this week. He did what I did—escaped. So with her gone, it's safe to visit Rimi."

Ming sighed, aching at memories Renasco had not troubled to erase. "My . . . mother died"—*Twenty years ago! Don't tell too much*—"recently. It seems recent to me, anyway. We were close."

"You were lucky, then," said Lyra. "I spend all my time avoiding mine. I'm sorry about yours being gone. Was that why you changed worlds?"

Ming tensed, then relaxed. In no way could she imagine Lyra Dusenfeld as a threat to her security.

Still, she should not advertise her status. "That, and a hope to be part of something bigger. My clan is badly inbred. Several of my cousins are crippled, and I've never been strong."

"You're wise to breed out. But as for strength, you're just skinny. Wait until you taste Rimi's raisinet pastries. I guarantee, you'll gain weight while you're there. Rimi's all right. Five kids are too many for my taste, but she's got a good heart. Jefta, her oldest boy, came along right after she and Coey were married. . . ."

Breed out. Sideswiped by an image of Tieg Innig, Ming forced her attention out the car's tinted window. On her right, a huge wheeled machine made its ponderous way across a field, chomping spindly bushes whole at one end and ejecting green-brown straw at the other. Even through the car's air filtration system, the musky perfume was overwhelming.

". . . and Salie, she's the youngest, is a terror. Only last week, she . . ."

It wasn't that Ming didn't enjoy hearing about Rimi's family, but she would meet them soon enough. Outside, the lush agricultural valley sped by. From time to time, Ming caught glimmers of sunlight off the Riddle River, winding kilometers off to the left of the turnless high road. The scent faded as her olfactory sense fatigued, to remind her vaguely of something, some woman's perfume, maybe, or some environment she must have known. Other vehicles whizzed past, appearing alongside for a bare second and then vanishing ahead. Lyra didn't seem to notice or care that they passed her by. Occasionally, in the oncoming lane, Ming saw vehicles painted the same silvery color as their staff car. More of Holjpip's employees? It seemed odd Zardir Huekk chose to send the parcel with Ming, then, instead of by regular messenger.

". . . do have trouble keeping teachers. I don't think the kids at Goodsprings are any worse than kids anywhere. Personally, I think the teachers get dependent on the nillies . . ."

Goodsprings. Huekk's contact, Rayman Dourthe. She imagined Huekk cloned and waiting ahead.

Think about him later. Ming continued to stare at the scenery. Another world. Another decade, twenty years in her own future. Here she lived, thrust forward in time, but this only occurred to her now, away from the villa. The two strangenesses had balanced one another. She was beginning to feel at home, here—and now.

"All right, this is where we leave HolLanCorp territory for a while," said Lyra. "These fields are ALPEX—"

"Lyra," Ming said slowly, "what are the other firms

developing? Anything new, anything different from Hol-LanCorp?"

"Oh. Um." Lyra drove on. "Nothing, Ming, I don't think."

Of course. How could Lyra know?

"All the best money is in the Goodsprings operation, and until Renasco tools up for offworld testing and synthesis, the Company has to deal with us."

"I see," said Ming.

"Not that Her Grace is independent. It's common knowledge she has a daughter somewhere that Renasco keeps tucked away in case Holjpip decides to shift her weight."

"A daughter. She's been married?"

"Not that I know of. A clone daughter, I think."

"What's that?"

"I don't understand how it works, exactly, but I think they somehow fertilize two ova with each other. Very touchy, very expensive, and illegal on most worlds. Most of the things malform and abort."

"Oh. Oh, how strange."

Lyra shrugged. "Never envy the wealthy."

True, thought Ming. *They have their own dreams—and problems.*

The road became a twisted, inky ribbon and began to wind toward a cleft in rounded hills dotted with herds of large grazing animals that never came close enough to the road to be seen clearly. Ming stared at springs, feeder creeks, and waterfalls, stared at lush greenery, stared at multihued ferns and flowers growing wild, wishing for time to stop and sketch some of these beauties. People back home, under Cabra Minor's polar dome, would never believe this. *Some day,* she promised herself.

Lyra stopped the car for lunch in a mountain town, where succulent-leaved trees provided shade Ming wasn't sure she wanted. Even in her heavy jumpsuit, she shivered.

"So eat," Lyra said, sensibly. "Then you won't chill so easily."

In the doorway of the small restaurant, Ming drew her pale green I.D. disc from her breast pocket. Cloistered in the villa, she'd never needed to use it. She ought to practice acting like a free woman. "All right," she said. "Let me pay."

At sunset they reached a gated checkpoint, where two men in familiar security uniforms examined their identification. A little farther on, as they passed through shadow-black forest, Ming asked, "What do you know about that mutant fellow—" *What did Lyra call him? Oh—* "Hookey?"

"Oh, Ming. You haven't had a run-in, have you?"

Ming crossed her ankles and lied firmly, "No. But you warned me about him. Why?"

Lyra didn't answer for half a klick. When she spoke again, she used a soft, low voice. "People taken to see him sometimes disappear, it's said. He's a snitch, a company weasel. We may work for Renasco, Ming, but we don't have to believe in everything it does."

That's the truth! Ming clenched her teeth at the thought of the collar in the back of her neck.

Forty years, she reminded herself, then realized Lyra waited in awkward silence for her answer.

"Right," she said quietly.

It was dark when Lyra shut down the car in front of a long, well-lit home. Ming sat still while the car sank, then stretched up and out of the passenger cabin, surprised to find tired muscles when she'd done nothing but sit all day. She plucked her duffel bag out of the car's rear panel by its white straps, then waited while Lyra pulled out a stiff-sided suitcase. Above, stars gleamed. Ming picked out two constellations learned at Anslanding, the Crown and Little Harry, but here they stood out against a far brighter starfield.

Somewhere out there, home . . .

A sense of hugeness rose in her, a swell of emotion. Sudden memory: stars that went on forever, projected on a viewscreen Ming saw with absolute clarity. Shan, her massive upper body resting against a vertical console and shriveled legs dangling from an acceleration chair, sat beside Ming in a silence just as awed as Ming's own.

"Ming. You okay?" Lyra took a step toward the house, then stopped. "Are you coming?"

"I'm coming." Ming stood still a moment longer and clung to the memory, then followed up the walk.

At the front door, Rimi and her children welcomed Ming like a long-lost clansman. "Come in, come in. Sit." Rimi, a short woman whose ample figure made Lyra's look slender, led them to a set table from which heavenly smells steamed upward. She held a chair for Ming. "Eat. You must be starved and exhausted, after your long drive."

"Oh, no," began Lyra, but as soon as Ming settled into the chair, Lyra lifted a knife and fork and sliced into a slab of juicy red meat, recounting details of the trip south. Ming listened, astounded. All this time she'd talked a green streak, and she'd still noticed things Ming missed.

She's made the trip before, Ming reminded herself as she ate. Still, it was intriguing to note the sparkle she always enjoyed in Lyra. She might sling casserole for a living, but she was not dense.

Rimi sat at the head of the table, leaning forward on thick arms. Children's voices began a squabble in the next room, but Rimi paid them no attention, concentrating instead on a pale brown pastry.

Ming tried to make conversation but kept falling silent and letting Lyra carry the burden of speech. The pastry tasted every bit as good as it looked.

"Have another." Rimi pushed a platter toward her. "Specialty of the house."

"Thank you," Ming mumbled, thinking, *Lyra was right. I could gain weight on these.* She glanced at Rimi Dusenfeld, her body stuffed into a beltless one-piece drape. *But not that much weight.* Between childbearing and pastries, Rimi had plenty of excuses for her size. Ming was filling out a little, too, she knew, but in ways her father and male cousins had always found attractive. It was nice to feel attractive. Nice . . .

"Ming." Lyra snapped two fingers together. "Yoo, hoo. I said, shall I show you to your bedroom?"

Ming jerked herself upright, then softly laughed. "I think you'd better. Rimi, this was wonderful. I'm just—"

"You're just done in." Rimi leaned forward, pressed away from the table, and stood. "Long drive, and altitude. We'll tuck you in and see you in the morning."

J

Tieg Innig sat beside the fountain again that night, breathing earth smells while nocturnal birds challenged each other. Holjpip had no performing for him, which was well, for as aggravated as he felt, he might not be able to play.

He had come close—so close!—to making the fatal decision about Ming Dalamani last night, when she sat here beside him. Who knew what she suspected?

Yet he read sincerity in her—yes, even attraction. He'd performed for enough females to read that. In her deferential but keen-eyed manner, a personality was beginning to shine through: intelligent but anxious to please, preserving a remarkable stability, considering the partial Renasco wipe. From her cringing attitudes on arrival, he'd thought he could control her with the threat of rumor-mongering. But now, with her spirit coming alive—

Blast! He clenched one fist. Now he regretted those threats. If he only dared to clasp those lovely hands, then take her in his arms and silence her with something warmer than a cyanite dart.

He'd put off the decision once more, perhaps with fatal results for himself this time, for she was gone. "Research vacation," said the work board at Staff Central, but Zardir Huekk's subscript approved the trip. Her Grace's mutant did not do that without reason.

Ming lay under Huekk's influence whether she liked it or not, whether or not she found Tieg attractive. One day, Huekk would pressure her beyond the petty loyalty of girlish attraction, and obviously Tieg felt her vitality far more strongly than she felt his.

Oh, come. Don't you think Huekk has had you under suspicion before?

It wasn't for himself he feared, but for the information he knew, which could be taken from him and used against others of the Old School. He plunged a fist into the pool, splashing his pants. The upcoming encounter with his deepspace probe made him jumpy. He had no right to make Ming Dalamani pay for his own tension.

Ancient Gods, he wished he'd never spoken to her.

The one thing impossible in life, he reminded himself, *is to change the past.* He stared off across the centrum.

He had been nineteen that summer, far enough along in Renasco training that half the cadets on this training ship saluted him at drill.

"Took you long enough," he chided as a thin, straight-haired man trotted into view, his dress uniform immaculate, pale blue with touches of copper.

"Only half a minute gone," Pell puffed. "We've still got two and a half. Dervis should signal in about fifteen seconds."

On and off through their childhood years, the friendship between Tieg Innig and Pell Panasuk cycled them back together like symbiotic creatures. Pell's indomitable cheerfulness gave Tieg a balance for his too-serious leanings, and Pell's medium-range test scores had been faked like his own, to avoid too much attention from Renasco supervisors.

The cool freight area stood empty, dim and quiet except for the two trainees, but in four hours it would fill with techs preparing to receive a million creds in fissionables for the starship's drive. In Tieg's specialty, drive technology, he hoped to harass the Company most effectively. The training crew's long run began tomorrow, and for the next two months, Tieg and fifty classmates would travel interstellar space.

Staring at his watch, Tieg smiled. With this airlock jammed, things would be delayed. Just a little minor sabotage by Tieg and Pell, a training run of their own.

A symphony of odd smells drifted from crates piled along two walls of this spacious receiving room: exotic composites, half-used reagents, acid sealing compound. Pell whistled a soft tune, caught Tieg's glance, then pushed the melody flat. Rubbing his hands together for warmth,

Tieg winced. Above Pell's head, mounted at three-meter intervals all down the freight lock's inner doors, red letters screeched, FREIGHT AIRLOCK—AUTOMATIC CYCLE—DO NOT ENTER UNLESS FULLY SUITED.

Fifteen seconds passed. If late for cadre dress inspection, they'd spend the next day microcleaning keyboards. "Come on, Dervis," Tieg muttered. Up in Engineering, their third conspirator should sit ready to shut off power to the airlock's momentum servo, to protect Tieg and Pell while they disabled the outer door.

"He'll come through." Pell flicked dust off one copper-threaded epaulet.

"I don't know. Maybe we ought to save this until we can carry it off ourselves. We can do our part, but—"

"Dervis can do his. Look, if I can trust him, you can."

Inside the airlock chamber, lights flashed twice. "That's it." Excitement raised the pitch of Pell's voice. He cranked the airlock's inner door several centimeters along and squeezed through. Tieg reached for the door to pry it open a little farther.

It whipped closed with a clang. Tieg pulled his fingers free barely in time to protect the tips from a crushing.

Dervis had cycled the airlock servo to "security" instead of "off," the idiot! Tieg smacked an override circuit and glanced through the chamber window. Inside, under flashing lights, Pell took a running start and rammed the inner door. Though the bulkhead shivered, the door did not budge.

Alarm switch? Tieg found one, hit it. Nothing.

Now Dervis killed the main power, with the flywheel counterbalancing gigantic freight doors already in motion. He couldn't possibly have botched it worse. Dropping to his knees, Tieg yanked a snap-bolt wrench from the small packet of tools on his dress belt. He twisted one bolt off the servo panel, then a second. Cover off, he began disconnecting wires with rapid, careful attention to the sequence he had learned.

Inside the lock, something thumped. Tieg's blood turned to clay, but he didn't stop until the wires lay disconnected. Then he stood up to the window.

The vast, empty lock lay open to space. Probably Pell had bumped the outer door as he spun helpless into the vacuum. Outside the ship, at this moment, Pell drifted, freezing, fighting the inevitable, then decompressing, exploding from inside.

Tieg shook; he could see it all too vividly. Bile rose in his throat. He swallowed it, gagged, then swallowed again. Unable to reassemble the servo panel, he collapsed against the bulkhead. How had he worked so calmly before?

Before, he'd thought he might accomplish something. . . .

Expelled from Renasco training with the "unsatisfactory" rating that excluded him from space-related employment, Tieg returned home to finish grieving and study music from his Company-widowed father. Through music, Old School had renewed his chance to fight Renasco, but neither music nor all the operatives of the Old School could rekindle Pell Panasuk's easy grin, nor bring back the gentle enthusiasm of Tieg's mother, taken by Renasco for purchasing a smuggled Cabran sunstone.

"Excuse me, Missar Innig."

A dark-haired woman stood bending forward near his seat at Holjpip's fountain, so pale-skinned he wondered if she ever ventured outdoors. Tieg swallowed bitterness one more time and ordered his features into a bland expression. "May I help you?" He motioned to the pool's tiled edge. "Sit down, if you'd like."

She wore the violet jumpsuit of Staff Central. "Thank you. I'm Jury Bertelsen, Missar Innig. The door guard gave me permission to speak with you here for a few minutes."

From her faint lisp he placed her as a Jarnik native, and he did remember the name. She was an Old School "watcher," one level less deeply committed than himself. He'd been directed not to contact her unless necessary. It was easy enough not to chat at SC; she answered only direct questions.

Jury Bertelsen sank down onto the raised green tile. "I've admired your music for some time," she said, then pressed her lips closed as if keeping secrets.

"Thank you, Mere Bertelsen. You're kind to say that."

She smiled and glanced down, not a flirtatious gesture but one meant to lead into flirtation. Tieg frowned. They ought not to be seen together, and another woman occupied his mind.

"My parents are coming later this year," she said. "Father's nearing the end of a government term, and Mother's paying for a circuit of four scattered children. Are you willing to schedule a private concert? They'd enjoy hearing you, I'm sure."

He'd just heard more words than Jury Bertelsen generally strung together. "I would be honored to perform for your parents." He rose and offered a hand to help her stand. "Madam Langelleik has scheduled a staff gathering next month and asked me to perform. Perhaps you'll hear something you'd like me to schedule into the later concert."

A quick wrinkling of her brow showed disappointment. She'd probably hoped for a private audition. "May I schedule the concert, then? Mother will cover your fee."

She could be the one who arranged all his performances, through Staff Central. "Certainly," he said. Dropping his hand, she stepped away. He stood ready to flick a hand in farewell if she turned around along her way through the door in the glass wall.

Ming woke with a sleeping tunic tangled around her waist. Sunlight streamed through a window above her, and she couldn't remember anything after leaving the dining table. She sat upright, glancing around at dresser shelves lined with soft animal figures and hard holo cubes of fairy-tale-costumed characters, mostly done in tones of purple and rose. No computer screen watched this room. In no way could anyone keep track of her.

Exhilarated by the knowledge, she swept out of the sheets and hurried to the window. Faded curtains hung limp beside it. Outside, she saw another house close beside this one, and above its roof, the jagged peaks of nearby mountains loomed dark and angular.

Two days lay ahead of her, their only imperfection the delivery she must make for Zardir Huekk. The sooner she did that, the sooner she could relax.

She found her duffel at the edge of her bed. Quickly she dressed and made her way up the single straight hallway to the kitchen, following the intoxicating scent of fresh pastry.

Lyra and her sister decided to show Ming the nilly pines as they grew wild. As soon as the children dashed off to school, Lyra chauffeured the trio to the valley's edge in Rimi's husband's car, a wider model. Close overhead the peaks glowered, white with black stone ribs. Ming had never seen so much rock and snow, at such angles—not even on vids—and they unsettled her.

Lyra stopped the car at a pullout and pointed. "There." A stand of dark trees nestled at the foot of a cliff, thirty meters from the roadside. Each tree's crown was roughly globular, its branches attached like tentacles to a central point. The yellow-green foliage looked spiky and brittle from this distance.

"Can we get out and walk to them?" Ming groped for a pencil in her heavy khaki jumpsuit's breast pocket.

"Sure," said Lyra, and she reached for the lock button on the driver's hatch.

"I'll stay in the car." Rimi leaned against the right-hand door. She didn't drive, she'd confessed. Ming was beginning to see why Lyra had run away from her family.

She followed Lyra across a weedy field to where the trees bunched together. The branches bore short, dagger-like leaves, broader than the "needles" she'd seen described in encyclopedia vids back in childhood science classes, but still adapted for a cold climate.

"And these—" Lyra bent down to the ground and delicately pulled up one long, flexible branch, "these are the prize."

Clustered near the branch's end, six conical fruits grew covered in dark brown scales. Between them, at the center of the cluster, a pale bluish-green parasitic plant nestled, its sucker thrust deep into the joint among the cones. "That's the mellow pod, then?"

"They used to pick them off and throw them away. I guess the active ingredients aren't all that chemically different, and the mellow one's made from the other." Lyra rubbed the parasite's glossy round leaves with one finger. "This one's immature. Let's see if we can find one with a pod. . . ." She let go of her branch and thrashed into the foliage for another. "Ouch! Watch these leaves, Ming! They bite!" Pressing one hand to the other, she shook her head.

Ming pulled out her sketch pad and swept a few lines onto the top page, suggesting the straight trunk, clustered branches, and narrow leaves. "Here," said Lyra's voice from inside the trees. Ming let her drawing pad fall onto leaf-littered ground and eased between branches to see what Lyra held out. In this cluster of cones, the scales had opened to drop their seeds; and between empty cones, the blue-green parasite sprouted a two-finger-long fruit of its own. A leathery cover attached itself to the pod and tucked tightly over it. Lyra pried open the wrapper. Inside were spiral rows of off-beige squares that looked like soft tissue.

"Interesting," Ming murmured. "Can you hold it a little longer?"

Lyra shrugged, and Ming hurried back for her pad. On the second page she made a detailed drawing of the mellow pod. "Thanks." She stepped back to complete her impression of the entire tree, as it clung to its pocket of poor soil at the cliff's edge.

Lyra peered over her shoulder. "Huh. You don't need to get *every* detail down, then?"

"No." In her drawing Ming suggested a branch here, a leaf cluster there. Satisfied at last, she tucked her pencil back into the coverall pocket and gazed around. When a dark streak flashed from one tree to another, she took a step backward. "What was that?"

Lyra giggled. "That is the Kokkeler's nutchucker. The critter that gave us the first hint there was something strange about the nilly beans. They live on them."

Ming peered into the grove after it. "I'd like to see one up close."

"That, you won't do. They never stand in one place long enough for you to draw one, if that's what you want. Rimi's got pictures at home, in the kids' schoolbooks."

Farther along on the valley "tour," Lyra drove past the new processing plant's front gate at a crawl. Unfenced, it looked like a small operation, its wide glass front incongruous on such a short building. "Coey works here, now."

"Most of it's underground," explained Rimi, "even

parking. We're pretty well isolated up here, and that's what Her Grace wants."

"Everybody on Mannheim knows about what we're doing up here. ALPEX and General do, anyway." Lyra steered the car back onto the residential avenue. Goodsprings was a one-story town, built low, without any need for packing of bodies into minimal space: an odd, stretched-out sort of place. The villa had felt much more like the cram-packed streets of home.

The women enjoyed a pleasantly quiet evening while Rimi's children cavorted in a downstairs room. The settlement, Lyra explained, was just shifting to individual housing from communal origins, an incentive offered by Holjpip to keep HolLanCorp's best workers contented, so the houses were all new, clean, and comfortable. Rimi Dusenfeld's husband, Coey Cooperson, had been sleeping when they left in the morning and now had returned to work at the plant's evening shift. Ming felt vaguely guilty about not having greeted the head of the household.

This is a different culture, she reminded herself, perched at one end of Rimi's sitting room. It was odd, too, to call a husband and wife by different surnames, and they showed no sense of clan identity at all.

As evening deepened, the sisters obviously wished to talk about the children, but tried hard to include Ming in their conversation. *Now is the time to finish Huekk's business.* "Would it be . . . all right if I went for a walk? My legs are stiff from all this sitting."

Rimi folded her hands across her middle and rocked back on her chair. "If you want."

Lyra selected a music tape from the file at the wall. "Sure, the neighborhood's as safe as any. Did you pack a coat?"

"It's in my room." Ming took a step toward the hallway. "Thank you for the tour, both of you."

"Good night," answered both sisters simultaneously, and then they glanced at each other and laughed. "We've *always* done that." Lyra gave Ming a final wave. "We're on the same beam-path."

In her room, Ming pulled her duffel onto the bed and drew out Zardir Huekk's brown, cube-shaped parcel. It slid with room to spare inside a breast pocket of her coat, though it gave her silhouette a weird, lumpy shape.

She started back out into the home's long single hallway. At one end, away from the bright living area, she slipped through a door into brisk mountain air.

Ming tried a frontal approach first, strolling to the aboveground, glassed-in entryway. Huge letters above the main door proclaimed the plant GOODSPRINGS ONE. The door slid aside when she stepped close. Down a hallway ahead, broad stairs descended; on her right, in a glass booth, sat a woman wearing purple and gray.

"I am looking for Mere Rayman Dourthe," Ming said. "May I go in?"

"No," snapped the—what was she? A receptionist? A guard? Hair cut short in a severe, squared-off style, she made no attempt at the usual glamour of receptionists, yet she didn't have the muscular build of Holjpip's household guards.

Ming shrugged. "Would you be able to call him out for me?"

"What for?"

"I have to deliver a message."

"From whom?"

Ming wondered if dropping Zardir Huekk's name might hurt her, and she hesitated.

The woman snorted. "I see. Another one of his skinny sluts." She reached down for her desktop. "He'll be off in an hour, sweets, at twenty-five even-up. Wait outside, all right?"

Face burning, Ming walked back out into the cool night. An hour proved a long time to think the situation through. *Another of his skinny sluts.* Did she wait in the darkness to be abducted alone? Twice, she stepped out to run back to the safety of Rimi Dusenfeld's house. Twice, she reached around the back of her neck to finger the metal stubs of Renasco's collar. She stayed.

Through the glass doors, Ming eventually caught sight of a cluster of women and men making their way up the broad exit stair. She braced herself. If need be, she could try to protect herself by invoking the name of Holjpip Langelleik.

Several lead workers shuffled by, glancing nervously sideways and behind. One looked Ming in the eye. Blank stupor gave him a grave-bound look. Ming winced, but the laborer ducked her glance, hunched his shoulders, and hurried up the street.

Another man hung behind the rest of the group, peering from side to side as he passed through the doors. Shorter than she, he wore the gray uniform coveralls on a stocky figure. That must be Dourthe, warned by Huekk to expect her.

She stepped toward him. A pungent chemical odor clung to him. It became stronger when he moved his head, as if his curly black hair carried a layer of dust. "I am—" She stopped dead. He'd had his eyes reoriented in the vertical, like the lizard-man shipboard. "I am looking for a Mere Rayman Dourthe," she finished with an effort. "Can you help me?"

With one motion, he pulled out an I.D. disc like her own but lettered in an ancient and gaudy decorative face, insular modern. "Will I do?"

She examined it. "Oh. *Missar* Dourthe. Excuse me. Here." Unnerved by his stare, she pulled the parcel out of her coat pocket and handed it to him. "From Missar Huekk, in—"

"Ah." Ming could feel the touch of those eyes traveling up and down her. "Where are you staying, Ming Dalamani?"

The smell must come from chemicals he worked with. His upper arms looked meatier than her thighs, making the coveralls bulge. "With friends," she said firmly, and she turned away.

"Come with me." He gave her a lip-smacking smile. "I have something to return to your friend in the villa. We can have a drink, talk about Anslanding. I miss the place."

"I . . . can't. I'm . . . expected. I'm already late. I had to wait an hour for you."

"This won't take long." He reached for her arm. "Is it the eyes that disturb you? It's the height of interworld style, Mere Dalamani. You'll find them most attractive. We don't have to have the drink, if you're in a hurry. Hot nillies, for two? They do make things . . . efficient."

She slid her arm free. "No! I'll . . . come back tomorrow night, this time, and pick it up then. Good-bye!" she shouted over her shoulder, and she took off running, visions of blinking vertical slashes giving her unmuscular legs new speed.

They ached within half a block. Expecting at any moment to fall, caught from behind, Ming dashed up the quiet avenue, past lights burning in house windows, as when she first arrived in the city. Left turn. She glanced back.

No one followed. Panting, she walked on.

If Rayman Dourthe expected her tomorrow night, he didn't need to chase her.

Chilled, she broke into a run again.

Ming woke to the sound of children laughing outside her doorway and lay in her borrowed bed, clutching a pillow. Zardir Huekk had set her up for this, she decided, using Dourthe to solidify his own control. If Huekk wanted her humiliated, why hadn't he done it himself?

Perhaps the mutant wasn't able.

Mutant! What did his repulsive quality say about men who sought out disfigurement as a style?

She rolled over in the bed, forced to remember the shipboard Renasco officials' callously given orders. Feeling uneasy, she changed from her tunic into a fresh jumpsuit, and emerged for breakfast only after the children's voices faded behind slamming doors.

"Ming." Lyra sat at the table, Rimi beside her, a plate of rolls between them. Morning light glared off the street outside; rain had fallen in the early morning. "What's the matter?" Lyra asked. "Didn't you sleep? You look awful."

"I—No, I didn't sleep well."

"Oh, I'm sorry." Rimi's broad face turned deep pink. "It must have been my cooking."

"No! My stomach's fine." Ming sat down across from Lyra and seized a roll, squinting out the window into the quiet street, at the dwellings across the way, and behind them, the looming peaks. Rimi poured her a cup of steaming c'fee.

"Thank you, Rimi. Your rolls are better than anything I ever remember tasting."

"What would you like to do today, Ming?" asked Lyra.

I want to go home! she cried silently. *Back to Father's little apartment! I knew peace there.* That one memory came easily, and she reeled it in and cherished it. It comforted her but intensified her sense of urgency. Her life was slipping away in a double time warp, both forward and back, and all of it out of her control. What could she see here at Goodsprings and nowhere else?

"What about—I'm curious about the nillies, and the mellows."

"Mellow *pods.* You want to try them?" Rimi asked.

"No. I am curious, though."

"A walk downtown," pronounced Lyra, "will show you all the nilly burnouts you care to see."

"I'll stay here and do dishes," said Rimi.

Strolling the settlement's streets, Ming did see all the burnouts she wanted: men and women who chronologically should have been in their prime, but walked bent, looking aged, standing in doorways or seated on benches along the shopping district. "They say the drug speeds up the metabolism," Lyra explained. "They get in just as much living as we do, but in spurts. They prefer to have their time in little pockets. Or something like that. I tried a nilly once. Didn't like it."

"Couldn't they counteract aging with the mellows?"

"Mellow pods. Maybe. I don't know."

They reached the town's central area. Green, open space lay unplanted and unweeded between domed shops, housing rows, and prefabricated-looking one-story office complexes. So much wasted space.

But why would they care? Ming glanced up at the peaks again. The mountain air chilled her ears, as if those peaks bent to watch her.

A black-haired man bearing a frightening resemblance to Rayman Dourthe dashed toward them, his arms flapping as he sped by, trailing that odd chemical odor. Ming stared. To him, she must have looked as if she were moving through mud.

Lyra ignored him. "Interestingly enough, they don't use nillies in the plants—the workers, I mean. Against company policy, just like the villa."

"That must say something about how safe they are. What about the other drugs, then? The mellow pods? Are they what gives some workers such a—a blank-eyed look?"

Lyra stuffed one hand into a hip pocket and stepped over a crumpled paper. "No, some workers here are criminals. Total memory wipes, sentenced to hard labor."

A chill caught Ming by the back of her neck. *There but for Renasco's "mercy"* . . .

"Even here," Lyra went on explaining, spreading her arms wide to take in all the valley and its shadowy peaks, and oblivious to Ming's moment of horror, "mellow pods are expensive. It wasn't that way when I was little. That's how they found out they stop aging. Some families used them to control unruly kids. Those kids stayed gap-toothed for five years, but they sure were mellow."

Ming got control of herself. "It's all legal, then."

"Yes. And research says both are nonaddictive, nonnarcotic in the physical sense: ideal, for people who want to use such things. But expensive. Even the beans are dear, outside the valley. Let's buy you a nilly or two while we're here, just to keep with you."

Maybe she could use one later, if Holjpip demanded a rush job. In a pharmacy along the street, Ming produced her I.D. disc and purchased a clear oval package containing three thumbnail-sized, dark round nuts.

Turning the package over and over as they walked back up the street, Ming shook her head. "They don't look like much."

"They taste worse. One thing Holjpip's got her people

working on at the plant is how to make the active ingredient palatable. Pills are fine, but she wants it marketable. Ultra'fee has been one attempt. What do you want to do tonight?"

Her friend's shift in subject caught Ming unprepared. Thinking of Rayman Dourthe, who would watch for her in the shadows of Goodsprings's main avenue, she drooped. "Lyra." She glanced both ways before stepping into a street devoid of traffic. "I have a commitment, believe it or not. I have to go to the plant tonight at midnight, to talk to someone for one of the . . . my supervisors, back at the villa."

"Oh."

Ming walked on, kicking at a pebble on the sidewalk.

"Could I maybe come along?"

About to refuse, Ming reconsidered. "Well, Lyra, the man—I've met him—has a nasty look in his eye, as if he were undressing me. I don't trust him."

"Oh," said Lyra. *"That's* what's bothering you. I knew it couldn't be Rimi's cooking. Is there something I can do to help?"

Ming hesitated. Though apprehensive, she found she wanted to protect Lyra. "No. Thanks."

"I'd be happy to come."

Why argue? She wanted company.

Huekk threatened dire consequences if she told Lyra about this delivery.

But I haven't mentioned delivering anything. "Well . . . would you, then?"

"A secret meeting? It'd be fun. Rimi would come, too," she added, "if you think numbers would make a difference. Rimi doesn't look it, but she's not afraid of any man that walks."

"Can Rimi walk that far?"

"For this, she would. It's been so long since she had a little excitement that wasn't on the telescreen. You can bet. Coey goes off shift at the same time, Ming. We can be walking down to meet him."

"It could make trouble for her or Coey with Missar Dourthe."

"I'll put it to her that way. If she'd rather not, you'll still have me. You know, Ming," Lyra said as they walked on, "you *are* a little helpless. You ought to learn to drive our cars."

True, thought Ming. *Look at the cripple Rimi has become. She can't drive her own car. When Lyra's not around, she must depend on Coey to take her for groceries and everything else.*

Lyra raised a hand. "We have the staff car and an afternoon to fill, and if you're doing something that takes all your concentration, you won't spend so much time worrying."

"I'm not worried."

So after lunch, Ming spent two hours guiding the silvery staff car up and down side streets in Rimi's quiet neighborhood. It nearly steered itself. Remembering Tieg Innig's cruise along the high road with both hands in his lap, she felt a little better.

Tieg. She would far prefer meeting him, instead of Rayman Dourthe. She sighed, wondering how his search for talent progressed back at the villa, and what he really wanted, and why.

As she shut off the car in front of Lyra's house, it sank down. "I give up," Ming said. "Why does it do that? Coey's didn't."

"Some special kind of adjustable air suspension, smoother ride or something. That's why they track so well, too. When we stop, the air bleeds out of the system. The whole staff fleet is like this. Takes a little getting used to, doesn't it? I think someone owed Holjpip money and paid off with a factory."

The women waited up together that night, Ming pacing. Rimi wouldn't hear of being excluded. Not ten minutes after the children were tucked away, one slender girl appeared in the hallway, short pale hair tousled around clear, fair skin and rose-colored cheeks. "Mum? Salie is singing in bed."

Rimi sighed dramatically. "Tell her I'll appear in about one minute if she doesn't quiet down."

The girl flounced back into the hall, trailing a too-large purple nightrobe.

"Kids." Rimi shook her head. "She loves camping on the floor in her little sister's room, and she knows I know it." She and Lyra returned to talking nothings like a pair of excited hens. At fifteen minutes to shift time, Rimi set an electronic watcher on the sleeping children and its beeper in her pocket, and they walked downhill to the plant.

As before, the blank-faced, frightened group hurried out first, banded together for security. Ming counted twenty-three.

Lyra touched her arm and muttered, "I hear this is a work-prison site for disgraced, wiped Renasco leaders. Easier to watch them all in one place." Holding Ming's stare, she concluded solemnly, "Moral of the story: Don't rise too high in the Company."

"Holjpip," Ming mouthed, remembering her orders.

Lyra shook her head vehemently. "Never. They need her too badly."

Rimi caught her husband's arm as he emerged through the glass doorway. Coey Cooperson, a huge man who walked with a stoop, stared down at her. "Why, Rimi. Has our guest talked you into a midnight stroll? Ming, it must be." He extended a hand. "Glad to meet you at last."

"And you." Ming clasped his rough fingers.

Behind the rest of the group, as before, came Dourthe. "Excuse me just a minute," Ming said in a loud, plain voice to Coey, and she walked toward the smaller worker.

Dourthe frowned; his disfigured eyes' sidelong glances at her weighty escorts emphasized his displeasure. "What did you do, bring the zoo?"

"These are my friends. I told them I was going for a walk, and they wanted to come along. We're going home for a special dessert," she added on the spur of the moment, certain Rimi could oblige with pastries. "Do you want to come?"

"Are you—oh, never mind. Here." He thrust a square envelope at her. "No one's eyes but Huekk's."

"Right," she said calmly, as if used to engaging in espionage. But as she turned away, she held her breath to keep from laughing. There stood a Renasco agent foiled by Ming-the-skinny, one half-spent factory worker, and two female cooks. If only all battles against the Company could end so easily!

Well, yes, she had delivered his package, and now she

clutched an envelope to go to Huekk. She hadn't exactly foiled the Company.

Even so, she felt like skipping.

Not caring for the solitude of his studio that night, Tieg ate in Staff Dining. Ming's absence still disturbed him. No one had come looking for Joash McMikall, and if random events tended to cluster, he was due for a run of bad times. When—if—Renasco caught him, would it bother to mind-wipe him after interrogation, or just kill him?

Striding back up the hallway toward his own room, he saw an entourage approach: two guards in black, with other trousered legs showing behind them. He stepped into a doorway to let them pass.

Holjpip halted. Two advance guards moved on a few paces to include Tieg in her circle of protection.

Tieg made a courtly bow. The ambassador brushed sleek hair back behind her shoulders with one hand. "You look tired, Tieg. Are you well? I have been meaning to speak with you."

She had a remarkable eye, too. "I am well, Madam. Working late, the usual. I promise I will rest. How may I assist Your Grace?"

She tucked her thumbs into shallow slash pockets. "I have begun, shall we say, a bit of psychological research. It has to do with cross-fertilization of the arts, the effect of one man's work on the craft of another." She paused to wait for his nod, then went on. "I wish to see that you play for our staff calligrapher. Frequently; often enough to affect her work. She will be the first subject of our research. She is young enough to be emotionally impressionable, yet her art is good. She has an instinctive sense of visual analysis. I will assign her some work to do while she listens."

"I see, Madam." Tieg maintained a straight-shouldered pose, but a sensation of impending disaster crawled along his spine. Was this the bad luck beginning?

Holjpip, whose normal polite expression gave the corners of her lips a slight upward turn, favored Tieg with a smile that would have melted polar ice. "Your help will be appreciated."

The ambassador owned his time, looked young, and was human, but she acted more like a mother than a lover.

Married to Mannheim, he thought again, *too busy for flirtation, even after five year's praise of my work.*

Which was fine. "Of course, Madam," he said, and he made a slight obeisance.

Holjpip proceeded up the hall, taking her guard with her. Tieg walked his own direction a little slower. His employer had unpredictable whims, but this was her queerest request yet.

Unless Holjpip wanted him watched by her personal calligrapher-spy.

Blast! Barbar Curan arrived on tonight's Renasco shuttle from *Anfis* station, and Tieg had to meet him, to make preparations for their rendezvous with that deepspace probe.

At least he had this day in Holjpip's grace, unwatched until Ming returned from down south. He had Her Grace's respect, even her fondness, and that must defend him.

In his own rooms, he showered. Then, dressing again, he turned away from the watching console and tucked the tiny dart pistol into a pocket of a plainer silver-trimmed black suit. He had spent three days on edge, carrying the gun everywhere, expecting a tap on the shoulder from Zardir Huekk or one of his henchmen. That one, he could take down with him and be glad. But now Holjpip said she wanted him together with Ming for a while, so wasn't he safe? They'd wish him free to move about, to give additional information, if he were being watched.

He ran a comb through his hair, yanking at tangles. When Ming returned, the worst thing he could do was threaten her. If she was truly on Renasco's side, that would only hurry her wish to betray and be rid of him—and perhaps gain her freedom in the bargain.

He bowed his head, acknowledging the temptation Ming Dalamani presented. So slender—born perhaps on a world of poverty, where thinness was not such an accomplishment as here on Mannheim. Food and flowers grew here in riots, and slimness was the mark of discipline.

Maybe soon he would have a single chance to see if her heart were soft enough to touch. Rubbing the skin of his arm, he briefly allowed himself the mental image of laying his hands on her shoulders and bending to kiss her.

*And who will watch Holjpip and her enterprises for the
Old School, if that's a mistake?*

All this would matter less critically in a few days, once
Barbar Curan got the probe data away. Tieg replaced his
I.D. disc and key clip in a pocket not far from the pistol.

Ten minutes later, he rode the high road west to Newport, intending to park the staff car at nightclub domes
clustered near the spaceport, in case of radio-tagging.
From there, he would walk to the port. Thanks to Ming, he
had two names for Curan's consideration, and it would be
good just to talk—about the probe, about happenings elsewhere in the Belt, and about Ming Dalamani.

All the way north to Anslanding, Lyra dropped hints.
She'd really like to know what was up, why Ming had to
keep that midnight appointment with Rayman Dourthe.
She was Ming's friend. She was good at keeping secrets,
she insisted.

Sure you are, Ming commented to herself, smiling at
her friend as the sun rose over low hills far off to their right.

She tried simple honesty. "I can't tell you," she said.
"It's not allowed."

"Oh, all right, Ming." But ten k's later, Lyra was hinting
again.

Finally realizing she could not escape that way, Ming
invented a story. "There are some . . . pharmaceutical
formulas Holjpip wants tested there at the villa, Lyra.
That's all. She doesn't want them going over the computer
net. Industrial spies, you know."

Lyra nodded solemnly.

"Swear you won't tell, Lyra."

"You have my word," she said, gripping the half-wheel
with both hands. Ming felt certain she meant her promise,
and just as certain she'd be unable to keep it.

Well, it probably wouldn't hurt Ming to have that kind
of rumor spreading.

Would it hurt Holjpip? To her dismay, she didn't want
that happening. Compromising her employer might
weaken her own standing, even before "further orders"
arrived.

Or what if word got back to Tieg Innig that she ran
secret errands for Renasco?

Oh, she groaned inwardly. *What did I involve Lyra for?*

Holjpip withdrew one hand from fragrant bath water, dried it delicately on the towel her chamber servant knelt to present, and took up a sheet of plastic from a poolside tray. Translucent white, the flimsy contained five lines of personal code from her agent in Vinnsing, capital city of the Nexos system.

Fascinating.

Ming Dalamani and her clan, it seemed, had been convicted exotic-jewel smugglers, originating at the small colony of Cabra Minor. Renasco's people on Nexos labeled that smallest Cabran colony "a crowded polar hovel. Deserved abandonment. Inbred, restive."

The same agent who delivered this message would find himself dispatched to the Cabra system in approximately one hour—

No. A second agent. Give Renasco nothing to suspect.

—to seek out anyone still surviving in that "crowded hovel" who knew how the smuggling was done, or any records still in existence of the act.

She dropped the flimsy back on its tray and slipped beneath the water, feeling it swirl, lift, and float her long hair. After a day's work, it was good to think about her gameboard in the quiet evening. Eyes open under chemical-pure water, Holjpip saw white all around her, the marble sides of the sunken pool. Down at her toes, a silvery ripple revealed the water inlet, banded in precious metal.

Her head broke the surface. She rubbed a sheet of moisture from her face. Holjpip's body might have seen nearly seven decades, but it looked twenty-five, smooth and white: at her prime, as she would be for years, thanks to rejuv treatments that prolonged external youth as well as internal health.

Holjpip's thoughts circled back to ivory skin and narrow black eyes, such a contrast to her own appearance, then to the flimsy at hand.

How would Ming react if she knew she had delivered a Renasco collar from Zardir Huekk to Dourthe, up in Goodsprings? Not even Zardir Huekk knew Holjpip had access to that information. She would keep it that way. Renasco demanded she keep Huekk around, but she moved circumspectly in his presence.

Holjpip gave a sigh and settled deep into the water again, then abruptly sat up, water streaming from her hair.

"Perris," she snapped. "Console, please."

The chamber servant brought a traylike remote unit, knelt at the waterside, and averted her eyes.

Holjpip keyed up a file and began to type notes in the user window. Difficult to trace the mind-wiped, yet if she could locate any of Ming's surviving sentenced kin, bringing one such person to Ming might be exactly the stimulation her memory required.

She bent to her work. Two searches of comparatively accessible files yielded nothing. She frowned. Perhaps tomorrow she would try other codebreaker/query sequences. There were other security systems, too. From a high-level military data base, that information would come easily.

Holjpip rippled the water with both feet, idly kicking. Renasco only brought military ships when it came on inspection, and she'd just as soon put off that inconvenience the full two and a half months until it was due.

Holjpip touched a temperature control. Beneath her legs, water began to warm and circulate.

"Perris," she called languidly, "you may wash my hair now."

7

Holjpip's order that she draw an expressionistic sketch series came as a surprise, but Ming accepted without protest. The second morning after her return from Goodsprings, she reported to the centrum and took a seat beneath a drooping tree while Holjpip received a succession of businessmen near the fountains. Beside the back wall, Tieg stood creating moods. He used the electronics boards again today.

Holjpip's order: *Anything the music suggests.* So Ming brought a pad and sat, allowing her hand to move freely on the paper, using pastels to create background washes and abstract movements. These new, luscious colors felt almost damp in their vividness.

Nothing Tieg played particularly stirred her, but she had raised a wall between her emotions and Tieg Innig during her trip south to Goodsprings, a wall tenuously built on the knowledge that she had nearly started to act silly over him.

During a break, he strolled down to stand beside her. "This is your new assignment, I hear. Did you enjoy your vacation?" He sounded distant, reserved.

"Yes, the mountains south of here are beautiful." She glanced up casually. "Her Grace initiates the most interesting queries about the arts. Would you like to see what I've drawn?"

He took a seat beside her on the red stone planter and listened while she described the music that evoked each of her five abstracts.

"Nothing marketable." She closed the pad. "But they're what she wanted." Tieg glanced toward the fountain. Holjpip sat bending forward, talking to a man Ming

119

did not recognize, while behind Holjpip's left shoulder, the shorter figure of Claude Yerren stared down on the others, and beyond the adjutant clustered the ever-present guards.

This is when he mentions the rumors Lyra started. Undoubtedly someone asked what she did down south, and a man with secrets will be sensitive to others' mysteries.

"I'm told to try something with a quicker tempo next," Tieg said blandly, and he walked away.

Well! Ming stared after him, one finger fanning the corners of her paper. *Maybe Lyra isn't as talky as I suspected.*

The music began again. Ming closed her eyes to concentrate. The perfume of johnnistars now pervaded the villa. Like the cryllia before them, the johnnistars' odor wafted through everything, but with a muskier undertone, a hint of high summer, excitement, and fertility.

Ming chose a rich green pastel. Turning it on its edge, she swept a curve onto the next blank page.

From Claude Yerren's standpoint, the morning ended well: lunch with Holjpip in a small, private dining room, the business of Mannheim walled out by massive wooden doors so her friend could relax. Holjpip sat staring away from her steaming c'fee, her expression unguarded and at ease. A huge light globe hung from the room's ceiling, complementing daylight from seaview windows with warmer tones of its own.

Yerren took a last bite of pudding and then pushed her bowl aside. "You noticed Mere Dalamani working?"

Holjpip smiled. "It's good to see her busy."

"Why Tieg?"

"Why not?"

"I know how well you like his work, but I'm tired of feeling on-edge about him. He holds it well, but really, Holjpip, that stress in him is going to burst loose some day."

"He channels it into music. That's one reason it's so good." Yerren opened her mouth, but Holjpip lifted a hand. "Claude, the man is intensely loyal, and his feelings run deep. He's willing to sacrifice the moment for long-term goals, and himself for a cause."

Claude Yerren sniffed. "That makes him dangerous."

"I can contain him."

Silence fell between them, the companionable silence of old friends free to disagree. Claude Yerren stared out the window, thinking, *The man's still a danger. Even without Holjpip's approval, it might be wise to take steps to see he's unable to hurt her—in any way.*

Holjpip watched a maid in copper-on-blue remove the table service, keeping only her cup. When the huge door shut again, she asked softly, "You heard about the new arrivals at Goodsprings?"

Yerren frowned. "No."

"Planetary rep to Little York and his top general."

Cringing, Claude Yerren shifted her own chair. "You're taking that lightly."

"There's no other way to take it. If Renasco wants to use my plant as a dumping ground, that's the Company's business. Philanthropy," she said caustically, "quietly converting death sentences to slavery."

"But, a planetary rep."

"No one ever accused Renasco of trusting its officials."

"So," snorted Yerren. "How many blank-eyed former shipping officers—and up—do we now have picking nilly beans from cones at Goodsprings One?"

"Do you really want to know?" Holjpip reached for a console inset into the dining table.

"No." *Blast. All she needs is one more pressure.*

Holjpip leaned back again. "We are building the unity of humankind again, Yerren, but only under our control. Remember that phrase?" Her eyes narrowed.

"Camel rot." Yerren pounded the table with an emphatically stiff fingertip. "The next major civilization will grow on strong—" Pound. "—local—" Pound. "—cultural units. No one can feel a part of a civilization so widely spread. Better to create worlds where the inhabitants can feel pride in who they are, and in those who gathered them. Then, strengthen those worlds."

Holjpip laced her fingers together and rested her chin on purple-tipped nails. "That too will cost lives."

Not yours, Yerren thought silently at Holjpip Langelleik. *Not yours. And if I have to take every threat from the*

*villa and set him to pick nilly beans from the cones, I'll do
it.*

Awed, Ming gazed down a long aisle. Beneath her feet,
an ancient carpet runner woven in filigree designs
stretched ahead fifty meters, and to left and right of that
runner stood ceiling-high shelves filled with books: antique
relics, freighted across space at incredible cost.

The young, black-haired guard beside her, Mere Able
Tatarka, cocked his head and scratched at his collar's violet
piping. "It's been a long time since she let a staffer in. Be
careful not to exert yourself."

Special low-oxygen atmosphere, Mere Tatarka had told
her. It smelled like chemicals and old paper. "I'll be careful," she assured him. "Thank you for your help."

"You won't take offense if I stay with you."

Ming laughed silently. She'd gained permission
through Staff Central to enter Holjpip's private library and
research typefaces and calligraphic hands, but not unwatched. Shrugging at the security guard, she stepped
toward the second stack of high shelves, shook her head,
and raised a hand to touch one blue-backed antique. "If I
owned these, I'd have them guarded, too."

She strolled up the tight aisle between stacks. On spines
alone, the lettering styles fascinated her. "Mere Tatarka?
Is there a catalog?"

He nodded toward the room's southeast corner.
"They're filed by order of acquisition."

"Definitely not by author or subject." Rounding the
end of the stack, she peered up to see an astronomical
treatise filed beside six volumes of poetry. Maybe that
made literary sense, but—

"True. I've read several ancient masters' fiction, and it's
either memorize-the-location-of-each-book or use-the-cat-
alog-every-time. You're a calligrapher, Mere?"

Ming eased down the astronomical treatise. It gave her
a chill in the pit of her stomach. Something in her was
trying to remember. Carefully she opened the volume's
bumpy-surfaced leather cover. Four typefaces on the title
page alone.

She slipped the book back onto its shelf. This was a

treasure house. What kinds of artwork might lie hidden, illustrating these books?

"My name's Ming," she said absently, strolling back toward the central aisle. He followed, step for step.

"Able, for me. Come often. I'm here Tuesdays on my rotation, and I'll help you find anything you'd like."

Startled, she paused to glance back. Small but burly, pleasant-faced, and not a day over twenty Standard, he maintained the wide at-attention stance of security staff. "I hope I have time," she said. "This room is magic."

"Innig," he said abruptly, scratching at his collar again. "I've seen you talking with him. The man's not what he seems to be. He's been investigated more than once. Dropped each time, by Her Grace's order. Be careful, Ming."

Ming started. Were her feelings toward Tieg that obvious, or was Able Tatarka sweet on her? If he knew her to be friends with Tieg, he'd observed her from a distance already. She had to discourage him without angering him; if she had security staff angry with her, that would be one more cause she had to please.

Why discourage him? Shocked by the thought, Ming tried not to smile. She might be able to use a friend in Security, so long as she didn't lead him on unfairly.

"Able, thank you for the warning. Would you show me the filing computer?"

After a week, the johnnistars still bloomed, and Ming had begun to look forward to her mood-sketching sessions. Relishing the scent, she walked up the hallway toward Holjpip's Operations room. Holjpip had questioned her in detail concerning her "mood pieces," and the nilly pine wire miniature—delivered yesterday—earned Ming a girl-ish, delighted smile from the ambassador, the first real smile Ming had ever seen on Holjpip. She would love to sketch Holjpip that way. It would be far more satisfying than manipulating thin wires in a shop area of the garage available for artisan use, but Her Grace never would have held the pose.

Holjpip sat behind her blond, white-grained wood desk this bright morning. Beside the long window, Missara Claude Yerren glanced away from the guard with whom she had been conversing. Backlight from the window gave Yerren's black curls a blue sheen.

"Sit," said Holjpip. "We have a problem."

Ming folded into one of the slender-legged chairs and took the proper posture. Her Grace certainly didn't grind stones to dust before getting to the point. On her desk lay a small, set gel plate Ming prepared the day before, an invitation scribed in a second personal alphabet designed by Ming and approved—with revisions—by her employer.

"To begin with, the color is wrong. What happened to your ink?"

Ming peered into the plate. The deep summer-green ink had faded overnight to a dull bluish cast.

Oh, dear.

Speak directly and make no excuses. "I used the precise mixture in your printer's reference file, Madam. My only guess is . . . some pigment in that ink mixture must react with the gel medium itself." She glanced down. On the sides of her fingers, the ink remained summer-green.

"Is this something you could have tested?" Holjpip raised a single eyebrow.

No excuses. "I should have thought of testing it, Madam." *No ink changed color before!*

Holjpip gave her a flat expression, as if placated. "You will, I assume, test future inks."

"Yes, Madam."

The ambassador leaned forward over the desk, her slender arms almost a match in shade with its color. "The other problem is serious. You used cijuli vines for a border. Our reception will honor the general staff of Podacan Interworld. We have used cijuli on Mannheim for ground cover, and in this environment it does just well enough. But on our homeworld, that vine is an ecological nuisance. It's a good thing," she added, "you'll have to redo the plate anyway, to get the color right."

The vines. Ming drooped a little. All those hours wasted: the work she put into each leaf, into each "clinger" tendril that spiraled off the main stem and pierced a leaf at its vein points.

"I am sorry, Your Grace. I found the greenery attractive."

"Mere Dalamani, I expect you to do your own research.

You cannot make mistakes like this in the future. Your service is an expensive luxury."

"Expensive," echoed Claude Yerren's voice behind Ming.

Ming faced straight ahead. Claude Yerren stepped up to the desk, touched one finger to the set gel, and shook her head.

Holjpip slid the invitation off the edge of her desk into a trash receptacle. "I'll still need it tomorrow for reproduction."

"Tomorrow." Ming gulped. "Yes, Madam."

Shivering, she marched to Staff Central, where from Mere Bertelsen's pantone book she requisitioned several packets of inks approximating the shade chosen for Holjpip's original plate. Clutching them like treasures, she hurried back down to her room.

On the work table she mixed and labeled them, then prepared a single gel plate. *Half an hour for this to preset, then a few minutes to chain a few circles of each color,* she told herself. *But how long must I let them season after I spray, to see if they change color?*

To wait out the preset period, she turned again to her computer. Under +BIO+ she ran a scan. Who might make interesting reading today?

Huekk.

She found a lengthy listing, headed by "Enforcement trained at the Renasco academy, twice decorated for Meritorious Service to Humankind." Ming grimaced. More of the same followed, but she didn't read it. Birthplace: Banneri, one of the Belt worlds hardest hit by the radiation storm, due to an abnormally thin natural ozone layer. Age, about fifty now.

There had to be something she could use against him, or at least to help toward winning her freedom, but it wasn't here in his past. Beautifully clean by Renasco standards, to her that past read "toad."

Time. She returned to her work table, dipped her pen into the first beaker, and filled its injection chamber.

A sharp *tat-a-tat* sounded at the door. Ming groaned, clenched her fists, then walked over and unlocked it.

"Lyra." She relaxed when she saw her friend. "Come in, if you want. I'm busy."

Dressed for work, Lyra wore her light red-brown hair shoved under a spiral headnet and carried a covered bowl. Its meaty-sweet aroma tantalized Ming.

"I have to test inks today, so I'll just . . ." It was easy, now, to manipulate the basic patterns. "I'll work while you talk."

Lyra stood close, her arm touching Ming's shoulder. As soon as Ming completed ten twisting circles in celadon green, each touching the circle on either side, she withdrew the pen from the medium. "Now. I have to clean the pen and change ink."

"If you have a minute, I brought you a hot midmorning snack."

"Oh?" Ming leaned toward Lyra. She rarely felt warm here, although summer had burst on Anslanding in full floral glory. With a flourish, Lyra cracked the bowl's lid open.

It smelled wonderful. Ming took the bowl in both hands.

A pink, gelid mass steamed inside. "Ugh. What is it?"

"Lunch for the upper-wing staff. Don't worry." Wiping one hand on her white coverall, Lyra smiled. "It's human-compatible, amino acids and such. It's a delicacy. I had to sneak this out for you." She poked at a long, thin, rosy tentacle with her spoon. "It's succulus, one of the native species on Mannheim. These succuli are fresh. *Really* fresh. They were netted this morning." Then, apparently seeing Ming's hopeless expression, she added, "It tastes much better than it looks. Try it." She produced a small fork.

Ming stabbed reluctantly at a tentacle, took a bite, and slowly chewed. The delicate flavor of the tentacle-laced gel could not distract her from the dish's appearance. Swallowing hard, she handed the bowl back. "Thanks, Lyra, but I don't think it's for me. You eat it."

"I'll be glad to." Drawing a second fork from a coverall pocket, Lyra set to. "That's lovely work you do."

"Just circles." Ming glanced ruefully at the gel plate. If Holjpip became displeased enough to dismiss her and send her away, Renasco almost guaranteed a second memory wipe.

"Honest, Ming, it's tasty," Lyra said around a mouthful. "Can't you forget what it looks like?"

Ming stared up at her. "It's my business to remember what things look like, Lyra." But even as she spoke, she wondered if the intensity of her reaction might imply something from her past.

Lyra pushed a curl deeper into her headnet and sat down in the desk chair beside Ming. "What's the real problem with your appetite today? I've seen you eat worse-looking things than this."

Swishing her injection pen in a solvent beaker, Ming detailed her encounter with Holjpip. "I worked two days, sixteen hours a day, on that gel plate," she finished. "And she wants another by tomorrow. With tested inks. It will take me all day to see which of these pigments cures to the right color. And then I'll be up all night lettering. It's all been going so well, Lyra. I guess I expected to go on pleasing her forever." She drew a deep breath and began chaining another row, this one using emerald nova, another shade not developed for gel work.

Lyra pursed her lips. "What about trying one of your nillies tonight, then, while you letter the plate? To make the work go faster?"

"Oh, Lyra." Ming spread her hands on the desktop. "I could, but I'd rather not. My life is passing too quickly as it is. And I can't help thinking Holjpip would be supplying those things to us, if she felt they would speed our production without risk." She began the third circle of the chain, touching its left edge to the right of the circle before. She had despised this drill in training. Now it seemed as natural as dressing.

"True enough," said Lyra. "Maybe it's better you don't decorate the plate, then, if Her Grace's worlders are going to be offended so easily."

"Mm." Ming twisted her pen thirty degrees and drew another arc, half completing the circle.

Lyra rose and pushed her hard orange chair toward the table. "I'll tell you what you ought to do. Go for a walk on the beach, while those set. Take an hour or two, get your spirits back up."

"I don't have time." Ming made the third arc meet the

second. "I need to get some more botanical samples to copy."

"*Make* time. Otherwise you'll be working into the night with hurt pride and no fresh air. I'll save lunch for you. Something other than succulus," she finished, smiling.

"Thanks," said Ming. "There." She drew out the pen.

"I won't feel good about you until you stop looking so hungry." Lyra took a step toward the hall door.

Laughing, Ming followed. "Lyra, you're a good friend. Thank you. And don't worry about lunch. If I miss it, I'll last until dinner." She let Lyra out and reached for the beaker marked terre verte.

Once the gel lay sprayed to set, she tried to stretch her aching back. She'd better give the curing process several hours, and meanwhile she needed to find a different kind of sample.

Maybe there would be something growing along the path to the beach. Her freedom might depend on the coming night's work, and Lyra was right: She was not in the mood. If she couldn't please her employer, back to the mnemonics laboratory. She shivered, recalling a cold metal table, clamps on her head. She had lain too sleep-sick and weak to resist as techs wormed long, probing electrodes into her brain, searching out the offending loci of verbal memory. The instants of searing pain—

No! She would not go through that again!

The black mood stole through her bones.

All right, Lyra. I'll try it. She snatched up her small knife and a windbreaker jacket and headed for the ocean-side tunnel.

M

The echoing corridor from downstairs women's quarters ended in a platform halfway up the cliff. At its edge, she paused to study the groundcover.

More cijuli, planted to slow erosion.

Ming almost went back inside, but at the railing she paused and stared downward. All that water.

She stepped down four flights of wooden stairs onto the sand's cliffside edge. There she paused, pulled off her shoes, folded them, and tucked them into one pocket. Overhead, four leather-winged gray creatures soared, each about half Ming's size, their eerie cries rising triple screeches. Kye-di-dees, Lyra called them. One plunged into still water just offshore, vanished, then popped cork-like to the surface, two long pink tentacles drooping from its toothy beak.

Succulus. Ecch. Ming padded barefoot down to firm sand near the shoreline.

Cool water swirled around her toes. She sighed at the feeling of fresh, free water. Never, ever would she get enough of it, not if she lived on Mannheim the rest of her life. And the patterns, rounded, intersecting, constant in change . . .

Raising one hand, she traced wavelets in the air.

"Ming. Good morning."

Tieg Innig stepped out from behind a boulder, today dressed in a flamboyant pink wide-sleeved blouse and sand-brown pants. Amused, she shifted her tracing hand to wave a greeting. A second later, he had strolled over. "Barefoot, Ming. You'll cut yourself."

"I love the feel of the ocean."

His thick brows dipped into a frown, but only for a moment. "You were a desert girl."

"A dome-rat." She stood still while another wave swirled sand between her toes. "Renasco left me that, anyway."

He looked out to sea. "I suppose taking all your memories would have left no psychological stability."

Remembering the Goodsprings workers, Ming shook sand off one foot. In a way, it relieved her to talk with someone about the frustrating blocks in her mind. Since her trip south, Tieg neither terrified nor fascinated her. Despite the suspicions that lay between them, a bond had formed here that she could not share with Lyra.

And certainly not with Holjpip.

No, she would not think about her employer. She had come down here to forget Holjpip for a while.

"What is it?" asked Tieg.

"What's what?"

"You're upset. Tell me."

Ming groaned. Apparently she had not won the reprieve just yet. "Her Grace," she answered, and she told Tieg about the cijuli vines and problem ink.

He raised one hand toward her shoulder but dropped it before they touched. "I know how that can be," he said. "She loves the arts, loves creativity, but she forgets she can't always force an end result. Too used to dealing with numbers and figures."

"How . . . forgiving is she?"

"One slip shouldn't do you in. Make that next effort a work of art."

"The last one," Ming said, "was art—just flawed. Let's talk about something else." She flicked a toe in the water. "What's the bottom like here? Is it safe for—that is, I've seen telescreen segments on—swimming?"

Tieg stepped away from the receding wave's foam as if it scalded through his shoes. "Have you ever seen anyone swimming here?" he asked, his voice strained.

"No," she admitted. *What did I say?* "I've never seen anyone swim at all. Not in person."

He bent down to pick up a pebble. "The bottom is sand and small stone, which would be a good footing for swimming, but the currents are treacherous, and that bottom drops away fast. The cliffs." He gestured upward. "They're only the part of the drop above the water."

"Oh. I see."

Tieg frowned and dropped the pebble hand to hand. "Not a good place for swimming."

She stared into the waves. It didn't look like a drop-off, but how could she tell? Foam lapped at her feet again. Tieg took several paces up beyond the waves' reach.

"Can you hear the music?" he asked, eyeing the foam.

It felt so good to be casual with someone. A rhythmic swish-lap-swirl: Was that what he meant? "Yes, I think I do."

"It reminds me of something I probably wrote once." His head came up, and he was smiling again. "That's a problem with this job. It's difficult to compose or improvise because when a melody starts to seem 'right,' frequently it's something I remember."

"Memory. Yes." Ming made a fist like the knot in her stomach.

He looked away. "You say you need more samples," he said abruptly, "from a different locale. I know a park in Anslanding that's well landscaped, where we could get a few bites of lunch."

Startled, she glanced up at him. "You have time, Tieg?"

"I think so." His small, slightly crooked smile looked friendly, ordinary, as he stuck the toe of one shoe into dry yellow sand. *Scatter* him, for being so handsome from this angle!

One kye-di-dee, floating on the water near her, rode a wave to shore and then began waddling up the sand toward the cliff.

"Yes, then," she said, "on one condition."

"What's that?"

"Will you warn me if I bring back any samples that might offend Her Grace?"

Tieg laughed loudly. "I'll do it."

Ming turned out of the wind, toward the cliff. The kye-di-dee started to pull itself upward, using the foreclaws on its wings, then its webbed hind feet; foreclaws, then feet. Ming walked to the platform, where she kicked sand off her feet and slipped on her shoes. Tieg led up the wooden stairs, paused at the tunnel entry, and pointed.

Clinging by all fours, the kye-di-dee craned its triangular head and peered back over a bony shoulder.

Ming stood up to the railing beside Tieg. "Do they take off from this low?"

"If there's an onshore wind."

Evidently unsatisfied, the creature pulled itself upward another meter, then twisted its short neck again. If Ming had blinked, she would have missed the takeoff. No sooner had it glanced out to sea than it arched, let go, and began to fall. Catching updraft in leathery skin between shoulders and hind legs, it took on a rounded shape, hovered a moment, then soared straight up along the cliff, wheeled at the top, and headed again to sea.

"That was incredible." Ming clutched the metal railing.

"For such gruesome creatures, they have their own grace."

She wondered, on the way to the garage, if Zardir Huekk might object to her going into town. One hand stole up to scratch the back of her neck. No. He'd let her go clear to Goodsprings. By comparison, this was only a hop.

Tieg selected a silver car from dozens parked in the garage. The long drop down into town afforded a broad view of Anslanding, and when she peered off into the hazy western distance she could see Newport, too, a shimmer of runways, pads, and domes. As soon as Tieg crossed the river bridge at Anslanding's edge, he turned off the main avenue onto a side street, then another, and soon Ming doubted she could find her way back. High buildings, some glass-sided and others a more conservative construct, congregated about the central part of the city, which they bypassed. Staring backward out her own window at a row of pyramids that might be apartments, she felt Tieg slow the car, and he pulled in beside a wide city block overgrown in green grasses and trees. A rustic sign fashioned from thin split logs proclaimed it DRAPER PARK.

To their right a blue pool rippled, and in it, several small, nearly naked children splashed each other with enthusiasm. "If you want to learn to swim," Tieg said as they strolled past, "this would be a better spot."

"Not as convenient."

Tieg looked away. "This way," he said, and he walked on. "Let's eat first, if you don't mind."

"I don't mind at all. Thank you again." She glanced around. A ring of foliage in twenty shades of green encircled the pool and a concrete pad. Beyond the pool, a white awning covered three rows of round white tables. Some of the restaurant's customers ate quietly—mostly couples—while others, seated in larger groups, punctuated their meal with bursts of raucous laughter. The table nearest a laid-rock retaining sidewall had room for six, but a single man sat there. He raised a hand.

"Oh." Tieg stopped dead. "A friend."

"Oh?"

"Well, yes." Tieg led toward a different table.

As he seated her, the stranger walked over. Dressed in pale khaki, dark-haired and fair-skinned, he had a well-groomed, indolent look about him. Tieg leaned both hands against the back of an empty chair. "Ming Dalamani," Tieg said, and when she rose in polite greeting, Ming saw that the stranger stood barely taller than herself. "Ming is Her Grace's new calligrapher."

The man's dark eyes narrowed minutely, deepening the lines around them. "Barbar Curan," Tieg said. "Electronics."

The hand Barbar Curan presented was wide, with short fingers and square nails, at the end of a large and muscular arm, and he pressed her hand firmly. Tieg used electronic equipment for his performing, Ming reflected, but Curan could be involved in Tieg's secrets, too.

"Are you with the General Co-Op, then?" she asked.

Curan shook his head. "Independent."

Maybe, she thought, and sat down again. No one she'd met on Mannheim was entirely on the level except Lyra and Rimi—and maybe Able Tatarka.

Tieg pulled a chair near Curan out from the table. As they sat down, Ming glanced aside. She could just see the children splashing in the pool. One screamed, but it sounded less like pain than delight.

A white-jacketed attendant appeared at the tableside, and Ming let Tieg order for both of them. "Just something simple."

"Soup Fresco, then," Tieg told the waiter, "and rolls. And your specialty, for dessert."

"Good choice," said Curan.

Ming glanced in his direction. From his weathering face, he might be ten to twenty years older than Tieg.

"Where are you from, Ming?"

Without looking at Tieg, who knew the truth, Ming began the litany explaining her missing past. "I was born on one of the abandoned colonies, Cabra Minor, but about two years ago, I got the urge to see more of the universe. . . ."

Conversation over the lunch that arrived was pleasant and meaningless; Ming felt secure enough in her role, with the previous life invented for strangers' benefit, to exchange pleasantries. Curan proved agreeable company, volunteering little but attending closely.

For a finale, the waiter brought each a tiny silver plate arranged with a five-pointed star of dark, glossy brown confections shaped like leaves.

Tieg curled his lips back from his teeth in a wicked-looking smile. "If you get addicted to these, you'll put on weight. Liqueur leaves."

Ming lifted one smooth candy and carefully bit off its tip. Inside the dark coating, she found a filling of some kind of cream. Greedily she licked thick sweetness off her teeth. "Oh. That is good."

"Deadly good." Barbar Curan popped a leaf into his mouth whole.

"And that reminds me." Ming pulled her tiny knife from a hip pocket. "I don't have a lot of time. Why don't you two talk while I look for leaves of my own? Would you mind?"

Tieg shrugged and leaned forward, the wild pink of his shirtsleeves bright against the white table. "Take your dessert plate with you. Otherwise, it will be empty when you come back."

"It's all right to take dishes from the restaurant?" She nibbled a second tiny bite.

Barbar Curan spread his hands. "Draper Park *is* the restaurant. Just don't leave the grounds with the plate, or you'll see what they use for security."

Carefully Ming picked up her little silver plate, and she laid her knife on its edge. Balancing them on one palm, she strode off toward the fountain.

* * *

Tieg studied her fluid stride until she passed out of earshot. "She's the one. Watch what you say."

Barbar Curan stretched his legs out under the table. "Yes. Lovely. She's interesting, Innig."

"What I want to know is, if they can block memory, can they inject false data?"

"Not by the same technology. This is locational electroconvulsion, the destruction of existing loci. And whether she has a real loyalty to Renasco, who can say?"

"When she first arrived, she sang the Company's praises."

"Naturally. Picture yourself in her situation. She doesn't remember what she did wrong. She had to please them. She had to."

Tieg lifted a liqueur leaf and examined its shining underside. Would Ming have carried her troubles with Holjpip to him if she were a Renasco spy?

Yes, if she hoped to catch him off guard. Curan often gave a sympathetic stranger the benefit of the doubt, and as Old School overseer for five worlds, he deserved Tieg's respect.

His respect, but not emulation. Tieg Innig had known betrayal too deep to ever trust easily again. Yet he might influence Ming while she flailed for support. He wanted to do right by her.

"I think," Curan drawled, scratching one knee through his trousers, "if you weren't half suspicious Holjpip knew what happened to your mother, you wouldn't have even questioned Ming." Before Tieg could protest, he raised a hand. "You've got just enough training and little enough experience at this to be dangerous. I think we could use Ming to run an occasional message. From the way she delivers the first one, we'll learn a lot. A test."

Tieg frowned at the self-image Curan projected back to him.

"There'll be nothing in the first one to incriminate either of us, and if she goes to them—" he made a piercing motion with one hand, imitating the shape of a Renasco collar, "she needn't know I can signal it, too."

Tieg pulled his chair closer to Curan's and cast another glance around the park. Ming stood still, facing into the breeze, short black hair swept back from her face. A high, reedy melody filtered out of creation's ethereal reservoir, gently settling in his mind's midrange. *Yes,* thought Tieg, reaching into his shirt pocket for a pencil and pad. *It would be sensible to test her loyalty.* If she passed, he could rest at night. Several measures of scratched notes decorated his staff before he spoke again. "So what's the news?" he asked quietly.

Watching two children trip a third into the water, Ming realized her tension had dropped. In one circuit of the fountain, she snipped several undergrowth specimens to copy, but as the third child gave a shove of revenge, she stared. If somehow she could capture the three-dimensional texture of water droplets in gel medium, that would impress Holjpip. It would be difficult, because each droplet would take at least three strokes, probably five. . . . Popping the last liqueur leaf into her mouth, she fingered the silver plate. It could work, if she managed joining the swathes. She couldn't wait to get back to the villa and try it.

Barbar Curan stared as she trotted back across the lawn, but he went on speaking as she seated herself. ". . . so we have to match a hyperbola. Easy enough."

Ming came alert inside. That sparked something: hyperbolic trajectory, an orbital term. Tieg could be looking for something not on Mannheim, his secret unrelated to the pharmaceutical concerns.

Be casual! She seated herself. "Spaceships, Missar Curan?" she asked off the top of her head. "You wouldn't happen to be a racer? I knew two system-clippers, back home."

"Business trip," he said, shrugging. The phrase echoed in her head. Match a hyperbola? It was another clue to her lost past. She *had* offended the Company in some spacefaring capacity.

And a clue to Tieg's hidden activities. Sweat made tiny beads on her arms, and the breeze cooled them. If Tieg and Curan thought she might endanger their concern, they might not let her go on watching both sides. She must not give them so much as a hint that she might have been . . . whatever she had been.

With a bland expression, Tieg offered the last liqueur

leaf off his plate. "Still hungry?" he asked. He watched her, his eyes shadows beneath curled eyebrows.

"I have a bit of a stomachache," she said, truthfully enough.

"And you ought to get back to work," Tieg added for her, picking up the last leaf. "I see. All right, then." He stood. "Thank you for lunch, Curan."

Tieg shut her into the car without speaking. As he got in on his own side, she slid her hand into her pocket and closed it on the cold metal case of her tiny knife. *What if he knows I've made a guess?*

It was an interplanetary crime to harm her. She was Company property.

Yes, perhaps he'd be punished if he harmed her. Much good it would do her, after the fact.

He pulled away from the curb. "Are you feeling better, now?" he asked.

"I do have to get back to work. Thank you." She stared straight ahead.

Tieg wrinkled one corner of his mouth. "Inspiration strikes, and you're away from your studio. I'll try not to distract you."

His sympathy melted her apprehension. She pulled her hand free of the pocket and went back to staring out into the streets of Anslanding. She could admire loyalty to a cause. It was a finer attribute to dwell on, at any rate, than his profile. Without slowing, Tieg drove toward the villa.

"Tell me one thing, Tieg."

"Yes?"

"Are Podacans averse to water droplets?"

"Is that your idea? Good. They're not—I don't think."

N

Ming worked on the new invitation gel far into the night. From experience she trusted manganese blue not to fade, and it suggested the summer season as well as any green. Managing variable-width nibs she had never used before, and making the rounded swaths meet—it took six to make a convincing droplet shape—was every bit as difficult as she anticipated.

She happened to be stretching, staring at the clock on the console, when its readout melted from 2532 into 0000, even-up. *No analog clocks on Mannheim,* she guessed. *Not with such an odd number of hours.* On Cabra Minor, the local minute had been recalibrated short to make the planetary-time adjustment.

Three hours later, satisfied and exhausted, she sprayed the invitation gel to set. Droplets surrounded the text, clustered here and there like natural spray. Ming twisted kinks from her shoulders. It had been a good day's work, even though she'd started late.

And been distracted by that phrase of Curan's. Hyperbolic trajectory? Rubbing at a blue stain on one ring finger, she tried to run those words backward and forward through fragments of memory, wondering what would bring recollection to the fore.

She tried the computer +BIO+ file once again. Tieg Innig was still the shortest listing in the staff directory. *Maybe he's publicity-shy. Or, hmm—if he's done something illegal . . .*

There had to be something in this data base she could use, and until someone stopped her, she'd keep looking. Cross-correlating recent Renasco convictions from +CURRENT EVENTS+, she found herself with an intriguing list of characters and even the name of an organization, the joining of which was criminal.

"Old School"?

Interesting.

She blanked the screen and hurried to Staff Dining, shivering with fatigue. After appropriating a snack, she lingered in a hot, spice-scented footbath and listened to music on the villa's open channel. She recognized some of the more commonly played pieces, now. This theme was Tieg's, one that suggested grandness and adventure. *They must play this late at night to keep darkshift people awake,* she mused, falling onto the bed. It felt so good to be certain she'd done well.

Ming slipped under the blankets. Behind her closed eyes, beyond her will, memory coalesced as she drifted into sleep, and Tieg's music played on.

Day faded slowly on the polar surface of Cabra Minor, the most sunward of the three Cabran worlds, the warm half-light of evening lingering like an apology for the day's scorching heat.

Ming pressed home the last bolt on *Opa*'s gleaming hatch, rocked back on her feet, and straightened. It felt so good to be certain she'd done a job well. She tossed her head to order her clan-tails and breathed deeply, then dropped the socket wrench into her pocket. Shan had already covered half the distance to the workbench wall, shuffling purposefully. The double black arrow of Shan's clan-tails whisked side to side over her gray suit's back.

Ming stepped onto the concrete, pivoted, and eyed the ship's tiled undersurface. *Opa* seemed an impossibility from the outside and would look ridiculous drawn on paper, but she might hang well as a ceiling piece. Gesture rippled in her underside, braces and feedlines leading the eye back and forth across her belly tiles.

Breaking the rhythm of labored steps, Shan looked back and up. "Coming," Ming called. Somehow it seemed right, that Shan was compensated for the effective loss of her legs by her brilliant intuitive streak.

Ming drew even with her. "All *Opa* needs now is an antimatter drive," Ming said.

Shan grasped the handle of a service cart and raised

one leg to stretch. "When you invent one," she answered in that low, gravelly voice, "cut me in on the patent. We can sell it to Renasco and retire."

At the dock's inner wall, Shan dropped a bundle of tools onto a sorting door. Ming laid her own beside them. When the panel opened, the tools vanished. Ming heard the hum of its inner workings, returning the instruments to their proper, computer-keyed places. She turned to lean against the bench, eyeing the far wall and its broad black outer gate. Through that gate they would take *Opa*. Tomorrow.

Shan closed her file and darkened the screen. "Want a ride home?"

Ming ran a hand along the bench's chipped, scarred edge. "Well." This would be her last chance for a long while to walk it. "No, I—"

A cart approached on the security screen, with the lean shape of Ming's father tall in the driver's seat. Beside him sat Jiadra Grazi, as sleek as ever in a tan duty suit that fit like her skin. "Looks like I'll stay a while. I should go over my orders for tomorrow once more, too."

"Suit yourself." Shan wiped her hands clean on a towel and dropped it into a bin. She reached the access door just as Lang Dalamani stepped through. Shan opened her hands and extended them in salute. "Good evening, Uncle Lang. Jiadra."

Jiadra folded her arms across her chest, accentuating already fine curves. "I'll call it good when I get adjusted back to darkshift. Hello, Ming."

Nodding, Ming brought the screen back up to full brightness. The door slid shut behind Shan.

"I'll be aboard." Jiadra headed across the streaky concrete toward *Opa*.

Ming centered her duty list on the screen. A track light flickered on its brace high overhead, and shadows wobbled. *There goes another one,* she thought.

"Ming." Her father's voice came over her shoulder. "I need to talk with you."

She turned and saw that he remained near the bench. Rotating her stool, she settled both hands in her lap.

Her father paced a few steps to the left, then returned. His large, ever-moving eyes came to rest on her. "Ming, you have your mother's way of staring."

Ming didn't answer. Her mother had died only recently of blistering–cold, a wasting disease she'd fought a year.

"How's *Opa*? Are you getting on well with the rest of the crew?"

Her father was an attractive man, sensitive and quiet. Rejuv treatments froze his appearance in mid-thirties, kept his hair black and young. "Yes, well enough." She thought back across the tiffs of the past week, all with Jiadra. "Why do you want to know?"

Lang gave an awkward little laugh. "Ming, you have no respect for your elders." He fixed his stare on the security screen.

Ming glanced up, saw the screen blank, then rocked her stool. "I'm sorry. I know you want me to develop more friendships."

He continued to stare. "I do wish to speak with you about . . . companionship."

His uneasiness began to affect her. Less assured, she said, "Certainly, Father."

He swayed from foot to foot. "For some time now, certain members of the Caucus have suggested I take a second wife. I want no lover," he added hastily. "My heart died with Ameena. But they insist I need company, that it is not healthy for a man still young to live alone with his marriageable daughter. They are right." His voice became so soft she had to lean closer to hear him. "I have been considering the idea for some weeks. I think my mind is settled, now."

Ming fumbled over words, her mind bouncing. Father? Remarry? Who might the Caucus suggest? Dalamanis preferred to keep within the clan, but the clan was declining. Her mother's sickliness, her own inability to gain weight, Shan's legs—all supported that conviction. *No,* she told herself, *that wouldn't be a factor. Father wouldn't want more children.* But as the thought faded, she realized she was not dead certain.

Shaken, she examined her fingers.

He thrust his other hand into a pocket. "I have asked—"

She woke sweating, the only point of reference in her dark room the clock blinking 0507 at the bottom of her screen. The music she'd been listening to, just before she fell asleep, still flowed in her mind.

That was no dream. There had been nothing dreamlike about it. It was *memory.* She crossed the room and keyed up the date. *I've been here twenty-three days.* Not quite a month, and memory was beginning to come back. They'd predicted *years,* when . . . Renasco stole these people from her. Her home, her identity. Shivering with fury, she seized her robe from the foot of the bed and waved on the room lights. So vivid . . . Father. . . . Pacing, she held the robe close around her body. Shan . . .

Had her father remarried, and whom? Why had she remembered this, in her sleep?

Ming reached back to flip her clan-tails, but her hand found a too-short, too-wide, undisciplined fringe.

Of course. They cut it when embedding the collar, and it grew out untrimmed.

In front of the mirror, she stopped.

Clan-tails: one more thing Renasco had wiped from her mind. Why that? Did they mean to take away her sense of who she was?

Craning her neck, still staring into the mirror, she fingered the too-long back hair. She longed for that sense of family. How would They react if she trimmed her hair properly?

She paused to weigh the safety of what she was considering. She'd seen all styles—shaved, curled, streaked, braided up, and braided down—on Holjpip's staff and guests and the women of Anslanding. Hairstyle did not carry identity for these people.

But to her, it did.

In the wet room, she found her small pair of utility scissors, then slipped the hand mirror into a wall bracket. Sitting on the sink's edge, she trimmed short the back of her month's growth of neckline hair, all but the lowermost layer.

Another echo of memory rose, as if lingering below her consciousness: the streets of Cabra Minor throbbing with traffic, workers trying to beat the change from dayshift to dark.

She held up the broad swatch at the center and trimmed away its edges. Letting down the middle swatch, she sighed. It felt so familiar and right to do this. They could take away verbal recollections, but not the tactile memories resident in arm and shoulder muscles that reached back to do this so many times.

Image: her own home stack, a newer construct on a busy boulevard, red-brown trim sprayed on its main doors. She lived on floor forty-two.

Snip. Left side into a diagonal. Snip, snip. A deep V from the middle. Snip on the right, and then, at the very center, she pulled up a three-cent swatch and cut it close to the nape of her neck.

Done. In the hand mirror, she saw a triumphant tight smile, and, when she shifted the mirror, clan-tails hanging low behind the raggedly trimmed neckline. They looked like man's tails, shorter than they should be, but they would grow.

With slow, heavy steps, Ming walked back into the outer room and laid the hand mirror on her work table. Renasco had let her live. Why no one else?

What a waste of manpower it would be, to execute an entire crew, when each could be mem-wiped and set to slave for them.

Staring into the mirror, she watched her mouth go slack. Those fright-faced workers at Goodsprings proved Renasco practiced memory wiping on a wider scale than she'd suspected. Odds were good her crewmen weren't dead.

Then she would look for them!

Her first joyous rush of resolve faded. *Where?* she asked hopelessly, glancing into the corners of her large, window-less room. Where, in all the worlds Renasco serviced? And what would she do when she found them?

A yawn began tamely but then seized her facial muscles clear up to her ears. Adrenaline, which had roared into her system during her dream and sustained her through her trimming, began to ebb.

The clock blinked on: 0532. Ming peeked at the gel, still bright, unfaded blue. She needed sleep, to face Holjpip calmly and proudly this coming afternoon, and show her the new water-drip design. She climbed back into her bed, waved off the lights, and pulled the blankets up to her chin.

If·they lived, where could they be?

Enough for now. Ming reached up to flip a clan-tail. *I will look for them, and that's a beginning.*

The following morning, Holjpip sat in her anteroom to the villa's main meeting chamber, waiting while other high Renasco personnel arrived and took their seats. She would enter on time, and any man or woman not at station had better have an excuse.

She stared once around the anteroom walls. The faint smell of fresh enamel lingered, and most of the furniture still was elsewhere. Holjpip sat down at a small desk. She had gone over her notes for the meeting well in advance, so she could afford a few minutes' speculation on other matters.

Ming, for example.

Under the additional pressure of the invitation deadline, Holjpip expected an emotional flurry, but Ming accepted the work and went to it. The Ops room techs, told to keep her under watch for the evening, reported Ming working late, finishing with all appearances of satisfaction. Holjpip laced her fingers together and rested her chin on them, elbows digging into the desk's edge. Ming seemed so delicate. Inner strength would make her valuable over the long stretch, if she didn't break under training.

A tiny twinge below her navel reminded Holjpip she was due for rejuv treatment.

At times, Holjpip almost wished she could spark sections out of her own recall. Tieg Innig, here in her employ, constantly called up one such memory.

She had seen it on the private Company net, so it had not been public news; still, the woman's death was too gruesome to forget. The victim's previous memory wipe for some unmentioned crime did not matter; even without an identity, no woman deserved such a death. Holjpip had vowed to control her underlings, to keep the strong from torturing the weak—vowed in the name of the dead slave, Abriel Innig.

Hiring her son had been a matter of responsibility; keeping her ugly death secret from him had been a matter of preventing Tieg from abandoning his work to seek revenge. Holjpip knew his violent side without having observed it, for as Claude pointed out, one heard it in his music.

Tieg Innig served three purposes for her: a nod to the dead woman she vowed by, the chance to watch the Old School, and—Holjpip let a smug little smile tug her lips— his professional capacity. He was the best in the Belt. How nice to have such a man for her private emotional possession.

She glanced at her watch and then stood, noted at the edge of her vision that her guard stepped out to follow, and pushed through double doors into the adjoining meeting room.

Chairs scraped as seven men and women in copper-on-blue rose. Without hurrying, Holjpip walked up the long table to the single chair vacant at its head. *Excellent. They all arrived on time.* The wall on her right supported an inlaid wood map of Mannheim, various pins and tags inserted through tiny joints into its magnetic backing. She gave this other gameboard a glance as she walked past. The guard who followed drew back her chair and seated her.

"Welcome," she said, laying her folio in front of her. "Begin, please."

Their names were on file in the folio, but she knew them primarily by branch titles. Dr. Sociology rose first, speaking with satisfaction regarding development of Mannheim's economic population pyramid. "With the recent growth in rural areas instigated by our improvement of medical and educational programs, we appear closer than ever to the desirable nonmanagement balance."

Missara Economics, a wire whip of a woman even thinner than Ming, spoke at length on trade balance among the three major exporters, HolLanCorp, ALPEX, and General Co-Op, but Holjpip heard nothing new there. "Research into the potential market for our newer products is beginning to come in as well, Your Grace." Holjpip raised her head. "The Belt worlds, particularly, seem ripe for any new brand of anti-aging compound, while relinked colonies such as Little York and Cabra Major, with their larger labor populations, appear open for a balance: anti-aging for management, stimulant for low-level workers."

It was coming, at last: the time when Mannheim could

maintain a decent trade balance. *Trade, via Renasco.*
Holjpip did not allow her expression to change.

A whistle on the desktop beside her punctuated the
end of Economics' report. Holjpip touched a control.

"Madam," said the quiet voice of Claude Yerren, on
duty as ordered in the Operations room. "A large craft
entering the system."

"Yes?" Yerren would not normally have interrupted
this meeting for such news.

"Preliminary communication puts it in the military
class."

"Thank you, Adjutant." Holjpip sat steady despite sick
dismay whisking through her. *Regular inspection isn't due
for over two months. We aren't ready. What are they looking for?*

Closing the communication circuit, she turned to the
next man at her table. "Half an hour's adjournment,
please."

O

Tieg caught only a nap the night of Ming's dream. Waking,
he shook Barbar Curan's hand off his shoulder. "All right,
all right. I'm up."

"You're not. You're lying down." Curan's voice sounded
hollow in the intersystem runner's small, windowless
cabin. "Once you're up, *I'm* going to lie down. Recheck the
drive for me, will you?"

Tieg had taken the first sleep shift after launch. He
pushed up to sit. "That was an hour?"

"Yes. We'll catch the Elleye in another half, probably."

Elleye, Little Eye: the probe, at last. After launching it

six months before, they would intercept it tonight, as its trajectory missed Mannheim's position in orbit. Opposite Mannheim (in that orbit), at a not-particularly-stable position in the astronomical time frame, circled the asteroid Mannheim's first settlers mined for palladium. It had a letter-number designation in the catalogs, but nowadays was allegedly disregarded. Curan, with experience in undercover positions, insisted they check it as a possible source of intermittent anomalies reported by two independent Old School watchers. It was too well hidden behind the sun to ignore.

Standing up carefully between two bulkhead cabinets, Tieg relinquished the bunk to Curan. "Sweet dreams," he mumbled as Curan dropped prone.

He drew a cup of c'fee from the maker built into one bulkhead. Cradling it in his hands, he sank into the pilot's chair, ran a glance over all the controls, then keyed through a check of the ship's drive and power units. Once certain the boards gave normal readings, he leaned back and poured half the barely cooled c'fee down his throat, pulled out a comb, and ordered his hair. He rubbed the sides of his legs. Plain broadcloth felt good, though it made him feel drab and self-conscious after four years serving an employer who insisted on finery.

Once he had always dressed this way, he and Pell together. It seemed such a good idea, to work the system from the inside, his own revenge for the way Renasco had taken his mother away. He'd hidden and kept her ring, a precious, bitter reminder of Renasco's ability to chase down "criminals."

Tieg grimaced. Pell Panasuk, dead; and Abriel Innig—probably dead, too.

He committed himself to the Old School as soon as he found it, an exile needing sanctuary, still believing Renasco could be circumvented. *Continue the music studies,* his supervisor ordered. *We'll have work for you soon.*

He did as told. At last they called him for training and made him an operative.

Given the high ground, Renasco held the vantage from which to eliminate all competition and monitor travel, so this little scoutship traveled unarmed. Too risky to arm it, and possibly catch the attention of some Newport Renasco crew. This trip, within the planetary system, was allowed by Renasco-enforced "interplanetary law." The danger was interception and questioning of the motives for their trip, and Renasco often took such actions.

Tieg drained the c'fee, glancing once more across the console. Then he rose and got another cupful. Short sleep shifts had been fine at eighteen, in school. Almost thirty, now, he liked the long Mannheim nights. Some said the twenty-five-and-a-half-hour day cycle suited humans better than any yet found.

Back in the pilot's seat, he went on thinking.

For this trip, he and Curan concocted a cover story about researching the sound frequency potential of this sun's natural vibration, what ancient man called "the music of the spheres," in case they were intercepted and questioned by Renasco. Tieg had little faith in cover stories, though. Better to get home before his two days' leave ended and his absence was noticed by Huekk or other Renasco eyes.

He glanced back at Barbar Curan, who already lay asleep. Curan's exploits as an attack pilot had once spread up and down the Jarnik Belt. Tam Barber, his name had been back then, Major Tam Barber. His home system, Lode, hadn't taken the decades of isolation well. Separated from markets for its rich metal wealth, Lode suffered war after planetary war until contact with Renasco brought the factions together out of the dark age, when every human lived in fear of global annihilation. Major Tam Barber's "death" in Lode's last war, ten years back, was widely mourned; Tieg had been astonished to meet him, alive and serving the Old School. Old School needed men like Supervisor "Barbar Curan," against the day Renasco could be challenged and fought. Most of his kind had been either shot down, bought by the Company, or forced into groundside retirement.

Tieg glanced again at the boards, then twisted aside and occupied himself with telescope functions. Even Renasco could travel so little of the galaxy. A populated corridor of systems and stations lay within refueling distance of one another, but that was as far as humankind could go. Astronomical technology had come near to mapping this entire spiral arm. The astronomers knew which

stars had planets, which white dwarf-red giant binaries—
no hazards at all to navigation—were approaching nova.
Radio astronomers had picked up transmissions from two
civilizations within the galactic plane, faint proofs of other
life, distant incentives to advancement. The Old School
stressed that technology always progressed more quickly
than humankind expected, if man took the position to
develop it, free from supergovernmental organizations
such as Renasco. He stroked his chin, wishing it were so.

Ten minutes later, he woke Guran. "I've got a signal,"
he said, and instantly Curan was standing. On the tracking
screen, at the center of the long instrument board that
curved around both seats, a flickering light crept closer,
sailing away from the sun, not quite approaching the half-
disk of planet that still loomed close behind them.

Activating a tractor as he slid into the instrument station, Tieg ran his fingers over a secondary set of controls
while Curan took the command seat. Curan brought the
runner closer. Deceleration and sideways maneuvers
pressed Tieg forward, left, and right. "Any minute, now,"
Curan muttered.

Leaning over beside him, Tieg reached for braking
controls. "I can do this, Innig." Curan touched one.

Tieg straightened, slid his hands into two hollows on his
own side of the console, and closed each on a pair of
crossed rods, controls for the runner's grappling arm. Staring hard at the probe's image on the external screen at his
left and a red superimposition representing the long,
hinged arm, he eased the two together.

The deck quivered. Curan reached for side maneuver-
ing controls, taking the probe's momentum out of their
runner's course. For a sickening instant, the ship's deceler-
ative pseudogravity flickered, but automatic compensa-
tion gyros reoriented the runner relative to its new path of
travel.

Tieg drew his hands out of the hollows and touched a
pair of console tabs. At the far end of the arm a switch
would close, and the probe would begin to fire data into
the runner's main computer, data it had gathered since he
and Curan launched it from this runner.

A brief tone sounded. "Done," Tieg announced.

He punched up the receiving file and smiled as numbers began to scroll by. "Got it, Curan. Stowing now," and he reached back into the hollows. This had to be done slowly, for the delicate equipment was old, the probe a snug fit in the scoutship's bay. He whistled as data fleshed out a picture on his small auxiliary screen.

"Tell," said Curan.

"Intense heat radiation, and highly unusual magnetic fields," Tieg said, letting go of the control rods to point at the screen. "The fields cluster, north pole to south, all around the asteroid."

"Our anomaly." Curan looked away from his own board. "Most of the heat is near the old mining site."

Tieg ran the pertinent data again. "Strange."

Curan rotated the control chair and stared at Tieg's computer screen. "Magnets—I know only one thing that has to be stored in a magnetic field."

"Antimatter," Tieg whispered.

"Right here in the Mannheim system."

"We don't know they've actually made any."

"But they're set up for storage."

Calla Whitney, Ming said in his memory, telling him about talents on the women's floor. *Hypermagnetic fields.* Holjpip Langelleik fumed at Ming Dalamani about a faded ink while taking experimental steps toward the next energy technology.

No! Not for Renasco!

Or else, what if one of her two rival exporting processors was involved? General Co-Op was supposedly resource poor. Yet, if it were investing capital offplanet, that might account for its perennial cash-poverty.

Or ALPEX?

No, he told himself, more likely Holjpip was working antimatter for Renasco, the better to consolidate its control of outsystem travel. The high ground would become more unassailable than ever.

A buzzer sounded near Curan's right elbow.

A hail? Tieg glanced at the tracking board. Nothing was in view, but—binary hells!—it was still set for near-space pickup, to magnify the approaching probe. Tieg dove for resolution controls.

Curan got them first. There, just beyond the planetary

horizon now and a bare three thousand kilometers away, drifted another ship.

"Halfway home," muttered Curan, "and no one to give the baby to." He flipped a lever beside the buzzing comm alert. "This is kay-ex-twelve-twelve." Calling out the runner's cover I.D. in a careless voice, Curan stabbed a finger toward Tieg's grappling controls.

The probe, unstowed while he speculated! Tieg seized the crossed rods. The arm was curled only halfway in; if they had to accelerate out of here, it would ruin their chances of bringing that delicate, expensive bit of technology into the bay.

"Kay-ex-twelve-twelve," answered a voice from the speaker on Curan's left. "You have been monitored docking equipment that is liable to inspection by interworld law. Stand by for tractor interception."

Interworld law. Tieg snorted.

"Like babes in the airlock, we will," Curan said without sending. "Not stowed?" he asked, aside. "Keep trying."

Twenty hundred klicks, now, probably just beyond its tractor range. Tieg worked the rods as quickly as he dared. Acceleration pushed at his seat.

The speaker buzzed again. "Kay-ex-twelve-twelve. Kill power or we will fire."

"And miss," mumbled Curan, one hand on directional controls. Renasco would never expect its target to understand evasion.

Another push of acceleration jarred Tieg, and his right hand slipped. He felt and heard something metallic strike the outside of the ship.

The probe. Wait—

"Elleye's still set to receive, isn't she?" Tieg asked.

"Of course."

"We've got to launch her out of this neighborhood. We can't afford to be caught with her if—"

"Right. Get her going, then."

"Kay-ex-twelve—" began the speaker again. Tieg shut off the phone.

"Leave it on. They might tell us something we want to know."

Tieg reversed the switch. "What about the probe?"

"Better send it into the sun. If they pick it up, and us,

we haven't the chance of an ice cube on brightside they'll buy our cover story."

True enough. They didn't need such a well-equipped probe for picking up nuances of solar phenomena. Tieg clenched one hand on the board. "No."

"If it makes you feel better, Innig, I'll make it an order. It's not your money we're sending into the melt."

"To save our lousy hides."

Curan bounced a fist off his console. "Think about that statement. Who values profit above human life?"

Warm with anger, Tieg gave a short nod, switched comm channels, and did it. "Into the sun she goes."

Freed of its burden, the grappling arm slid home, and the doors of its bay shut.

Renasco's watching that asteroid, Tieg thought. *If so, they're defending it.*

The scoutship shivered.

"Ye Gods," gulped Tieg. "They're firing on us! They're not even going to try to intercept."

"I've got full meteor shielding on," Curan said in a low voice. "See if you can read what they're using."

Tieg ran the data at max speed. "A missile, class bee-two-three."

"That's no scoutship, then," Curan exclaimed. "That's a warship."

"What the bloodied—" the little runner quivered again, "is it doing in the Mannheim system?"

"Right." Curan held down both shield and acceleration controls.

"What can I do?" Tieg cracked his knuckles.

"Leave me alone," Curan answered tightly. "I'm busy."

Tieg turned back to his computer and ran a few figures. Then, with a terrible, sinking feeling, he ran them again. "Curan, we're accelerating faster than they are, but by the time we get behind the horizon, full shields will have depleted our power. We won't be able to retrofire for re-entry."

He sat still, watching the tracking screen. On that glowing board, their assailant drew away behind.

"Run that check using half shields," directed Curan.

Tieg obeyed. "Energy remaining, if we do. But, Curan,

half shields won't deflect that class missile, and I can't see
the things coming."

Acceleration pressed him still deeper into his seat. The
console lay smooth beneath his fingers, and sweat itched at
one temple. Behind the little runner, the flickering probe
floated backward in vacuum.

He reached for controls he had recently switched off
and reactivated reception. Numbers sped past him.
"Curan. Elleye could show us when they're about to fire.
We could save shield power for when we need it."

"Say again?"

"She ought to be able to give us warning of each firing
about a quarter-second before the hit."

Curan frowned, his forehead glistening too.

Tieg glanced back down. "There! Firing—"

An instant later, the scoutship bucked.

Barbar Curan drew his left finger back a centimeter
from the shielding switch. "Do it. We need that power."

Tieg waited, staring at numbers on his screen, while
acceleration continued to mount.

Inspired by the success of her revised invitation, Ming
stood over her work table in the early afternoon, practicing her new raindrop technique in a spare gel plate. Although Holjpip acted preoccupied, she had praised the
effect, even called Claude Yerren from some other work
across the Ops room to show her the invitation, its message
surrounded by minuscule drops and the likeness of a tiny
bird at the center, shaking its wings dry. Ming smiled at
the memory.

She'd found the official file on Old School this afternoon, too. Its aims, according to Renasco: sedition and
piracy—disturbingly familiar. Was that what she'd been?
They were out there somewhere, maybe even here in the
villa. If that cause were the anchor for Tieg's loyalty, she
understood his singlemindedness. Perhaps even Holjpip
was involved.

One stroke, twisting the injection pen to taper—ah,
good! Second stroke, joined at its edge. It was good work,
and original. She was approved. She was part of the—

The floor vanished beneath her feet. The pen disappeared in her hand, or seemed to. All sensation gone below

her chin, she collapsed on short carpet beside the work table. Her skull rang with the force of her landing. One arm lay immobile across her chest, and her head lay facing the ceiling. Her legs—she couldn't feel them, nor move her head to see if they lay straight or twisted.

All she could do was breathe, and she did that hard, slowly, terrified. The collar. That wretched, condemned Renasco collar.

No! Tears sprang from her eyes and trickled off her face into her hair.

What in all the worlds had she done? Huekk? Had he learned she was shielding Tieg Innig, or was this the penalty for too much curiosity at the computer?

Calm. Be calm, she commanded herself. It hadn't killed her. She was only paralyzed.

Only? she wanted to cry. She would almost rather die than live this way.

She had to be calm. A female voice shouted out in the corridor, halted, then shouted again.

Something smelled bad. *Probably me,* she moaned, glad she could not feel whatever mess she might have made.

Running feet passed by outside. Ming lay listening for a long, long time. At one point, her fingers itched to draw. She laughed bitterly. At another, the old religion of her clan brought up hope, a reward for those who sacrificed self.

Small comfort now.

Time dragged on. To help it pass until someone found her, she began to count panting breaths, but each came so slowly that counting only intensified her fear of suffocating.

At length, her door slid open and heavy footsteps approached on the thin nubbly carpet. They paused. Unable to turn and look, she bit her lip.

All at once her body returned—except her right leg, which lay numb, twisted under her. She could move again! Wriggling her fingers was a kind of new ecstasy.

"Get up," said a male voice.

A deep voice, not Huekk's. She pressed up with her arms, her soaked, soiled clothes dragging. Once she'd struggled to her feet, she saw a tall guard in black.

"You were at your work," he said, pointing at the plate. Her pen lay half drowned in unset gel, a black pool of ink darkening the medium around its nib.

"I was. Sir," she added. "I mean Mere. Excuse me." The numb leg began to tingle painfully, but that was nothing, compared with what They would do with her, now, if They wanted.

"Very well. I'll send Custodial down to clean the floor." Without another word, he marched out.

What was going on?

She couldn't walk on her right leg. Swinging it, clutching the table against needling sensations that grew stronger with every swing, she clenched her teeth and concentrated on putting the pain of returning circulation out of her mind. Then, dropping to all fours, she crawled to the shower. After cleaning up, she put her clothes to soak and struggled into a fresh jumpsuit.

She could move again! The paralysis was not permanent. Was the collar mechanism more complex than a simple spinal squeeze?

There had been a voice shouting out in the hall.

Perhaps a malfunction in someone's transmitter. No, if it'd been a malfunction, they'd never have come for her. The command had been sent.

Agh. It was useless to try to think over the pain of that leg.

Putting weight on her foot felt like stomping hot coals, but she marched herself across the room several times, then stopped at her computer screen. First she checked the time. She had been immobilized for nearly an hour. It seemed like ten.

Staff Central, she keyed in.

+SEND+

What's going on?

The cursor blinked in rhythm with the time at the screen's corner, but Staff Central did not reply.

Oh, scatter them, anyway, she grumbled, and she headed out through the door.

The silent downlevel corridor echoed back her steps, but beneath the high banks of lights at Staff Dining, loud voices drowned out taped-in music.

Lyra stood at her station behind a serving counter. "Ming. Good to see you. Thought you forgot to eat again."

"What's going on?" Ming asked, then realized she dared not explain to Lyra that her Renasco collar had closed. "I was outdoors for a while, and when I came in, it was as if someone stirred the beehive."

With a deft hand, Lyra mounded pale brown rice flecked with green on Ming's plate. "You said it. The Queen Bee had a scare today, I guess. There's a warship in the system. One of ours, fortunately," she said. "That is, Renasco's. I guess it was chasing somebody or something. No idea if they caught it. For an hour every door in the place stayed locked. I was in the glassware closet. What a place to get shut into. Just me and the goblets, and nothing to drink. We're running lunch late to make up for the hour down."

Ming reached for her plate and found her hands shaking. She tried to laugh sympathetically at Lyra's plight, but the result was pitiful. Gripping the plate as she hobbled to an empty spot at one table, she tried to keep her ears open for news. No individual voices rose above the din.

In three minutes, she wolfed the meal. Leaving her plate in a tub beside the door, she hurried back to her room. No matter if there was a warship in the system, she had work to do.

After ten tries at chaining a simple row of circles with clumsy hands, she flung herself on her bed and cried. What if this happened again? Angry, terrified, she let tears spend her emotions down to numbness. She didn't want to move, now. Two nights ago, she'd stayed up all night. Last night, she'd been too excited to sleep after that dream. Her eyes closed.

Her body was destroyed. She fell, reduced to atoms. Fell, screaming, knowing no one could hear. Fell . . .

Followed closely by a tumbling Renasco warship.

"Hot sweat," muttered Lur from somewhere, near, in the void.

Jiadra clenched missiles in both hands, her sequined body quivering with rage. "Ming. Get over here."

Obeying blindly, Ming unlocked her acceleration

chair, slid it along the narrow metal track to Jiadra's ordnance board, and locked it in place.

Sudden pain blazed in her right cheek. She wheeled to see Jiadra's arm rebounding, hand open, ready to slap her with the other missile.

Across wormhole space blazed a wash of music, shimmering overtones mixing like colors on a palette.

"Tractor!" screamed Lur as he dissolved before Ming's eyes. "We're caught!"

Shan's legs shriveled into wriggling stubs. "No," she pleaded. "Ming, help me. I can't move. The collar's closed. Ming . . ."

P

Ming buried her head beneath an acceleration cushion. . . .

No. The "cushion" was her pillow; the "tractor threads" twisted around her arms were gray blankets. Trembling, sweating, grateful to wake from the hateful dream, she curled her body into a ball beneath warm covers and forced her panting to slow. Then, rolling onto her back, she pulled the blankets tight and stared upward. Her family had sought to beat Renasco in space. They had . . .

It was coming.

She squeezed her eyes shut.

Opa . . . passed through the wormhole . . . into range of a second Renasco ship, and was caught in the ship's tractor field. Jiadra ordered the ship destroyed, Lur resisted—Shan refused—a scuffle broke out on the deck. . . .

Ming's eyes burst open. She didn't want to remember

any more. She wasn't supposed to have memories like these for years, yet! What made these dream-memory links, as perfect as telescreen bios?

She thought back. High emotion? The terror of that passage had been like what she'd felt this morning, when the collar had closed.

Had there been a waking-sleeping link with the other dream? She couldn't remember, but she did recall music.

Ming threw off the covers, her eyes burning from having cried, and then slept. Had this memory vanished under the block, as when Huekk flung names at her to torment her?

No, she remembered them, now. She had shipped with her uncle and two cousins, not just Shan. And Renasco had been chasing them. Chasing them, on the way home from . . . where?

Oh, Shan. In vivid dream-memory she watched those pitiable, twisted legs shrink to nothing. If Shan were dead, Ming was entitled to grieve.

But was Shan dead?

Yes . . .

No!

Ming rolled over on the bed and pressed up to check the computer screen. Midafternoon, now; if she could intercept Lyra and practice driving for an hour, this vague black ache might fade.

Lyra murmured encouragement as Ming steered downhill and through the first intersections of the city. "Whoops—no, you've got to give *him* the right-of-way."

"Sorry." Releasing the brake, Ming turned off the main boulevard. "That's enough of that. Do you know how to get to Draper Park?"

"Of course."

"Then, would you like a dessert?"

"Ooh. Ming, would I."

"Fifty-five-point-two-six creds remaining on your account, Mem. It's getting a little low."

Ming pocketed her disc and thanked the waiter. *Actually, it's getting respectable at last,* she thought.

"Over here," called Lyra.

They sprawled on long chairs, sharing a single silver

plate of liqueur leaves and watching the fountain play. No raucous children's voices provided background noise today, and Ming guessed she hit a vac day when she came with Tieg. Three toddlers kneeling beside the pool splashed fingers in the water, instead. Warm breeze swept through Ming's short hair. The dream crept back, less excruciating, but it sobered her.

Shan must live, somewhere, and perhaps the others did too. Clan honor obligated Ming to look for them. Where to begin? On the data base?

"I met a nice fellow yesterday," Lyra said in a vague, dreamy voice. "His name's Sperry, and he's on the Security force. Ever seen him?"

Letting the dream fade while sun warmed her face, Ming kept her eyes closed, which heightened the sensation of fluttering seabreeze. "No, of the guards I've only met Able Tatarka. What's this Sperry like?"

"Blond, tall, and friendly. I think he's, um, looking, too. Stable job with a little class, and he's even a little . . . heavy. Just my style."

Ming chuckled. The breeze gusted again, and she lay still, letting herself float on contentment.

"Excuse me, Mems." A waiter popped between their chairs, snatched up the silver plate, then hurried on. Lyra had passed nearly five minutes without speaking. Ming glanced aside. Lyra hadn't fallen asleep, but her half-closed eyes gave the impression she would drift away any second.

A young woman came dashing across the green lawn. Still running, she scooped up a child and carried her away.

"That's odd." Lyra rose onto her elbows.

Ming frowned. "Certainly is. Dessert's gone. Do you want to head back?"

"Yes. Ming, I don't like that."

Passing through the business district, Ming made a right turn. Lyra craned her neck to look behind. "Uniforms. Twenty of them—oh, no. Ming, we've seen this before and I thought Her Grace made them quit."

"Quit? Do I need to stop?"

"No," Lyra said vehemently. "Get back to the villa. When Renasco drops in on its client worlds, sometimes it takes what it wants."

"How do you know that's it?" Ming concentrated on negotiating an intersection, avoiding pedestrians dashing in all directions.

"You recognize it when you've seen it." Lyra's voice sounded uncharacteristically grim.

Ming drove on. "Could this have something to do with that warship?"

"Could. We all thought Holjpip had insisted to the higher-ups she wouldn't stand for this. Something's happening, Ming. I don't like it."

"Then why didn't that waiter warn us?"

"Us?" Lyra laughed. "Two villa employees in dress?"

"Oh." Ming had grown so accustomed to living in uniform she'd forgotten. For this two-hour break, Lyra had simply slipped a long vest over her coverall, and Ming wore blue and amethyst.

"Lyra. What's this?" Ahead, something blocked the road. More copper-on-blue: A black air scooter was parked across the boulevard's center, so only one vehicle could pass, and leading up to it, halted passenger cars formed a line.

"Roadblock."

"What do we do?"

"We could walk uphill off the road, back to the villa." Ming wriggled her feet. "I'm game."

"We'll have to come for the staff car later."

"I don't mind. I don't want to have to deal with those people."

"Neither do I."

In front of a shop, Ming parked the silvery car and jumped through the driver's hatch before the vehicle finished sinking. "Come on." Lyra hurried out into the street. Once across, they jogged uphill as quickly as Lyra could push, into an area that reminded Ming of Goodsprings: domed shops, spread-out office complexes.

Two blocks along, Ming halted. "Look." Parked ahead, a second black air scooter blocked this narrow avenue. "Hot sweat," she muttered.

Lyra leaned over, swinging her arms and panting. "They've ringed the town, then. Well. Do you want to spend the night here or try to make it back to the villa?"

You're a coward, Ming scolded herself. "What are they doing at the roadblocks?"

"Looking for valuables. The thing that worries me is that they have a reputation for taking women, too. I've eaten my way out of the desirable category. I'd be concerned for you, though."

"Oh, come on. I'm a bag of bones." Ming began to trot back downhill toward the staff car.

"They *like* women skinny here. Haven't you noticed?"

"I think I know how we might get through," puffed Ming.

The wait in line played Ming's patience to its end. When at last they reached the black air scooter, a uniformed man directed them toward its starboard fin. A second brown-haired young man stroked his copper belt as he peered into the car. "You." He pointed to Ming. "I think we need to talk."

Ming slid the I.D. disc from her breast pocket and held it up in her palm. "I'm on assignment for Madam Langelleik, Missar. I am expected back momentarily."

"Oh-h-h." He raised both eyebrows. "Personal staff?"

Keeping her face expressionless, Ming nodded.

"Good. I'd like a message carried to Madam Langelleik."

Ming slid the disc across the dash to Lyra and clenched the half-wheel. "I'll take it for you."

Like lightning, he reached through the window and struck Ming in the face. "Tell Madam, 'Never forget who owns this world.' Get out of here, staff."

Only Ming's inexpertise kept her speed down once she'd steered past the air scooter. Gradually the road wound uphill toward the villa. "I'm all right," she insisted to Lyra, although the cheekbone under her left eye throbbed, and her eye kept twitching. "Let's just get back."

Lyra clenched the car's curving dash. "You're not delivering that message, I assume."

"Only to Staff Central, and only as a report."

"I think . . ." Lyra began, then paused for a quarter-klick. Ming ignored her, driving on. "I think we were lucky," she finished as Ming steered into the cutting that

led into the staff garage. "I think we—you—we nearly
didn't come home."

"How many people don't come home, tonight?" She
shut down the car beside the blockhouse.

"They like cripples, too. They—Ming! Your eye's going
black!"

Returning the car's key clip to the blockhouse attendant, Ming avoided his stare. "Go ahead," Lyra offered at
the elevator. "You go first. Get Medical to give you something for that eye."

"Thank you, Lyra. I'm sorry I got you into—"

"I went along gladly, Ming. Now get going."

Mere Bertelsen sat again at Staff Central, her stare as
cool as ever. "Who should I see about this eye?" Ming
asked directly.

"Medical. Room thirty-oh-six." The dark-haired woman
stared up at Ming's face.

"There's some kind of looting or something going on in
town," Ming began, but Bertelsen cut her off. "We know.
Steps are being taken. What happened to your eye?"

Amazing. She asks questions, too. "I was asked to give
Madam a message, but only by a man at a roadblock, and I
think he was flexing his muscles."

Mere Bertelsen touched a tab below each screen above
her terminal, and the images went black. "Was there a
message, then?"

"He said to tell her, 'Never forget who owns this world.'
I don't think it's worth bothering Her Grace about."

"That's for Staff Central to decide. Thirty-oh-six for
Medical."

Ming took care of her bruise, but Medical's curt atten-
tions left her feeling comfortless. Wondering if it might be
a mistake, she went looking for Tieg Innig.

Room 835 was uplevel. Seaside, too, she noticed from
the odd number. The court favorite would have choice
rooms.

She stepped into range of the motion sensor in the door
frame and saw his entry alarm light. Five seconds later, the
door slid away.

He wore the red-and-gold tunic over slim black pants.
After a startled look, he raised a finger to touch her cheekbone. "What happened? Come in."

"I've already been to Medical about it, and they put a fader on. There's some kind of mayhem down in town." She walked forward to sit down in a broad, comfortable-looking wicker chair that he held for her.

"Just a minute." He crossed to the opposite wall.

The rooms, far larger than her own, gleamed with natural daylight that filtered around the brocade curtains of a long sweep of windows. Through a door on her left she saw another, smaller room, lined with black instrument boxes, its drab curtains shut, and when she twisted around to look at Tieg, an arch on his right showed a windowed bedroom.

"This is lovely," she said.

"I suppose things down in the windowless zone are more spartan." He offered her a glass of pale yellow-green juice. She sipped as she described her encounter in Anslanding. Slumped forward on a short white couch along the left wall of this main room, he looked hollow-eyed and weary, but before she could · ask what ailed him, he clenched both fists on his knees and said, "You have no idea how close you came to spending an afternoon as a . . . what they call a 'sportswoman.' You bluffed well."

And why had instinct drawn her here?

"I guess I just wanted to make sure you weren't in town," she said.

"Thank you." He gave an awkward short laugh. "Believe me, this villa will be the last bastion of any storm that breaks on Mannheim."

She caught the glance toward his studio door. "You're busy." She raised a quivering hand and drained her glass. "Thank you. I should go."

He followed to the door. "You don't have to leave. That's tickle-me juice, from Nexos, my homeworld. Would you like more?"

"I—no, you have work to do. I have work to do. Maybe the whole thing will pass."

"Maybe." Tieg exhaled heavily and reached for the locking panel. "I hope to the Ancient Ones it's over now." As he reached for the panel, his expelled breath carried a protest.

Ming spun instantly. "You're hurt, too. I knew it. How did it happen?"

"I'm all right," he insisted.

"Have you seen Medical about it? What happened, Tieg?"

Dropping his arms to his sides, he exhaled again. "Frankly, if you'd look at it for me, I'd appreciate it. I can't see back there."

"Of course I will." Ming stepped away from the door. "You have first aid supplies in the wet room?"

"Underneath the sink," she heard him call as she stepped into the small room and waved on its light. Inside that panel she found a small red cubical container. Touching one end made it spring open; inside lay tapes, dressings, and plain bandages. She carried the kit back out to the front room.

Tieg lay on the white brocade couch, face down, wearing only the snug black pants. Ming stood where she was for an instant. His body was muscular and attractive without baggy camouflage. He looked—he looked—like a man, more full of life than any man she had seen like this, and for once he did not frighten her.

Kneeling beside the couch, she touched the long, red, ragged-edged bruise that began halfway down his back, near his spine, and crossed to the hip near the waistline. "Tieg," she whispered. *How did you do that?* she ached to ask again, but he'd already refused to tell. Silently she reached into the pouch for a deep-pressure analgesic dressing, and she unwrapped it quickly. "Deep bruise," she murmured. "But your rib's in line. The kidney's not in danger. I'm pretty sure about that. My father used to compete at pole dancing."

He tried to turn his head toward her, grunted, and lay back down. "It worried me a little."

Carefully she read the package's instructions, then tore open the inner cello and applied it. "You're right. You never could have reached this."

As she pressed the edges hard against his warm, silken skin, he sighed and laid his head cheek-down on the white cushion. "Better already. Just bruised?"

"You could've seen it in a mirror."

"I did," he said slowly. "What I saw concerned me."

With an artist's eye, Ming studied the line of his spine from curling dark blond hair to the point where it vanished under his waistband. Leaning her left hand against the couch, she sat beside him for several moments. At last, her hand slipped down and rested on his shoulder. Only a touch, skin on skin, but it felt wonderful, as if she had not touched another person's skin in . . . well, other than handshakes it had been twenty years at least.

"Call me tomorrow, Tieg, will you?" She straightened up, laying the medical kit on the wicker chair.

Rolling to his side, Tieg pulled his legs under him and got up. On his chest, the hair grew thicker than her father's. Ming made herself look only at his eyes.

"I'll let you out. Thank you—" He caught her elbow, and she remained stock-still.

The moment stretched into a minute, and still he stared. At last, he touched the locking panel. "Take care of that eye, Ming."

Q

Tension at the villa remained high, and Ming kept to her rooms for three days, emerging only to join Lyra at Staff Dining. Holjpip seemed to lose interest in music drawings. *She's busy with whatever called in the warship*, Ming guessed as she stared at the console on her desk. Neither "further orders" nor word regarding the warship she now knew as *Doran* reached Ming, though shuttles came and went with visible regularity over at Newport. She did not see Tieg, either, who she hoped to ask about it—cautiously, though!—and without hint or mention of the mysterious Old School.

She stretched out her feet and scrolled the screen downward. This early Friday morning, she sat studying a series of artworks by Podacan masters. With a *whish*, the

hallway door slid open. Startled, she pulled her hands away
from the keyboard.

Zardir Huekk stepped through, a blue tunic covering
his barrel chest and hanging over stubby thighs. "Mere
Dalamani. Shut down and talk to me."

Clamminess settled in her fingertips. Ming canceled
the remaining requests from her series, blanked the
screen, and rotated her chair so she could face Huekk.

He seated himself at her work desk and stared at her.
"Aren't you a mess? Been boxing? And do you need the
hairdresser's room number? You have a problem in the
back." He snickered, then frowned. "What do you know
about our little excitement last Tuesday?"

She exhaled a short breath. He was ignorant of Cabran
customs, then. And on the count of Tuesday, she was safe.
She crossed her ankles firmly to keep her legs from shivering. "Very little, Missar Huekk. I was here at work when
. . . while the crisis passed. A little later, I went to town
and—"

"And brought Her Grace a message. I heard." Huekk
rocked the chair. "There is a Company inspection team in
the system, and men from on board are asking me financial
questions. Extraneous employees are high on their list to
eliminate. You have as yet proven singularly useless to me.
Perhaps you should be replaced. By an artist with eyes for
watching other things than a computer screen." Flapping
one hand in front of his face, he shook his head. "So far,
you've given me nothing. It has been nearly four weeks."

Ming touched her still-tender cheekbone. He couldn't
expect skillful spying from her. Huekk simply enjoyed be-
littling, and she provided an easy victim. How far would he
take this? "I . . . can't think of anyone," she said slowly. "I
. . . don't think you're reasonable to ask, Missar. I work
alone."

Huekk got up off the chair and strolled toward her, a
smile crooking his face. "Give me your fingers."

Reluctantly Ming held out her left hand.

He seized her right. "What would it take . . ." he held
it palm-upward between both his own, "how much pressure . . ." As his bottom hand made a fist, the other began
to press hers backward, against her joints. She gasped.

". . . to break these fingers and make you as much use to Madam Langelleik as you have been to me?"

She tried to pull her hand free, but with powerful leverage, he held it locked between his own.

"Unless she chooses to pay for an extensive reconstruction?"

Her knuckles stretched and strained between strong, heated hands.

"Why aren't you looking harder, Mere Dalamani?"

"No time," she insisted. "Missar, I've been working."

"Fagh." Flinging down her hand, he stomped aside. "You enjoyed your little spell without feelings, then. It could be done again. It will be done again, if you cannot find this spy for me within a month. You will be paralyzed, and taken to Little York, and this time we will take all your memory." He stepped toward the door. "And set you to thinning cabbages in a hydroponics vat."

Boom.

Ming folded around her arms, curling her throbbing hand into a fist and stroking it. No one could help her if Huekk came again, wanting sport.

Tieg had been questioned, too, by a young assistant to Zardir Huekk.

He lay on his bed, behind the arch in his bar-shelving wall, and stared up at the ceiling. Outdoors gray sky stretched, and the winds of a storm front swept in from the sea to rattle dust and sand against his window.

Huekk's lackey had released him. Therefore, Ming Dalamani had not cast suspicion his way.

He curled up off the bed, crossed to his small refrigerator, and chose a bottle of juice. Sipping at it, he stared out at the ocean. It would be months, now, before he and Curan dared risk another offplanet mission.

They had barely put the mass of Mannheim between themselves and that warship in time. Then, with Curan dodging near-misses, he'd endured the wildest ride of his life, as Curan took the scoutship down in a meteorlike trajectory. Tieg never wanted to live through that heat again, the vibration, the terror. One-handed, he rubbed his back.

So, inspection came early this year. Perhaps Holjpip

suspected her competitors of illicit activity on that asteroid, or maybe Renasco was preparing to guard it.

Someone was trying to make antimatter. That fact was
at least as critically important to Old School as decoding
the Renasco shielding, and here he sat, with no way to get
that information past the warship to anyone who could use
it against Renasco. What if antimatter technology *and* radiation shielding passed into Old School hands, and Old
School could match Renasco at its own game?

Competition. Exploration and trade flourishing again,
humankind given the stars, as in his great-grandfather's
day.

A flock of kye-di-dees plunged in formation into a shoal
of roiling water, and each bobbed to the surface drooping a
silver fish from its beak. Tieg leaned away from the window glass.

Ming had not given him away. She became lovelier
every day, more of a temptation, more of a distraction; and
he could not afford distractions, not now, not ever.

He wanted to trust her, so he must give her the chance
to prove he could. Tieg checked the time on his console
screen against the performing schedule at its center. He
had half an hour free. It would be pleasant to talk, and
there were ways of conversing privately, even here.

Arriving back in her rooms from lunch, her nerves still
rattled by Huekk's intimidation, Ming jumped when she
heard her computer screen buzz. She turned to shut it off.

+MING. WOULD LIKE TO SPEAK WITH YOU. TIEG, 835+

She took a moment to freshen herself. In the mirror,
she eyed her reflection. With Lyra encouraging her, meal
after meal, to fill her plate and clean it, she really was no
bag of bones any more, and with treatment, the bruise was
fading toward yellow. Did he find her pretty?

Tieg met her at his door, dressed, for the first time she'd
seen him this way, in an ordinary pair of dark blue coveralls. They made a staggering change in his appearance, but
the mocking smile was all Tieg Innig. "Well, come in."

She started as a gust of wind spattered his windows.
The light outside seemed dimmer. He motioned her toward the short white couch, taking his own seat on the
wicker chair, pulled close.

"You're lucky to have so much room." Ming went on staring at the window. "Though I'm not complaining about my quarters. The entire apartment where my father and I used to live was smaller."

"Your eye looks better. What happened to your hair?"

She reached up to finger one clan-tail. She hadn't stopped to wonder if he would like the style. "I'm experimenting. What do you think?"

He pulled a page-sized rectangular board off the floor where it lay beside the chair and did something to it with his index finger, while he said, "I suppose I've seen stranger hairstyles. You're art staff. You can dress as you please." When he handed the board back, she read, *Keep talking. Tuesday, early: you caught then, too?*

Ming glanced around. Sure enough, his console sat oriented toward the bedroom, away from her line of sight. Holjpip's trusted favorite was not watched as closely as other staff.

She touched a finger to the board's frame. His message disappeared. "I've seen stranger styles, too, I suppose," she said slowly. The flat of the board darkened where she touched it. She tried writing by pressing the slick, dark-green surface with her fingernail. It worked. *I was drawing,* she wrote, began to give back the board, then remembered her suspicions. *Doran? Why here? How were you hurt?*

"Like mine?" he asked, working quickly with one finger. "Believe it or not, Ming, this streak is natural. My grandfather on my mother's side had hair like this. It went white in my mid-twenties." He handed her the board.

Company inspection. Regular but early. Heard Holjpip grounded everyone she could Tuesday. Uncomfortable?

Very cautious, Tieg. She fingered the white brocade on the arm of his couch. Tuesday evening, both had been too spent for questions. He hadn't even noticed her clan-tails, back then.

"Don't stare, Ming," he said softly.

"And you?" She blinked, momentarily forgetting hairstyles.

He flicked a finger upward, then touched it to his ear and reached for the board. "People remember the hair," he said. "It's become a personal trademark." *You questioned, as well?* she read, when he handed it back.

Ming nodded, then returned the board.

He grasped the chair's armrest. "I've never had a chance to simply sit and talk with you. Tell me about your homeworld."

"Hot." She folded her hands around her knees, determined to carry on this conversation as well as the other. "Crowded. We were never planted for independence. The Company is . . . was, back then . . . helping, with trade items we'd done without for decades."

"But at Company prices. I see." He was writing again.

More water hit the window. Tieg stretched his legs out, staring upward, and offered the board. *No memory of crime?*

Hoping he cared and was not just trying for information, she took the board while he picked up her cue and began to prattle about import tariffs. *I dream. They help— give back a little.*

He kept talking while he read her message, then wrote again. *Of what?*

Ming accepted the board and wrote furiously. *Family: several arrested together. Huekk reminded—their names— said "executed."* She scratched out the last phrase and re-wrote, *most likely executed. I mean to search—see if any alive. Maybe I'm only one, partial wipe. Would you help?* She gave back the board.

No longer talking, eyes glittering, he began to write. Remembering herself, she began to quote some of the Renasco prices she recalled from twenty years ago, but she feared her extemporaneous speech would fool no one, if the Ops people chose to listen.

He slipped her the board and took up the tariff litany of his own. *Not possible to find someone Renasco takes. Cold sleep twenty years—maybe died, other causes.*

Ming wrote her reply. *If they're alive, I want to find them.*

I'd need names.

She hesitated, glancing up. He stared at her over steepled fingers and continued to talk about nothing.

She'd given away too much to stop now. *Ashan*

Dalamani, she wrote reverently, in a neat, two-dimensional castil hand. *Lur Dalamani. Jiadra Grazi.*

His lips moved as he read the names several times, committing them to his memory. Then he wrote again and handed back the slate, his face a mask. *What if you found them?*

What would she do? What was the chance a collared laborer could offer them any help?

It wasn't a matter of help, but of love and honor. Shrugging at Tieg, she pulled up off the couch and walked to his window to look out at the rain.

A few seconds later, he said, "Stay there for a minute. I want to play something for you." From the studio around the corner she heard a soft rustle, then music drifted down from speakers she couldn't see, a synthesizer's reed setting over a soft, lutelike thrum. It sounded like a warm breeze smelled, though outside, beneath the overcast, steady windless rain fell.

When the song ended, he came back out to stand beside the couch.

"Evocative," she said. "If I knew more about music, I could talk more intelligently about it, but . . . I like its colors."

"You inspired it."

"Me?"

Tieg stuck one hand into a coverall pocket. "You've been sketching me. Why shouldn't I sketch you?"

Her fingers tingled, remembering the silky sensation of touching his back. It would feel so natural to touch him again. She glanced down.

Without looking away, he stepped close and drew her into the window corner near the couch, both hands on her shoulders. Here was her touch, but she didn't know if she liked it, after all; it made her heart pound. He stared down at her, though, kindly . . . more than kindly . . . he was going to kiss her. . . .

Instead, he pressed her head against his shoulder and lowered his arms to cross her back. "Little Ming," he whispered. "Little, lost Ming. Life hasn't been good to you."

Being held by her father had felt warm and secure like this. In memory she could almost smell her father's shaving rub. To her surprise, Tieg wore no scent.

Was her father the only man who ever embraced her? One of Tieg's hands stole upward to tug gently on a too-short clan-tail.

"You'll help me?" she whispered, then pushed away, careful to avoid the unwinking Eye. If that embrace went on much longer, he would need no music to manipulate her emotions.

Still he stared, eyes bright.

"Thank you." She strode to the door. "Would you let me out, please?"

Too young, too innocent of men, to see a physical move as anything but frightening, Tieg observed as he crossed the room. He had to respect that fear of degradation. Apparently it was an ancient fear, drilled into girls at their mothers' knees.

She needed his help, risked her own security to ask for it. She would not betray him, now. "Good-bye, Ming." The door slid open, and she hurried away.

He glanced at the console. If he didn't dress quickly now, he'd be late.

Here was one, and the date looked right.

Holjpip leaned back on her desk chair and pressed her eyes closed.

With three days gone since *Doran* arrived in the system, she judged it safe to use her computer uplink and tap the ship's connections with Renasco's master bank for secure ownership records. The company owned thousands of memory-wiped slaves, but the name "Dalamani" was not common, and Ashan Dalamani was property as of 4512 New Age.

To breach the woman's history more deeply would require excruciatingly careful codebreaking. Holjpip shook her head. Not necessary. Transfer of ownership would suit her needs. Holjpip would offer just over the going rate to the owner, a fueling supervisor on the nearby station *Anfis,* through an intermediary. With her thumb, Holjpip stroked the underside of her chin. She could imply a connection with her nilly bean research.

A new piece for the gameboard.

And if it's the wrong Dalamani?

Holjpip mentally shrugged and began to compose a letter of intent.

A voice rose at the door. She blanked her screen as Zardir Huekk marched in. "Madam," he said in clipped syllables that sounded queer delivered in his high-pitched voice. "We have a difficulty."

"Yes?" She laced her fingers on the desktop.

He took a seat. "The inspection team has asked me directly to check on the previously unreported disappearance of an employee. McMikall is the name. Have you heard of him?"

Asked Huekk, directly? Holjpip maintained her perfect pose. Her investigation of Tieg Innig's sea-abandoned corpse had turned up the name, but she felt no compulsion to tell Huekk. "I shall put security onto the problem immediately," she said.

Huekk's lips curled in a false smile. "I and my staff would be willing to undertake the search. You are busy."

He demanded the job. Did Renasco suspect a cover-up? "Do it, then." Holjpip touched a tab on her desktop console. "Dismissed, Missar Huekk."

She watched him out the door arch. Was it time to withdraw her protection from Tieg Innig? One employee was not worth jeopardizing her work here at Mannheim. If Renasco had begun to move through Huekk, the Company could mean to stir trouble.

Yes. But that would not negate the need to explore Mere Dalamani's past. So before worrying about Tieg, finish this letter.

R

Holding her breath, Ming leaned forward with her makeup brush. Beginning at the edge of Holjpip's jaw, she feathered a narrow line of iridescent black makeup she'd applied with her fingers, widening it to the penciled outline, ending at a point just below the eye.

She flicked a glance to her sketch. Holjpip stared through Ming into a large salon mirror. Behind her, Yerren and a uniformed woman Ming thought might be a hairdresser watched, hovering. It felt queer to have to ignore an audience while she worked, particularly when the most important member of the audience served as her canvas.

At the other corner of the jaw, she began again.

Six days since the Renasco sweep into Anslanding, and still no official visitation. Unquestionably Holjpip's net watched the inspectors' housing at Newport, but tonight's masquerade went forward as scheduled.

Carefully Ming applied a line of white, now, with her fingers. For six days, she'd expected Renasco's "further orders" to arrive at any moment. Her nerves were wearing thin.

When she finished, after cleaning the hairline and throat with a short-bristled makeup bright, Holjpip's lovely young face looked inhuman, black and white in brazen diagonals. Tonight, in a costume Ming designed from hair to slippers, she would wear black trimmed in white. Her flaming hair was lacquered black already, to cover with tiny white jewels.

Facing the mirror, Holjpip smiled. "Hah. You wouldn't know me yourself, Yerren, would you?"

Ming backed away to lay the bright on her tray, gave the ambassador a short bow, and took up a tiny spiral brush. "Thank you, Madam. Close your eyes, now." Ming touched the brush to a container of golden gel, then to Holjpip's lashes. "One moment more." She lifted an atomizer of fixative and carefully, evenly, sprayed the makeup to set it. "There, Madam."

The hairdresser pushed forward. Ming lifted a hand towel and straightened to gaze around the salon. In several other chairs sat high-ranking members of Holjpip's staff, each being painted. On some, the pigmenting went on far below the jawline. The wide, airy salon seemed to extend forever, surrounded by mirrors reflecting unending visual tunnels, and the air hung heavy with fixatives, dyes, makeup, and conflicting perfumes.

Irritated male voices filtered through the nearest mirrored door. As Ming turned to see, it burst open. Three men rushed forward, the one in the lead broad, red-haired, and red-faced, an easy caricature.

Holjpip continued to pose while the uniformed woman seated behind her combed glittering white jewels into her blackened hair. Ming wiped her hands rapidly.

"I am looking for Madam Langelleik," shouted the red-faced man. "Is she here?"

"Look in front of you," Holjpip said in a soft, sarcastic murmur.

He hesitated for several seconds, then marched forward. "Madam Langelleik, Voy Torben, secretary-director of Allegiance Pharmochemical—"

"I know you, Secretary-Director Torben." Holjpip waved one hand out from under her makeup robe. "Sit down."

The hairdresser relinquished her stool beside Holjpip, but portly, red-haired Torben remained standing, breathing hard. "What is that warship doing in our system? What do you mean to do about the Renasco gangs marauding in our streets?"

"How long has it been since they last disturbed your people?" Holjpip asked, calm as ever.

"This morning, Madam. This very morning, two took the payroll chits from our main office and destroyed them. Destroyed half the office's currency, then drove off with the other half."

Holjpip frowned, curving the diagonals painted on her

face. "Torben, I am doing what I can. If I overstep my superiors' limits, they can replace me."

Chilled, Ming thought of the blank-eyed ex-officials at Holjpip's Goodsprings plant. She dropped her towel into a receptacle.

Torben's face grew redder. "Madam, why did they come in the first place? Did you instigate this sequence of events? I warn you, you might be Company rep, but you have no right to stifle competition. General Co-Op stands with me—"

Holjpip waved him to silence. "I am certain this has nothing to do with you, Secretary Torben. This is a regular inspection, early for once."

Speaking a little slower, he took the stool. "Taking your little secrets offworld in a big way, then? It's true, the rumor your new pharmaceuticals are your ticket to the top of Renasco, and your share of ownership of humanity?"

Ming half expected Holjpip to fly off her salon chair at the ALPEX man, but Madam the ambassador remained as cool as ever. *She's not so young and volatile as she looks,* Ming reminded herself.

"Perhaps," Holjpip said. "That is one reason I must move cautiously with the inspection team. I have years of experience dealing with these people. Let me handle Renasco in the Renasco way. When my patents are secure, you may license rights to the mellow pods, of course. There will be business enough for all of us, Secretary Torben.

"Meanwhile," she continued, "what do you intend to do with your shares of the Newport Authority, under the regulations passed last month?"

With growing amusement, Ming listened as Holjpip spun a web around a bait of shares in mellow pods, withdrew the bait, dangled it again, and then pounced on her prey, while he sat glowing with promises of wealth. Even under pressure, the woman's genius was obvious.

At last, Holjpip dismissed him. His cronies guarded his flanks as they left.

Holjpip watched them go, the slight narrowing of her painted eyes the only sign she too appreciated the situation's resolution. The hairdresser moved in again and sprinkled a last spoonful of jewel flecks onto the back of her hair.

"Amazing," Ming whispered.

"What was that?" Holjpip spun her chair and raised the thin double-arch of her eyebrows.

Ming shook her head, smiling. "Well done, Madam."

"Finished, Madam," said the hairdresser.

Holjpip rose out of the chair, black and white elegance, catlike in her grace. Her Grace. Impulsively, Ming curtsied.

Holjpip laughed raucously, but it was a well-meant laugh, a sharing of pleasure. "Ming Dalamani," she said, "continue your sketchwork at the masquerade, and come to me later. I shall have a gift for you. A thanks, for services rendered—including the empathy I have no right to demand, but which you have shown me this night."

One hairstylist glared at Ming before removing Holjpip's cape, then bent to tidy her own tray. A dresser moved forward, Holjpip's iridescent gown draped over her forearm.

Ming felt as if she had swallowed something too big for her throat. Protecting her makeup, the attendant draped Holjpip's gown down over her shoulders, drawing it tight at the waist, straightening it on her hips. Once Holjpip stood costumed, Ming helped her into matching shimmering black gloves. No purple tipped her nails tonight. *Because she planned to wear gloves, or because of the inspection team?* The seamstress had truly done beautiful work on the costume.

Holjpip's attention had shifted from Ming to the costume, so Ming collected her tools and left the salon through the nearest mirrored door.

She had barely stepped onto the hall carpet when she heard, "Ming. Good day."

Startled, she turned back toward the guard at the salon's door, then recognized his face. "Able Tatarka." The one who'd been so protective in the library. "You rotate different stations *and* shifts?"

"Yes, I'm a rover. I hear Her Grace chose you for her own costume designer. Congratulations." He smiled, flicking the piping on his collar, and Ming stepped sideways on the hall's deep carpet.

Reaching down inside herself, she found a new poise. She had been someone, once, and in dreams and flashes it was coming back. Pressing her palms together, she glanced up into Able's eyes: pure violet, like the trim on his uniform. "Thank you, Able."

"May I see you tonight, when I'm off shift, about two hours from now?"

Half cringing, wishing he hadn't asked, yet flattered by his attention, she shook her head. "I'm assigned to attend the masquerade, Able, to continue a series of abstract drawings. Thank you, though. You're kind. I mustn't keep—"

"Next week, perhaps." His chin set earnestly.

"Yes." She turned a trusting smile up at him. "I mustn't keep you from your duties. Stay well."

"And you." He touched her elbow, then returned to attention.

Claude Yerren chose not to attend the masquerade. As Holjpip finalized her preparations for the gathering, Claude made her way to her own rooms. Striding down the hallway, she met Tieg Innig, evidently on his way to the centrum. He wore no facial paint, but the black caftan that was his attire for the most formal gatherings shimmered to his ankles, and he carried a black instrument case draped with a small cloth bundle. They nodded to one another as they passed.

Once in her own suite, which occupied a third of the villa's northernmost end (Holjpip's suite took up the other two-thirds), she slipped off her shoes, turned up her room receiver, then switched it from environmental rainfall to quiet music. Beyond the windows of her spacious lounge, the sun set in dusky shades beyond Anslanding, and city lights began to compete with the sky for brilliance. North windows past the room's corner showed greenery that did not move in tonight's summer stillness.

The inspection came too early this time, but Holjpip's contacts moved swiftly, and thus far Claude heard no negative reports. When the heads of Renasco's visitation team came to the villa, signaling the inspection's completion, she and Holjpip would know if they'd covered evidence quickly enough, or if they'd end their lives at Goodsprings.

Claude passed into her bedroom and slipped into a soft housedress. As she laid her amethyst ring, Holjpip's gift, on her dresser top, the holographic likeness of a young man's face caught her glance.

It always did.

Gaetan Ortola, her husband, had died twenty-seven years ago, the only perfect man she had ever known—perfect, except for his susceptibility to stress. He'd worried himself into the early grave, or so her friends said, all of them but Holjpip.

Holjpip alone had offered a position instead of too-late advice, and had given her good honest work to keep her mind off guilty misery. In time, Holjpip's business concerns drove off the grief. With Holjpip, Claude Yerren ascended the corporate ladder.

Belting a robe over the housedress, she went to her food bar and touched in a dinner order. It would take Staff Dining some time to bring her meal, so she poured a liqueur and took it to her favorite chair. Opposite the windowed corner of the living area, she could watch out both windows at once. As she relaxed into the chair, a guard strolled past the west pane, rounded the corner, and marched eastward.

Inspection teams had come and passed since their arrival on Mannheim.

Yes, but never two months early. Claude scratched the finger that usually wore the amethyst. And the gangs, still roving—though today they'd raided ALPEX, leaving small business alone—irritated her.

Claude Yerren knew most of Holjpip's real ambition and guessed more, but she kept her guesses to herself. Holjpip had too many worries, and Claude Yerren vowed never to lose another anchor. Gaetan's cancers had yielded to no treatment, as if his body, exhausted in worry, could no longer respond.

Holjpip is far stronger than Gaetan ever was. It had taken years to admit the fact, but she no longer was bitter, not even about the mellow pods. Thirty years too late for Gaetan, that discovery that might have saved his life.

Saved him, yes, but over the long term, ruined him. Nothing was without its price.

So Holjpip took Gaetan's place in her life. She admired

her friend's genuine appreciation of the arts. Holjpip's re-
creations, such as her quest to uncover Ming Dalamani's
past, might ease her over the tense week ahead. For
Holjpip, no recreation existed without usefulness. Holjpip
spun enormous pleasure out of testing her own intelligence net, which was not yet a rival to Renasco's—

It will be. Claude Yerren swallowed a tiny sip of burning melon-flavored liqueur and watched the sun's thin rim
vanish beyond hills. *Soon. It will be.*

What about Innig, then?

*Not yet. She'll want him to entertain the inspectors,
when they deign to greet us. Two weeks, and this will end.
Villa employees have vanished before.*

Standing at one corner of the centrum, Ming watched
Holjpip's guests cluster in, admire one another's costumes,
give false names, and form new clusters. At first, the centrum resounded with soft recorded music, but Tieg appeared in his corner before the expanse half filled and
reached for his string synthesizer.

A mysterious minor triad began to whine under the
trees. Tieg's elegant black suited the centrum's evening
ambience, and a black turban concealed all his hair but the
white forelock. When he turned his head, the turban sparkled iridescent subtones of blues and greens.

Though the villa rang with frightened rumors, she sat
here on assignment once again. Careful to disturb no one,
she settled in with her sketch pad to create another mood
piece. Tieg created a stir by playing one long interlude on
a triangular-bodied, ten-stringed lute from a position on
the fountain pool's edge, and Ming sat awed by his fingers'
precision. Several women in red-and-yellow Podacan uniforms mingled with the masqueraders. Ming wondered if
Holjpip's worlders had come with the Renasco officials.

Much later, with identities revealed, Ming heard gasps
from the crowd when Holjpip, pseudonym "black lady,"
rose to acknowledge her subjects' admiration. They may
have been truly surprised or stroking Holjpip's pride, but
Holjpip curtsied and ordered the refreshment table refilled. When that achingly sweet, seductive end-music began, Ming recognized it and hurried away of her own
accord.

In the hallway, she heard her name. Recognizing the strident voice, Ming turned to see Holjpip, followed as usual by one huge woman and a pair of well-muscled men in black. She had gone unguarded through most of the evening for the sake of her masquerade, although Ming doubted she was helpless.

Ming lifted the cover of the sketch pad. "Madam, I have another mood piece for you."

Holjpip took it, glanced at it, then flicked one finger. "Come in here."

Ming followed Her Grace into the Ops room, where Holjpip keyed up a floor map of the villa, made a change, then smiled, the eerie diagonal design on her face lit from below by the console's gleam. "You will have to move your things. I have put you in eight forty-eight. Get your recoding chip from Staff Central."

An uplevel room. Upstairs, with windows . . .

"Madam," she stammered. "Thank you. I've done nothing to deserve—"

"I respect the arts, and I reward those who choose to serve me well. Good night."

In a daze, Ming made the long trip below the centrum to Staff Central—which, she had found, remained open like Staff Dining all day and night. Chip in hand, ten minutes later, she approached the assigned doorway, loaded and recoded the lock, and stepped in.

She did not face the ocean, but beyond her window, Anslanding glittered between tossing boughs. She flicked on the room light. One wall looked as if made of framed cloth panels. She stepped around it—it was a room divider, after all—and sank on her windowside bed. It was a wide one, and she assumed from experience that the closets held all she needed to move in. Soft light shone through the divider's panels, making it gleam rose, amethyst, and deeper purple, the hues beautifully balanced. Near the head of the bed, two doors stood open. Through one, she could make out the edges of shelves, and the other led into the wet room.

What luxury! Ming returned around the divider. Opposite, on the far wall, was a long desk she could make serve as her working table. She needed all that storage space, having collected drawers full of supplies since her arrival, not all of them necessary for calligraphy. On one end of the desk perched the ever-present console—she would have to activate it right away, but not just yet—and beside the window sat a deep, soft chair.

Her own, so long as she went on pleasing Holjpip. She wondered how often Holjpip received friendliness, freely given. What if Holjpip could give her access to information on surviving crewmates?

Ming didn't dare ask yet, but perhaps later, when—if—she continued to win her employer's approval. This deeper move into Holjpip's favor might even supersede Huekk's "month"—

Yes, but what happens when Renasco tries to contact me now? I've become as close to Her Grace as anyone could.

A sharp rapping sound broke that discouraging train of thought. She stepped to the doorway and tried the interior locking panel. The door slid aside, and there waited Tieg Innig, holding the turban at his side.

She gaped.

"I heard the neighborhood was improving," he said with a glance of gray eyes to each side, "when I checked out at Central. Congratulations."

"Thank you." Waving him in, she shut the door. "I'm just looking things over." She jerked her head toward the blank console. "And that's still off."

"You learn quickly." Tieg laid his turban on her long desk. "Though they have other ways of observing, if they choose."

Ming felt awkward in the ensuing silence. "I heard a new theme tonight," she said, trying to fill it. Self-consciously, she hummed the tune. "Very soothing. All I could draw to it was spirals. That must be how mellow pods make a person feel."

Tieg paused halfway to the window. "Ming. You're not using those, are you?"

Surprised, she stood with her back to the door. "No. I don't know enough about them."

"You're smart to be cautious." Crossing the room, he glanced out the window, then recrossed and pulled the padded desk chair away from its place at the blank console.

Ming took the soft chair closer to the window. "Before you go on, what do you hear from down in town?"

"It's eased up some. Apparently, Holjpip had the road-blocks taken down."

"That's encouraging."

"Yes, but don't sidetrack me from mellow pods. If you don't know about them, you need to." He rested his elbows on his knees so the caftan made a black tent over most of his body. "So far as anyone knows, the nilly beans have a single side effect: burnout. But mellow pods are more subtly dangerous. At first, people thought they halted aging by preventing the breakdown of tissue. There's evidence, now, that the active substance halts changes in the nervous system's structure."

"That's bad?" Ming leaned against the chair's deep backrest. "It would stop memory loss."

"True enough. But also learning, and emotional development."

Ming spread her hands, fingering the velvety arms of her chair. *Her room!* A long silver car whisked past the window. "Holjpip knows about this?"

"One assumes. She'll market them with full and appropriate warnings. But how many people have you known who dreaded rejuv treatments?"

"They're supposed to hurt. That's one reason so many put them off for so long." The other reason was that once on rejuv, you had to take the bimonthly treatments the rest of your life, or else go into a rather nasty accelerated aging syndrome.

There was the expense, too.

"So here's a simple, painless way to get the same physical effect. There'll be a market."

Ming guessed Tieg spoke truly. Here in Anslanding, and so probably all up and down the Belt and on all the new Renasco colony worlds, there would be people eager to painlessly prolong their youth, disdaining future potential for learning and stability.

Then she remembered the Renasco gangs. "Will we be here to see it happen?" she asked.

"I think we will. This has happened before. The raids ease off, then in a few days there's an official visitation at the villa." Tieg rose and glanced left, at the door. "I have something for you, before I go."

Ming pressed out of her chair. Tieg came forward a few

steps, then stretched out one hand. The caftan rippled down his side. "An . . . apology gift."

"Apology?" She reached back to flip a short clan-tail.

Tieg held his right hand extended. "A minor thing, maybe, but my conscience doesn't think so. I've distrusted you. I don't trust easily; it's hard for me. I want you to have something to help you dress your role."

Into her hand he dropped something small and sharp-edged. Ming peered down. In the dim light of the room's overhead panel, a pair of amethyst crystals mounted in white metal barely glistened.

"I'd noticed your ears are pierced."

Ming laughed. "And did you know that on my homeworld, touching an earring is the gesture of apology?"

He raised one curly eyebrow. "No."

She set the earrings down. "You don't wear purple."

His lips tugged up, then outward in a controlled smile. "You've noticed. My contract has other dress standards."

Ming stood staring at him, then glanced over her shoulder at the dark console and asked, "Do you trust me now?"

He took a half step back and looked directly at her eyes. "Yes," he said. "I've begun to, though you've probably always deserved it."

Did she dare go on, then?

Clan honor. She plunged into deep water. "Then tell me about the Old School."

Tieg Innig backed two steps away and groped into his ebony sleeve band.

Quickly, she went on. "It's not what you might think. I've—"

"Softly," he hissed.

Ming lowered her voice. "I've run queries on the data base ever since I arrived, wanting to know more about this world, about you, about Mannheim's problems." She raised both hands, palms toward him, to shoulder height. "I know nothing more than the name, and that its activities are reported to be sedition and piracy." Pausing, she frowned. "That was my conviction, Tieg. Sedition and piracy. What do they do that I used to believe in? Did I work for them, once? What can I do to find out more?"

Still his fingers rested at that sleeve, and Ming realized

he was armed. Armed, violent enough to frighten Lyra, and—at this moment—afraid she endangered his position.

Tell it all quickly, then. "Renasco has asked me to spy for them," she blurted out in a whisper. "Tieg, I could have mentioned your name to Zardir Huekk the day I arrived. I never have, I never will. I want my freedom, but—" Her voice began to tremble. Hating the stagy effect, she sucked air and got it under control. "Not at the cost of what I believe in. They want me to insinuate myself into Holjpip's favor, too. I don't know why, but I don't want to know, anymore. With the inspection coming . . ." She trailed off. "I want to help you, and I want to help Holjpip."

"And if it came to a choice between her and me?"

She had to strain to hear him. She'd dreaded the question, but she had her answer ready. "I'd help you, Tieg."

"How certain are you?" he whispered.

"Sure enough to risk my life admitting all this."

He reached two fingers into the sleeve band. "You understand, then." Ming held her breath as he drew out a tiny weapon. Holding it in one hand, he took a seat on the desktop.

Ming stayed exactly where she stood. "They . . . sent me here, to . . . await further orders. That was a month ago, and I'm afraid those orders will come from the inspection team. They've . . . threatened to remove me, if I prove useless." Ming tried to force sarcastic humor into her voice but couldn't. Things were drawing too close to their climax now.

"Well," he said, and he laid the pistol on his lap, where it looked silvery on the black fabric. "Well."

For nearly a minute he sat that way. Ming watched his hands, and the gun. He could use it quickly from there, but showing it was one step toward openness, and she was glad to be able to see it.

And to know for certain what it implied: Tieg was Old School.

8

Tieg beckoned her closer. Wondering what kind of listening device he feared, then remembering overhead monitors at Staff Central, she walked forward until she could have easily touched his knees.

"I don't envy your position, Ming—the memory wipe, the collar, nor that kind of assignment. We could help you." He paused and crinkled his mouth, then whispered, "They always finish their inspection before calling in any operatives they mean to replace. If it looks like they're moving you, we'll be ready." He still kept the gun in his lap. "What did they make you, Ming, when they stole your memory?"

"What did they make me?" After careful thought, she answered literally. "A servant, I suppose, with holes in her recollections. But they didn't take my mind away. I remember the things I used to believe in, and I still believe them. They put a hold of fear on me, and they offered to reward me, but since they didn't change me, I—I guess they've failed."

"Thank you," he murmured.

Confused, she reached out and almost touched him, then quickly dropped her hand.

"My mother was taken by Renasco, you see. Questioned, they said. Questioned, and then memory-wiped like you. We never heard from her again. But it would be good to know she might still be herself. I've only met the . . . totally wiped, before."

Mother: Old grief choked her. She suspected it would be better not to inquire into his mother's crime—not yet, anyway. "And that's how you guessed it had happened to me."

186

"When I was old enough, I tried channels, looking for her."

"Why do you tell me about her?"

Tieg raised one finger to point her way. "If that means anything to you, if you understand pain, Ming—loss—if you're the least bit tempted to go to Renasco, go now. Leave this room alive, and don't come back. You have enough information to buy their favor, I think. Only . . . if that's your choice, tell me you're going, and grant me a running start."

"You haven't been listening."

"Ming, I'm giving you the chance to change your mind."

The chance to be spared the terror of watching him fire —because he would shoot from behind? By Able's claim, he'd been investigated for violence before, and shielded by Her Grace. "I'm staying," she murmured. "With you."

He tucked the pistol back into his sleeve band, slipped down off the desktop, and took both her hands. His fingers spread warmth through hers like desert heat. "I'm glad," he said quietly. "I could never hurt you. I'll help you escape them, if I can."

She nodded, waiting, almost afraid to breathe.

He leaned his cheek against hers, so close that his whisper tickled her ear. "Our goal is to reopen space travel for mankind. And we need people who owe Renasco a debt of honor."

"Yes?" she asked, her pulse running quickly. "What can I do?"

He gripped her hands. "You must swear to keep our very existence quiet, to start, no matter what you've found in the data base."

"I do. By my ancestors," she added solemnly.

"It might mean—" He hesitated. "Well, if they do call you in for questioning, and we can't get you away—"

"I understand. I'd never let them strip my memory again, knowing they'd come next for you."

Pulling back to stare down into her eyes, he waved off the room lights. Warmth slid around her. Aware of breath on her cheek, she trembled but held her ground. Ming leaned into Tieg's kiss, tentatively at first, and then, as she caught her body's cues, with ardor. Her hands splayed on his hard, muscular back. Stars danced inside her head, as when she once caught a fever, and strange tinglings told her there was more to come. Tieg's arms clung warm around her waist, and when he drew his lips away from hers, his hand pressed her head against his shoulder. *I could never hurt you*, he'd said. Was it truth or just poetry?

Below the hill Anslanding sparkled, and the intense white light of a shuttle floated downward, southward in the western sky, toward Newport.

"Ming," he whispered. "Ming, I have wanted that for weeks. Renasco would spare none of us if they knew Old School operatives worked on Mannheim. And Old School is my life. I would never dare . . . get close to a woman who was not one of us."

First she closed her eyes and held him, feeling his heart beat against her chest. Then she stood a little straighter and murmured over his shoulder. "I wondered. I mean, I did have enough of my memory back to understand you'd been to space."

He rested his cheek on her shoulder, and his breath came warm against her throat as his lips pressed beneath her ear.

She gulped. "Isn't . . . Holjpip . . . ?"

When Tieg laughed, the soft explosion tickled her neck. "Yes, she's jealous. But she has never been my lover. She treats me like a son, if anything."

She felt so relieved she had to tease. "A match for her clone daughter, maybe."

"Her daughter would be twenty years older than I am."

"Is she married?"

"Not that anyone knows of."

"There you are. A little rejuv . . ." She shrugged.

He laughed again, then abruptly his head came up. "There is something you can do for us, right now. I need a message taken to Barbar Curan in town, one I can't use normal lines for."

Ming reached for his hand, wishing she could always go on touching him. "Is Missar Curan—?"

"Yes."

Ming had lived for so long in a role that kept her out of compromising situations that she had nearly forgotten something of deadly importance. Her fever dropped in an instant. "The collar, Tieg."

Tieg drew his hand away and walked toward the window, silhouetted by city lights in the darkened room. She followed. "Curan has used sentenced laborers as couriers before. He has what's called a 'jammer.' Have you ever heard of one of those?"

She rubbed her hands together, feeling cold and isolated, apart from him. "No."

"A jammer can keep a collar from activating, within its range. So long as you were working for him, you would be safe. If you see any sign of roadblocking, though, turn around and come back. Or if you can't, go stay with Curan. There shouldn't be any by now, but . . ." He shrugged.

"It's good to know of a safe place in town." *Why won't he go himself?* Miffed for a moment, she reconsidered. Perhaps he wished to test her commitment. She would hope others' loyalty had been well tested, if her safety depended on them. "Yes, Tieg. Let me."

He drew her back into an embrace. "I suppose you have to get on with your moving-in, though," he whispered. "Want help?"

Ming pulled away, her senses raw. "There's not much. I can do it. It won't take long."

"I'll draft the message and bring it here to you. Meanwhile, you'd best switch on that screen."

"One minute more?" She leaned her head against his shoulder and traced a spiral up his back. He held tightly.

At last she walked toward the desk. Flick: The console came on. She reached for the room light panel.

Air swirled past her, and Tieg stopped at the door just as fine gray bars began to glow on the screen. She touched the lock to let him leave, and he walked out without glancing back, a rustle of black fabric following him.

He can't afford to be seen here. Naturally. Oh. Tieg. Her hand shook as she reached to close the door, then she stood against it, trying to force her whirl of thoughts into sensible organization. Remembering the warm press of his body, she twisted her fingers together and clenched them.

Where did I put those earrings? Thrusting one hand into an overblouse pocket, she frowned. *Now that I've offered to work for Tieg's Old School, what happens when Zardir Huekk comes back?*

She turned back toward the window. There the amethysts lay, on her long new desk. Disquieted, she went in search of a service cart to move her belongings.

Ming drove through Anslanding as midnight passed. Around her, advertising lights winked on and off or spiraled toward space to drop and climb again. When she crossed one side street, more lights glared far down the block. Crowds clustered on the sidewalks. *One good place to stay away from,* she guessed, *with Company gangs in town.*

The notion of Curan's jammer kept tantalizing her, while she counted streets as Tieg directed. If she owned a collar jammer, she could try to escape Huekk. Never mind that she had nowhere to go, that she would far rather stay with . . . her body warmed at the memory of heady new experience.

At the specified corner, she turned into a dark, quiet lane lined with two-story row houses and squat single dwellings. She counted those singles carefully. *This will be it.* She pulled over. *From this moment, Ming Dalamani, you're the traitor Zardir Huekk is looking for.*

Troubled by an image of the arrogant mutant bending over her, Ming sat motionless in the darkened, quiet staff car, collecting her nerve.

You've been that traitor for two hours, she reminded herself, toying with one clan-tail. *In fact, you were a traitor to Renasco long before Rimi Dusenfeld bore her first child. Nothing has changed.*

She stepped up and out of the car. Even in soft shoes, her footsteps sounded loud on the walkway. Glancing up and down the street, she hesitated, but nothing moved except back at the boulevard, where lights whizzed by.

A yellowish, pale lamp lit one end of the house's short porch. Ming took a deep breath of smoky, salt port-town air. Following Tieg's instructions, she rang the bell twice, waited half a minute, then rang twice again.

The door swung inward without a sound. Barbar Curan stepped away inside, dressed in a long, dark green nightrobe. "Ming." He sounded surprised, but motioned her inside, then pushed the door closed. Two worn couches lay along two walls, and a dark doorway loomed on her right. The house smelled musty, but Barbar Curan managed to look trim and poised, though she'd surely just wakened him.

"I have this for you from Tieg." She presented the folded, sealed slip of paper.

"Ah. You're a messenger now?" Curan tucked the paper into a pocketed fold of his robe.

"He's told me about . . ." She glanced all around.

"No ears here," he said. "Come in, sit down for a minute."

The shorter couch, beneath a green landscape panel on the room's inner wall, looked old and frayed after Holjpip's opulent villa. Ming sat. "Old School." Despite his assurance, she felt she should whisper the incriminating words. "I want to be involved, Missar Curan."

"You're involved now," he said bluntly, walking toward a wooden desk across the room from her, beside the front door. From a drawer he drew a small black box. "Forgive me," he said as he recrossed the room. "I must ask the rude favor of looking at your collar."

"You knew about it?" She turned on the couch so he could reach the back of her neck.

"From Tieg," he said, the tone of his voice calm and steady. "Of course."

She lifted her short clan-tails. Close to her ear, something whirred.

"I'm reading the transmission frequency. I can't jam something I haven't quantified. There." Another short whir. "You're safe now, within about two city blocks of this. Beyond that, you have to rely on your wits."

She shook with a sudden wild surge of joy. Freedom—a little bit of it. She hadn't realized until this moment how shackled and caged she felt. Even at the Cooperson-Dusenfeld house, down south in the Pomona Valley, she had known Zardir Huekk could close her collar. "At any distance on this continent," he'd said. But here, for these brief minutes, no one could hurt her.

She would pay soon enough, she reflected, as soon as she left the jammer's range.

If only I had one of my own!

"How does the collar work, Missar Curan? I thought it

compressed the spinal cord." She settled back around in the couch to face him. "Then I found the effect wasn't permanent."

"The hard way, I assume."

She folded her hands in her lap. "Yes."

"It's more a matter of electrical disruption, as I understand it: neutralizing nerve impulses, so none pass."

Aware Curan watched her, she lifted her chin. "Do you want to return anything to Tieg?"

"Wait just a minute, and I'll let you know." He walked across to the desk again, and she stood to follow. "No. Stay there, if you don't mind."

She sank back onto the couch and waited while he broke the letter's seal along one edge, read, and then dropped the paper into a cylindrical container beside his desk and kicked it. Bright, blue-white light shone from its depths. "Just give him the word *approve*, Ming. Have a safe trip back."

"Missar Curan?" she ventured.

Thrusting his thick arms under the green robe's folds, he stepped toward her. He was of the age, she guessed, to go on rejuv soon. Fifteen, perhaps twenty years older than herself—*than the years I have lived,* she corrected herself.

That makes him my chronological age mate, more or less. For a second, she stared at the lines gathering at his dark eyes and flecks of gray in his hair, which was otherwise as black as her own.

Barbar Curan's thoughts in that instant were eerily similar to Ming's. *Had we lost the war back on Lode, had I served the sentence we imposed on the rebels, I would be her physical age now. Would I trade these years I've known for the appearance of youth?*

He pitied her. Perhaps he understood a little of what she had been through. So Tieg saw fit, at last, to let her prove herself? "Innig wishes to write Huekk theme into final bars of next week's production. Approve?" That had been the text of the message. Had Huekk intercepted it, the mutant would have undoubtedly gone to Tieg for answers, signaling Ming's infidelity.

"Yes?" he asked her.

Ming pressed her palms together in a gesture foreign to

him. "Missar Curan," she said again, "why did you join the Old School?"

He took a seat on the other couch and arranged his robe over his lap. "Adventure, at first," he admitted. He wanted to speak plainly with this young woman, trusting impulses that had served him for years. "With the wars ended by Renasco's arrival, there was no place in Lodan society for a former fighter pilot. Oh, Renasco wanted me, but they couldn't force me to serve them."

"Monkeys," she said vehemently, her oval face animated. "That's what we called them back on Cabra Minor."

Since their meeting at Draper Park, she had gained self-confidence to better match that exquisite, ivory-skinned beauty. Ming Dalamani had begun to draw Tieg Innig free of his convoluted shell.

"Yes. Monkeys," he answered. "And the more I saw of their worlds, the happier I was I had chosen Old School."

"Curan," she said, her lips pursed in an expression of hesitancy. "This is silly. Forgive me for being juvenile, but . . . I like you."

She has just committed to us. Barbar Curan rose and offered her the open hand of friendship. She clasped only his fingertips. As they touched, he fought back a yawn.

"I'm gone now." She moved languidly toward the door. "Thank you for . . . jamming my . . ."

"You're protected within about two blocks. Good night."

Pausing at the doorway, she drew a deep breath. "Good night, Missar Curan."

He shut the door behind her and went back to bed. Loyal for the moment, soon she would be tempted, really tempted, to give them away. Trained in psychology, he knew the enthusiasm of "conversion" faded rapidly, followed by second thoughts. The dangerous time had begun for Ming Dalamani, and Tieg would need to watch her.

She stepped off Curan's porch and glanced skyward. The night gleamed with stars, and longing caught her by surprise. She must be closing on the forgotten secrets, now.

She put the staff car in motion and steered up toward

the boulevard, then turned toward the villa, where Tieg waited.

Sweet seductive music she'd heard twice, now, rose in memory to distract her. Vague images teased, too, a golden future linked with Tieg Innig's past, a past to substitute for her own lost years. It seemed cowardly to drive along the dull, stony streets of Anslanding. She felt as if she should be flying toward the sun.

It's too good to be true, she warned herself, as the street leaped the wide bridge over the Riddle River. *Something's bound to go wrong—with Renasco, most likely.*

No roadblock waited at city's edge, and she laughed her relief to the quiet night. The daydream of flying, far too pleasant to squelch, danced in her mind with hints of the Ming she had been. The two notions had set together like a finished gel plate, and there was no untangling them any more. If music roused emotion and—yes!—if emotion initiated these "dream" memories, Tieg Innig might own the key to her wholeness.

Tieg sat on the stool in his studio. On his left, the tape of a recent composition transferred itself onto a performance disk for presentation tomorrow evening. Accustomed to late hours, tonight he felt more awake than ever.

After tonight, he would be able to rest at last. Huekk would never be able to resist coming to him if Ming repeated the contents of the message. Tieg had a "Huekk theme" prepared to fit the message, a clashing twelve-tone melody with power in its bass line to titillate Zardir Huekk's taste. Tieg would use it, too, if need be, at that upcoming engagement, though the necessity of using it would mean Ming had—

Don't borrow trouble. Tieg recrossed his feet on a rung of his stool. *She won't go to him, not this time.*

Two green lights blinked on his disk recorder. He shut down the transference mode and sat still, eyes closed, remembering Ming's warm, if stiff and inexperienced, embrace.

And why are we being inspected early?

Tieg had wondered about *Doran* and its passengers so many times over the past week that that thought's emergence evoked only dull dread.

He shut down the equipment and took himself to his bedroom to undress. Automatically he reached inside the black caftan's sleeve band for his dart pistol. He had carried it for so long, now, that he hardly felt it any more—

Startled, he groped deeper.

It wasn't there.

He pulled off the garment and shook it, then sank onto the foot of his bed, mentally retracing his steps.

Ming's room.

Tieg went rigid. If she had taken it while distracting him in her arms, then she was smooth—too smooth—and she had gone to Curan armed.

He frowned. *Stop that, Tieg. For once, put your suspicion away.* He'd checked on an instrument in the centrum after leaving Ming. It could be there, worked loose while he concentrated on something else. If someone found it, they picked it up with his fingerprints all over it.

He groaned.

Check here, first. Tieg ordered himself up off the bed and peered or groped into every likely cranny, then all the unlikely ones.

Sinking on the wicker chair, he laced his fingers. If anyone came looking for Joash McMikall, and if that pistol turned up, it would take them to Tieg Innig. Jury Bertelsen at Staff Central would be anxious to help, but until he spoke with her, he needed an alibi for possessing an unregistered weapon. Tieg closed his eyes.

Hunting might suffice. He could have been hunting up north, during his two-day leave. The port from which he and Curan left was north of here, and if his movements weren't checked too carefully, that might cover.

Might's not good enough. He yanked his caftan back on and hurried to the centrum.

T

"Joash McMikall. Come in." In a dreaming haze, Tieg stood at the freight lock of the training ship *Lucci*, cranking open the inner door as the momentum servo ground into motion.

Shaven head painted in concentric circles of copper-on-blue, Joash McMikall stepped through, carrying a hideously contorted, decompressed body. Thin, straight-haired—

"Pell." Lovingly Tieg took the corpse in his arms. "You found him. Thank you, Joash. Oh, thank you."

"Three hundred creds a month," McMikall reminded him; he brandished his dart pistol, then stepped back through the airlock into space.

Like wax melting and reforming to fit an invisible mold, the corpse's face changed from male to female, hair curling as he watched, to frame a face now square-jawed with large, soft, vacant eyes. "Mother. Mother, you're so light." She began to float upward, out of his grasp. "Mother, don't! Mother—"

He opened his eyes to darkness, forced his fingers to release their clutch on his blanket, then swung his feet onto the floor and paced across the living area to his wet room. He had to wake up.

Waiting for another gel to preset, Ming turned back toward her console to continue her queries on the database system. Beside the keyboard, a reasonably recent mathematics text lay open. She'd found it in the library and received permission from Able Tatarka to borrow it for three days.

She glanced toward the other end of the long table. In a

shallow bowl, scattered over a nest of smooth black pebbles, lay ten pure white johnnistars. Able had brought them with the math text. Feeling vaguely guilty, she seated herself on the swivel chair.

"Old School" proved a dead end, but suspecting as much, she abandoned that route of inquiry (in case the Ops room techs watched) and found an official Renasco history. Ponderously composed, it still held her attention while the half hour passed.

Scrolling past a section on import-export quotas for client worlds, Ming found herself sitting up straight. Her fingers wanted to fly automatically through a letter-number-command combination. *I wonder what it is.*

Quickly she blanked the screen and let her fingers run across the keys, almost twenty strokes in a sequence so automatic it must have been drilled into her.

Nothing happened. She repeated. Nothing again.

She seized a sketch pad. Seating herself at the keyboard again, she jotted down the sequence so she wouldn't forget it. She'd worked and worked to regain wiped numerical skills, but didn't trust herself to remember this now.

Then, on a hunch, she punched up the +BIO+ program. She keyed in +TIEG INNIG+, but before entering the request, she added that mysterious sequence.

A screen full of data appeared, ending with a partial notation that overflowed screen space available.

It was a codebreaker sequence! She peered close. To her astonishment, Tieg had begun training at the Renasco academy, but hadn't graduated. Expelled, instead, for "manslaughter of fellow student" and "destruction of Company property."

Manslaughter. Then, he had . . . he had killed, according to Renasco. How much credence was the Company's judgment worth?

"Mother, Abriel Innig, convicted on accomplice-to-smuggling charges, N.A. 4512."

The same year as my conviction. Dear clancestors, there could be a connection. The entry followed his family back two generations. The sole child of siblingless parents, raised in Vinnsing, Nexos System—

His file was edited for the public because his record's not clean, she realized with a shiver. Beneath her con-

sciousness, memory was rising. She blanked the
screen . . .

No. No, it would not come.

Frustrated, she shut her eyes and pulled one deep
breath. Beside the keyboard lay the scribbled codebreaker
sequence.

What else might it open?

Earlier in the week, she had come upon a blocked directory. She dug for it, keyed it up again, added the mysterious sequence, then entered the request.

Ten subdirectories appeared. She chose one at random.
When it did not open, she tried it again with the
codebreaker.

Twelve additional keywords.

Ming sprang off her desk chair. She couldn't begin lettering the gel yet, but she had to think. What kind of illicit
security-foiling code had she stumbled upon? Who taught
it to her? She might be asking for all kinds of trouble if she
went on pursuing these avenues. Leaning over the johnnistars, she sniffed their heavy, sweet perfume.

Then she would proceed cautiously, for she had fed in
that sequence five times already. She glanced at the
screen. Almost time.

*Time, yes, time. How long will it take them to come for
you?*

Maybe they won't.

Returning to the work table, she set to lettering. An
hour passed, then two.

*The access must have held without activating alarms.
Where did I learn this—how was it used before—?*

Her conviction. Blessed All, this had to connect. She
considered destroying that incriminating scrap of paper,
then decided to hide it instead. Crossing to the console, she
tore the sheet free from the pad, folded it in quarters, and
studied her beautiful new room for hiding places. If
Renasco wanted to find it, it would be found. But perhaps,
in some innocuous place, it might escape notice for some
time.

Eyeing the window curtains, she shook her head. She
examined divider screen, carpet, wet room, cabinets. *Under the console?* No, too obvious.

Where?

She tucked it inside the math text and shoved the weighty volume into a cabinet. That would cover her for now.

Two days passed, with Tieg unarmed while Renasco occupied Anslanding. But he began to breathe easier for another reason: Ming must not have given that test message to Huekk. Curan's return signal he found slipped into a computer note regarding a portrait sitting time, but he remained too busy to look her up personally. Frustrating.

Returning from breakfast at Staff Dining, he rounded the hall corner and swung into his room.

Every cupboard door hung open, the couch cushions lay crooked, and the area carpet had been flopped over. After one glance around, he sprang toward the inner room, hoping to find his life's work intact.

The files lay open there, too, processor boards unsnapped from consoles and strewn atop instrument cases. He leaned one arm against the doorway and groaned.

A short laugh spun him toward the hall door. Just inside its frame, Zardir Huekk rocked from one foot to the other. Had Ming betrayed him, after all?

No, McMikall's missed. An icy shiver danced down Tieg's spine, but he didn't dare let Huekk see discomfiture. He must be innocent, outraged.

Outrage? Easy. "Missar Huekk." He took a step toward the mutant. "What have you had to do with this disruption in my private rooms?"

"You might well ask." Huekk's reedy voice carried a sneer. "There's a disappearance reported, and Her Grace is under pressure from her supervisors to find the man. Apparently he worked for Renasco under loose control. A housekeeping employee saw the missing man in this area, so all the rooms along this hall have been searched by my subordinates. This evening, when the main shift is done and twenty-two employees get home at once, this hall will be an entertaining place—but the real entertainment will come when Her Grace finds out what happened."

All the rooms. He, then, was not particularly suspected yet. "Searched for what?" he asked, burying damp hands in his pockets.

"Things," Huekk drawled. "Traces. Unfortunately, the

man was gone quite a while before anyone reported him
missing. Must have been a very loose contact. And you,
Innig. Just because you're Her Grace's prize pet doesn't
mean you're invulnerable to general search. You remember that."

Steadily Tieg returned the little man's gaze, until
Huekk backed out through the open door.

Tieg shut it. He should work in the studio now—compose in a script book—and clean the rooms later, when he
was calmer. *They must not have found the pistol. Oh,
Ancient Ones, have I had a close call! If someone had
found it in here—*

*Or were they looking for something else, and is all this
a cover?*

In a cupboard, tumbled inside a packet of odd souve-
nirs, he found his mother's ring.

Relieved, he held it for a moment, letting it warm in his
hand to the glow point, fondling the memory of the first
time he saw it: his mother's open, beautiful joy, his own
delight.

Angrily he closed it away.

Huekk's men were looking for what, then? Old signs of
a struggle, scrapes on the walls? Bloodstains? He checked
under disarrayed couch cushions. There was his pressure-
writing slate, undisturbed.

Perhaps even Huekk is nervous with Renasco in town.

Returning to the studio, he began to inventory his
wreckage.

It wasn't as bad as he feared: nothing stolen or dam-
aged. The circuit boards would take an hour's testing and
reinstallation, but that was not major.

He leaned against the window and stared out.

Unexpected mayhem: like the day he'd arrived home
from school to find their home in disarray, his father dis-
traught, and his mother gone.

All for the sake of that pretty bauble. He'd smuggled it
to school that cruelest day to show Pell. The eerie dream
rose back into his mind, McMikall's face melting, trans-
forming into the one face he had always loved. He kept the
ring in memory of her, but wasn't it time to move that
crystal witness of the past into present reality?

He'd wanted to try an experiment with its odd qualities

for some time. Perhaps now was the moment, to help heal his memories, and begin new ones.

Ming finished drawing a character and drew her injection pen free from the gel medium, then hunched down beside the working table to eye the letter from another angle. From down here, the twists of ribbon transformed themselves into the letter *S*—crudely, but legibly. She had done a row of *A*'s, now, and from the low angle, each appeared as a different letter. Holjpip had asked for this project, so one set gel could carry a double message.

Straightening, she stretched her tired shoulders and snapped the pen's cap on to keep the nib from going dry. Seven letters more, and she promised herself a short break with the chapter on conic geometry.

She'd gotten a late start this morning, after following Huekk's aides through her room from closet to cupboard, tidying after them and asking questions they refused to answer. Her codebreaker sequence, slipped into a jumpsuit pocket hanging in the closet, escaped attention. The aides' comments concerning some missing man encouraged her. She suspected it concerned the mysterious, violent "inspection team."

Last night she searched the data base, entry after entry, using the codebreaker. Some she blanked immediately, finding lists, sets of coordinates, bits of nothing.

Now, an *A* that would become a *T*.

Just before noon, aching for a rest, she arched her back and headed again for the screen. Another list appeared. Guessing anything vital lay concealed under an inconspicuous heading, she chose the least descriptive title, "Oneday."

Another list. Ready to blank the screen, she paused with her hand over the keyboard.

Along the left margin, names; to their right, instructions—no different from many she had seen.

But those names, and those instructions . . .

Larris Donahoe, Central Enforcement, activate reserves and await orders.

Garren Eden, HolLanCorp Hydroelectric, to emergency status.

There was more—a page more. Breath caught in Ming's windpipe as she read on:

Axis Taylor, Newport Comm Downlink. Shut down except on direct order. Broadcast prearranged declaration of . . .

Instantly Ming blanked the screen, but she remembered what she had seen, and the keystroke sequence that raised the file.

Holjpip was planning insurrection.

Oh . . . my . . . clancestors. . . . She rocked back on the swivel chair. It would be wonderful if this world went independent, free of Renasco.

Free: The second thought made her quiver. *This is it, Ming. Your ticket to freedom, now, today. Take the codebreaker to Zardir Huekk. Bring up this "Oneday" file and walk free, board a shuttle without luggage, collect your reward.*

On the other hand, Holjpip could be sending someone this moment to check on the file's activity, or could be reaching for her collar transmitter.

Only one thing Ming could do against that possibility. She wasn't going to make a stinking mess of herself again. She paced into the wet room, took care of business, then ambled out again.

Now. If she chose to tell Renasco, to fulfill the orders that had brought her here, she must hurry.

Could she? She fingered a pebble near the edge of Able's flower bowl. Freedom . . .

Never. Not after all she'd seen and learned at Holjpip's villa. If anything, she owed Holjpip her help.

Hastily she glanced at the time. Only two minutes gone. She paused at the window and stroked a pale tan curtain. Could this information benefit her clansmen who survived? She had found something others would want to know about, at least three powerful others. If she could wait out the five minutes it would take a guard dispatched from the Ops room to reach her, she would know if that knowledge was hers and free.

If They came for her, she could hide nowhere, wearing the collar. Better, then, to be caught practicing.

She refilled her pen with manganese blue. Capital *F*, now—turning it to *A*, *B*, and *C* from ninety degrees away

came easily, but to make it appear from the low angle as a
D took painstaking work. After six twisting strokes, she
pulled the pen free and checked her work.

No.

Try again.

Despite her resolve, a vision of Huekk's congratulations
stirred her most selfish desires: a glimpse of freedom, of life
without the Renasco collar. She had to tell someone about
"Oneday." Why not gamble with it for all she could gain?

But once she told anyone, it would set activity in motion she'd be helpless to stop. There was no real escape,
only a choice of people to throw in with, and a confidence
given could never be recalled.

So, think. What do you value?

That made the choice easier. She stood, pen in hand,
steadying the nib over her cellose block. She could never
take this information to Renasco with a sure heart. If she
followed her first urge and chose to tell Tieg, he would
offer Her Grace the aid of the Old School. The notion
made her vaguely jealous—-and nervous. If he'd killed
someone, might he do so again?

*Stop being silly. This has nothing to do with that.
Think.*

Ming clenched her pen hand and started another letter. If she did nothing at all?

Things might go on as before. So long as she could keep
Zardir Huekk away, she could live contentedly here. The
notion shocked her, and she straightened again. Not long
ago she had passionately wanted freedom, but with Tieg,
this could be a good life, and she could go on looking for
her crewmates.

Unable to work and argue with herself at the same
time, she sat down beside the table and worked. The row
of letters began to stretch below the gel's surface. From
the top, each *F* looked slightly different; it would never be
an elegant hand, but it would approach rustic beauty, particularly if text required no double letters. Bracing her
hand against the working frame for the entry stroke of an *F*
that would metamorphose into a Zed, she shifted her seat.

Now, consider the final alternative. Consider going to
Holjpip.

That did it. She thrust her pen into the solvent beaker

and rested her head over crossed arms on the desk. Holjpip would have her killed or memory-wiped, if she came alone with what constituted the ultimate threat to Her Grace's security. Anyone who'd seen the overview of that plan would be a danger to Holjpip, particularly with inspectors in the area who could interrogate at will.

Coming with the offer of Old School assistance, though, she might survive the encounter unthreatened. Holjpip had hidden that program, therefore must want it hidden for some time yet. Insane to have filed it on the villa data base, at all? Maybe not, when personal codes were allegedly invulnerable.

Where did I learn that codebreaker?

She glanced over at the console. An hour had passed. Time for lunch, and They hadn't come. She was safe.

Ming eyed her letter row from down at its side. Here the letters looked less plain, but without doubt she had an entire alphabet—almost. Quickly she tried a manganese blue *F*-Zed. *There.*

A message alert buzzed on her screen. She crossed back to the computer.

+WOULD YOU BE FREE FOR A WALK ON THE BEACH?— T.+

She exhaled relief. *Certainly,* she typed back. *Ten minutes to clean up.*

Swirling her pens in the solvent, she tried to finish the mental argument. *Easiest,* she told herself firmly as she snapped one pen back into its case, *to do nothing. Say nothing.* It felt uncanny to hold this kind of control in her hands for once. *As soon as you choose, you're Ming Nobody again, caught in swirl currents. Until then, you hold a key.*

He met her at the bottom of the stairs, wearing a fantastic new outfit, layers of fabric shading from intense spring green over his shoulders down to black forest near his heels. His fingers twitched when he pulled them from its pockets, as if he had just seen an ancestor's ghost, but he watched her descend the last flight, then took and pressed both her hands.

She squeezed back, then bent down for one shoe.

"If you'll keep them on, we can walk along the bottom of the cliffs today."

He held her hand as they walked up the beach's stony

head. Waves' crash, kye-di-dees' cries, and the warmth of Tieg Innig's hand filled Ming's senses. Yet his hand trembled whenever his grip loosened momentarily, and it occurred to her that Huekk's aides said the search this morning was general. Maybe he was in trouble. "Is everything all right?" she asked finally.

"Oh, I—" He pushed white hair back from his face and squinted up at the sun. That outfit looked hot. "Well, the search this morning didn't help anything. I was afraid they'd destroyed all my recordings, but they're just jumbled. I needed some distance from being angry, before I could get back to work."

Silent again, they picked a path along the cliffs' base toward the point where the waterline curved close. There, huge irregular boulders replaced the small fallen stones they'd crossed. Ming braced a hand against a jagged black behemoth and carefully stepped around it.

Tieg lowered onto a long, flat rock and kicked off his shoes. Ming joined him, not too close. Afraid she'd tell everything if she opened her mouth, she concentrated on watching the waves, tracing shapes with one finger in a thin layer of sand blown up onto the rock, waiting to hear why he'd called her down.

"Ming," Tieg said, speaking loudly over the swash of waves, "I'd like you to do some work for me. Nothing to do with . . . Curan. But I have a jewel that's been in my family for some time. I'd like it reset."

"Wire work?" she asked. "What do you want made? A ring? A pendant?"

"No, not wire work. Something more complicated."

She shifted her seat on the boulder so she could study him. High above his face, the cloudless sky shone nearly manganese blue. "I give up."

"I've had the stone for years. And for years—my father showed me the effect—I've known bringing it near certain circuits sets up resonances of its own, superimposes odd rhythms on my recordings."

She flicked hair out of her face. "Why?"

He pursed his lips. "No idea. I can't wear it performing, and I've kept it away from my instruments for that reason, so it's been put aside for a long time." Drawing his feet up, he wrapped his arms around both knees. "It was my mother's, you see, so I haven't had the heart to tamper with the setting. But . . ." His voice trailed away.

Ming sat waiting for him to finish, staring upland over his shoulder at long trailers of cijuli vine that dangled from the cliff's edge. Each leaf, she knew, would be pierced at vein points by its clinger tendrils. She wished she'd had a chance to save that rejected invitation gel.

"Well." He thrust his feet out again. "I want to find out how it does this. I think the search this morning made me realize how badly I've wanted to know, but for years I've put off the experiment."

For sentimental reasons, she understood. Spray from a breaking wave blew mist into her face, and she wiped it dry.

"I've been wondering," he went on. "Suppose it could be set in an amplifier circuit of its own. Something that looked like something else, in case anyone from the Company were to see. A plaque, maybe, or a nameplate, done in calligraphy. Generally available circuitry is microscopic; no one would look twice at something this large."

"With metallic inks?" Ming asked. It made sense. "And the hardened gel would provide insulation."

"Exactly." His eyes lit. "Exactly. I can draw you the circuit I need, from setting to switch. But can you get the inks, and the time to carry it off?"

"Inks, certainly. Her Grace asks for sparkle and gleam effects often, so I know the inks are available. And time, well, anything like this counts as exercise, when I show Staff Central my work schedule. I have several practice projects on my timeplan, but I can move them. This sounds much more interesting. What kind of a stone is it?"

"It's a ring. I assume you can return the stone to its setting when we've finished the experiment?"

Evaded again. She tried a different line of inquiry. "As long as it doesn't melt at twist-welding temperatures, I think I should be able to. Or you could have a jeweler do it."

"I'd . . . prefer to keep it quiet."

His mother had been convicted on accomplice-to-smuggling charges. The stone was probably illegal to possess. Ming brushed dug-in sand grains off her palm, sending a finger-length crustacean scuttling under a rock.

"Willing to try?"

"Yes, of course. Did you bring the ring with you?"

"No. As I said, it's locked away. But I'll have it for you later."

He had already eaten, so she lunched alone. In an hour, he called her to his room.

"And the power cell? Where does that go?" Leaning over Tieg's workbench, she followed his tracing finger across a paper while he explained each crossing and connection.

He rubbed his lip. "If I understand this right, the stone will provide its own power."

"Radioactive?"

"Something like that, apparently."

"No problem, I guess," she said. Her shoulder rested against his.

"I'll pay for silver inks."

She smiled; this would have halved her cred balance. Resting her eyes, she glanced up at the drab brown workroom curtain, then from side to side at electronic consoles. "All this must have cost you plenty."

"Some, yes. Some is Holjpip's, some was my father's. He never did find a patron. As far as I know, he still works the odd concert, the occasional sponsorship. I've . . . lost touch with him."

Ming nodded, thinking, *If you and your Old School are ever caught, he won't be taken in for questioning.* "I understand." It would be so natural to kiss him, comfort him. She leaned closer—

Tieg's screen buzzed. "Just a minute," he said.

Irked, but careful not to touch, Ming gave the board on her right a close visual examination. Dials, slides, tab controls; all this equipment, plus a set in the centrum, constituted quite an investment, no matter who paid for it.

The sound of his step turned her around. He wore a mocking expression as he recrossed the studio. "The official inspection team will come to the villa the day after tomorrow, Jury at Central tells me, and I'll spend the next several days on call."

For some reason, she still felt she ought to console him. She laid a hand on his arm. "The centrum is a pretty spot."

"Yes, but I won't be able to help you with this."

Ming spun her stool, took hold of his desktop with both hands, and examined his diagram again. "If I start work on it now, maybe I can finish tomorrow, before They arrive."

He cocked one bushy eyebrow. "It looks like a lot of work."

"It will be. That's all right, this is interesting."

"You will sleep."

"Oh, yes . . . father." Ming laughed at his protective expression. "I'll sleep."

W

Tieg scowled when he met Ming at his door late the next morning. "You didn't sleep. Your eyes are almost black again."

"I slept enough. Here's your nameplate."

"Nameplate?" He shut the door behind her.

Smiling, she held up the thin, hard slab she'd finished in the night. It was true she'd slept—two hours right at dawn. She hadn't eaten since lunch the day before, but she didn't need to tell him that.

Tieg took the slab. Just larger than his spread hands, from the top it gave his name, followed by a quote from one of Holjpip's ancient books:

> *Just as my fingers on these keys*
> *Make music, so the self-same sounds*
> *On my spirit make a music, too.*

"I like that," he said softly. "Thank you."

"Now look at it from the side."

From that angle, he'd see the circuits. He was visibly

startled. "Ancient Gods, Ming," he breathed. "It's incredible. The design work alone . . ."

Staring back at him, she shrugged. "It took most of yesterday afternoon to dream it up, but I've been practicing this kind of thing. I'm beginning to think from two angles."

"Amazing," he whispered.

He'd never reacted so openly to her previous work. "Let's set your stone, then."

"Shh. I'll meet you in the studio."

Ming took back the small slab and crossed in front of the console to his private room. A space lay cleared near the window. She waited, clasping the gel. It felt warm. One minute, then two, then he slipped through the door and held out his right hand. On the smallest finger gleamed a ring. Pure red at its center and citron-gold at the edges, the jewel glimmered in the dim room. "Listen." Touching three buttons with his left hand, Tieg activated an amplifier, then drew his ring hand close to its front panel.

Buzz-zzt-zzzzzzz-t: The irregular pattern reminded her of distorted speech. "Tieg. That's strange."

He touched two more controls, and a soft recorded suite began to play. Her head felt light, as if something she almost remembered fought to surface. She blinked exhausted, burning eyes. Perhaps if she stood up, she'd stay more wide awake. "Do you want the stool?" she offered.

"No. You're the one who's going to work. Did you bring—"

Ming pulled one hand free of her pocket, holding her fine metalworking tools.

"Here, then." Tieg jerked the ring from his finger and held it out.

It came from his mother. No matter how illegal this is, it represents something he's lost. Ming took it reverently by the gold band, careful not to touch the pulsating jewel. "Do you have a clamp?"

Securing it to the workbench, she saw an eerie vision: hundreds of such crystals, tumbled together into a small metal locker. *Dreaming, Ming. Wake up and work.* She reached down to loosen a prong. As she touched her tiny jeweler's knife to the stone, her arm tingled. "Oh."

"What's wrong?" Tieg leaned close.

"I guess I am a little tired. If you'd bring me a glass of water, I'd thank you."

Five minutes later, just after the music changed from major to minor, she locked a pair of tweezers around the loosened stone and eased it from its mounting. "It's lovely," she said. "Look at it pulse. How does it do that?" She glanced up over her shoulder.

Tieg stood close by, his white tunic falling open at the neck. He shrugged. "I guess you understand these are not exactly legal."

"Of course. Slide me the nameplate, now."

Between the words "Tieg" and "Innig," she'd shaped a socket into which four threads of metallic ink protruded for contacts. Cautiously, she dropped the jewel into place.

A wave of dizziness threw her off-balance. Careful not to jar the amplifier circuit, she leaned back on the stool. "Tieg, I have to lie down for a minute."

He supported her out to the white couch. "Thank you for doing so much work on this. But I wish you'd sleep."

"I enjoyed it." She slipped off her shoes and propped her feet up. "You can probably finish the rest. Here." From her pocket she pulled a thin net of silver threads. "Slip this over the slab and warm it with your breath. It should seal things in place, but it's removable with solvent."

"Good," he said. "The stone usually shines brightest when it's warm, anyway."

Carrying the thin net, he vanished around the corner. Ming lay still, her eyes closed. The locker of jewels—something to do with Shan—and—Tieg's mother—? *Sweat. If only I weren't so tired and hungry.*

"I think I have it," she heard from the next room.

She used the back of the couch to pull herself upright. "Let me see."

"Listen." As she drew close, he tapped the tiny silver switch she'd embedded in the capital *T*.

Pure light exploded through her head. Blinded from the inside, holding both hands over her eyes, Ming reeled back toward the couch.

Tieg seized her shoulders to guide her. "What's wrong?"

The room faded in, out, in. "The slate," she whispered.

"Where do you hide it?" It wasn't Tieg standing over her, but her father. *They'd like you along as apprentice, Ming. If it's what you really want, I won't stand in your way.*

She locked her fingers together and gently said, *I do. It will pay all our debts and bring honor to the clan. And I want to see space, Father.*

A locker full of glimmering stones.

She grasped it in both hands. Too flat, too light—it had shrunk, was empty—

It was a pressure-sensitive slate, and Tieg Innig crouched beside her. "Should I call Medical?" he whispered.

"No!" With shaking hands, she traced two words on the slate's surface: *I remember.*

Ming! You will follow orders or I will have you disciplined! Arms crossed, Jiadra took another step toward her. Weapons officer.

Communications. She had been communications. Sound echoed through the tiny spaceship, an irregular buzzing like distorted speech, like that of the—

Sunstone.

Her eyes flew open again. Tieg still knelt, shaking his head. *Sun*—she wrote onto the slate, then, *Shan. Lur.*

"What?" His lips formed the word.

She wrote again.

Ming's pupils dilated as if she were drugged. Tieg read the slate once, twice.

Twenty years ago, it said. She'd been in cold sleep for twenty years. Twenty years ago, his mother brought home this sunstone.

Had Ming Dalamani brought it to Nexos?

He jerked to his feet and crossed the room.

Because of this stone, his mother had been taken. For an instant, he wished Ming had never been born.

Easy . . . easy. Even if it's so, it's not her fault.

The sunstone crystal made her remember, somehow. Amplified, it threw her silly. He glanced back over his shoulder and saw her write again. When she dropped the slate, her arm limp, he crossed to read the drifting scrawl.

Father. Don't marry Jiadra.

Quietly, gently, he cared for her the rest of the day,

while she slipped between past and present. Her pulse and
breathing remained steady; she didn't seem to lie in any
physical danger, so he'd take her to Medical tomorrow, if
she hadn't recovered. For now, he put the music back on—
loudly—and tried to make sense of her mumblings. She
had smuggled sunstones, though those brief references
came between long discussions with lost family members.
Within an hour, Tieg knew her father, deceased mother,
and cousins all by name. Uprooted from a clan system,
Ming lay absorbed in memories of old security. Thank the
Ancients that couch lay hidden from his console.

He poured a glass of milk and sipped at it. Obviously
the amplified sunstone did this to her. But how? He'd
turned off the switch without effect. Ming still lay in her
trance.

Her left, verbal hemisphere had been selectively
blocked. That was a "known." But as an artist, Ming possessed a right hemisphere as highly developed as most
individuals' verbal sides, and links between hemispheres
most people lacked. Somehow, the amplified crystal must
have stimulated that linkage. The radiation it emitted, that
irregular, speechlike pattern?

He glanced down once more. Her face wore a raptured
expression. Whatever memory she held now, temporary
loss only hallowed it.

When his midday meal arrived, he met the staffer at
the door and took the tray from her, then shared soft bites
with Ming. She ate greedily, not speaking, then drew farther from the world and deeper into a nearly catatonic
state.

Not long after lunch, her eyes closed, and she began to
snore softly.

Tieg returned to the studio and tapped the amplifier on
again. The crystal pulsed and buzzed, confined in its wire
net. He tapped the switch. It darkened and grew quiet.

Ming woke at dawn the next morning, tightly wrapped
in a blanket, to find Tieg lying beside her on the floor.

She shook her head to clear it. One eye seemed to see
her father resting in his tiny sleeping cubicle over their
apartment's living area, but the other eye saw Tieg. His
blanket had slipped from bare shoulders, and brown stub-

ble covered his cheeks and chin. No other man *had* held her, except her father. She remembered, now.

He rolled over and looked up into her eyes. "Ming," he said softly. "You're awake."

"What did I do?" she murmured, wondering if the Ops room knew or cared where she was. "Sleep all day and night?"

Tieg rolled free of his blanket. Beneath it, he wore silken-looking trousers. He stood and scratched his head with both hands, then sat down on the couch's edge and ran one finger along her jawline. "Some of it didn't look much like sleeping. You talked."

Evidently, hiding her presence didn't concern him. She reached for his wrist and caught it as his hand touched her ear. "I remember," she whispered.

He took up the slate from where it lay beside his feet. *I know. Heard you. Glad for you.*

Blinking away the vestiges of sleep, she watched him cross to the wet room.

It had been a long time. She scrambled to her feet. "Me first, Tieg? Please?"

After she finished, he showered. On his console, she read, +READY 0800 EVEN UP, CENTRUM.+

"I have to go out," he said on his way out of the wet room, tightening a cuff band on an iridescent blue shirt and dropping the slate on the couch. "I play all day for the inspection team. I'm glad to see you coming around. Little York wine sneaks up on you."

You're welcome to stay, the slate read, *if you're not ready to live in both worlds at once.*

She did remember. She remembered everything, now, from the day the Clan Caucus set *Opa*'s departure, through capture and trial, training, and thirty-two days' service in this villa on the hill. Old School, too, and the mysterious codebreaker: Shan's, she realized. She blanked Tieg's slate and wrote quickly. *TX—fine now, must talk soon.* Standing, she found herself steady, and famished.

On his way out of the wet room again, Tieg paused. "You're welcome," he said. What he wrote was: *Tomorrow, at earliest.*

"I'll go now," Ming said. Tieg's concerned expression warmed her. *Scatter* his obvious hurry; she wanted to take him down to the shore and tell him everything. "See you tomorrow morning, Tieg?"

He hooked one arm around her shoulders. "Ming," he whispered, "I'm so glad for you." He kissed her, and she marveled that a touch so brief could carry so much meaning. Then he hurried to the door. She wouldn't be able to open it from inside. If she wanted to get out, she had to leave now.

Lyra eyed her suspiciously while dishing a double breakfast of cereal and fruit and a roll of mixed meat. "What are you doing up this early? You don't look like you've slept."

"I caught a touch of something yesterday and slept most of the day, so I wasn't tired last night. I'm all right now, I think." She felt jumpy, as if she wore a sign on her back lettered, I'VE SUDDENLY REMEMBERED MY ENTIRE PAST. ASK ME ABOUT IT.

"I heard from Rimi yesterday." Lyra paused while both held the plate. "They've had gangs at Goodsprings, too. Taking things. Our friend Missar Dourthe was killed when Renasco people stampeded a herd of drone workers."

"Killed?" she asked, thinking with relief, *Then he won't be able to harm Rimi or Coey!*

Lyra nodded. "I know," she said solemnly. "Doesn't seem real, does it, when someone you know dies?"

"N-no." Balancing her tray, Ming wandered off to find a seat. Memories faded in and out while she ate: her mother's last illness; sleepless nights grieving beside a tiny cubical urn of ashes. Days spent fasting, wondering what to do with her life and odd talents. After eating, absorbed in sorrow as fresh as yesterday, she didn't notice her route until she nearly reached the centrum wall.

She stared through glass and trees at the elegant series of fountains. She must have come this way unconsciously looking for Tieg. Bless him for letting her sleep off the worst of this disorientation!

Beyond the fountains, motion caught her eye. A man and a woman in midranking Renasco security uniforms marched slowly along, each gripping an arm of a small, defective form—

No.

Blood congealed in Ming's veins. All her muscles went flaccid.

This was surely more memory, surfacing in a hallucination. The small, broad-shouldered woman between the guards had gray hair and shriveled legs far spread, dragging along while the others tried to hurry her.

Shan! Ming wanted to scream. *Shan!*

She pressed one palm to the glass wall for support. Footsteps passed behind her back, and she realized she was loitering. Trembling, she turned aside and sauntered up the corridor along the clear wall, staring through glass. It *was* Shan, with this uniformed couple. How, in all the worlds of the Belt?

From this distance, her cousin looked impossibly old and almost emaciated. Renasco had given Shan no respectable occupation for her "modicum of dignity," the way they trained Ming for use. That made sense, though. Shan —*Shan!*—had cracked Renasco's codes to commit the theft. Shan's memory must have been wiped clean.

Executed, hah! Indeed, Renasco hated waste—the waste of a pair of hands—"drones," Lyra had just called the totally wiped. Perhaps Shan had been such a one, twenty years ago. By now, her memory might have returned. Shan would be little more than a slave *(but with all the native intelligence she ever possessed,* Ming reminded herself). How she must have suffered, these long, long years.

Who were those people with her? What did they do for Renasco?

With her best effort at unobtrusiveness, Ming tailed the trio until they vanished into the Ops room. She couldn't follow there, nor could she loiter in North Upper under the stares of Holjpip's security staff. Neither knowing nor caring if the query was proper, she rushed to Staff Central.

Mere Jury Bertelsen fielded her questions with curt answers, her arms folded in a hostile pose. From Ming's description, the man and woman were transfer guards, conveying a prisoner or newly purchased servant from one owner to another. No, said servant/prisoner had not yet been logged in. Mere Bertelsen didn't know her name. Yes, the three were lodged together. Guest suite number thirty-one seventeen.

Ming reeled back up the hall. If Shan were being added

to the villa staff, she needed only to wait until those guards left, and then she could—

No. Her insides curdled. She couldn't wait. Shan had not been logged in as staff. Suppose she was meant as a gift for the Renasco inspectors? "They like cripples, too," Lyra had said.

No, no. Holjpip was above slave-giving. But how long could Ming count on remaining here at the villa, now that the inspection looked imminent, and "further orders" might come with it?

Ming fingered the short hair between clan tails. She must see Shan, speak with her, see if memory did return after years passed, help her if she could. Suppose Holjpip meant to put her on staff, and treat her as well as Ming had lived over these weeks?

Well and good, but if the inspection team took Ming away, she'd never have more than that single glimpse of her cousin.

Seeing neither the hallway nor the people she passed, Ming wrestled with herself.

At her own doorway, she reached a decision. Somehow, under some pretense, she'd wait in room thirty-one seventeen until they brought Shan there.

Holjpip rose behind her desk as the pair of employees passed her door guards. Between them limped the shriveled, gray-haired woman. Holjpip blanched. For years, she had surrounded herself with men and women who, if not actually young, looked young. She hated facing disfigured cripples of age or radiation. In this creature, Holjpip saw a woman she herself might have become, given a minor chromosomal breakage, and had she not gone on rejuv early.

The uniformed woman bowed. "Madam, the mere you requested."

Dressed in Renasco colors herself today, for the inspection—the black officer's uniform with blue-trimmed copper collar band—Claude Yerren thrust herself away from the wall of screens and swept one arm forward in an imperious gesture. "She should have been taken to Staff Central, not here. She offends the ambassador."

"Wait." Holjpip gestured impatience to Yerren. "Name and business?"

The uniformed woman stepped forward and saluted formally. "Major Dubio, Madam, and Captain Eillis. We are transferring the property-person of Ashan Dalamani." The major gestured seaward with a broad-fingered hand. "Your operation is magnificent, Madam. I apologize for the delay. Company staff intercepted our shuttle from *Anfis* station and advised us to stay shipboard on *Doran* until today, warning that its officials needed to bring a looting situation under control. We sincerely hope your people suffered no damage."

Holjpip acknowledged the major's salute, staring at the crippled legs and grotesquely overdeveloped shoulders of her new servant. Apparently her offer had been accepted. She wrenched her attention higher. Soft chin and ivory complexion did suggest a blood relationship with Ming Dalamani. "Mannheim is one of the most comfortably habitable worlds colonized thus far. We like it well—and, yes: Today, the city will be still. Staff Central." Holjpip delivered her usual speech without bothering to soften her voice. "My doormen will direct you."

Then she looked away from the retreating trio. She would have to deal with this second Mere Dalamani as soon as she got the inspectors out of the way. Fortunately, Ashan was distinctly recognizable. She would jar Ming's memory, if it could be touched.

Claude Yerren bent over the desk. "I assume you have a good reason for purchasing that one."

"Yes, Claude. A long-term goal."

The adjutant nodded. Yerren knew what goal she referred to, though they did not speak openly of it. Goodsprings One had room in its dormitory for many more. Nodding, Holjpip stretched her back, ignoring cramping in her midsection again. She couldn't take time out for a rejuv treatment this week. "But we must work with her later. As soon as we finish with . . . our inspection team."

Yerren glanced at the time.

Patiently she followed, all the long slow way across this huge building, until they let her sit down. Then, once her legs could rest from bearing her body's weight, it didn't matter how long the handsome people took.

It had been a long road back. Her original master had struck her the first time she volunteered a deduction from some conversation he'd thought her too bleary-brained to comprehend. But in time he came to value her powers of observation, because he could use them. People tended not to see her. They didn't want to see her; her presence made them feel awkward. So she vanished, and watched.

Her oldest memories were of the Camp, a training ground where she was treated with all the dignity of an animal. There, she'd been retaught to walk, to speak, to think. Teachers at the Camp had led her to believe they ruined her legs, and would ruin her arms as well, if she defied them. She had been glad to escape when that fueling-station officer bought her service, and after he'd tired of abusing her, his treatment hadn't been so bad, only wearing and tedious. She learned her defect was congenital. That comforted her, now.

For twenty years, watching and learning to pretend stupidity, she coped with a life she knew was not her first. Dreams, memories—aching, she always fought down the glimpses of past that occasionally came. Rarely shipboard, she still gleaned more from those trips than either of her previous owners guessed, and she took care to keep it so. Her talents lay in that direction, she sensed. She wished to know more, but her longing for dignity, security, and peace was stronger than curiosity.

A third owner, now. She would adjust. The female transfer guard stood. Shan heard the elegant, well-fed woman in purple say, ". . . conclude later, over a bite of lunch," and the pair clasped hands over the desktop. Shan eased up into the most comfortable standing position, where she could balance her weight between her legs, and waited for her transfer guards to lead her out the door.

V

As soon as Ming returned from Staff Central, she sat down on her bed, pulled her feet up under her, and spread out the villa map she'd obtained her first day here. Outdoors, greenery tossed in an offshore breeze.

Room number thirty-one seventeen, visitors' quarters, would be easy to find.

And the lock coded to someone else's palm print, she reminded herself, fingering an amethyst earring, *just as some transmitter is keyed to Shan's collar.* Lyra had mentioned access to master chips, once. Guests received room service, and for that the food crew needed entry.

She had long expected Lyra to spread rumors stemming from the midnight encounter at Goodsprings, but no word returned. Perhaps Lyra did know how and when to keep silent. If Ming asked her to help get into that room . . .

No. This time, you'd endanger her by including her.

Tieg? He would work all day, but this business with Shan would interest him keenly.

She certainly couldn't hope for help from anyone else on Holjpip's staff. Huekk's face appeared in her mind. . . .

A hand closed on her shoulder and dragged her to the courtroom's center floor. Dazed by the terrible spectacle just past, she looked up. High behind a shimmering glass window, a judge in copper-on-blue peered down as if wishing to examine the living face of the child-woman he was about to order killed.

So long as he hadn't pronounced the sentence, a part of her could pretend it would not happen to her, but Lur, Jiadra, Shan—she'd seen each given the injection, on the metal table . . . right there, in the front of the medico-legal chamber. Could she ask for life, when . . .

She flung her arms wide to shake off the belligerent Renasco guard and opened her eyes to the sunlight of Mannheim.

They'd given Ming the injection, too, a tourniquet's painful squeeze and a pin-thrust without the dignity of sterilization. A fake, all of it. After experiencing "death," Renasco's victims belonged to the Company with no memory of the terror.

Only . . . she remembered, now. Thinking of Huekk made her recall that most terrible intimidation of all, their mockery of a trial. She briefly considered destroying the incriminating paper with Shan's codebreaker written on it, then changed her mind. Here on Mannheim she felt safe, but it couldn't last. She would start looking for Shan at Staff Dining, with a second breakfast.

And she would get to Shan, whatever it took. Her best option was to try alone, without involving anyone else. She walked around the cloth room divider to her work table and drew open the top drawer. Inside, untouched between two sizes of metal rods left over from her nilly-pine sculpting, lay her clear packet of nilly beans.

Perhaps part of one. For the half hour, real time, it would affect her system, she could still blend in with other people, and for bursts of energy, she would be able to move quickly.

Maybe a quarter. Just once wouldn't burn her out.

Carefully she split the seal on the packet and pulled out one oblong bean. A whiff of its acrid odor turned her head. With her penknife, she halved it. Inside its hazel-brown skin gleamed dark creamy meat. She split each half a second time, then tucked the quarters into a hip pocket of her duty—

She faltered. Jumpsuit. The "duty suit" term had come back with the rest of her memory.

Well, it is a duty suit. She glanced around the room and tried to imagine escaping into Anslanding with her crippled cousin. Now that she could drive, she might check out a staff car alone. If it became necessary to get Shan away, she must hide her well and quickly, then return to explain to Tieg. Beyond her I.D. disc and a handful of local money she'd received as change down at Anslanding, she could offer Shan nothing except her own wits. Where . . . ?

Lyra's sister, Rimi! "Rimi's not afraid of any man that walks," Ming whispered, quoting Lyra, *and Rimi doesn't know either of us wears the collar.* They could hide the staff car near the Goodsprings One processing plant, where it might remain unnoticed, parked underground among rows of silver vehicles, while she took Shan up the short hill to the Cooperson-Dusenfeld home. For weeks, maybe. That would give them time to plan an escape from Mannheim, too.

Well. First, see her. Speak with her. Perhaps seeing Ming's clan-tails might jog a memory in Shan.

Seven minutes later, Ming sat at a corner table in Staff Dining with a fresh, sugary roll and c'fee. The hall had begun to get crowded. Like the home she and Shan had lost, it smelled of queerly mixed food and crowded bodies, jostling, hurrying, each individual on some private assignment. Lyra was busy on a far line and did not see her. From inside a near pair of serving doors, five couriers departed with covered trays for other parts of the villa.

Deliberately Ming swept her cup from the table. It clattered to the floor. "Sweat," she grunted. Nearby, a few workers turned her way, then ignored her again. Pretending irritation, she made for the double doors.

In a preparation room as vast as the serving area outside, long rows of countertops emitted clouds of steam, and grain smells mingled with those of meat and scrubbing compound. No one paid her any attention.

She turned left and searched along the slick metal wall. Wetvac—she seized one from an open rack. She might need to snatch it quickly, take it back, and clean up, if anyone challenged her presence here. There—on a low white counter, couriers' supplies lay: a stack of trays, a pile of covers.

"Here, now, what are you doing?"

At the approaching voice, Ming spun around. Between aisles of cooking pots, a guard stalked toward her. Blood drained from her hands, and then she recognized Able Tatarka—just as he brightened, recognizing her. The luck she'd begun to trust had just paid off in full.

She smiled, sincerely glad to see him. "I want to take a surprise to my friend Lyra in twenty-twelve. What's the chance I could borrow one of . . ." She let her voice trail off, glancing down into a small bowl full of blue chips the size and shape of the pink ones she'd used for coding her locks. They had to be the master keys Lyra mentioned.

"Lyra?" he asked, pursing full lips. "That wouldn't be a name for Tieg Innig, would it?"

"No," she exclaimed. After sending the bowl of flowers and shining pebbles, he must have seen her with Tieg again, about the villa. "No, Lyra works in here."

Apparently he read her genuine surprise. "I should escort you, but I'm on duty for ten minutes more. Can you wait?"

"N-no. Lyra's off in ten minutes, too. I have to beat her."

"Well, I trust you, Ming. You're a fine artist, and if that means so much to Her Grace, I can follow her lead. Here." With a broad hand, Able slipped a chip into her side pocket.

"Thank you," she whispered. "When Lyra asks how I got in, I'll tell her how nice you are." Then she seized a lightweight wetvac.

It took her one long minute to clean the mess off the floor, and she wondered if violet eyes watched. Leaning the 'vac against her empty place, she hurried from the dining room.

I trust you, Ming, she heard again. He'd never trust her after this, if word got back to him she'd lied. Kind Able. Feeling ashamed, she silently begged the All, *Please, let me catch Shan at the room!*

"See you in a while, Lyra."

"Bye, Amidel."

Clutching a covered bowl, Lyra left her workmate at an elevator and rushed along the skylit upper corridor toward Ming's new room. If she hurried, she might catch—

"Mere Lyra?"

At the sound of the male voice, she spun around. A guardsman stalked toward her, but not her friend Sperry. Smaller, black-haired, and slender enough to look more like a gymnast than a weight lifter, he paced closer. *Oh, dear. Caught smuggling succulus. Maybe he won't ask.*

"Yes?" she asked, gripping the bowl against her body.

He clasped his hands behind his back. "Ming Dalamani's friend Lyra?"

She laughed, and to her it sounded guilty. "Why, yes. Um, is there something I can do for you?"

He gave her a small, secretive smile. Deeply relieved, she smiled back, and as she did, she got a good look at him. He was better-looking than Mere Sperry, with intelligent movement to his . . . oh . . . *violet* eyes.

"No, not really. I've just gone off duty, too." He shook his head. "Are you taking a surprise to her room?"

"Well . . ."

Above his smile, one eye winked. *Oh, my. Arrest me. Please!*

"I was going to take this to her." She wedged open the bowl's lid. "I tried it on her once, and she couldn't eat it. I was trying again, but—well, I don't suppose you'd want it? She'd probably choke on it anyway."

Pursing expressive lips, he peered down into the bowl. "It smells wonderful, Mere Lyra. But I should report you."

"It's only a little bowl." She must find out this man's schedule. TATARKA, read the tiny nameplate on his chest. Hadn't Ming mentioned him?

"You're sure she doesn't like it?"

Lyra glanced up and down the long upper hall. "She didn't, the last time."

"Well. It happens this is my favorite, Lyra, and Ming's friends are mine, too. I'll take it. Next time, though, watch out for Security. All right?"

Solemnly, Lyra nodded.

He made a fist on one hip as he turned away. "The inspection team is due to arrive momentarily. I'd stay out of the hallways all day, if I could."

"Oh. Thank you, Mere Tatarka. I will."

The corridors seemed more crowded than usual for this time of the morning, and Ming marched along nervously. Someone might see her trying to enter. She might have brought a tray and cover—but no, she was dressed all wrong to be taken for kitchen staff. *Housekeeping. I'll be a supervisor, inspecting their room.*

Along the hallway, she forced herself not to glance from side to side except to check room numbers, ignoring a black-garbed guard as if she belonged here on business.

There: thirty-one seventeen. Press the panel.

It slid out from the wall. Drop in the chip, press again. The panel slid back out. At first Ming feared it hadn't worked, and she would have to begin again with a new plan. She worked the slippery chip free of its slot.

The door slid aside. Ming pocketed the chip and stepped in. No one was here. The apartment was even larger than Tieg's, done in blues and pale sea-foam green. The screen through which the Ops technicians might be watching her stood on her left, along the wall. She'd stand . . . right . . . here, near the door, to wait for Shan and the others. But first she snatched a towel from the wet room and draped it over one arm. A new floral scent tickled the edge of her sense, sharper than johnnistars.

Footsteps: The hall door slid open, the light flicked on, and a man strode in. Sapphire-blue gleamed on his collar. Tall, black-haired, and frowning, he carried an envelope of flimsies.

"Good day, sir." Ming glanced behind him for the others. "We've been . . . having trouble with one of the maids, so I was asked to inspect before your arrival." A second inspiration struck her, and she spoke before considering consequences. "Is everything to your satisfaction, here? Will your colleague require anything special?" *Oops. Where do I find extra supplies, if they want them?*

"No, no." He shut the door. "You needn't worry about the others. My colleague is taking the newly purchased servant to the cafeteria."

Ming thrust one hand into a duty suit pocket. *So much for luck—I missed Shan at Staff Dining!*

"But as for my satisfaction . . ." He crossed to the bed, sat down on it, and patted the covers next to him, smiling with what he must have thought was suavity. "Sit here and talk to me." Ming maintained her poise. For Shan, she could endure almost anything. Surely she'd be back soon.

He grinned as she sat down. "Tell me about Madam Langelleik, Mere, ah, I don't believe I caught your name."

"R-Rimi," she improvised. "Certainly, Missar—"

"Captain Eillis. Now, about Madam?"

"Madam Langelleik," Ming answered quickly, "is a fine manager and patron of the arts." He patted her hand, and her resolve to wait here for Shan weakened. *How can I get out of this bedroom?* "Do you know, Captain, the centrum of this villa is the loveliest place of all. There are any number of private nooks, where we could . . . talk." She tipped her head to one side and smiled into his eyes.

He grinned, showing gold-banded teeth. "Very, very nice," he said. "I did see your centrum, although I had little time to explore. Let's do that. Who knows when Madam will call us?" He touched a paging button pinned to one wrist.

Now what? Ming felt clammy as she let the captain guide her from his room, one hand at the small of her back. She knew no nook in the centrum would suit his intentions, so she ought to be safe—but if she hoped to see Shan, she must stick to this man like a ship's tractor.

As they turned one bend in the hallway, Eillis swept one hand around her neck, backed her against the wall, and kissed her. Caught totally unprepared, Ming did not resist for several seconds.

"Ah," he whispered. "That kind of housekeeping. I'd hoped so."

Spotting movement off to the left, Ming was startled to see Jury Bertelsen striding toward them, evidently on her way to work. One hand on a broad hip, Mere Bertelsen paused.

Captain Eillis's hands scalded at her waist and throat. Ming edged away, too late.

When she looked Mere Bertelsen's way again, the staffer had vanished. Ming's cheeks flamed as she led the Renasco man on up the hall, and she tugged at an amethyst earring.

W

Holjpip stood at the villa's front door, flanked by guards at the pillars. Claude Yerren waited at her shoulder as the motorcade rumbled closer. Holjpip tugged at a blue-trimmed cuff; she too wore Renasco colors for today's inspection.

One long cerulean limousine pulled into sight, then a second and a third. The inspectors could have come from Newport more efficiently by air bus, but this show of force through Anslanding's streets, like the looting and roadblocks, was a calculated display.

As the third car pulled into the emptied parking oval, five intensely blue air scooters dove in close formation from the wind-whipped seaside. They swept low over the motorcade, pivoted as a unit to the right, then peeled upward again to land one by one on the villa's roof.

Yes, thought Holjpip, keeping her chin pointed precisely ahead. *We see you. We are impressed.*

Uniformed drivers sprang from hatches to stand at attention. Two male passengers stepped from the first car, a man and a woman from the second, and with them . . . Holjpip frowned at the unmistakable form of Zardir Huekk. They'd met with him before inspecting her villa once before, too.

Another man and one more woman emerged from the third car. This woman caught Holjpip's attention by appearance alone: Her close-cropped hair was the same coppery shade as Holjpip's, and though she wore a man's style, no one could mistake her femininity. She carried herself proudly, head held high on a long, beautiful neck.

"Yerren," Holjpip whispered straight ahead, hands pressed against rough cloth at her thighs.

"Yes," Claude Yerren hissed in her ear. "It is."

Holjpip maintained that posture of attention while the first pair of officers strolled up the white walkway between vine-spiraled pillars, but only years of practice made it easy. *Galoubet. Renasco let you come.*

The first pair accepted her salute. "Our compliments on the lodgings at Newport," said the nearer man. Chief inspector's laurels gleamed on his black tunic's breast. "Most pleasant. Of course, you understand we felt the need to wait until Anslanding calmed down a bit, before we wished to enter it ourselves."

The underchief beside him added, "Yes, the forces, cooped up shipboard for weeks—" He clucked his tongue. "So uncontrollable."

Holjpip growled inside. "Welcome," she said.

Claude Yerren stepped from her place in formation, and Holjpip noticed she'd found time to have her curls trimmed short and neat. "Gentlemen, we shall begin your tour in the villa's centrum."

Holjpip gritted her teeth. Thrown off guard by seeing her daughter again after almost thirty years, she hadn't introduced Yerren. She would make no more such mistakes. "Yes, go with my adjutant."

The men swept through the villa's huge main doors, following Yerren.

The second pair stalked closer, Huekk between them, laughing raucously at some joke. The male inspector's ears, sliced and stretched into spirals, resembled long fruit-peelings, and his eye slits had been rotated ninety degrees by cutting through the brow bone and rebuilding skin and muscle, so whites showed above and below the irises, instead of side to side. She'd seen the new fashion, but its repulsive quality still struck deep at her sensibilities.

His female partner's blue eyes lay reoriented in the vertical, too. As Holjpip saluted and Huekk returned the gesture, the woman blinked, lids creeping inward from both sides. Renasco meant to rattle her, knowing she hated disfigurement: all standard inspection procedure. She wondered what other surprises her superiors held in reserve.

"Welcome." Holjpip swept one hand aside. "We welcome you with our best. Do go with the others into our centrum."

Finally, the third pair swaggered up the pillared walkway. Holjpip gave her clone-daughter the slightest of smiles. Galoubet had sought no such surgery, yet as she walked closer, age lines showed dark and scarlike, and Galoubet did not smile back. *My own child. No response?* Perhaps she'd been memory-wiped, or she feared mistreatment. Renasco had held her apart for years. Today, Holjpip guessed, was her debut.

A puff of wind carried the sharp scent of newly blooming pegsbreath. Holjpip's stomach twisted. She saluted the pair. "Welcome to Prime Row," she said. "Galoubet, it is good to see you on Mannheim."

Her shoulders square and her waist slim, Galoubet's expression showed intelligent reserve, and on her, the dress uniform looked attractive. To Holjpip's shock, she also wore chief-inspector's laurels. "Madam, you have not changed. I see this is your home, now."

"This is my home." Half dazed, half offended by Galoubet's lack of reaction, Holjpip flicked a glance to the man beside her daughter. He, too, had his eyes realigned to the vertical, and a compact pistol under his arm. Was he a bodyguard or a hostage-keeper? Again Holjpip waved inward. "Come into the centrum. We await your report with keen interest."

Galoubet laughed, a raucous, ugly-sounding crow. "Yes, Madam, we feel certain you do." Swaying along close to her escort, Galoubet passed through the doors.

Holjpip kept her posture erect and followed.

From her position, hidden from Tieg behind a high planter, Ming saw them coming and turned her sigh of relief into a little alarmed cry. She wanted this tête-à-tête interrupted before it went further, and she could not afford to be caught here by Madam Langelleik and a Renasco inspection team.

The tall captain grunted displeasure, too, and scrambled to get his footing on the tiles. "I'd just as soon not spend time with these people, Mere Rimi," he said to Ming. "Their idea of pleasure with underlings is watching them scream."

"Very good, Captain." Ming backed toward the glass wall. She couldn't make out details of rank from this distance, but she remembered those uniforms from sleep-sick days shipboard. Hurriedly she led the captain out the centrum's southern doors, throwing one last glance over her shoulder. Was that Holjpip, walking nearly last beside Zardir Huekk, her hair shorn off?

No, Her Grace followed the others.

"There you are." The second, female transfer guard marched up the hallway alone. "I have a job for you, Eillis."

Ming's shoulders sagged as the Renasco major led her aide down South Upper. The woman must have left Shan. Where, Staff Central? Once again, Ming scurried toward Mere Bertelsen's domain.

But Shan wasn't there, and Mere Bertelsen glowered as Ming stood wondering how to inquire.

Best, she decided, to return to her room terminal.

Nothing, nothing, and nothing, on the rosters she accessed using Shan's codebreaker.

Hot sweat!

Ming wiped perspiration from her temples. Memories of Shan rose to taunt her: Shan as she'd been on their doomed smuggling voyage, helping and encouraging all the way, while Jiadra put her best efforts into underscoring Ming's incompetence.

Father hadn't married Jiadra: Ming remembered, now. Jiadra must live somewhere, Renasco's slave.

Goodsprings?

Ming dismissed the notion. Only disgraced Renasco personnel lived there. Jiadra had been excruciatingly lovely by Cabran standards. Ming leaned back on the chair, thinking she could guess Jiadra's fate: a company "sportswoman." She half decided Jiadra deserved it, then silently scourged herself for thinking such a thing.

She wrestled memory aside, sank down on her bed, and fingered its tapestry cover.

What to do, then?

Work while you think. The inspection team might possibly appear in her room. After considering her sketch pad, she mixed one gel tray and laid it aside. The faintly acidic smell made her wistful. This month working for Her Grace Holjpip Langelleik had been good, an interlude between perils.

She would letter "Mannheim" at the gel's center, then decorate it with johnnistars and water droplets. With the lettering done, she could show it with as much or as little illumination as she had time to execute.

She poured a second plate, arranged her inks, and set to work.

The delegates' visit looked to Holjpip as if it had opened a four-day examination, room by room and line on line, of every department of the villa, her activities in the Newport Space Authority, her secretly held shares in AL-PEX, and every other activity conducted over the past two years.

Galoubet, coleader of the team, was shock enough.

Following the inspectors through humid staff kitchens while personnel standing at rigid attention let food shrivel in their ovens, Holjpip stared hard at the back of her daughter's neck. Half the reason for their visit, she understood now, was to rub Holjpip's nose in the woman Renasco had made of Galoubet: Renasco to the core, every word the perfect Company line, and she didn't even wear a collar.

Walking the halls at the rear of this procession, Holjpip mulled over memories. At Galoubet's seventh birthday, Holjpip had ordered the child transferred from crèche custody to her own. She'd seen intelligence and deep affection in the child; but Galoubet, ripped from her crèche mother, became a tiny demon who rebelled furiously and called her natural parent "enemy"—for a month. Then a relationship began to form, a mutual sharing of thought patterns and reactions.

For the happiest three years of her life, Holjpip played the mother role, aided of course by her staff, but finding joy in the winning of a daughter who was more her heir than any naturally conceived child could ever be.

Then Renasco snatched her away.

She knew, now, the brief time together had been engineered so the Company might more effectively set up the hostage situation. For forty years they had controlled her this way, allowing only rare visits.

Now watch Galoubet, look at her. If this woman was hostage for Holjpip's good conduct, that conduct warranted rethinking. She couldn't bear the notion of harm coming to her daughter; yet Galoubet, past the age of majority decades ago, made her own choices, and Holjpip could hire another heiress conceived. Rejuv assured it.

How did Galoubet feel about looking twenty years older than her natural mother? Perhaps Renasco prevented its hostage from taking rejuv treatments, or meant to remind Holjpip of her mortality.

Galoubet's understanding of the Mannheim operation impressed her, too. Renasco might be grooming Galoubet to take over here, when it promoted Holjpip on—or removed her.

The split-eared inspector paused beside a wide-eyed young woman in cook's white coveralls. "I don't like her looks. Missar Huekk. Search her for weapons."

Another strip search. If her colleagues tired of the human body, they never tired of human fear.

Holjpip maintained attention and said nothing. In conceiving Galoubet, she had hoped to ease her fear of mortality, to multiply her leadership to posterity.

Something had gone awry.

Six hours later, they arrived at Ming's room. In late afternoon light from her window, Ming hunched to decorate her second "Mannheim" plate. Her door slid open and she took a stiff, proper posture.

Claude Yerren entered first, glanced around, and evidently found the room's order to her liking. She stepped aside.

Ming gaped while the lizard-eyed men and woman followed through, metallic perfume wafting before them. Then came the short-haired woman, Zardir Huekk, a grim- but normal-eyed man, and finally Holjpip.

"Sirs, Madams," Ming said, looking at Holjpip for safety. If she stared at the others too long, her reactions would surely show, and that might spell trouble.

"Our calligrapher." Holjpip walked forward.

"Yes, we've met," said the short-haired woman.

Ming peered closer; then, shocked, she recognized the red-haired woman who issued her original orders on board the Renasco transport ship.

Holjpip looked unfluttered by the familiarity, but Her Grace was Her Grace. "What is your work today, Mere Dalamani?" She looked ominous in Renasco colors, and Ming wondered if she was mistaken in feeling a loyalty to the ambassador.

Ming stepped backward from her station and turned half aside. "Knowing your guests would arrive today, Your Grace, I am preparing a gift." Carefully she lifted one gel, sprayed and set.

For an instant, Ming saw thanks in Holjpip's hard eyes, then the haughty mask dropped back into place. She accepted the gel and displayed it to the others. Again, Ming stared. How could any human endure surgery to look like a reptile?

"Ribbon calligraphy." Holjpip handed the slab to the slender red-haired woman. Ming judged from the others' deferential postures that she was their chief. "Three-dimensional work. Given time, Mere Dalamani may become one of the art's rare reasonably capable practitioners. Note the droplet work."

"One for each of us?" the woman whined.

Clancestors, she talks just like Holjpip. Then Ming remembered, weeks back, Lyra's description of the clone-daughter. This was the one! If she had met this official shipboard a month ago, Holjpip's operation was definitely under watch, the early inspection no accident. What was the woman's name? She had read it, and vowed to remember, but back then it seemed irrelevant. . . .

"Yes, Madam." Ming made a bow to Holjpip's offspring. "Only two are finished, but I shall have the others delivered to you as soon as possible."

"How long do they take?" The other woman's blue eyes blinked like slowly opening slashes.

"The illumination takes the longest, Madam. I could do the lettering in a few minutes, but several hours' handwork went into the surrounding details."

The man with . . . spiral ears . . . stepped up to the plate she'd nearly completed and peered down into a spray of droplets. "Hours?" He dipped a finger into the gel and stirred vigorously. "Oh. You should feel this, Galoubet. It's like eye jelly, only thicker."

Galoubet. That was the name. Watching her work destroyed, Ming maintained attention with an effort. Hours of tedious work, gone instantly.

Spiral-ears turned up and leered at her. The Renasco judge had leered like that. Obviously, her discomfiture entertained him more than her work did.

Holjpip's voice took a raucous tone. "We shall have those plates delivered." Without a word of thanks, she led her colleagues from Ming's room.

Huekk lingered over the ruined gel, staring into the swirling, graying whirlpool. "You'll have useful work again soon, Mere Visual," he called over his shoulder as he hurried after the others.

Ming shuddered. *Eye jelly.* She rubbed an earring. *If ruining a gel is the worst they do while they're here, I'm lucky.* Dumping the medium down the sink, she stared at her own mirrored eyes, dark and small, but human. She guessed she'd have nightmares tonight. After cleaning the tray, making the effort an exercise in discipline under stress, she poured it fresh, mixed five more trays, and sat down on her bed to wait out the presetting period.

Lunch? She examined her spotted fingers.

No, she'd missed lunch three hours ago, and she wasn't hungry. Staring at the cloth screen, she shook her head. Holjpip's superiors, Holjpip's daughter. Holjpip, in Renasco dress uniform.

Holjpip, planning to throw off these people— "Oneday."

She picked at a black stain on one thumbnail. No wonder Holjpip had to move so carefully. A month ago, Ming had planned to serve Renasco as well as she could. Now, the notion seemed a travesty of real loyalty.

Ming wandered to the console and turned up the sound channel. She heard something new. The channel probably carried live music from the centrum, or wherever Tieg sat playing for these creatures. She sat on her desk chair, staring.

Then she roused herself. Perhaps Shan was back at that room, again; at least, she could hope that Captain Eillis's superior officer had returned, and that his Major didn't want him dallying with staff.

Ming checked her deep pocket. Besides her nilly bean quarters, she still had that blue master-chip. She'd try it again.

The room was not merely unoccupied, but empty now of personal belongings. Alarmed, Ming leaned against the door. Gone already?

Staff Central, then, again—quickly.

The staffer on nightshift shrugged and agreed to run Ming's check. Ming stood, absentmindedly tapping one foot, relieved Mere Bertelsen had finally gone off duty.

"One moment, Mere Dalamani." Ming glanced back across the office to see the staffer turn aside and answer an on-screen communique. She thought she heard the woman mutter "Innig" under her breath in a soft laughing tone while keying a response to the unknown inquirer, but since Ming wasn't certain she heard Tieg's name, she said nothing.

Finally the staffer completed Ming's check. "Yes, another Mere Dalamani has been logged in. As property, though, not staff. There's no room assigned to her yet. She could be bedded with someone else."

"Do you have any idea who?"

The blond woman shrugged. "She *could* be, I said."

Rattled, but as determined as ever, Ming wandered back out into the high-ceilinged hallway. Now where? No logical avenues remained to try, but she wouldn't be able to sleep. On the chance Shan's new keeper might take her on a late villa tour, she roamed the halls, checking and rechecking Staff Dining, until her feet ached from walking and her jaws from yawning. But she found no sign of Shan.

Half an hour before Ming came to Staff Central, Jury Bertelsen had scooted out of her work station, her mind made up after a day's soul-searching. Over the past weeks she had seen Tieg alone with Mere Dalamani, sketched by Mere Dalamani, watched by Mere Dalamani; and now Ming hid out in the corridors, returning the favors of a Renasco transfer guard. Tieg was in danger.

Soon she sat in Tieg's room for the first time, her delight accentuated by the sensation of sharing deep, dangerous secrets. The rooms smelled of wet soap and electronics gear, of Tieg Innig. Delicately she fingered a pattern on the white brocade couch. He sat nightrobed in a wicker chair.

She told what she had seen, finishing, "She inquired about Captain Eillis's room number, then evidently went there directly. I would have come to you immediately, Missar Innig, but it smacked so badly of carrying gossip that it was a difficult decision."

"I understand," he said, his blue-gray eyes narrow.

Now, she thought, dealing with Ming as a potential security breach would be his responsibility. *Let's see what he does.*

Instead of offering explanations or refreshment, he saw her with professional courtesy to the door. She stood in the hallway, surprised to have it done so quickly and wondering if it'd done any good.

Tieg returned to the wicker chair and sat brooding. *She's jealous, that's plain, to speak for that long without being asked.* One hand cradling his chin, he fingered the thin twiggy weave on the chair's arm. Ming had feared the inspection team's arrival signaled the end of her service here, and a "removal," one way or another. Perhaps the transfer guard had abused her because he was aware of her tenuous status.

Abruptly cold with anger, he crossed to his desk and put in a call to her room.

After two minutes' wait, he clenched both fists. Had they taken her away?

Staff Central answered his next query with odd humor: Yes, she was still "quite within" the villa.

He drummed his fingers on the desktop. If she suspected she was about to be removed, it was time to get her to safety.

Another call to her rooms brought up only the cursor. After half a minute's thought, he checked Newport Space Authority's schedule.

The next shuttle flight Newport-to-*Doran* was not scheduled for two days. This was the lull period, with the final inspection under way. They couldn't take her away yet. That gave him time to contact Curan.

He tried Ming's room once more, and again the cursor blinked balefully.

X

Ming dropped exhausted onto her bed without changing into her sleeping tunic, and knew nothing—no falling-asleep period, no nightmares of reptilian eyes—until she woke to infant morning light. A man wearing the security uniform of Holjpip's staff shook her by one shoulder. Out of reflex, she jerked away. *Security? Here?*

"You're to come with me," he said, and nodded toward the hallway door. She blinked downward, saw she had slept in her clothes, and finger-combed her clan tails as she followed him. She had little time for confusion. Around a bend from the transfer guards' room, he stopped. He did not knock, but the entry alarm light came on over the door.

Afraid a pair of transfer guards waited inside for her, she considered turning to run.

It took exactly that long for the door to open. When she peered through the arch, she saw two people on a long black chaise. One was Galoubet.

"Go on." The guard nudged her shoulder.

From a place behind the door, Zardir Huekk appeared, a Renasco tunic belted in copper around his stout middle. "Good morning, Mere Dalamani." He seized her by one elbow and drew her into the room. Galoubet lounged, nightrobed, against the shoulder of the lizard-eyed, spiral-eared man. Like her, he wore only a thin white robe. In front of the lounge, separated from it by a low frosted glass table, a stool sat drawn close, and Huekk pushed Ming toward it. She thought it wise to bow before she sat down. Huekk stood behind her, one hand on her shoulder.

"Well, Mere Dalamani." Galoubet pushed away from her companion and leaned forward, elbows over her knees. Clancestors, she looked like Holjpip, now that Ming knew to look for the resemblance! The same hard eyes, though the telltale skin around them looked younger; identical angles of cheek and chin. Other than those eyes, the face looked far older than her mother's.

The haughty air was the same, and with this woman, she could not count on a respect for the arts to protect her. Ming sat stiffly, ready for anything. Catching a whiff of something sweet, she glanced down at the table. On a silver dish, rows of sliced mellow pods lay on a bed of tiny pink blossoms.

"We are ready for your report," Galoubet said. "Obviously, your calligraphic work has been satisfactory."

Beneath the stool, Ming crossed her ankles. "Thank you. I . . . shall have those 'Mannheim' plates lettered for you and your colleagues, as soon as—"

"You needn't consider them a priority. Tell me, instead, if you feel you have fulfilled those other orders. Are you within the ambassador's favor?"

She could have gotten that information from Huekk. She's manipulating me into saying something, Ming thought, and with her next breath she realized she must play Galoubet's game and give the appearance of full cooperation, or never leave Mannheim with her mind intact.

"Yes, Madam," she said, twisting her fingers together and nodding with her whole upper body, trying to give the appearance of greed. "She often praises my work—"

"Good." Galoubet drew upright with a gesture that was so much Holjpip's Ming knew the next words would carry the meat of her message. "Are you prepared to win your freedom?" she asked, touching the edge of one finger to her chin. "Now?"

Zardir Huekk's hand shifted on her shoulder, and he flicked the stubs of the Renasco collar. Ming shivered and did her best to ignore him. Galoubet's companion snatched up a handful of pod slices and slunk off toward another room, a powerful, sweet perfume drifting behind him.

"Absolutely, Madam," she said firmly. "I have had enough of servitude to last at least forty years."

"Well said." Galoubet laughed, reached onto the low glass table, and tossed something into the air. Huekk caught it as it passed over Ming's shoulder and dropped it into her hands.

It looked like an open frame made of brown metal, just larger than her two palms together, just smaller than the standard fifteen- by twenty-centimeter tray for gel work. She looked up toward Galoubet.

One shoulder of the loose white robe slipped down her arm. Galoubet ignored it. "You're to embed it in a gel as a gift for the ambassador. Make it a personal gift. You've given her such before, have you not?"

Galoubet would be able to check, if she hadn't done so already. "Yes, Madam. It seemed a good way to impress her."

"Good. Make certain Holjpip has this in her possession before five local days pass, or . . ." She gave Ming a flat-lipped smile like Holjpip's. Huekk's fingers wriggled in Ming's neckline hair.

"That will be easy, Madam."

"No longer than five days."

"Done, Madam."

"You will be watched."

"That is nothing new here, Madam."

Galoubet rubbed the backs of her hands together and laughed raucously. "You are either a consummate liar or a true friend of humankind, Mere Dalamani. You may go."

Consummate liar—me? Ming stood, keeping her face expressionless, and tucked the odd framelike object into her musty, slept-in duty suit's large pocket, to nestle beside nilly beans and the blue master chip. Zardir Huekk made a mock grandiose bow to Galoubet, then followed Ming to the doorway. She half feared he would escort her back, but he boarded a single-passenger elevator and vanished.

Ming rushed the rest of the way to her new room. On screen, the time blinked 0627: too early for others to be waking, but she called Tieg's room anyway. This call might be monitored; still, if she didn't reach him now, she might miss him—and without his help, she doubted she'd find Shan again. Who watched her? Huekk at Staff Central, some tech in the Ops room, or one of Galoubet's lizard-eyed aides in some other place? Uneasily, she fingered the mysterious frame. He'd probably know what that was, too.

Within two minutes, an answer blinked onto her screen: +MING, WHERE ARE YOU?+

On my way down to inquire about another setting. Even as she entered it, it looked lame. She wanted to send Renasco to town, looking for her, but draw Tieg to the spot where they had talked about setting his sunstone.

+FINE+ appeared as rapidly as it could be typed. It looked like he understood.

Moving automatically, Ming mixed enough gel medium to fill one standard-sized tray. Standing where her hand movements would be visible to the screen, she held the brown metal frame down into the tray, checked its fit, then turned her back again to hide her movements. With her right hand, her elbow protruding past the line of her body, she poured the medium into the tray—but with her left, she slipped the mysterious frame back into her pocket.

Then she ran a comb through her hair, strolled past the console to her door, and dashed to the beach elevator.

Resting on a boulder, Tieg watched a summer storm front creep shoreward over the sea, that eternal hiding place. A glance over his shoulder showed Barbar Curan making his way down the vine-trailed cliff. Tieg watched, glad for the distraction. Curan moved like a spider on rock. One limb at a time, he descended nearly to the bottom, then dropped the rest of the way.

Tieg walked up into soft, dry sand cluttered with sea kelp and driftwood.

"What's this about?" Curan shouted over waves crashing on the rocks.

"Ming." Tieg tugged one long sleeve of his red-and-gold tunic. "Either she's in trouble, or we are. One of my contacts at Staff Central saw her, embracing—being embraced by—a uniformed Renasco patrolman, and she was gone from her room last night until . . ." He explained Ming's fears about the inspection team, then shook his head hard. "She hasn't been taken away yet, but she might need our help soon, to go into hiding."

"Either that, or you're afraid this team could be an intercept, and she's been working against us all this time."

"Yes. In that case, we're waiting here in a trap." Tieg stared out into the water. Two kye-di-dees popped beak-first from the waves, battling for possession of an eel-like fish. Binary hells! Which was it? If Ming had betrayed them, how long would they have to make an escape?

Far beyond the kye-di-dees, the dark line of cloud hovered. "She's on her way here, anyway. Could we . . . just try to get her away, whichever turns out to be the case?"

Curan looked as uncomfortable as Tieg felt. "We'll hear what she's got to say, first."

"I need another dart pistol. Can you find one in town?"

"Give me time. The weapons market is tight, with *Doran* in the system and uniforms in the streets. Everyone's a little nervous."

"Nervous." Standing just out of the surf spray, Tieg tried to laugh.

Curan pulled his hand-sized black collar transmitter from his jacket pocket. Tieg nodded, then Curan tucked it away.

Ming darted out onto the broad porch. From here, she could look far out to sea. With the full memory of her upbringing on scorched Cabra Minor restored, she felt the water's call more powerfully than ever. Between long, rolling breakers and a wall of thickening clouds floated a distant speck: some barge, probably bringing lumber down the coast to Anslanding.

She had loved her arid home, but here she felt a sense of belonging almost as deep as her old clan ties. She didn't want to leave this sea, this villa, this environment drenched in the arts—and particularly, Tieg Innig.

Far up the beach, cliffs bent to meet the water. She couldn't see him on his way. If he wasn't there already, she'd miscued him. At least her gel-pouring ruse had put off Renasco pursuit temporarily, she told herself. She trotted down the stairs and then jogged north, clan-tails slapping her neck.

Breathless, she rounded the cliff. "Tieg?" she called. He appeared from behind a boulder, rushed forward, and pulled her close. The rough, metallic gold of his collar rubbed her cheek. "Ming. You're safe. I tried to call your room all last night."

"I was looking for Shan, my cousin. Oh, Tieg, everything is happening at once. I'm afraid—"

Barbar Curan stepped out from behind another boulder, a pistol dangling from his hand. She exhaled, almost as relieved to see him as she was to see Tieg. "Sit down, and we'll talk," Curan said.

"First," Tieg said abruptly, "who was the man in the Renasco uniform?"

She stepped backward, bumped a large rock, and sat down on it, finally recognizing the fear of betrayal in his eyes. From the jumble of far-past and recent-past memory she'd lived with for two days, she remembered Mere Bertelsen, catching her with the Renasco guard. Who else might have seen? "Tieg, listen." She licked salt from her lips. "Shan, my cousin, is here. That man was one of the transfer guards who brought her. Shan is the one who stole Renasco's shielding, Tieg. We have to free her."

Frowning, Tieg fidgeted with something in one pocket. She wondered if he was armed again, and whether he believed her. "What does that have to do with embracing Renasco men in the hallways?"

"I was trying to find her. I tried his rooms, and got trapped inside with him." She brushed a pebble off the rock.

"Wait," said Curan. "Start at the beginning—which, for me, is: How did your memory return?"

"It was Tieg's—" She halted. Tieg drew his hand from that pocket and handed her the nameplate. With a deep breath, she held it up and showed it to Curan. "This," she said softly, pointing to the crystal that gleamed under its silvery net, "is what my family was smuggling when Renasco caught us. It's called a sunstone. The heart is a soft fluorite mineral, the outside related to amber, which makes it hard enough for gem use."

As its mounting warmed in her hands, the stone began to glow, facets catching and reflecting lights from its depths. "It almost looks alive," Curan murmured.

She glanced significantly at Tieg. "That's something else I've remembered. Some people believe they are alive in some primitive way, absorbing warmth and emitting odd energies as waste."

"The buzzing sounds on the amplifier?" Tieg asked.

"Yes," she said. "That radiation, plus whatever it did to bring up my nonverbal memories. Everything seems to have crossed over again."

"It put her away for hours—unconscious, at the end." Tieg shook his head at Curan. "I can imagine what she was going through, with that much reorienting happening in the brain."

"All right," Curan said. "I think I understand enough of that to know what's going on. Then what? A cousin?"

"Yes. There's a woman at the villa, right now—or," she faltered, "at least, she was here last night—who is one of my cousins. We were smugglers together. That's why Renasco collared us."

Tieg slowly rubbed his palms together.

Twisting an earring, she glanced at Curan. "Her name is Shan Dalamani. If we can restore her memory, she's worth all the Old School stands for. She broke Renasco security and got our clan their radiation shielding, Missar Curan. What would be the chance we could take her south to Goodsprings, where my friend Lyra's sister lives? We could hide her there, for a while."

Tieg reached for her hands. "Broke what security?"

Ming inhaled. "That's the rest of it, Tieg. I remembered her computer access sequence that got inside Renasco's protection codes. My fingers knew it. She drilled me." Ready to explain that this had happened days ago, she changed her mind. Let him think this returned with the rest of her memory. "So I tried it. The codebreaker opened . . . all kinds of programs. And listen . . ." She gripped Tieg's hands and leaned closer. "Holjpip is planning to move for independence. There's a file in her personal directory called 'Oneday,' and it's a blueprint for insurrection. It looks like she has contact people all over this planet sworn to her, programmed to move simultaneously. Not one of them could know about the master plan, but—"

"Could you bring this file back up?" Tieg thrust his nameplate back into a pocket.

"I don't know if I dare, today. There are so many Renasco people, all over the place—"

"What's the codebreaker?" Curan rubbed his chin.

Ming hesitated, thinking, *There goes my last big secret.*
A wave crashed on rocks nearby. She drew out the folded
paper and gave it to Tieg. "I wanted to go to Her Grace
and throw in with her. She's a capable leader, but she'll
need help to shake off the Company. I didn't dare approach her with this until I had you, because—can you
imagine what she'd do if I came alone and announced,
'I've found you out'?"

"Easy." Curan peered over Tieg's shoulder as Tieg un-
folded the page. "She'd have you quieted, one way or the
other. She's lived without a calligrapher before."

"Exactly. But with the Old School's help to offer
her . . ." Curan's face went blank, and she halted. "Your
people would support her if she made a bid for independence, wouldn't you?"

A swirling gust of sea breeze made Curan's dark hair
stand up. "I'm authorized to speak for the School. But it
would be better to wait until *Doran* left the system. It
could destroy Anslanding from orbit."

"No! Holjpip wants to capture a warship. She has a crew
on call, ready to shuttle up."

Tieg, too, stared at Curan.

"There's one more thing."

Both men eyed her.

"This." She drew the brown frame from her pocket.
"What scared me this morning is that Galoubet wants it set
into a gel for Holjpip within exactly five days. As a gift. I
have no idea what it is, but if I read Galoubet at all, it's
dangerous, and in five days it will—"

Curan snatched it and ran with it toward the cliff.

"What—?" Ming looked to Tieg.

Tieg watched closely while Curan deposited the frame
between two reddish stones well above high water. "If
you've been monitored running away," he said, "and if it is
dangerous, Galoubet could have it do its damage sooner."

She swallowed. "That makes sense."

Curan trotted back down toward them. "I'll come back
for it and have it analyzed. Did you go back to your room
after they gave you this?"

"Yes, and—"

"Did you call Tieg from there?"

"Yes," she admitted.

"Then we're in a hurry." Calmly, Tieg reached for her hand again.

Barbar Curan kicked at a stone. "Innig," he said, looking down. "Ming's call to you could have been monitored, but of the three of us, you're the safest one to send back to the villa—and the one with quickest access to Holjpip. Take Ming's codebreaker. Wait however long you need, until you can get Her Grace alone, and tell her—tell her we have it in our possession and can access all her files, but that she can count on the Old School's support if she chooses to move on this 'Oneday' sequence."

Tieg's jaw clenched. Ming understood. His undercover position would vanish in an instant, but he had an order.

Curan pulled a pen from his pocket and bent over Ming's paper, recopying the twenty-command sequence. Tieg drew Ming to her feet. "I'm sorry," he said softly as wind whipped his hair into her face, "about the way I reacted to the Renasco man. I never thought I'd be jealous, but . . ."

She wrapped her hands around the back of his neck. "If you're jealous, I guess I'm glad." He bent toward her. Shutting her eyes against distractions, she worked her lips against Tieg's, pressing her chest to his and realizing: *This is what it is to love a man—and he's going in to danger.*

Pen-scratching noises behind her stopped, and Tieg's arms loosened. Curan tore the paper in thirds and pocketed one piece. Tieg reached for the second. "Hopefully, at least one of these copies will get through, either to Holjpip or the Old School," Tieg said. "Holjpip will have to believe we're serious when she sees what this can do. If . . ."

"It will," said Ming.

Curan offered Ming the third paper. "I'll take you south and come back for your cousin. While you're at Goodsprings, you can get a place ready for her with this friend of yours."

Tieg reached for Ming one more time. "Forgive me?" he asked, the arch of his eyebrows entreating.

"For what?"

"For distrusting you still. After all you've—"

"Of course. Good luck, Tieg. If there's anyone Her

Grace likes, it's you, but oh, be careful. She's really trapped, if anything brings 'Oneday' to the inspectors' notice."

"I know that." He clasped Curan's hand and shoulder, then turned and dashed back around the bend in the cliffs. Ming wanted to cry.

"All right, then." Curan dropped his pistol into a windbreaker pocket and zipped it closed, then drew something black and metallic from the opposite pocket. Ming recognized it as the collar frequency jammer. "I have this, in case you're wondering." He dropped it in again. "We're going to have to hurry, if I'm making two trips south in one day. My car is right above these cliffs. We'll take the long way around."

With a start, she remembered what lay in the pocket of her none-too-fresh clothing. "Just a second." She thrust a hand deep inside. One of the bean fragments had fallen out, but three remained. "Nilly quarters. Do you want any?"

Without hesitating, Curan seized two quarters and began to chew. "Forgive my greed—two for me. The other is yours."

If Barbar Curan considered them acceptable, Ming Dalamani was going to try one. She tossed the last piece into her mouth and bit down hard, then gagged down pulverized fragments mixed with horrible-tasting saliva. Curan pulled one hand. "Come on."

She ran. Spray carried onshore by the wind chilled her legs, but she kept them pumping. "Wretched beans aren't making any difference," she grumbled.

"No? Look at the water."

The waves did appear to creep up the shore and then wash again to sea as if they had all the time in this world. "Oh," she said, then pushed herself to run harder.

Tieg reached the villa with an hour to spare before his scheduled performance, though he seriously doubted he'd give it. Half walking, half trotting, he approached the Ops room, one hand deep in his pocket, clutching the incriminating scrap of paper.

A burly security man stood at the hall door. "Mere,"

said Tieg. "I must speak with Her Grace, if it is at all possible."

The young man glared up at him. "Only on urgent business, Missar Innig."

"It is." Tieg saw hostility in the guard's eyes and wondered what he'd done to offend him. Jealousy, perhaps, of the art staff—or rumors of romance between Tieg and his employer—or simple nervousness, while the inspection team lingered.

After a long hesitation and a fast frisking, the guard stepped aside. Tieg straightened the tunic's belt, glad he'd dressed for work. Her Grace disliked seeing him plainclothed. Processed air cooled his sweaty arms. Holjpip sat behind her desk, Claude Yerren standing close, both wearing the black Renasco dress uniform. On Holjpip black looked elegant, but Claude Yerren became dark and foreboding. At the screens along the near wall, Ops techs flipped from room to room, trying to keep the entire villa under observation while the inspection continued. Holjpip looked careworn, the lines at her eyes deeper than usual. Perhaps the dark uniform deepened other shadows' appearance.

"Your Grace." Tieg stopped short of Holjpip's blond wood desk and bowed, feeling hot and disheveled. "Is there any way we might speak alone for three minutes?"

Claude Yerren rapped on the desk with the finger that wore the amethyst. "Missar Innig, this is not the time for asking special favors. Her Grace has been—"

"Let him speak." Holjpip waved her adjutant aside. "Good morning, Missar Innig."

"Alone, Madam?" Tieg glanced aside at the technicians. "I never have asked the favor before, and I doubt I'll ask again." That was true enough. Once he gave her this news, he was more likely wiped than not. He'd had time to think it through during his run up the beach.

Holjpip made a slight jerking motion with her head. Claude Yerren walked behind the desk and touched something. A door Tieg had never noticed slid open near the center of the office's long, light-grained back wall. Claude Yerren stepped inside, and Holjpip followed. Tieg came last, composing sentences in his mind as he caught his breath.

Bare white walls surrounded an unfurnished, carpeted cubicle so narrow Tieg could touch three walls at once. "Alone, Madam?" he asked, one more time.

Claude Yerren positioned herself between Holjpip and Tieg.

"No." Holjpip dipped her chin. "Say what you wish with Missara Yerren here, or leave."

Tieg leaned against one white wall, both hands behind him. "Hear me out before you react, then, Madam. Ming Dalamani's memory has returned." Holjpip's hiss of indrawn breath and the whip of Yerren's head startled him, but he plunged ahead. "She and three cousins stole Renasco's shielding to make a smuggling run—and, Madam, she has recalled the keystroke sequence that enabled them to break Renasco's encryptions." He paused. "Madam, she asked me to tell you that, using her cousin's codebreaker, she found the program titled 'Oneday' and would like to be included. As would I, Your Grace."

Youth's high color drained from Holjpip's cheeks. Claude Yerren stepped forward to block the narrow exit, drawing the pistol from her belt holster. "Madam, this is enough. I have warned you about this man."

"Wait," Holjpip barked. The muscles around her mouth worked for an instant, then her control returned. "Tieg. Surely you understand I cannot let you go free, when you talk like this. But before I give you to Missara Yerren, is there more?"

He guessed the decision to silence him had come in that pause. Yet if Holjpip created her own dominion, with antimatter drive and ships fitted with radiation shielding, Old School's aims would come to pass even if the tide of events stranded him. He had to help her now. He rubbed his forehead dry. "Yes, Madam, there is more. I spoke this morning with a district supervisor of the Old School. You know of the organization."

"And I have known for years you are a member. What of the supervisor?"

Tieg swallowed.

"He's *what*?" Claude Yerren's free hand closed over the other on her pistol.

"At ease, Claude. Why do you think I keep him around?" Her stare bored into Tieg. "For several reasons, not the least of which is a link to the Old School, should I need one. Go on, Tieg. I must chair an emergency meeting in ten minutes."

Tieg kept leaning back on his hands, hoping Claude Yerren was not too eager to shoot. "He offers you the support of the organization, Madam, when you see fit to implement 'Oneday.' They too have a copy of the Dalamani codebreaker, now, and access to all the secure files on Mannheim.

"Meanwhile, the crippled woman, Shan Dalamani, just brought to the villa, is Ming's cousin who stole the shielding in the first place. If her memory could be brought back, she might recall the mechanism. Madam, Old School knows someone is making antimatter here in the system. If you had the shielding secret here, too, and could fit your own ships without sending to Little York—"

Holjpip raised a hand to interrupt him. "Ming's memory." Her voice rose. "How was it restored?"

Tieg explained the sunstone and its amplifier setting. "Where is it?"

Now he understood Ming's visible reluctance to give up her scrap of paper. He groped into his pocket and pulled out his mother's netted, remounted jewel. "It has to be warmed to reach its maximum effect."

"I see. Yerren, bring the crippled woman. At once."

Claude Yerren made no move away.

"Now, Claude."

"Madam." Claude Yerren pressed one hand against the doorjamb. "You must have the Dalamani women and Missar Innig locked away. Quickly, or word of that program will spread."

"And the Old School supervisor, as well? How do you propose I find him?"

"Question Innig. At Medical, or use *Doran*'s facilities."

Tieg gripped the nameplate gel, flicking the net's seam. Holjpip gave Yerren a curt nod. "Claude, if you love me, get that woman here now."

Stiff-shouldered, Yerren handed Holjpip her pistol, then stalked out through the tiny room's sliding door.

Despite her businesslike grip on the weapon, Holjpip's forward-inclined posture gave her a more approachable look as soon as Yerren had gone.

She took the netted crystal delicately, peering at it, her hair falling forward over one shoulder.

"One thing more, Madam. Your clone daughter has given Ming some kind of device. She was to set it into a gel as a gift for you. My supervisor will analyze it, but I fear—"

Holjpip's hand holding the gel dropped to her side. "You fear they mean to remove me. It is either that or a promotion I would have to decline, Tieg. Where is Ming, and how *did* she access 'Oneday'?"

He was as good as wiped already, with nothing left to lose, and Ming wanted him to convey this trust. "On her way to Goodsprings, Madam. She asked me to give you this." He handed across the folded slip of paper. "This is the codebreaker she used."

Holjpip laid the sunstone on a ledge in the wall. Left-handed, she shook the folds from the paper, then she examined it character by character.

"When Mere Shan comes to you, you might show it to her."

Holjpip rocked her hands like two pans of a balance, one holding the paper, the other gripping Yerren's gun. "I will give you a tracer," she said carefully, "to find Ming. Get her back to the villa quickly, and I will detain her for her own safety. Send your supervisor on to Old School, to make his connections. Goodsprings will not be secure. Renasco will counterstrike there, if anywhere."

"Counterstrike?" Tieg let himself begin to believe he might escape the memory-wipe.

Holjpip plucked something off her right sleeve and shook it to the floor. "If I should implement the 'Oneday' plan, the Company is certain to strike back, and there is more happening at Goodsprings than nilly bean research."

"Antimatter?" Tieg whispered.

Holjpip leaned a hand against the wall, wincing as she nodded. "R and D," she whispered hoarsely.

"Madam?" Tieg reached for her shoulder.

"Nothing," she said, and shook off his hand. "Overdue for rejuv. Bring Ming back. Thank her and tell her I accept her offer of service. And don't let Yerren see you. She'd probably shoot you on sight now, no matter what I said."

Tieg stepped away hastily. *She does treat me like a mother!*

Holjpip led the way out into the office. She set the paper on her desk and weighted it in place with the gun, then drew a hand-held directional receiver from a desk drawer and placed it on his palm. From another drawer, she lifted a plastic-coated capsule. "Swallow," she said brusquely. "This is a tracer, too. We will follow your movements."

He forced the capsule down a dry throat, watching Holjpip for any flicker of emotion.

She returned his stare, her eyes alert within their network of tiny lines. "Now, hurry."

4

Five minutes after Tieg left the cubicle, Claude Yerren marched back into the Ops room. Holjpip stood behind her desk, fingering the jeweled nameplate in its silvery net. Holjpip had owned many gemstones in a long and wealthy life, and never one quite like this quiver-lit jewel. From five minutes closed in her fingers, it already gleamed brighter than before.

Her mind leaped to a phrase from an ancient song. Drawn from a faith that flourished on Podaca during the gamma-ray storm, each verse ended,

And all the stars shall sing together, together.

Odd, how isolation turned her people into believers. Grounded by deadly radiation, the faithful decreed the stars themselves lived, nearly forever, and that their seed was everywhere, a witness to their majesty, for those who could see it.

"Star seeds," she mused to her friend. "Do you know, I

think I can guess who owned this before Tieg Innig. Where is—?"

A man in the uniform of her private guard backed through the door arch, pulling the Dalamani woman, trying to hurry her while she balanced on withered legs. Yerren came to attention beside Holjpip. "Bring her here." Yerren indicated one chair.

Is this the one? Holjpip thought at the stone, adjusting a black cuff as the woman dragged herself closer. *Might we pull off independence?*

Ashan Dalamani held her head erect, but the vague terror in her eyes confirmed her total memory-wipe. Over twenty years, the sparked-out loci would have recovered physically, but the fully wiped never lost that look.

Not in Holjpip's experience. "Sit," she ordered.

The guard hurried forward to assist the crippled woman into a white-cushioned chair close to Holjpip's desk. Wisps of gray hair escaping the tight knot at the base of her neck dangled below her ears. (A knot to hide collar stubs, Holjpip understood. How many thousands of sentenced laborers would flock to build Holjpip's dream if she could return memory and remove those collars?) *Sing together, together.* One felt awkward admitting one's spiritual inadequacies in this age of action and transaction. Her stomach cramped violently, making her diaphragm flutter and breathing difficult for two full seconds. *Next week!* When she could get a steady breath, she spoke to the nearest guard. "Pull the curtains and turn down the lights." Alarmed by the cramp, she finger-combed long hair back from her face and found ten long strands uprooted by the gentle tug. *Next week!*

After peeling the hairs off her fingers and shaking her hand, she sat back down in the dimmed room. She slid the netted nameplate across her desk. "Have you ever seen something like this stone, Mere Dalamani?"

The woman lifted and examined the gel, turning it over and over with broad, strong-looking hands. The crystal's light, diffracted by the gel, made the entire transparent block glimmer faintly. Holjpip watched, first eagerly; then, as seconds passed without effect, with growing concern.

"Is this a switch?" The woman touched a ragged-nailed finger to one spot on the lettering.

Holjpip glanced up at her adjutant. Crossing her mouth diagonally with one finger, Yerren shrugged. The techs along the wall kept flipping room to room, intent on their duties.

Ashan Dalamani still bent over the slab. "Am I to switch it on, Madam?"

"Try it," Holjpip said shortly. If all this effort had gone for naught, she'd wasted invaluable time while the inspection team camped in her home.

The woman tapped silver with one finger.

An eerie, low voice began to hum between Holjpip's ears, its rhythm irregular but unending. She blinked away fogginess. The crippled woman slumped in her chair; her guard caught her, propped her up, and looked to Holjpip for instructions.

Holjpip hurried around her desk, took a companion chair, and seized Shan's wrist. "Mere Ashan," she said in a low voice. "Do you realize what that crystal is?"

The woman clenched her mouth closed, deep lines surrounding her wincing eyes.

"You will not be harmed." Holjpip closed her other hand around the gel and Shan's fingers. "Do you remember—"

Shan groaned. "Too . . . bright."

Holjpip dropped her voice to a whisper. "You stole Renasco's shielding."

"No—yes!—They took us all—"

"The shielding," Holjpip interrupted. "Can you remember how it operated? Did you refit your own ship?"

The woman shook her head as if fighting vertigo. "No—yes!" Her voice dropped in pitch and became calm. "Lur, give back the wrench, now. One more connection, and—"

"Not now." Almost dizzy with triumph, Holjpip squeezed Shan's shoulder. The guard watched, intent, as she motioned to a second Security officer. "Take her to Medical, twenty-five-hour watch. No one is to come near her except by my express order. She's to talk to no one except by my order, either. Clear?"

"Madam." The first guard scooped Shan into his arms. Accompanied by his fellow, he carried her out.

Holjpip sprang back behind her desk, gripping the set

crystal. Her hand quivered as she touched up a key sequence.

Claude Yerren smirked. "You're locking everyone in, again?" she asked.

"We have our 'Oneday,' Claude," Holjpip whispered, running fingers through her long hair and dropping strands to lie unnoticed on the floor. "Dalamani's shielding will give us a fleet of our own. Cancel that emergency meeting. Get those air scooters on the roof secured—

"Wait." She touched the inscribed gel again. "First, take Galoubet's room. Double-guard her. Get her away from the rest of the inspection team if you can, but keep them locked in, as well. We may want them, if we can pull this off. For messengers."

"I understand, Madam."

"Offer her a position—you'll think of something. I haven't time. She's crazy for power." Holjpip touched a tab that reopened the curtains, relit ceiling panels with a wave, then made a hard decision. "But . . ." Gods, she hated to say the words. "Galoubet's life is not priceless if you meet a hostage situation, Yerren. Do you understand that?"

Her adjutant nodded once. Holjpip scrolled priorities across the back of her mind. "When you're done, you do have a subject for questioning. Get an interrogator, and pry all the information you can from Ashan Dalamani—before Renasco finds her."

As Yerren swept out, Holjpip bent to the "Oneday" program and began activating long-formulated commands. Once Renasco knew or guessed a rebellion was under way, the Company would issue nilly beans universally. Therefore, her forces would use them, too—this single time.

Holjpip glanced out into the rising morning storm. Could Galoubet be spared?

Sing together, together.

Star seeds? She felt queerly comforted by the stone she held and memories it renewed. Her "Oneday" dream was a posterity far beyond Galoubet's life span. If that dream grew to fruition, some day her name might be remembered on hundreds of worlds.

Why then were her eyes watering?

* * *

Accompanied by two security staffers, Claude Yerren found Galoubet alone, studying a portable console on the glass table. "Madam," Claude said formally, "I need to speak with one of your colleagues."

"Then you'll have to wait," Galoubet said absently. "I think they're in Stoner's room. They're conferring on certain of my orders, at any rate."

For the benefit of Ops room watchers recording this confrontation, Claude maintained attention, though she wanted to smile foolishly. *She's alone! This is too easy.* "Then, Madam, it is my pleasant duty to inform you Her Grace has placed you under house arrest."

Galoubet laughed, her shoulders stiff with indignation. "Her Grace has no such power, Missara Yerren, and you'll find our in-room intelligence net—"

"You'll find, Madam, all your lines of communication disrupted at any moment, if they're not already. The Renasco colony of Mannheim is as of this day declaring its independence. This is a plan long laid, and Her Grace means to spare you the brunt of the uprising's violence. She asks me to tell you, Madam Galoubet, that she would be pleased to offer you a lucrative position within her sphere, in return for your cooperation."

Galoubet reached again for the console, then snatched back her hand. With a quick sideways motion, she went for something on the table, something beside the silver dish of mellow pods.

Watching for just such a move, Yerren whipped out a tranquilizer dart-pistol. The security guard hurried forward and took Galoubet's weapon off the frosted glass.

"Madam," Yerren said again, still making certain her body did not block the console's viewing field, "all this is being recorded for Her Grace's later viewing. She offers you preferential treatment, as—"

"You can all tell Her Bloody-handed Grace precisely what I think of her, then." Galoubet sprang up off the chaise, her thin white robe parting down to her waist. "She is a manipulator of lives, a vain wastrel, and a figurehead of meaningless pomp, grasping with rejuv and mellow pods and every means at her disposal for an immortality she'll never win." Down at her sides, her hands shook. "Either she or I will be memory-wiped before this uprising of hers ends."

Yerren would have liked to shoot the woman for that speech, and not with a tranquilizer. If Galoubet had any idea of Holjpip's tireless work . . . "That's as it may be, Madam," she said, making her voice sound disciplined. "For now, you are to consider yourself under protective custody—"

"I have nothing else to say to her, Claude Yerren. And you—"

Claude tightened her finger on the firing stud. Holjpip's daughter dropped a second pistol and slumped back onto the chaise.

"She should wake after about half an hour," Claude told her escorts. "Search her to the skin, and then check under that. Thoroughly."

Barbar Curan grabbed Ming's arm to help her uphill. "That way," he said, spending little breath on speech.

A steep-banked cleft split the cliffs. Ming made for it, stumbling in deep sand while the sea roared in her ears. Though the nilly bean hadn't quite worn off, her legs weren't in shape for this. If she had Curan's athletic build, running might be easier. "When you see Shan," she puffed, "ask if she remembers me. Lyra will help you. Lyra's great."

"Where do you know this Lyra from?"

"Staff Dining."

"Oh. Makes sense."

A snarl of wind gusted up the draw, and Curan gave her hand a squeeze; that, or he pulled harder than before. A few meters, and they would reach solid ground.

"Stop!" Eerie voices echoed around her. "One step more, and you'll die. Both of you."

Ming whipped her head up. Adrenaline gave her the energy to run again, but she didn't dare. Perspiration trickled down her chest.

Zardir Huekk stood five meters up the trail, straggles of hair blown back from his face by the onshore wind, and he held a weapon at the ready.

"Interesting," the mutant shouted, his echo-chorused voice deeper and slower than she had heard before. Was that a fading nilly bean effect, too? He halted at the firm ground's edge and squinted downhill. "Major Tam Barber, himself, of Lode. I had heard things about you, Major Barber. You'll have answers for us."

Ming glanced behind her for the strange name's owner. *Tam Barber—Barbar Curan?*

Curan dropped to a crouch with obviously trained speed, reaching for his pocket. A *crack* echoed down the draw. Curan's throat exploded in scarlet. He toppled backward and landed heavily; deep, yellow sand sprayed around him.

"Curan!" Ming cried, kneeling. So much blood. . . . Curan's eyes squeezed closed in an expression of pain, his hand open and stiff-fingered.

"You hold still, Ming Dalamani. Just where did you think you were going, when you had orders to fulfill?"

She stared down at Curan a moment longer. This was no clean courtroom fake, but violent—horrible—death. Grasses fluttered in the sand; the smells of blood and her own sweat mingled in an instant of still air. She felt sick.

With deliberate slowness to counter the fading stimulant, Ming turned her face back up the winding, grassy cleft. Huekk swaggered down the path, one child-sized hand raised. She eyed his black weapon. Was it a long pistol or a short rifle? *Curan. . . .* Ming glanced down once again, then stood utterly still.

Zardir Huekk stopped a meter short of her and gestured with the gun. "Mere Visual, how do you know this traitor to humankind? I would have liked to question him. What made him refuse me so quickly?"

"What did you call him? I thought his name was Curan." Ming spoke with as much control as her pounding heart allowed. "He was—"

"Shut up," Huekk said through clenched teeth. "I don't even want to hear your answer. I don't even want to know why your collar didn't close when I signaled it. It's time you learned exactly how much you are worth to Renasco, *Mere* Dalamani. I warned them you'd turn traitor."

The jammer must still lie in Curan's jacket pocket, set to keep her collar deactivated. Grasses bent low, but there were no other movements to give her hope of a passing stranger or chance of rescue, and Curan lay, his blood soaking the sand in a crimson halo.

"Come here." Huekk brandished the long black gun. She stared up its hollow barrel—a projectile weapon, tearing, ugly, and cruel—as she went to him, silently protesting every foot-sinking step. Finally she stopped, shivering, at the shingle's edge.

He snatched her right hand. "I assume you're thinking of running away." He made a fist with one of his own hands, forced her palm open, and bent it backward. "You probably could run faster than I can." His eyes looked eager, his smile no longer crooked but straight and tenselipped. "But you'll need my help to get medical assistance." He pressed her palm further open.

"No! I won't run, I promise!" Ming grabbed for his arm with her other hand and tried to pry him away as discomfort became intense, then unbearable. "No," she begged. "My hands—if you break my hands, I'm no use to—to Renasco."

"Renasco—" her middle knuckle burst, and stars danced in her vision, "doesn't need you." He shifted his hand and pushed harder. Another finger left its socket. "Unless there's anything you've been meaning to tell me, Mere Dalamani?"

Tell him! she wailed to herself. *Tell him about "Oneday" and go free!*

"No!" she shouted. Twice in quick succession, her joints melted, and she passed beyond distinguishing one pain from another.

Her knees wobbled. Huekk shook her arm hard, so she did not faint, but she fell. Still gripping her injured hand by the wrist, Huekk knelt, twisting her arm. He dropped her hand on the solid, packed path and wedged it down with one sandaled foot. Standing on her wrist, he raised the other foot high. "I think you do have something to tell me, Mere Dalamani."

His old intimidation game. She could stop him this instant by betraying Tieg and Holjpip—

"No!" she shrieked, and she tried to pull away. If Renasco meant to remove Holjpip, knowing of "Oneday" would make no difference.

Huekk's weight crushed her palm. Agony licked up her

arm. She tried to rise but could find no balance. He reached down and seized her left hand. "Now, this one," he purred, wrenching her up close, breathing quickly in her ear.

Ming flung herself out of his grasp and threw her right arm out to break her fall.

He laughed as she landed on the crushed, disjointed hand. "You're not going to escape, Ming Dalamani," he said. Taking one step onto soft sand, he seized her left arm and disabled her other fingers—moving faster, this time, or else the nilly bean was wearing off.

Although she fought to evade it, Huekk's heel plunged down once again, and she screamed. Storm winds began to whip at her.

"You're going nowhere now," his voice oozed through a blur of cold pain, "except with me. Come along."

She lay staring up at him as through a tunnel. "I can't . . . get up, Missar Huekk."

"Want me to help you?" he asked in a husky, excited voice.

Slowly, fearing at any moment he'd kick the support out from under her, Ming struggled to a kneeling position. A spatter of rain stung her face. She folded her arms across her chest. It didn't ease the shrieking pain but seemed better than letting her hands dangle unsupported. She got her balance on one foot, then tottered upright. Dizzy, her breath coming in gasps, she stared at Renasco's insect-headed mutant.

Huekk pushed something against her lips, and she gagged on the flavor of another nilly bean. "Get it down," he said. "It's not going to speed you up in the shape you're in, but it'll keep you from going into shock—for long enough to get back to the villa." Choking, she tried to chew before she swallowed. Huekk smiled crookedly again and gestured inland with the weapon. "Go," he said. "We'll take my car. It's parked closer than Major Barber's."

She stumbled a few steps up the path. Before she rounded the first bend, bile rose at the back of her throat. She slowed, panting and looking down frantically for a place to be sick.

Pain shot into her back. She straightened, pivoting. Clenching his weapon in stubby hands, Huekk leveled it at her body's center and jabbed again, this time catching her stomach with the sharp barrel. "I told you you'd need my help to get back. I'll take one of those hands clean off, if that's what it takes to inspire you to move."

Adrenaline served her well, now. Ming plodded uphill, mastering nausea. She rounded two curves where steep earthfalls bent the trail, then stopped. Footsteps, running down the draw from uphill, grew rapidly louder.

"Up," Huekk grunted. He grappled her waist and forced her up a steep dirt bank, still jabbing the weapon into her middle with his other hand. Upward off the trail, she struggled alongside him, as raindrops raised puffs of dust like tiny thunderclouds.

The echoing steps drew nearer. Ming twisted her neck to stare down over her shoulder. Pounding into sight, his red and gold tunic making him an easy target, Tieg Innig ran hard, arms and legs pumping.

Huekk's hand tightened around her waist, and he raised the barrel into her right cheek. "Stop," Huekk shouted, his reedy voice resounding off both banks of the draw: "—op—op."

Tieg halted, stared upward, and froze, arms caught in the middle of a swing. One hand worked the air. Distant thunder rolled, echoing around them.

"Drop it," Huekk crowed, "whatever it is."

Something that looked like another collar transmitter fell into the dirt.

"So you're the other, are you, Innig?" Huekk shouted, thrusting again with the gun barrel. "You and Major Tam Barber? Now we know who's going offworld with the Renasco inspection team. Very, very good. But first—" the barrel jabbed again, deeper, to hit Ming's teeth through her cheek, "I think you value this woman, Innig. Unless you want to watch her head explode, you have talking to do."

"No," Ming cried, squeezing her eyes shut. "Don't!"

Huekk laughed into her ear. "There, Innig. She gave you away. Who else on Mannheim do we call in? Tell me, or I shoot. She just saw Barber die the way she will. Didn't you, Mere Dalamani?" He shook her violently. Her hands burned, and she wanted to vomit. "Unless . . ."

"Derwin Watts," shouted Tieg, "at Ansland Electronics. He's one. Let her go, Huekk, and I will tell you the others." She stared down the steep bank, not believing. He couldn't do this—betray other Old School members?

No, Ming, idiot! He's trying to distract Huekk! Do something!

"Derwin Watts," repeated Huekk, twisting a handful of clothing at Ming's waist. "Very good, for a start. Give me another."

Ming stopped resisting and leaned into Huekk for balance.

Tieg bit at his upper lip. "Shuttle-Down Lounge, Newport. Everyone on staff."

"Another, Innig," Huekk taunted. His clutching hand slid up Ming's arm to her throat.

Ming pushed off.

Her world tumbled. She threw out both hands. A blast resounded close to her ear, and something red plunged past her. Pain shot up both arms, so intense she nearly blacked out. Hand-over-shoulder, she bounced on the hard dirt track. When she rolled to a stop, she wanted to lie down and shut her eyes, but pushed up dizzily with shoulders and elbows.

Two meters away, his tunic torn open down one side, Tieg crouched over Zardir Huekk, both hands at the mutant's throat. He raised Huekk's misshapen head—Ming saw terror caricatured in Huekk's features—and then crashed it down on stone with a stomach-twisting *crack*. Again. Ming tried to shut her eyes but couldn't keep them closed. Huge raindrops splattered the ground beside her, though she felt no sensation but pain. Huekk's hands flailed, then flopped. Tieg lifted the barrel-chested body clear off the ground and flung it down violently. It bounced and lay still.

A shudder shook Tieg. He fell to hands and knees, gasped twice, then crouched low to the ground.

Ming's stomach answered Tieg's. Then she fell in darkness.

On the way to breakfast shift, Lyra hesitated three doors up the hall from work. Staff Dining's massive doors slid together, shutting her out. "Wait," she called, breaking into a run, but heavy, black metal panels clanged home.

Panting, she pressed an ear against one. Faint voices clashed inside.

Lyra leaned away, pushing stiff-set hair deeper into her headnet. Lock-in, again? What could this mean? Another warship in the system?

Irked, she glanced up and down the hall. Black door-walls stood at both ends of vision, trapping her in a thirty-meter-long box of soundproofed corridor.

At least it's not with the glassware, this time. She sighed heavily and looked for a place to sit. *I've got the run of a hallway. I wonder if this is part of the inspection.* She slapped one thigh. *That's it. It's a drill.*

Sitting on the carpet, soft as it was, gave her leg cramps, and after five minutes of vainly sniffing the faint odor of sausage, she stood and began trying room doors. None opened to her palm, not even those normally public. Something passed over the skylight, and she flinched, then laughed derisively at herself. This wouldn't go on for long. The last lock-in had been for an hour, but that had been a real emergency.

As if to prove her guess correct, the security doorwall ahead began to grind open again. Lyra pushed away from the rough fabric-covered wall, relieved. A single security guard squeezed through and then did something to the wall beside the door. It shut with a *whump,* and as she gaped, the man hurried toward her.

An instant later, she recognized him. *Him.* "Mere Tatarka," she exclaimed. "What's going on?"

Able Tatarka's black hair shone, and the flush in his cheeks glowed warm and ruddy. As he trotted past, he turned his head. "Oh. Lyra, hello. I can't talk."

He remembered her! "What's going on?" she repeated, hustling alongside him. "Is it a drill?"

Able frowned and fingered his collar without breaking stride. "You'll be all right, here in the hall—no, wait," he said, turning abruptly. Lyra almost tripped, trying to match his change of speed and direction. Able paused outside one door. "When I open this, get in fast and don't let anyone out, or it'll mean my neck. There's a net hookup in here. At least you could follow whatever's getting out on the news. Ready?"

If this wasn't a drill, what was it? Able bent toward the

door's locking mechanism. Lyra almost protested being locked into a smaller space, then realized Able meant to do her a kindness by giving her access to news. Probably he wasn't supposed to unlock anything for anybody.

The door began to slide, and she wedged into its opening. A thinner woman might have slipped right through; Lyra struggled for an instant. A strident female voice clipped off in midword as the door slapped shut behind her.

Lyra recognized no one. It looked like a gathering of midlevel supervisory staff. A long-legged man whose copper-ribboned blue tunic hung partway open took two steps toward her. "How did *you* get—"

"I was locked into the hall," she said, puffing for breath, "and a security man let me into here. Said it'd be safer." These management types would probably feel less irritated with her if she acted the menial. "I think he felt sorry for me," she added, deliberately wiping her hands on the fronts of her overlaundered coveralls. "Would somebody please tell me what's going on?"

"Shh." Long-legs jerked one thumb toward the terminal. Lyra took a place at the crowd's edge. The unseen woman began to read loudly again, with comments.

"Chorus Kay Satellite Company, declaring compliance. She's got the communications net locked in, now."

Lyra gave the thin man a helpless look.

"We're for it now," he said, sullenly picking at a fingernail. "Her Grace has snapped. She's declaring independence."

What? Lyra tried to ask, but she choked inhaling.

"Yes." A pale-faced man with blond eyebrows, wearing Podacan red and yellow, stared him down. "And would you rather work for Renasco or Holjpip, friend?"

The Renasco man worked his lips, but the woman close to the terminal raised her voice again. "For heaven's sake, Goodsprings!" She began to chant, reading. "Plant employees have barricaded themselves inside and are refusing to open to Renasco supervisors, though nightshift workers are getting in somehow. Official estimates put the number of striking workers at six hund—"

"Goodsprings?" Fed up with politeness, Lyra tried to

shove forward a little. "I have a sister there. Let me through."

The blond-browed man backed out slightly to let her into the press, but from those two steps closer, she still couldn't see the board, and no one else moved except to rock back and forth, keeping balance. A woman bumped Lyra's hip.

"Hah!" the shrill woman laughed. "Look at this—the net's in contact with Renasco outside *and* the employee spokesman now." Lyra still couldn't see the reader, but her voice wavered in pitch as if her nerves had endured all they could. *Mine will go soon, too, if I have to listen to her for very long.* "This is great—they're arguing. Cooperson, the man inside, who just got there, is really telling them—"

Rimi's husband Coey, a rebel spokesman—for Holjpip, against Renasco? "Yee-eeh!" cried Lyra, and the people closest to her shrank away. Lyra muscled into the gap they left. "That's my brother-in-law," she exclaimed. "Let me see!"

Able Tatarka arrived at guest quarters just in time to see Claude Yerren vanish into a room two doors north. Standing outside the Renasco supervisor's door, three other uniformed guards waited, and from up the skylit hall five more arrived. "Ready?" snapped Able's captain. "Ops reports three inside here. The rest of them next door will wait ten minutes. Do it right. Conscious prisoners, if possible."

Able drew his tranquilizer gun and heard seven other pistols click ready. The captain hit the lock. Able pushed forward with eight others into cloying, perfumed air.

Inside, the lizard-eyed woman was standing on a table and shrieking. One man stood below her, brandishing a fist and shouting back. Long, fleshy spirals of ears quivered as his head shook, and his black dress tunic showed sweat stains. Another man stood off to their right, hands at his sides, turned half away from his shouting colleagues. Able and two other guards went for him.

He wheeled toward them. Able saw a pistol in his hand and underchief's laurels on his uniform breast, in that order.

"Good." Speaking soberly, the underchief kept his gun

hand low. "*You* can quiet my friends down. Perhaps you'll also tell me why we've lost power and communication."

Able answered: "Sir, Her Grace has placed all of you under protective custody. To be absolutely honest, I'm not entirely certain what's going on," he admitted, frowning at the man's pistol, "but it looks to me as if she's had enough of this inspection business. Sir," he added, for the man nodded and handed over his pistol grip-first by the thumb and forefinger. Maintaining a straight face although he tingled with surprise, Able holstered it at his own belt. Behind him, a shriek rose and faded as a tranquilizer took effect.

"I see," said the underchief. "In fact, perhaps I see more clearly than you do, if it's not obvious to you what has happened." He sniffed, glancing right. Able's partner cocked one eyebrow, and Able looked, too. Their captain bent over a prone form beside the table. The heavy perfume seemed to come from that direction.

Raising both hands onto his head, the underchief submitted to frisking. "When Her Grace has a moment to speak with me," he said as one of Able's partners removed a sheaf of flimsies from his breast pocket, "please inform her I am willing to talk."

Fully straightening his shoulders, Able gestured for his prisoner to move toward the door. As they passed the captain, he glanced up and then stared. Able grinned. *This* prisoner could answer questions immediately.

He had a good feeling about this. One that included promotion. Soon.

Z

Nine A.M.: Holjpip wiped a tired, burning eye. A rejuv-delay tremor danced across the knuckles of one hand, but she kept watching the net. Her procrastination of treatment was taking a week off her life every hour, but this time she must make the sacrifice or have a long life come to nothing. Beside her, Claude Yerren moved with unnatural speed, tracking the movements of loyal people into command, police, communications, power supply. Her Ops room techs, too, sounded dizzy and looked like marionettes operated by madmen.

Holjpip wrinkled her nose at the pungent row of nilly beans lying on her own console. She didn't dare use one, this far into rejuv sickness, but obviously, Yerren knew her orders.

Radio voices in Holjpip's left ear babbled, uplink to *Doran*—now passing over Mannheim's nearside—and aboard. It was happening so fast it took Holjpip's breath away. It took all her concentration to follow. It—

It was over. "Helmdecksecured,personnelundercontainment," the voice in her left ear clipped out. "Madam,weawaityourorders."

Yerren swiveled toward Holjpip, grinning like a teenager. Holjpip pursed her lips and gave Yerren the quickest nod. In weird, speeded-up tones, Yerren began to trill off orders for *Doran*'s deployment to the system's edge, where it would orbit on guard against Renasco reinforcements, watch the antimatter facility, and contact *Anfis* station to open diplomatic relations.

On a gleaming screen set into her desktop, Holjpip inserted tic marks beside objectives accomplished. Hydroelectrics, satellites, police—tic. She suppressed a yawn. Warship—tic—and then she clenched the quivering hand on her desktop. Cashflow system and taxes, programmed in place and ready to instigate, could wait a day, and Mannheim's citizens would notice little difference in their routine.

Leaning back to stretch, she winced through one more abdominal cramp, then touched up data she'd not seen before. It had come from Ashan Dalamani, and it looked genuine. Now, to deliver this technical information to the Goodsprings research and development facility and her antimatter asteroid. Under *Doran*'s protection, her crews there would shortly begin construction on a new kind of intersystem craft.

Shan pressed a shoulder deep into her mattress and shut her eyes, weary but satisfied she'd remembered everything vital. Claude Yerren had left her in the hands of a dark-uniformed questioner, who proved willing to accept freely given answers at face value, if she swore to their verity. Five minutes alone with Claude Yerren converted Shan's dizzy dread of the copper-haired woman—who'd restored memory all against her will—to support. Here on Mannheim, everything her clan had sought to accomplish would shortly become reality. Weaving from past to present with the questioner's help, she had rebuilt in her mind, and then on his portable terminal, the shielding system that once protected little *Opa*. With Holjpip's resources, it could be constructed properly now, with high-quality tools and the best materials.

She inhaled. Fresh paint, in this room; a fresh life, once she left it. She had a proud past now, after twenty years fighting to wall it away.

Her door slid open. The questioner in black slipped back into the dim light of her bare holding room. "Are you awake, Mere Dalamani?"

Shan pushed up onto one elbow. "I'm awake. What is it?"

He made a fist on one hip. "I am to ask if you would accept a position on Mannheim Interspace's prototype shielded ship. We mean to recruit, develop, and deploy as rapidly as possible, and establish Mannheim as a power effectively able to compete with Renasco."

"Absolutely." Shan shivered. She'd believe *that* when it happened. It couldn't be real—but she'd be an idiot to turn it down.

"I am also to offer immediate removal of your Renasco collar. Such devices were outlawed on Mannheim forty-one minutes ago."

Gulping, Shan pushed all the way up and flung a short, ugly leg over her bedside. "Take it. It's yours. Get rid of it. Give it to some deserving Renasco monkey, with my regards."

He shrugged. "Can't. Against the law now, though I see your point. There will be some discomfort—"

Shan rubbed the back of her head, pulling down hair from the loosely bound knot. "Yes, yes," she said, "I don't care. Get it out."

The questioner called something up the hall, then poked his face back in toward her. "The doctor will arrive shortly. Let him know if you have any medical allergies."

Ming woke muzzy-headed in a long, narrow, institutional-smelling room. Blinking away horrible dreams, she reached out to sit, but nothing responded. Both hands and arms lay splinted and tightly swathed in opaque bandages. They didn't respond, nor would her feet, when she tried to wriggle them. Ming could neither move nor feel below her shoulders.

They've closed the collar again. We've lost.

"Ming!" Tieg's head appeared in the doorway, and he hurried in. "They weren't expecting you to wake for an hour yet. How are you feeling?"

"I'm not," she groaned. "Tieg, the collar—"

He touched one hand to her shoulder. "The doctor said you would be paralyzed temporarily, because your spinal cord was bruised when they took the collar out."

"Out? Tieg, what—"

He interrupted, stroking her cheek. "Holjpip instituted 'Oneday,' Ming. Anslanding is boiling, *Doran*'s crew has been reshuffled—it's a mess out there. You're being zealously guarded by a gentleman named Able Tatarka. Know him?"

"Able?" Ming laughed. "Yes. He doesn't like you—"

"I've noticed. Apparently he decided to trust me, how-

ever, when I brought you in and confessed to killing
Huekk. It turns out . . ." Tieg shook his head. "Getting rid
of the mutant was scheduled for 'Oneday,' so I'm not being
charged."

That morning, that terrible morning . . . what day
was it now? "Missar Curan," she whispered.

Tieg's eyebrows arched. "They found him not long after he was shot. Later—not now, Ming—I need to know
. . . what happened between him and . . . Huekk."

Ming squeezed her eyes shut, but even then she saw
blood darkening yellow sand. "I don't think he—"

"*Later.* When you're feeling—"

"I don't think he suffered, Tieg," she pressed. "It came
so suddenly—though he'd just eaten half a nilly bean—oh,
if he hadn't moved for his gun so quickly, he might have
lived."

Tieg stroked her chin, and she looked up. "Maybe," he
said. "But if he thought he'd face Renasco questioning, he
would have rather died. We all would."

Something she could neither reach nor identify for certain itched. Ming gritted her teeth. "Did you go back for
the . . . frame?"

He nodded brusquely. "Disruption field, miniature and
powerful. Would have killed everyone in the room with
it."

Ming gulped. "Shan. Where's Shan? Is she still here at
the—"

Tieg pointed across the room. "Asleep. Same surgery,
but she's recovering rapidly. She's been awake twice already. Holjpip promised her a new education, and a nice
position with HolLanCorp's new branch: Mannheim Interspace."

"Oh," Ming breathed. "Excellent. What about that
daughter of Her Grace's?"

From near the doorway, Ming heard a familiar harsh
voice. "It's amazing, what people do when they're offered
power."

"Your Grace?" Ming whispered.

Holjpip strode up the windowless chamber. The black
Renasco dress uniform abandoned, she wore pale amethyst once again. From her easy, graceful stance and the
shimmer of hair around her shoulders, Ming guessed she'd

just emerged from a rejuv treatment. "Galoubet," she said, "is insisting she'll be mind-wiped before she'll work with me.

"But I've come to thank you, while I have a moment, for your assistance: your refusal to cooperate with her, and what appears to be your support with the codebreaker, through Old School."

"Yes, Madam. I meant it as support." Ming pressed her head against a deep, soft pillow. "Your Grace, the collar— thank *you.*"

Holjpip shrugged, making the gesture dignified. "We still could lose. Wait and see. We have one warship, and Renasco has ten. We're in a rush to build new ships, but our people have the incentive of freedom."

Lying on her bed, Ming exhaled through a broad smile.

Holjpip glanced side to side, then spoke on. "About your sunstone therapy: evidently, the crystal emanates some kind of energy in addition to light. My psych people are calling it eta-wave, for now.

"If Renasco learned to spot-convulse both hemispheres of the brain, our crossover stimulation effect would become useless, of course." She crossed her arms, displaying purple-tipped nails. "But for now, we'll have a flood of talent wanting treatment, starting with those high-level Renasco people sent to Goodsprings as manual labor. Tieg, you'll head south in the morning to get a technological staff accumulating. Ming, as soon as you're able, I want you in charge of that enterprise. You're my most reliable employee who's lived through memory wiping."

Useful work. Zardir Huekk had spoken prophetically, though he meant something different. "Yes, Madam. Gladly. I . . . believe I still owe 'humankind' just over thirty-nine and a half years."

Holjpip gave a clear, ringing laugh of pleasure that made the featureless room sparkle. "Serve me as a free woman, and you're released from Renasco's claims. Naturally, if we go down, we go together, so I believe you will do your best for me—as will others we'll offer a haven to here."

Ming looked up into the deep, hard eyes of Holjpip Langelleik, framed by the face and hair of a woman her own age. This *was* a woman she could serve—not with a whole heart, perhaps, as she had served her family, but with pride, and a hope there was something worth building here on Mannheim.

Then she pursed her lips. "Will they—my hands—be as good as before?"

Holjpip uncrossed her arms, bent down, and closed long fingers around Ming's bandaged wrists. Her expression was alarmingly sincere. "On Renasco worlds, they made a particular study of regenerative medicine. Yes. Your hands will heal, in time." She pulled back and gave a more typical gloating smile. "Meanwhile, Missara Shan has consented to run a request for additional sunstone crystals back through the wormholes to Cabra Minor as soon as her own spine has healed, and we have the prototype antimatter-drive ship shielded. It will make a most appropriate test for the design."

"Shan," Ming murmured. "She'd be so happy to do that. I almost wish I could—"

"You," Tieg said, "will stay here until Medical says your hands are healed. They are too shapely and accomplished for anything less than complete restoration."

"They're just trained. But I'll stay." Ming glanced at Tieg, then at Holjpip. "If we have a new world to build, Your Grace, I'll be needing full use of them."

PART THREE

Epilog

Ming flexed her hands on Holjpip's conference table. They were still too stiff for calligraphy, but in the months since "Oneday," she had been kept too busy with Holjpip's memory-restoration program to even consider artwork. On her right hand, her sunstone glimmered: Reset in Abriel Innig's ring, it stood for a new promise.

Down the table, Barbar Curan's Old School replacement rose from his seat. "I have little new to report, Madam. The failure of Renasco's first attempt to retake *Doran* has apparently discouraged them from harassing the system. We have our warship's crew to thank, and frankly, you should rename that craft. I might suggest *Renaissance*, old spelling."

From her position heading the table, Holjpip accepted the flimsy the O.S. man passed via the new Podacan ambassador. "ALPEX?" Holjpip asked the man and woman sitting next to Old School. "Co-Op?"

"No report today, Madam." Secretary-Director Voy Torben attended for ALPEX, still a comic picture with ruddy face and red hair, but he took a respectful stance and tone of voice nowadays. The General Co-Op woman shook her head. There they sat, on Holjpip's "First Planetary" council, looking to Her Grace for protection. Though she'd stirred the economic situation violently, even her competitors now admitted she'd improved it. Any day now, florals and pharmaceuticals would begin to flow offworld more cost-efficiently than ever aboard Mannheim Interspace ships, and currency chits from six worlds—

Holjpip already had the trade guarantees—would decrease Mannheim's debts

"I report for Missara Shan Dalamani." Ming came alert as a younger woman across the table brandished another flimsy. "This came via wormhole canister. Returning from the Cabra system, her crew evaded Renasco pursuit to drop uncoded schematics for the radiation shielding on Jarnik itself. The antimatter drive continues to function within tolerances, and she recommends we institute full production. And, Madam, she forwarded . . ."

From a velvet-covered box the woman spilled an amber-and-ruby stream of sunstone crystals. Ming caught her breath: At least a hundred gems lay on the table, a grand gesture of support from the clan's Caucus of Elders.

She's done it—we've done it!

Voy Torben of ALPEX turned to whisper in Missara Co-op's ear. The Old School man rose and applauded, while ten other men and women stared at the glowing pile. Sight of it brought to Ming's mind the scent of Cabra Minor's deserts, blasted into the dome through briefly opened gates. She would go back one day, but only as a visitor. She was home now, on a wet, blue-and-green planet.

Holjpip smiled, not the flat-lipped smirk of four months ago, but the genuine expression. "Missara Ming Dalamani," she said. "Your report, please."

Ming stood, feeling self-conscious. Holjpip had appointed her to this circle, but she hoped eventually to step down and let a genuine leader take her place. "South Upper has nearly filled," she said, displaying her own flimsy. "Refugees are still coming in shiploads, and we're treating and sending them on to Newport and the new southwestern plantations as quickly as we can. Not everyone responds to treatment; the high percentage of successes who remember some kind of arts training supports our theory." She nodded toward the tumbled pile of sunstone crystals. "Those will certainly help, Madam." Ming handed the flimsy up the table.

Half an hour later, the meeting broke up. Ming passed Staff Central on her way to the centrum. As she peered through the door, Jury Bertelsen looked away.

She met Tieg at the head of the fountain pool. A whiff of

sea air caught her by surprise, and she glanced into the water. Scores of tiny silver fish turned in a school and fled for the pool's low end. *Fish? Here?*

With an artist's delicacy, Tieg took one of her hands and kissed the side of her index finger. "Her Grace is toying with saltwater art, now. I have a sea symphony commissioned, due next year. But it's time for you to rest awhile."

She nodded. They planned a wedding trip south as soon as she could get away.

"My staff's trained now," she said. Her new chief assistant, the Renasco inspectors' underchief—locked in for "Oneday"—had joined up the day Holjpip gave him the chance.

Galoubet, at the other extreme, still fumed in luxurious quarters. Holjpip refused to wipe her memory, though Galoubet behaved as if certain the wipe was imminent, hurling food at her room servers, ignoring opportunities to research the data base. The high-strung, inbred temperament, Ming guessed, nullified Galoubet's inherited strengths. It looked to be a long, interesting standoff, and she wondered if Holjpip would ever find the courage to have another heir conceived.

Reaching for Ming's shoulder, Tieg pulled her into a tree's shadow. "Look," he whispered.

Lyra passed through the door on the opposite side, dressed in pink lace and a pale amethyst skirt. The black-haired guard who admitted Lyra seated her in a white webbed chair near the fountain, then stood bending close, one boot on the tiled brim. After a few moments, Lyra laughed.

Both Able and Lyra had visited often while Ming recuperated; she guessed they'd eased one another over the shock of learning their friend had worn a Renasco collar. Ming thought back to a long conversation en route to Goodsprings, and Lyra's determination to find a husband who was not a plant worker. Rubbing at the healing scar beneath her clan tails—no metal protruded there, any more—Ming silently wished her friend happiness. *I think you've found a nice one, Lyra.*

Tieg touched her elbow. "We were discussing our vacation."

"I think I'm ready."

"For all of it?"

Ming took his hand again and sniffed the mingled odors of jungle and shore. Anticipating Mannheim's first independent-born generation, Holjpip offered expanded housing and pay increases to villa staff who married. That hadn't affected Ming's decision, but it would keep them comfortable.

With a hand that daily became stronger, Ming squeezed Tieg's fingers. "Yes," she said, teasing. "All of it. Today I lost twenty years, once. I'm not waiting around for you."

About the Author

Kathy Tyers, a California native, settled in Montana chiefly to see if she would find wilderness as inspiring in reality as in J.R.R. Tolkien's works (she did, and she stayed). She has an amateur radio license and a SCUBA certificate, and has worked as an immunobiology tech and a primary teacher in a private school—but as the daughter of a flutist and a brassman, she has always considered music a necessity of life. Kathy performs on flute and Irish harp with her guitarist–music teacher husband, Mark, and they have released two folk albums, "Leave Her, Johnny" and "The Very Best Dreams."

"Excellent hard science fiction . . . Ideas splash out of Zindell's mind and flow across the pages of this book. . . . Not just a brilliant novel, but a strong and serious view of human potential."
—Orson Scott Card in *The Magazine of Fantasy and Science Fiction*

NEVERNESS
by
David Zindell

"One of the finest talents to appear since Kim Stanley Robinson and William Gibson—perhaps the finest."
—Gene Wolfe

It is a world unlike any man has ever known before, teeming with life and stunning in its complexity. A world where the evolutionary possibilities open to humanity are evident in rich detail. The world where Pilot Novitiate Mallory Ringess will navigate the Solid State Entity—a nebula-sized brain composed of moon-sized biocomputers analogous to neurons—the world where he will confront his future—and the very fate of Mankind.

"Grand in scope, vivid in evocation . . . This book suggests that Zindell has just embarked on a major career in science fiction."
—Michael Bishop

Buy **Neverness** now on sale wherever Bantam Spectra books are sold, or use this page for ordering:

The novels of
SHEILA FINCH

☐ **The Garden of the Shaped** (26801-5 • $3.95/$4.95 in Canada) On the world of Ilia where the inhabitants are the products of genetic engineering, a war begins between two of the three new races of humanity. The fate of Ilia lies in the hands of the young but uncommon Queen Sivell, whose very uniqueness could bring peace to her world . . . or death to her people.

"An intriguing look at bio-engineering from the point of view of the *engineered*."—Gregory Benford

☐ **Shaper's Legacy** (28167-4 • $3.95/$4.95 in Canada) Two generations after Queen Sivell's time, war looms once more on the horizon for the people of Ilia, as the fierce and primitive Rhodarus rise against their sister races.

And coming in November, 1989 the stunning conclusion to Sheila Finch's exciting trilogy!

Buy **Garden of the Shaped** and **Shaper's Legacy** on sale now wherever Bantam Spectra books are sold, or use this page for ordering:
